IN THE
SHADOW
OF POWER

IN THE
SHADOW
OF POWER

VIVECA STEN

TRANSLATED BY MARLAINE DELARGY

SANDHAMN MURDERS

amazon crossing

Text copyright © 2014 by Viveca Sten
Translation copyright © 2019 by Marlaine Delargy
All rights reserved.

Previously published as *I maktens skugga* by Forum in Sweden in 2014. Translated from Swedish by Marlaine Delargy. First published in English by AmazonCrossing in 2019.

Published by AmazonCrossing, Seattle

www.apub.com

Amazon, the Amazon logo, and AmazonCrossing are trademarks of Amazon.com, Inc., or its affiliates.

ISBN-13: 9781542007665 (paperback)
ISBN-10: 1542007666 (paperback)

Cover design by Damon Freeman

Printed in the United States of America

To my darling Lennart

"Fatso, fatso, fatso."

He lay on his side without moving or protesting. If he tried to do anything, it just made things worse.

Please let recess end, he prayed. Please let the bell ring.

The leader of the gang, the king of the schoolyard, delivered a vicious kick, the heavy boot striking the base of the spine. His victim felt his body jolt, but managed to suppress the cry of pain before it could escape. The situation always escalated if he reacted.

His nose was blocked with mucus and tears, but he mustn't give in and start crying. That would be fatal.

The bell rang. Finally. The shouts died away.

He waited for a minute or so, then opened his eyes and looked around. He was alone in the yard. He wiped his nose, which had already begun to swell; his hand came away smeared with blood.

The bell rang again.

Getting to his feet was agonizing. He knew he'd get a black mark for being late, but he didn't dare go in until the others had taken their seats.

"I will have my revenge," he whispered to himself. "I'll show them."

The words reverberated in his head.

"Fatso, fatso, fatso."

CHAPTER 1

Monday, April 29, 2013

Maria Svedin waited in the spacious hallway, shifting anxiously from foot to foot while Celia Jonsson helped Oliver put on his navy blue school blazer. Should she fetch Oliver's bag, which he'd left in his room? It was often hard to know what Celia expected of her.

Celia fastened the shiny top button and brushed back a strand of dark hair before straightening up.

"Maria," she said in Swedish with an English accent, "I'd like you to drive Oliver to school; I have other things to do today. You can take Carsten's car—he walked to the office."

The request took Maria by surprise. Celia always did the school run in the mornings, but she was clearly stressed. There were dark shadows beneath her eyes, and her mouth was a thin line.

Maria had heard raised voices the previous evening. Even though the apartment was large and her room was a long way from Carsten and Celia's, she hadn't been able to avoid hearing the angry words coming through the walls. It had sounded as if they were quarreling about Carsten's plans for a vacation home in Sweden.

"Maria?"

She nodded and headed for the door. The elevator came all the way up into the apartment. She pressed the button several times to show Celia that she understood. She would have preferred not to take Oliver to school; she still had problems with driving on the left in London, and the roundabouts made her nervous.

Celia didn't notice her reluctance. Or maybe she just didn't care.

"If you get the car out, I'll be down with Oliver in a few minutes," she said. "I want to fetch his new mittens."

She used the wrong Swedish verb, but Maria made no attempt to correct her. She simply put on her jacket and picked up the keys.

"Hurry up, Oliver!" Celia urged her son. "You mustn't be late for school—you know what Daddy will say."

There was a click; the elevator had arrived.

"See you down there," Maria said.

The lights usually came on as soon as someone entered the underground parking lot, but when Maria stepped out of the elevator, nothing happened. The doors closed behind her, and she was in darkness. She turned to press the button to open the doors, but the hum of the mechanism told her she was too late.

She moved forward, stamping her foot on the gray concrete floor, but still the lights refused to cooperate. Was there a power outage? No—in that case, the elevator wouldn't work. There must be something wrong with the automated lighting system, but she had no idea where the switch was or how to find it.

She knew that Carsten's car was around the corner, at the end of the line about fifty yards away. She reached into her pocket, intending to use the flashlight on her phone, but her fingers found only a packet of gum and some loose change. She must have left the phone in the apartment. She edged backward until she felt the elevator doors against her shoulders.

She turned around; thank goodness for the tiny pinprick of light that showed her where the call button was. She pressed it hard, keeping her index finger there as if it would make the elevator arrive more quickly, get her out of here.

Come on, come on.

What was that? A faint sound behind her made her jump. It was so brief that she wasn't sure if she really had heard it, but the impression of a metallic clang lingered, as if someone had dropped a tool, maybe a wrench or a hammer.

Maria glanced over her shoulder, peered into the darkness. She thought the sound had come from the other side of the wall, somewhere near Carsten's car. Was there someone else down here?

"Hello?"

She held her breath, felt her heart racing even though she was standing perfectly still.

"Hello?"

An oily smell drifted by, so fleeting that she barely had time to notice it. Her eyes were beginning to get used to the gloom, and she was able to pick out the shapes of expensive cars neatly parked in their spaces. It wouldn't be hard to hide behind one of them.

She tried to pull herself together, but the pounding of her heart meant she was breathing way too fast. Celia was waiting for her. She had to hurry and get the Land Rover, otherwise Oliver would be late for school.

She inhaled deeply, clutched the car keys tightly. It wasn't far; surely she could fumble her way over there. She could feel the sweat trickling down her back beneath her thick jacket and sweater.

Resolutely she took a step forward, then another. Almost there. The sense of relief was enormous.

She could smell gas now, or was that just her imagination?

Was she alone down here, or not?

"Hello?" she called out again, though her instincts told her to keep quiet.

Then she heard another sound, as if something was dripping slowly onto the concrete.

A flash, and the world exploded in a burst of fire and smoke.

CHAPTER 2

Tuesday, April 30

Julia let go of Nora's hand as they reached the area outside the Sandhamn Inn. At least a hundred people had already gathered there, waiting for the torchlight procession to begin. Nora knew most of them and waved to a group of neighbors who were standing, chatting.

It was a lovely evening, but not particularly warm; the chill of the unusually long, cold winter still lingered. The snow had arrived in November, and the ice hadn't melted until the middle of April. It had been Stockholm's longest winter in over a hundred years. The waters around the jetties had frozen solid, and the bitter wind seemed to have been blowing nonstop for months.

Out of the corner of her eye, Nora saw that Adam and Simon had each grabbed a torch and were holding them up in the air.

"Can I have one of those, too, Mommy?"

Julia tugged at her arm, and Nora knelt down. Her daughter's blond hair was braided into two rats' tails, sticking out behind her ears. Her blue eyes were full of anticipation.

"You're not old enough to carry a burning torch, sweetheart. You'll have to wait until you're a big girl."

Nora knew exactly what was coming. Julia clamped her lips together, disappointment written all over her face. She really was ridiculously like Jonas. They both had the same narrow upper lip that almost disappeared when frustration kicked in. Julia's top lip reappeared and began to tremble as tears of anger took over.

"I want one!" she screamed, hitting out at Nora.

"Julia! That's not OK!"

Adam handed his torch to Nora. "Want to ride on my shoulders, Julia?"

He lifted his sister with ease and placed her securely on his shoulders. Julia beamed; disaster averted. Adam went over to join some friends, the little girl draped over his head like a sack of potatoes.

Nora watched her oldest and youngest children, feeling a wave of love so powerful that her eyes filled with tears even though she was in the middle of a crowd.

My precious children. Darling Julia.

To think that she'd had a daughter, become a mother of three.

Jonas came over and interrupted her thoughts.

"They're cute together," he said, nodding in the direction of Adam and Julia.

Nora cuddled up to him. "He sometimes seems so grown up." Adam would soon finish his second year at high school, and the taciturn teenager had become a kind and considerate young man. "It shows there's hope for Simon, too," she added.

"Thank goodness for that."

Was Jonas tired of Simon? That wasn't like him, but there was no denying that Simon would try anyone's patience. Without warning the sunny-natured little boy had metamorphosed into a grunting thirteen-year-old who spent most of his time sitting in front of the television. All winter Nora had been dealing with Julia's tantrums and Simon's sulky behavior. It hadn't been easy, and occasionally she wondered if she was too old to cope with children so far apart in age.

"Isn't it almost time to start moving?" Jonas said, glancing over at the chair of the Friends of Sandhamn, the group responsible for organizing celebrations on the island. She was holding a megaphone and seemed to be getting ready to speak.

When Jonas turned his head, his hair brushed against his collar. It was still brown, without a trace of gray. *I'm the only one who needs to dye my hair,* Nora thought as the age difference between them hit home once more. This year Jonas would be thirty-nine, Nora forty-six.

The chair of the Friends struck up a song, and the procession slowly began to move, past the Strindberg Café and into the old part of the village. The destination was Fläskberget, the hill above the shore on the northern side of the island where the Walpurgis Night bonfire would be lit to mark the arrival of spring.

Nora was still holding Adam's torch. She raised it high above her head, taking care to keep it away from anything or anyone. It was madness to allow all these people carrying burning torches to make their way along the narrow lanes between the old wooden buildings; it wouldn't take much to start a fire, and the single fire engine on the island would be of little use.

However, tradition was tradition.

By the time they made their way up the hill, the bonfire was already ablaze, fed by the torches the revelers threw onto the pyre. Orange and yellow flames flickered against the blue evening sky, and in the distance, a white Vaxholm ferry sailed across the shining water.

In the chilly air, every contour was crystal clear.

"It's time to sing along with the choir to welcome the spring!" announced an elderly man who'd taken over the megaphone.

Nora searched for Simon in the crowd and spotted him on the other side of the bonfire with his friends. She waved, but he didn't see her. Adam came over to join her and Jonas, Julia still perched on his shoulders.

The fire crackled loudly and sent a shower of sparks raining down toward the water; it looked like a waterfall of fireflies against the darkening sky.

Julia held out her arms to Nora; she wanted to get down. Nora took her and got a big hug in return. She felt the warmth of the little body, and her nostrils were filled with the scent of her soft, fair hair.

Darling Julia, she thought again.

Jonas was now carrying Julia, who had tired eyes and her thumb in her mouth.

"I guess we ought to go home," he said quietly. The Brand villa was only a few hundred yards away, perched on top of Kvarnberget like a beacon. They'd left some of the lights on, and a warm glow shone from the downstairs windows.

"You go on ahead. I'll just find Simon, check where he's going."

Nora had not seen her younger son for quite a while. Before dinner, he'd made it very clear that he wanted to stay out until midnight on weekdays, one o'clock on weekends.

Nora had been horrified. Midnight was way too late for a thirteen-year-old, and one o'clock was out of the question. Simon's face had darkened when he saw her reaction; none of his friends had to go home early. Why did he have to be the only one?

Nora looked around; the fire was dying down, had become little more than a pile of embers glowing softly, with the odd charred branch poking out. There was no sign of Simon, but she caught sight of Eva Lenander, whose son Fabian was Simon's best friend. Eva was holding a plastic bag and waiting patiently for Marco, the family's black poodle, to do what he had to do among the trees at the edge of the forest.

"Have you seen the boys?" Nora called out as she went over.

Eva shook her head. "I think they've already left; Fabian said they were going to the Richardsons'."

They also had a son Simon's age and lived just past the chapel, only a few minutes from the Brand villa.

"Thanks—at least I know where he is!" She sighed and pushed back a strand of hair. "It would have been helpful if Simon had mentioned it before he took off."

Eva laughed, the dimple in her left cheek deepening.

"Like Fabian would have bothered to tell me if I hadn't grabbed him just as they were leaving! I can't get two sensible words out of that kid these days. All I hear is bad-tempered mumbling."

Nora realized she was smiling. It was good to hear that she wasn't the only mother of a teenage son who was acting up.

"By the way, have you heard the latest?" Eva said eagerly. During the winter, she had had her hair cut short with blond highlights; it really suited her and drew attention away from her round cheeks to her eyes instead.

Nora frowned; what had she missed? They'd spent very little time on Sandhamn over the spring because Simon's soccer training had taken up most weekends.

"A new house is going up on the point at Fyrudden," Eva informed her. "And you'll never guess how much the owner had to pay."

Nora hadn't even been aware that the extensive plot on the south-western side of the island was for sale.

"I'm assuming you know," she said, unable to suppress her curiosity even though she would have liked to pretend she wasn't remotely interested.

Eva held up both hands, fingers spread wide.

"Times two." She waited for Nora's reaction.

"Twenty million! You're kidding me, right? That's crazy!"

"That's what I heard—from what they call a reliable source."

"Who the hell's paid that much?"

"I don't know their names, but I believe they're Swedes who live overseas."

Of course they are, Nora thought.

"I think they live in London," Eva went on. "Apparently work started on an enormous house back in the fall. The build won't be cheap either. It's supposed to be finished by the summer."

Nora looked over at the old boathouses at the bottom of Kvarnberget. They reminded her of a time when the islanders went fishing in order to put food on the table and used the boathouses to store their nets and equipment. These days, most of them had been renovated into cabins or saunas—a development that certainly wasn't unique to Sandhamn, but she still found it depressing.

"So fru Sjöberg must have finally passed away," she said. No one had lived at Fyrudden for years. The widow who owned the land had spent the last ten years in a nursing home while her house gradually deteriorated. Ida Sjöberg must have been close to a hundred years old by the time she died.

"Yes. I think it was the winter before last, because apparently the sale went through pretty soon after that. She didn't have any children, so it's her nephews and nieces who'll be laughing all the way to the bank."

Marco let out a loud bark; he'd finished snuffling around and was tugging on his leash. Nora glanced at her watch.

"I have to go. Jonas will be wondering where I am." She gave Eva a quick hug. "Good night. If you happen to see my son, tell him I want him home by eleven."

It was dark now, with only a few pink streaks showing where the sun had gone down. The sky was strewn with the distant sparkle of countless stars. Nora shivered as she hurried home.

So Fyrudden had been sold. It had to happen eventually, of course. The plot was enormous, probably one of the largest on the island. It was in a fantastic south-facing location and included a significant stretch of the shore. It was worth a lot of money, but even so, twenty million sounded ridiculous.

The former owners had never even considered fencing off the area. Respecting the tradition of open access along the coastline had been a given.

What would happen now?

People who were prepared to spend that much were unlikely to be considerate of old customs. That had become clear over recent years, as many properties on the island had changed hands.

Would it still be possible to walk along the shore and enjoy the beautiful view? What would the new owners decide to do when they settled on Sandhamn?

One thing's for sure. If they do put up fences, there'll be trouble.

CHAPTER 3

Thomas Andreasson gently touched Pernilla's shoulder. She'd fallen asleep on the sofa with her head on the wide armrest. Her mouth was half-open, but she wasn't snoring; instead she was making little sighing noises at regular intervals.

"Pernilla? Don't you think you should go to bed instead of nodding off in front of the television?"

Slowly she opened her eyes.

"It's almost eleven thirty," Thomas went on. "You've been asleep for quite a while."

"How did the movie end?" Pernilla asked, yawning and running a hand through her tousled red hair.

"Same as always. The good guys won, and the bad guys got what they deserved. No basis in reality whatsoever."

It was meant as a joke, but he could hear how bitter he sounded. Pernilla sat up and stroked his face.

"Is that how you feel?" Her hand rested on his cheek. Thomas knew she'd been worried about him lately. He shrugged. The words had just come out; he hadn't really given them much thought, and he didn't really want to talk about how he was feeling. Certainly not at this hour.

"OK, let's go to bed," Pernilla said with another yawn.

"I'm not tired. You go. I'll be there in a while."

"Don't stay up too long."

Pernilla opened the door of Elin's room and peeped in. Thomas knew their daughter was fast asleep; he'd already checked on her several times. The constant worry that something might happen during the night never left him. He went over to the kitchen window and looked out at the silhouette of the jetty, the shadows cast by the small lantern at the far end, and the water covering the seabed like a shining lid.

It had been a quiet Walpurgis Night. Nora had asked if they'd like to join in the celebrations on Sandhamn, but they'd decided to stay on the smaller island of Harö. Thomas's parents had come over for an early dinner, then gone back home.

Spring is in the air at last, Thomas thought.

Soon everything would begin to grow, and the lilacs would bloom. He and Pernilla and Elin would spend the summer on Harö as usual; he was hoping to extend his vacation by using some of the paternity leave he'd saved so that Elin could enjoy more time out in the archipelago. Thomas's parents would be in their summer cottage and were always open to babysitting.

He ought to be feeling good now that the long, cold winter was over.

Instead he was at a very low ebb, drained of energy.

He took a cold beer out of the refrigerator, returned to the sofa, and picked up the remote. He flicked from one channel to the next until he settled on an old action movie he'd already seen several times.

He had nothing to complain about. He was happy with Pernilla and deeply grateful that they'd found their way back to each other after the divorce eight years earlier. The fact that Elin had come along was a miracle in so many ways.

Every day he looked at his daughter, amazed that she was part of his life.

And yet he was sitting here, brooding. Why couldn't he just be . . . happy?

This year he would turn forty-six. He had a long way to go until retirement. Could he really continue working as a detective inspector for so many years?

The thought of constantly being faced with the various expressions of human stupidity and evil was sometimes difficult, sometimes almost unbearable. Having to deal with despairing relatives and victims, cynical lawyers making unreasonable demands . . .

He wasn't enjoying his beer. He turned off the TV and put on his jacket. He needed to get out of the house, clear his head.

It was wonderful to fill his lungs with cool sea air. Thomas took a few deep breaths as he made his way down to the jetty. A fine layer of dew covered the oiled planks. Across the water lay the island of Storö and Hagede jetty, invisible in the darkness. In the winter it was possible to walk there across the ice.

Only weeks ago, icicles had hung from the eaves, and patches of snow still lingered in the crevices of the rocks. He hadn't even put his aluminum boat, a Buster, in the water yet; everything was delayed this year.

You have nothing to complain about, he told himself yet again as he pushed his hands deep into his pockets.

His former partner, Margit Grankvist, had promoted Thomas to the position of team leader when she took over the department a year or so earlier. His salary had increased, as had his administrative duties; unfortunately the former didn't compensate for the latter.

He and Margit operated on a firm basis of mutual respect. She gave him a great deal of freedom and trusted his judgment. Even so, the past months had been challenging, with a number of difficult cases and a seemingly never-ending stream of budgetary cuts.

Something wasn't right with him. When the alarm went off in the mornings, he just didn't want to get up.

Is this how it's going to be? he asked himself sometimes as he drove to work, wondering how he'd make it through the day.

Thomas turned around and gazed at the house.

Pernilla and Elin were sleeping behind those walls. The two most important people in his life.

I'm a lucky man. So why wasn't he happy?

CHAPTER 4

How could he possibly have missed the call from Russia? Carsten Jonsson stared at his cell phone and realized it was on silent. He must have forgotten to change it after the meeting at the bank, and now it was too late to call back. He'd had a few drinks in a bar, and it was almost midnight, even later in Moscow. He'd have to wait until tomorrow.

He went into the library and poured himself a small whisky. He'd earned it. Everything had gone well at the bank, things were going according to plan, and the loan would be repaid in October as agreed.

Carsten sank down into the leather armchair facing the huge picture window. It had stopped raining while he was walking home, and now the clouds had dispersed, suggesting that tomorrow might be nice. It was about time; it had rained almost every day throughout April.

The apartment was silent; Celia and the children were in bed, as was the nanny. Marianne? No, Maria. He found it difficult to keep track; none of the girls stayed for long.

Maria was made of sterner stuff, though. She'd made a speedy recovery from the accident in the underground parking lot.

Accident.

Carsten considered the word. The car had been completely destroyed, and it was pure luck that no one had been hurt. According to the insurance company, the explosion had been caused by an unusual technical fault that had made the gas tank self-ignite. No one was to blame.

He ran his fingertips over the armrest.

There had been considerable interest in the Russian share deal. And he'd had to play hardball in a number of other business matters.

What if it hadn't been an accident?

He didn't want to go back to all that hassle with United Oil, the nights when he didn't know if he could continue, the mornings when he needed to use a little something extra to get him out of bed. Everything that happened afterward.

But he was a different person now. He hadn't taken anything for years, although he made sure he had a supply nearby, just in case.

His glass was empty. Carsten got up and refilled it.

Hopefully the insurance company was right, and the incident in the parking lot had nothing to do with his business affairs. Maria seemed fine now, and she was good with Oliver and Sarah. Carsten checked from time to time to make sure she always spoke Swedish with them. It was important for the children to be comfortable in his mother tongue. They had to learn about their heritage, be able to talk to their grandmother.

That was why he'd built the house on Sandhamn. At least that's what he told himself, even though he knew better. The image of his father's face came into his mind, but he pushed it away.

It had taken a lot of negotiation before he'd been allowed to buy the extensive plot of land, but in the end, money had won the day.

As it always did.

The vendors' talk of selling to locals or turning the area into a nature reserve had died away when they saw the size of the wad of cash he was waving in front of their noses. On the day the contract was signed in the lawyer's office, he had seen the greed in their eyes; they were already thinking about what they were going to spend it on.

The dark-blue night was illuminated by beams of light playing across the sky. London sparkled before him.

As a young man, he had lived in New York, trading in stocks and shares for one of the biggest American investment banks. That was long before he set up the venture capital fund and started making investments of his own, but he'd never felt at home in the US—unlike London.

Carsten ran a hand through his hair, wondering what kind of car he should go for when the Russian deal went through. A new sports car, maybe. If he wanted it next spring, he probably needed to order it now, get in line.

He'd never gambled so much on a single investment, but the setup was brilliant, and he'd immediately realized that this was a unique opportunity to make a grotesque amount of money.

It was all thanks to Anatoly Goldfarb, his former colleague at the bank in New York. After a few years Anatoly had been lured back to Moscow by a newly founded Russian investment bank offering huge bonuses, but he and Carsten had kept in touch. It had been well worthwhile.

Carsten shook his glass, clinking the ice cubes.

Russia was volatile. He wasn't unaware of the risks involved in doing business with the former Soviet state, the need to grease the palms of key individuals and pay out significant sums in "commission." However, with Anatoly by his side, there was no danger. Carsten would never trust his old friend completely, but he did trust his desire to make a profit.

The investment in the Russian technology company had begun with a call from Anatoly two years earlier. Carsten had been sitting in the library with a glass in his hand, just like now. Anatoly had asked if Carsten was interested in getting involved with a company that was showing great—no, amazing—potential.

As was so often the case, whether the country in question was the US, Sweden, or Russia, it was all about a team of smart young computer engineers who'd come up with a brilliant idea.

Ten or fifteen years ago, Russian investments had focused on gas and oil. That was at a time when Russian national treasures were being sold off for next to nothing. The former KGB guys had been on the front line, the ones who gradually emerged as a new upper class: the enormously wealthy oligarchs.

Today the Internet was key. There was mind-blowing potential in a country with 140 million inhabitants, where global giants like Google and Facebook were nowhere near as dominant as they were in the rest of the world.

Carsten had flown to Moscow almost right away. He'd spent several days in meetings with Sergei and Roman, the two founders who'd begun to hone their business plan when they were college students.

He'd gone into every detail, met the other board members, examined every calculation, and eventually he was convinced. Sergei and Roman were most definitely whiz kids who could work magic with computers.

Carsten already knew that Russian programmers were considered to be among the best in the world and always came out on top in international competitions. However, these two had something even more important: an inner drive, a hunger he recognized within himself. Both Sergei and Roman wanted a slice of the pie, the incomprehensible payoff that was accessible only to the superrich in Russia. Sergei in particular practically drooled whenever the stock market flotation was mentioned.

They had also managed to secure GZ3, a Russian bank and investor with an excellent reputation. It now owned twenty-five percent of the shares, guaranteeing a successful flotation.

Carsten refilled his glass for the second time.

Sergei and Roman's idea was to create a safe payment method for the e-commerce firms that had begun to appear throughout Russian society. The ability to pay safely online was still a major problem in the country, and although a vast number of firms had started up in recent years, customers were hesitant. The fear of being scammed was still widespread.

KiberPay had developed a solution that made the problem disappear. It enabled the buyer to feel secure; the payment didn't go through until the goods had been delivered. The technology behind it was also smartphone-based, and that was the key to its success.

The payment system was accessible to Russians who still didn't have a credit card but did have a cell phone. It opened up a channel to millions of customers and would revolutionize the Russian market, perhaps even other markets, such as those in Africa.

The fact that it also provided a huge amount of data such as individual telephone numbers and personal preferences wasn't exactly a disadvantage either. Carsten could already see the potential in the customer database that would quickly grow. The marketing opportunities capitalizing on that information were endless.

He inhaled the aroma of the whisky in his glass.

It hadn't taken him long to make up his mind after that first meeting. This was an extraordinary investment that would double the size of the venture capital fund in one stroke.

With Anatoly's help, Carsten put everything in place, making sure he fulfilled the additional demands placed by the Russians on a foreign investor. His lawyers set up a purpose-built structure; the holding company in Guernsey guaranteed that the profits could be brought home gradually with minimal taxation.

Over the past two years, all the forecasts regarding the Russian business had been met or exceeded, and everything had gone according to plan. Each time Carsten checked, he was surprised at how positive it all seemed. More and more customers were signing up, the income streams were growing fast.

In September they would float the company on the stock market, and he would more than recoup his investment.

That was why he'd increased his exposure to risk when Anatoly contacted him in January and offered him another bundle of shares. One of the original investors needed to reduce his commitments at short notice; was Carsten interested?

It didn't take him long to make up his mind, not least because plenty of others were beginning to sniff out the potential in KiberPay.

A few weeks later, he had acquired an additional portion of the company. This time he bought the shares privately; it broke every rule in the book, but he didn't care. He had to borrow money to facilitate the deal, using all his assets as security, but he knew it was a sound investment. The loan wasn't due to be repaid until October, which gave him plenty of time after the flotation.

The profit would give him a platform of his own, the freedom to do exactly what he wanted for the rest of his life. A personal loan of twelve million dollars made his head spin, but he knew this was the chance of a lifetime.

He could see the beam of the headlights as a lone car crossed Chelsea Bridge. Nice and steady, like Carsten's plans. By the fall he would be richer than he could ever have imagined.

And he would no longer need Celia's money.

CHAPTER 5

Thursday, May 30

Nora nodded at the security guard sitting at the reception desk of the Swedish Economic Crimes Authority on Hantverkargatan. She swiped her pass card to open the glass doors and thought, not for the first time, that her photograph looked like a police mug shot.

The sun was shining in through the windows when she reached her office on the second floor. She was hoping for a quiet morning; she had no meetings booked and wasn't due in court until the following day.

She had only just put down her black briefcase when there was a knock on the door. Åke Sandelin, chief prosecutor, was standing there, holding his glasses in one hand.

"Good morning. Can you spare a few minutes?"

His checked shirt was open at the neck. No tie, which meant he wasn't in court today either. However, his well-polished black shoes shone, and Nora glanced at her own well-worn loafers with a certain amount of embarrassment. She waved in the direction of the nearest chair. Her office wasn't large, but there was room for a desk, two chairs, and a side table in pale wood.

"Take a seat."

Åke sat down and crossed his legs.

"So how long have you been with us now?" he asked in his distinctively deep voice.

"Let me think . . . I started in August 2010, just after the holiday period."

Nora had gone for the temporary post with the Economic Crimes Authority when Julia turned one. In the spring before Julia was born, she had stepped down from her post at the bank where she had worked for ten years; the decision had been made by mutual agreement, as they say.

In return for a generous severance package and excellent references, she had gone quietly, without reporting her former boss for sexual harassment.

Had she done the right thing? She would never know, but she hadn't been able to face a long, drawn-out legal mediation. The financial settlement had kept her afloat for quite some time.

"Are you happy here?"

Nora gave a start and realized she'd been lost in thought, transported back to the misery she'd felt when things went so wrong.

"Absolutely, happier than I could ever have imagined. I actually feel that I'm contributing to making a better society."

She was upholding the law in the best sense of the word, however banal that might sound.

"It's good to be working on something meaningful," she added, "instead of putting all my time and energy into a project just so that it can be included in a quarterly report. I like the fact that this isn't about consumerism; we're not selling shampoo or lipstick."

She saw a glint of recognition in Åke's eyes. *He understands me, because he feels exactly the same. It's important to believe in what you do. How did I overlook this in my job at the bank?*

The last few months in her previous job had been difficult. The management had tried to force her to give the green light to a dodgy deal.

When she refused, she'd been sidelined and then harassed. Eventually the scandal broke when one of Nora's colleagues in the legal department discovered what was going on and decided to blow the whistle. Nora remembered the headlines and the media frenzy. Both her former boss and the vice chair had had to leave in humiliating circumstances, but she was already gone by then.

"We're more than happy with you," Åke assured her. "Your background makes you ideally suited to the work we do."

He broke off and put on his horn-rimmed glasses, which magnified his eyes. His gaze looked more intense, dark and piercing, which no doubt gave him an edge in court.

He smiled and leaned forward; Nora automatically did the same.

"We have the opportunity to take on another district prosecutor. I don't know if you'd be interested?"

District prosecutor? That would give her the opportunity to make a real difference. She felt warm inside.

"I'd love to stay on here, I really would."

"Excellent." Åke leaned back. "We'll need a dispensation from the prosecutor general, and of course the selection committee will have an input, but I'm sure it'll be fine."

I must call Jonas. Buy a bottle of wine to celebrate. He's not on duty until the day after tomorrow; a few bubbles tonight should be OK, even if he's flying on Saturday.

"It's the usual procedure," Åke went on. "We were thinking of an application period of a few weeks, with a start date of July 1." He smiled again and got to his feet. The conversation was over.

"I appreciate your confidence in me," Nora said, suppressing the urge to skip around the room.

Nora gathered up the documentation she needed for tomorrow: a small-business owner had been cheating on his taxes and his value-added tax payments. She had familiarized herself with the details and was ready to go for a conviction. As she was locking everything away, she glanced at her watch. Jonas was picking her up in half an hour, just after six.

"We're going out to celebrate," he'd said as soon as he heard her news. "The boys can watch Julia."

Nora stared at her computer. There was no point in starting anything new at this point, so she clicked on the home page of one of the country's leading daily newspapers, *Dagens Nyheter*, and scrolled through the headlines. An article about wealthy Swedish expats caught her attention, and her thoughts turned to the building project on Sandhamn.

What was it Eva had said about the people who'd bought Fyrudden?

Nora knew she shouldn't be so nosy, but she couldn't help googling *Fyrudden + Sandhamn*. She soon discovered that a limited company was listed as the buyer. That wasn't particularly unusual in itself; expat Swedes often put their assets into a company in order to avoid tax.

However, the person who had named this company hadn't exactly used their imagination; it was called Fyrudden AB. Nora did a little more searching and found that someone called Carsten Jonsson was behind the purchase. Sounded like a Danish first name.

She checked public records, feeling slightly ashamed as she looked up Carsten Jonsson, but she was too curious to back off now.

Jonsson's mother was born in Copenhagen, while his significantly older father came from Rimbo, north of Stockholm. The father had been a sea captain before transferring to the Customs Service. He had died many years ago, in the late 1990s, but the mother, Kirsten, was still alive.

Lars Carsten Jonsson was born in 1975, so he must be thirty-eight now. After graduating from high school in Vallentuna, he'd studied at the Stockholm School of Economics before traveling to the US to do his master's in New York.

She didn't find anything else out about his life in Sweden until he popped up as the new owner of Fyrudden, but Nora did manage to find out what he'd been doing in the meantime.

Carsten had stayed in New York and started his career with Morgan Stanley, the major investment bank. After a while he'd moved back to Europe and settled in London, where he worked for a smaller investment bank. But he wasn't a current employee.

Maybe he'd started up some kind of fund and was making investments of his own? That was a pretty common move for a venture capitalist. The Swedish Economic Crimes Authority kept a close eye on those guys—almost as close as the IRS.

The trajectory for successful venture capitalists was laughably standardized. First they got themselves a sound education in economics before serving their time with a major bank in London or New York. Gradually they started investing privately, often with one or two associates. All with the aim of becoming stinking rich.

The king's youngest daughter, Princess Madeleine, was soon to marry a man with exactly that kind of background.

Nora decided to take another look at the mother, see where the money came from.

Judging by his mother's tax details, Jonsson hadn't grown up in a wealthy household. Vallentuna wasn't exactly a luxury suburb, and Kirsten received only the state pension. His father didn't appear to have left them anything either, so Jonsson must have done really well overseas if he'd made enough to buy Fyrudden.

Twenty million—unbelievable. And how much was the house costing? Every time she was on the island, she'd heard the locals complaining about the construction workers' trucks constantly shuttling back and forth with materials.

She kept searching and discovered a photograph. It must have been taken at the English gala premiere of a James Bond film; she could see a cardboard figure of Daniel Craig in the background and the title of the movie in big black letters.

Carsten Jonsson wasn't what she'd expected at all. He was wearing a well-fitted black dinner jacket and was tan and muscular, his slightly too-long blond hair flopping over his forehead. There was something impatient about his posture, as if he was on the way to somewhere else and didn't really have time to stand still for two seconds.

The woman next to him was in a lilac silk dress. She had dark wavy hair and was very slim, bordering on skinny. His wife? Impossible to tell, but a huge diamond sparkled on her left hand, and there was something very relaxed and confident about the way her arm was tucked under his.

They made an attractive couple, but Nora couldn't imagine them on Sandhamn, where jeans and faded shorts were the norm. She scrolled down the page, but there were no more pictures.

Maybe a media-shy venture capitalist wasn't so unusual these days, given the attitude of the press toward those involved in finance.

She shook her head and logged off. She knew quite a lot about her new neighbor on the island now—a lot more than the gossip Eva had passed on. Should she be ashamed of herself for having spent half an hour poking around? Maybe, but at the same time it was important to understand what kind of person Carsten Jonsson was. Plus she hadn't accessed any unauthorized databases. Everything she'd found was either online or counted as public information, available to anyone.

In spite of all that, she wasn't entirely comfortable with herself as she got to her feet. She felt as if she'd secretly peeped in through the window of her neighbor's bedroom.

CHAPTER 6

Thomas was in the middle of a huge yawn when Margit Grankvist poked her head around the door.

"Are you busy?" she asked, waving a bundle of papers. "I think our bosses have finally gone completely crazy. Sometimes I just get so tired . . ."

She pushed back her short hair, which was now peppered with gray, and dropped the papers on Thomas's desk. He could see from the letterhead that they came from the National Police Board, so were unlikely to contain good news.

The expression on Margit's face confirmed his suspicions.

"What's happened?" He read the title: *Streamlining Police Work.*

"A streamlining and efficiency consultant will be joining us and monitoring our work in order to . . ." Margit broke off and picked up the first page. "In order to identify comparison figures that can be used in the development of a methodology within the national police service with the aim of securing and optimizing a coherent resource allocation and competence provision in a cost-effective way."

She sat down and leaned back. "Sometimes I wish the Old Man was still here so I wouldn't have to deal with this crap."

"As far as I'm aware, no one forced you to take his job when he retired."

Thomas immediately realized that his words weren't going to improve Margit's mood. Anyway, he wasn't convinced that their former boss, well known for his uneven temper, would have handled the demands from on high any better.

"How much damage can one consultant do?" he added quickly, hoping to take the sting out of his words.

"Who do you think should have the honor of looking after the idiot when he gets here?" Margit went on as if he hadn't spoken. It was obvious that she had Thomas in mind.

No, thanks. Thomas was about to suggest Aram Gorgis, his partner since Margit's promotion, but knew Aram wouldn't thank him for it.

"How about Kalle? He's pretty diplomatic," he said instead.

"That's not a bad idea," Margit said slowly.

Thomas still thought of Kalle Lidwall as a young detective, even though he'd recently turned thirty-six and they'd worked together for many years. Maybe it was because of his colleague's reserved manner; Kalle didn't make a fuss about anything. But he was far from a novice, even though he looked like a young Coastal Ranger with his cropped hair.

"Plus he's good with IT; he'll be able to produce any stats that are required," Thomas went on, underlining Kalle's suitability.

Margit's shoulders dropped a little. "By the way, guess who I saw in the newspapers the other day?"

"No idea."

"Erik Blom. There was a big article about the firm he's working for now, Eagle Security. They've won some major contract with the city of Stockholm. Erik's security chief of the division that handles the public sector."

Thomas couldn't tell whether Margit was impressed or critical.

"He seems to be doing well. In the picture they had of him, he was wearing a significant amount of hair gel, and his watch must have cost a fortune."

Erik had always been something of a high flyer, cooler than most. He hadn't been a bad cop, far from it, but he was a guy who liked the good things in life.

Karin Ek, their admin assistant, had sadly informed everyone of Erik's departure, adding that the unit would never be the same, but Thomas knew exactly why he'd decided to go. A few years earlier, he'd lost his only sister to cancer. A month after the funeral, Erik had come into Thomas's office late one evening when they were both working overtime.

"Life's too short," he'd said when he'd told Thomas about his decision. "I'm tired of risking my life for a pathetic salary, fighting for a bonus of a couple of hundred kronor. I want a decent income. I want to be able to travel, to afford a nice apartment."

Thomas had picked up the slight unsteadiness in his voice, the grief seeping through.

"Look what happened to Mimi," Erik had said quietly. "You never know what's waiting around the corner."

Margit picked up her papers and got to her feet. "OK, so that's settled: Kalle will babysit our consultant."

After she'd gone Thomas just sat there, staring into space. Erik's words echoed in his mind. Maybe he'd had the right idea.

Life *was* short and unpredictable.

He saw his face reflected in the computer screen. His hair was still mostly blond and hadn't yet begun to thin. He exercised regularly and kept himself pretty fit. But his temples were graying, as was the stubble he could see when he shaved in the mornings. The lines in his forehead had deepened.

I'm only forty-six, he thought, wondering why he'd put it that way. *You'll soon be fifty*, a voice whispered.

"I want a different kind of life," Erik had said.

So do I.

CHAPTER 7

The door closed behind Sarah and Maria. Celia had asked Maria to take Sarah with her when she went to pick up Oliver from school, blaming a headache even though she really didn't need to explain herself.

Maria got along well with the children—almost better than she did.

There weren't many years left before Oliver would be sent off to boarding school, and Celia knew she ought to make the most of the time they had. But she couldn't do it, couldn't cope with Oliver's babbling and his constant questions when her mind was filled with Carsten and the way he treated her.

The pleading look on her little boy's face when he wanted attention was too much for her. It was better if Maria took care of him; then at least Celia didn't have to disappoint him.

She went into the bedroom and drew the dark velvet curtains, then fetched a Sobril from the bathroom. She knew she shouldn't do it, but it was necessary. It wasn't as if she was some kind of addict; she just needed to alleviate the pain for a little while.

She lay down on the bed and pulled the soft cashmere throw over her. She'd found it in Harrods, and it was a perfect match with the other colors in the bedroom, Champagne and Bordeaux.

She was oppressed by the thought of the holiday home in Sweden. Carsten's new project on Sandhamn.

Sandhamn. The name made her feel anything but positive.

They could have bought a villa in the south of France like so many of their friends, but Carsten had refused to listen. Instead he'd spent a ridiculous amount of money on a plot on some little island in the Baltic. She'd seen the total cost on the contract, which he'd accidentally left out on his desk. When she converted it into pounds, she was shocked. Carsten hadn't even given her a sensible explanation, apart from insisting that the children needed to spend time in Sweden and become fluent in the language. But there were plenty of other ways to learn Swedish.

She'd seen pictures of the construction site; the new house was completely isolated by a stretch of shoreline with a dense pine forest behind it. There were no neighbors nearby, and the small village was some distance away. No cars were allowed on the island, only bicycles.

Celia swallowed and wished she'd taken a double dose to stop the bad thoughts creeping into her head.

She'd done everything he'd asked of her, even learned Swedish for his sake. And still it wasn't enough. She knew he had other women; she was smart enough to realize what was going on when he went off to his business dinners and came home in the middle of the night with unfamiliar perfume on his jacket.

She'd once had herself tested, terrified that he might have infected her with something he'd picked up. The humiliation still made her feel sick.

She curled up under the throw.

Over the last six months, Carsten had made frequent trips to Russia but had refused to go into detail about them when he came home. It had to do with investments, and that's all he would say.

Celia was worried that he'd met someone else. There were plenty of rumors about beautiful Russian women who were looking for a meal ticket in the shape of a rich Westerner.

The more Carsten stayed up late making phone calls, the more anxious Celia became. She'd even considered mentioning it to her father, just to find out whether he knew anything about these Russian investments, but Carsten would be furious if he found out, and there was already enough tension between her husband and her father.

In the beginning she'd believed that the money she had persuaded her father to put into Carsten's venture capital fund would form a solid basis for their relationship, but instead it had opened up a deep rift between them. It had made Carsten financially dependent on her family, and she knew he hated the situation.

Celia's eyes filled with tears. She'd never really been in love until Carsten came into her life at that wedding. They'd danced together all evening, and she'd known right away that this was the real thing.

He'd made it clear that he was prepared to fight for her, even though her parents were wary and had tried to persuade her to take it slowly.

"I'll never let you go," he'd declared when she told him how her mom and dad felt.

The proposal had been unexpected and had made him even more attractive. When she was finally standing at the altar with her hand in his, she had been convinced that her parents were wrong. It had been the happiest day of her life.

She couldn't face the idea that they'd been right all along. They'd warned her against marrying someone from a different social circle and had been afraid that Carsten was more interested in Celia's money and connections than their darling daughter.

The thought of admitting how bad things were between them was unbearable. She simply had to grit her teeth and make sure her marriage survived.

A single tear trickled down her cheek.

Maybe Sandhamn was exactly what they needed after all; maybe spending a summer on the island would help them find their way back to each other, make the family whole again.

She so wanted Carsten to look at her the way he used to.

And she wanted the children to run to her instead of to Maria.

CHAPTER 8

"Hi, I'm home."

Pernilla closed the front door with a soft click.

She sounds so happy, Thomas thought before he left the kitchen and the dirty dishes. He and Elin had eaten without her because Pernilla had had a late meeting.

"Hi, sweetheart." He kissed her gently on the lips. "Do you want something to eat? There's goulash."

"I'd prefer a glass of wine. You're never going to believe what's happened today!" Pernilla was beaming. "I've been offered the most fantastic job—that's why I'm late. I thought it was an ordinary meeting with a major client, but it turns out they want me to take on the responsibility for all branding issues in Scandinavia. I'll be leading a team of four, it's really well paid, and I'll get a company car!"

Thomas was still holding the tea towel. He pulled Pernilla close and gave her a big hug.

"Congratulations! Let's open a bottle of wine to celebrate."

Elin came running in and Pernilla picked her up. The little girl nuzzled into her mother's neck as she always did. The back of her blond hair was tousled.

"Hi, honey! Guess what? Mommy's so happy today!"

Thomas went back into the kitchen. "Red or white?" he called over his shoulder.

"Either is fine."

He inspected the top shelf in the pantry. There were two bottles of red wine; one was Pernilla's favorite, a Merlot. As he unscrewed the cap, he could hear her chatting away to Elin. She sounded so excited; the words came bubbling out. He was pleased for her, he really was. She worked hard, she was good at her job, and she deserved an opportunity like this. Absolutely. Now Elin was a little older, so it was easier for Pernilla to focus on her career.

"Problem?" Pernilla teased him, pointing to the bottle in his hand. She opened a cupboard and took out two glasses.

"Leave the dishes, we can do them later. Let's go and sit on the balcony. It's a lovely evening, quite warm out still."

Thomas followed her through the living room, where Elin was curled up on the sofa in front of the TV, watching the last children's show of the evening before the news.

The turn-of-the-century apartment block in Södermalm was made of brick, like so many other buildings in the area. The balcony was big enough to accommodate two wicker chairs and a coffee table. Thomas had covered the concrete floor with dark-brown wooden decking.

"So tell me all about it," he said when they were sitting down with a glass of wine.

"They want me to start as soon as possible, preferably in September. The guy who's doing the job now is leaving in midsummer. The idea is that I'll have an overarching brief throughout Scandinavia, dealing with branding and content."

"What?"

"I know, it's all jargon," she said with a smile, taking a sip of her wine. "It's about developing the brand in the future, finding out how it's perceived by clients, suppliers, and the market as a whole. What's the first thing you think about when you hear names like IKEA or Volvo?"

"You have to remember I'm just an ordinary cop," Thomas said, half joking and half serious. "We're not very good at discussing branding and consent."

"Content. Sorry, I got carried away." She pushed back her hair. "The idea of working in depth on a brand gives me such a buzz. At the moment everything I do is targeted—we go in, we run a campaign, we disappear. There's no follow-up. This will give me the chance to work on every aspect from beginning to end."

Thomas nodded as if he understood exactly what she meant.

"Their head office is right by the Globe, which is perfect. I'll have a shorter commute than I have now, and I can still cycle as long as there's no snow."

A group of children was playing down in the courtyard, and the sound of their laughter filled the air. The leaves of the old weeping birch were already a darker shade of green; spring was turning into summer.

"It'll mean a substantial salary increase too," Pernilla added, giving him a look that was difficult to interpret.

"Great," Thomas said quickly.

A little *too* quickly?

There was no reason not to be happy, but at the same time the knowledge that the gap between their salaries would be even greater made him uncomfortable. He reminded himself that they lived in an equal society, in one of the world's most egalitarian countries.

"That's wonderful," he went on, wondering who he was trying to convince. "Here's to your new job!"

CHAPTER 9

Monday, June 3

Carsten Jonsson stopped on the edge of the forest and allowed his gaze to sweep slowly across the area. The morning sun was already high in the sky; the shore was bathed in sunlight. There was the odd patch of reeds or lyme grass, but there were no buildings to spoil the view. Apart from a few terns circling overhead, he was completely alone.

He felt the hairs on the back of his neck stand up. This was good, better than he could have imagined. Slowly he took in the house, just yards from the water's edge. The huge panes of glass reflecting the light, the turret on one gable end.

The renowned architect had been worth every penny.

The external walls consisted of panels painted dazzling white, creating a dramatic contrast with the black metal roof. The windows ran from floor to ceiling—double height in the living room. Every detail had been carefully planned. Carsten had spent a ridiculous amount of time on the architect's drawings, and it had cost a fortune, but he'd been determined not to hold back on anything. After all, the expense was peanuts compared with the money that would come flooding in once the Russian deal was signed and sealed.

Stylish, he thought. It was exactly what he'd dreamed of when he was a little boy and knew that one day he would stand here like this.

Something hardened in his pants.

"It's perfect," he murmured to himself, refusing to allow the memory of his father's voice to seep through.

The dull roar of an engine could be heard in the forest. It grew louder, and soon a quad bike appeared, pulling a trailer with several men on board.

Carsten recognized Mats Eklund, the project manager, bent over the handlebars. When the bike stopped, Eklund raised a hand in greeting and switched off the engine. His double chin wobbled as he clambered down. The builders disappeared behind the house, chatting quietly as they headed for the shed that was used to store their tools and equipment.

Carsten walked to the steps, studying his project manager. He knew that Eklund had a good reputation, but he was also aware that he paid just enough tax to avoid the suspicions of the IRS. The foreign workers probably didn't earn much.

"You've made excellent progress," Carsten said, holding out his hand as Eklund came over.

"I brought in some extra bodies, just as you asked." Eklund unzipped his dark-blue fleece jacket and produced the key from his inside pocket. It was shiny and new, just like everything else in front of them. "OK, let me show you what you've paid for."

Eklund opened the door, then took a step back.

"After you—it's your house."

Carsten walked in, and the light struck him right away, a flood of sunshine illuminating every corner of the house. Reflections of the sea danced and shimmered in the air. Sun, wind, and water only yards from his feet.

"You're going to need plenty of blinds," Eklund commented.

Carsten wasn't listening. He moved into the huge open-plan space, well over six hundred square feet. He could already picture the generous sofas next to the open fire. They'd place the dining table, with Arne Jacobsen chairs, by the south-facing glass wall.

Newport and Danish design—he could already hear Celia's protests, and the thought made him smile.

The wing housing the family bedrooms extended from the living room at a wide angle. Each one had a stunning sea view, and the master was at the far end with windows directly facing the water. Deep built-in closets would give Celia plenty of room for her clothes.

In the opposite direction, a smaller wing provided accommodation for the nanny.

It had been the architect's suggestion to distribute the bedrooms in this way. At first Carsten had been unsure, but now he understood. The different sections of the house balanced one another while screening the interior living space from the shore. "Two bird's wings protecting the nest," he'd said.

"The major appliances won't be here until next week," Eklund said. "But everything's ready. It won't take long to complete the installation. The electrician has practically been living here recently."

Carsten folded back a section of protective wrapping to admire the shimmer of the pale-gray Italian stone floor tiles.

"It's fantastic. But don't forget, it has to be finished by midsummer."

"I know what's in the contract—you don't need to remind me." Eklund adjusted a strip of masking tape on one of the window frames. "By the way, the local council came to visit."

Carsten closed his eyes. The council had raised objections from the get-go. The drawings had had to be redone several times, and he'd been forced to fly to Sweden in order to attend the meeting with the Planning Committee in person. The architect had been there, too, and charged him a whole day's pay for his trouble.

The application had been rejected, and Carsten's only option was to get his lawyers to complain to the county council in order to push through what he wanted.

"What was it this time?" he asked, thrusting his clenched fist into his pocket with such force that he scratched himself on the zipper.

"We found two old women creeping around outside when we came back from lunch on Wednesday. They were busy measuring and taking notes—said they were carrying out an inspection."

"What happened?"

"They claimed we haven't followed the approved plans. They think the footprint is too big."

Carsten relaxed his clenched fist. He knew they were right, but that was irrelevant. He had no intention of allowing a bunch of underpaid pen pushers to dictate what his new house was going to look like. He was done with Värmdö local council.

"What did you say to them?"

"I told them they had no right to be here. We've been granted permission from the Planning Committee, and we're following those plans. End of story."

Carsten's eyes narrowed as he thought about the gray-haired chair of the Planning Committee. The condescending look on her face.

"I realize it's been a long time since you lived in Sweden," she'd said. "But Swedish laws apply here, and the kind of building you're intending to erect isn't appropriate in a place like Sandhamn. Plus it's too close to the water."

As if she'd never made an exception to the rules regarding the preservation of the shoreline. Carsten knew exactly how many times the committee had ditched its so-called principles; his legal advisers had provided him with a long list. A list that proved very useful when he complained to the county council.

"Did you get their names?"

Eklund nodded.

"Good. I'll call my lawyer, get him to report them to the police."

Carsten went over to the kitchen area and opened one of the cupboards. He admired the solid wood, the softly curved handles in brushed steel. They'd been specially ordered from France; it had taken six months to get ahold of them.

"Say they were trespassing," he went on without turning around. "That should keep them away. They've got no business coming onto my land."

It would teach them a lesson if nothing else. The police might well dismiss the matter, but there were other options. He could take them to court, file a private prosecution against them as individuals, prevent them from hiding behind their professional roles.

That should keep them up at night, but above all it would send an important message: *Don't fuck with me.*

"Won't that cause even more trouble?" Eklund said, running his hand down the edge of a freshly painted door until he brushed against the square handle.

"That's my problem."

Eklund went over to the glass wall; an orange pilot boat was passing by.

"Are you happy with the jetty?"

"Very happy."

Carsten gazed with satisfaction at the huge structure, which would easily provide berths for four or five boats.

"By the way, have you heard anything about the planning consent? One of your neighbors came over the other day to ask about it."

Carsten sighed. Fucking assholes.

"We haven't built a *new* jetty," he explained. "Therefore we don't need planning consent. This is just a redesign."

He'd checked this out, too, with his lawyer, who'd assured him that he'd win if anyone decided to take him to court. Soon his legal bills were as high as those from his architect, but he didn't care. Nothing was going to stop him.

Carsten gave the cupboard door a little push. It closed gently and without a sound, exactly as per his specifications, which put him in a slightly better mood.

The locals were bound to object. Good old Swedish envy. What else had he expected?

"Don't worry about it," he said with a shrug. "I'd like to take a look at the bedrooms now."

He headed along the hallway to the master suite.

"What the fuck?" he yelled.

Chapter 10

Carsten was pointing to the big window. There was an ugly mark in the center, and the glass was crisscrossed with cracks.

Eklund walked past him to take a closer look.

"It wasn't like this when we left on Friday."

"How the hell did it happen?"

It wasn't too difficult to figure out, but Carsten wanted to hear Eklund's explanation.

The other man's forehead was beaded with sweat.

"It was too expensive to employ a security guard over the weekends," he muttered. "The boys don't want to stay around unless they're getting paid more."

"If you'd told me that before, this could have been avoided."

Eklund stared at the window, his expression troubled. "You know this project isn't popular on the island. People say we're destroying the forest by driving back and forth on the quad bike, crushing heather and blueberry bushes."

"And are you?"

"We've brought in most of the materials by boat, but a certain amount of driving is inevitable. We can't walk from the harbor, carrying everything that's needed for the project."

Eklund stuck his index finger under his black knit hat and scratched the back of his neck.

"We've had complaints about the jetty, too. Your new neighbor, Agaton—the guy who lives over there." He pointed northwest. "He came over the other day and went off."

"Agaton?" Carsten frowned. "He's the guy who wrote all those letters." He turned away from the broken window and shrugged. "He needs to stay away from my property."

"He claims the new jetty is partly in his waters."

"And what did you say?"

"Nothing, just that it was none of my business, and he'd have to take it up with you."

Eklund peered at the window again. "Maybe it was just kids. A couple of bored teenagers who'd had too much to drink. There's not much to do on this island before the season gets underway."

Carsten pushed aside a shard of glass with his shoe.

"Get this cleaned up and make sure a new window's fitted as soon as possible."

He walked out of the room; he couldn't look at it any longer.

So there were objections on the island? It was hardly a surprise, but he knew how to get the locals on his side.

CHAPTER 11

Tuesday, June 4

Carsten was walking through customs at Sheremetyevo, Moscow's international airport. Automatically he looked for the sign for Aeroexpress, the train that would take him into the heart of the city. Moscow traffic varied between total gridlock and complete chaos, and as a seasoned traveler he rarely took a cab into town.

The stock market flotation prospectus for KiberPay was safely tucked away in his briefcase. He'd read through the whole thing one more time during the flight just to make sure that all was as it should be. The SEC, the US financial regulator, was well known for its meticulous approach. There was no room for any errors in the documentation required before flotation on Nasdaq. They'd been working on the prospectus for almost a year, but there were still many questions that needed to be fixed.

A female voice made an announcement over the PA system, first in Russian and then in English. An electronic board informed passengers that the next train to Bellorusskaya would depart in ten minutes.

Carsten had arranged to meet Anatoly for dinner at Café Pushkin at eight o'clock, which gave him a few hours' peace and quiet in the hotel.

He needed to order a car and driver for the following day, and he could also do with some sleep, if he could manage to relax.

He bought a first-class train ticket and headed for the elevator.

The brightly lit façade was as impressive as ever when Carsten's driver brought the Mercedes smoothly to a halt outside Café Pushkin. Carsten had always liked this place, and it served top-quality Russian cuisine.

An elegantly uniformed attendant opened the beautiful glass doors, and it was like stepping back into the nineteenth century. It was hard to believe the restaurant had opened only fifteen years ago. The deep gilt-framed mirrors on the ceiling, the richly decorated bar made of dark wood, the curving staircase, and the shelves of books with gilded leather bindings—the whole thing could have come straight out of an aristocrat's mansion in the days of the tsar.

Anatoly was already seated at the round table, but got to his feet as soon as he saw Carsten.

"Welcome to Moscow, my friend."

He held out his hand and patted Carsten's shoulder with the other.

"Champagne," he said to the maître d'. "Dom Pérignon 2000."

The maître d' bowed and returned in seconds with two crystal glasses and an ice bucket. He poured the drinks, then handed Carsten a leather-bound menu. As usual all the dishes were listed in both Russian and English, although Carsten knew it was an old-fashioned colloquial variation of Russian that few native speakers could read. However, there was no denying that it looked impressive.

"The duck pâté is pretty good," Anatoly said. "I had it a few weeks ago when I was here with a group of investors."

Carsten much preferred duck liver to goose; the thick slices of foie gras that were so popular among the nouveau riche Russians were much too fatty in his opinion.

"I'd like us to meet up in your office first thing," he said, jerking his head in the direction of the other diners. "I've highlighted a number of points in the prospectus that we need to go through in detail; this environment is hardly conducive to that kind of discussion."

At the next table were two men in their thirties; Carsten didn't like the look of them at all. He thought he could see the outline of guns beneath their shirts. Had Anatoly decided to surround himself with bodyguards? He knew it wasn't unusual in business meetings over here, but thought it would be inappropriate to ask.

The table on the other side was occupied by a man in his sixties accompanied by a strikingly attractive woman. Carsten reckoned the age difference must be at least thirty years. A diamond necklace sparkled every time the woman moved. Her blond hair was arranged in a messy up-do, with a few strands tumbling softly around her face. She was wearing a close-fitting strapless dress, drawing attention to her bare shoulders. Maybe he should consider finishing off the evening at Egoist, one of Moscow's more upscale strip clubs?

The maître d' took their orders and replenished their glasses. He held up the empty bottle with an inquiring look. Anatoly nodded, then turned to Carsten and cleared his throat.

"We've had an offer."

"What do you mean?"

"For your shares in KiberPay. We have a buyer."

Carsten couldn't help laughing. He raised his glass in a toast to Anatoly.

"There'll be plenty of buyers as soon as the company's floated," he said. "We both know that. When KiberPay goes up on Nasdaq, the shares will be worth billions, whatever currency we're talking about."

The company had been valued at four hundred million dollars in January, when he bought his shares. Now it was worth two billion, which meant his three percent had gone up from twelve million to sixty.

Easy money. It had been ridiculously simple.

Anatoly gave a discreet cough. "I haven't expressed myself clearly enough. We've had an inquiry about your personal shares. The person involved is wondering if you'd be interested in selling before the stock market flotation."

"Are you kidding me? Why the hell would I want to offload my shares at this stage?"

Another private placement? That was how he'd gotten into KiberPay, through a private arrangement where shares changed hands with the help of a financial adviser who conducted the transaction. Anatoly had acted as broker for everyone involved, but that phase was behind them now. They were so close to Nasdaq that Carsten could almost feel the money in his hands.

Was this some kind of Russian humor that he didn't understand?

"If you sell now, you know how much you'll get," Anatoly said hesitantly. "You can never be sure what will happen with a flotation." He broke off and said something in Russian to a passing waitress. He continued with no explanation. "Sorry. The introductory rate won't be set until the day before. We both know that. There's no guarantee that it will hit the right level."

In theory Anatoly was right, but the valuation was based on a meticulous analysis of KiberPay's earning capability and market potential, the stream of clients signing up, and not least the company's track record.

"You were the one who mentioned a rate you'd be happy with," the Russian pointed out.

They'd sat up late one night in Moscow, drinking vodka. Carsten had had a little too much and had talked more openly than he usually did. He'd let slip the share price he was hoping for.

An amount that would pay off all his debts and make him a very wealthy man.

A moment of weakness.

He had realized the very next morning that he'd left himself exposed by telling Anatoly about the extent of his loans and commitment but hoped the other man had also been too drunk to remember.

Apparently not.

"So who's asking?" Carsten did his best to keep his tone casual.

A pianist began to play in the background, a melancholy tune that he vaguely recognized. Shostakovich?

"The inquiry came via a legal practice, Beketov & Partners."

Carsten had never heard of them, but then he was no expert on Russian law firms. At the same time, he wasn't surprised; this was typical of Moscow. Many private individuals, investors who preferred to remain anonymous, chose to be represented by discreet lawyers.

The waiter arrived with their starters. He poured the golden Sauternes they'd chosen to accompany the duck pâté, then bowed with one hand behind his back.

"Have they mentioned a price point?" Carsten asked, even though he had no intention of selling.

"Not yet. They wanted to see if you were interested first."

So very Russian, Carsten thought; he couldn't help smiling. There was always someone wanting to jump on board when the sweet smell of success was in the air. No doubt the rumor that KiberPay was a real goldmine had spread around Moscow by now.

But whoever was hiding behind Beketov & Partners would have to stand in line along with everyone else. They could either sign up for shares before the flotation or wait until it was possible to trade publicly on Nasdaq.

"So what do you think?"

Anatoly seemed to be slurring his words a fraction. Admittedly they'd gotten through a bottle and a half of wine, but he wasn't usually so easily affected.

Carsten shook his head, amused by the whole thing.

"No deal."

"Are you absolutely sure?"

Why didn't Anatoly just drop it? They knew each other well enough. He must realize there was no point in persisting.

"Tell that lawyer there's nothing to discuss. There's no reason for me to sell at this stage."

"Apparently this guy's worth listening to. He's . . . well connected."

Carsten felt his stomach muscles contract. The corruption of the legal system in Russia was no secret, nor was the political control of the country's courts and prosecution service, but it wasn't something he'd ever worried about. The state exerted political and financial pressure in certain contexts; it was well known that public money was widely misused, and there was a lack of clarity and fairness when it came to business matters. Many investors had already been frightened off.

But that also opened up opportunities.

So far any inroads into private property had been largely restricted to companies it was in the nation's interest to control: steel, oil, gas fields. Carsten had been convinced that the e-commerce sector was safe. His investment was too small to arouse any interest.

Had he been wrong?

The thought of what had happened to Mikhail Khodorkovsky crossed his mind. Khodorkovsky had been the richest man in Russia when he was arrested and charged with fraud. At the same time his oil company, Yukos, was taken over by the state. Many believed that the charges were fabricated in order to justify the nationalization of Yukos. Khodorkovsky had been in jail for almost ten years.

Anatoly kept his eyes fixed on Carsten, who glanced around to check that no one was listening. The men who might be carrying guns were sitting in silence. The fat man at the other table was enjoying blinis, sour cream, and black caviar while the attractive woman was merely picking at her food.

"Have you really no idea who the buyer might be?" Carsten asked quietly, feeling beads of sweat break out along his hairline. In the labyrinth of corrupt officials running the Russian state, there were many who tried to exploit the situation, sometimes by pretending to adopt a position of power that didn't exist. He had no intention of allowing himself to be spooked unnecessarily.

"Obviously I've asked the question, but the lawyer refuses to reveal any names."

No need to act hastily, Carsten thought, wiping his forehead with his napkin.

Anatoly struck a match and lit a cigarette.

"How high up might these 'connections' be?" Carsten asked.

"Hard to say."

Anatoly muttered something in Russian, the long syllables giving emphasis to the words Carsten couldn't understand. However, the tone was unmistakable.

"What did you say?"

"A fish rots from the head down."

"Sorry?"

Anatoly shrugged. "It's an old Russian saying. You know how things are here."

You should clean the stairs from the bottom up, Carsten thought. *In Sweden we tackle the issue from the opposite direction.* The symbolism of the two different sayings wasn't lost on him.

"What do you think I should do?"

"You should at least listen to what they're offering before you dismiss the idea."

"And if I don't?"

Anatoly made a noise that was somewhere between a laugh and a cough. "There's no point in speculating on such matters."

Carsten wasn't prepared to leave it at that. "What happens if I don't do what they want?"

"That depends on who the client turns out to be." Anatoly took a long drag on his cigarette. When he exhaled, the smoke curled slowly above the flickering flames of the candles. "But if they're willing to pay a good price, as good as you'd get otherwise . . ."

He was right. Carsten had nothing to lose. If the price was high enough, then of course he could sell his shares now. The bank wouldn't complain if they got their money back early, and it would enable him to release the properties he'd used to secure the loan: the apartment in London and the new house on Fyrudden.

That would enable him to sleep better at night.

"OK, talk to them. You can act as middleman. Find out what they're willing to pay and who's behind the offer. If they're not prepared to reveal any more details, I'm flying home tomorrow evening as planned."

CHAPTER 12

Friday, July 5

Thomas made his way down the hill to the restaurant where he'd arranged to meet Erik Blom. It was on the quayside by Nacka Strand, just a few minutes from the police station. However, Thomas rarely went there to eat; the prices were considerably higher than the cafés he usually frequented for lunch, and the clientele was made up of the sailing fraternity rather than pen pushers.

The two of them had been trying to get together for weeks. It hadn't been easy to find a mutually convenient date, but Erik had sounded very keen on the phone, not wanting to put it off until after the summer holiday season.

It seemed as if all the outside tables were occupied, and Thomas tried to spot Erik in the crowd. The hum of conversation filled the air. Eventually he saw his former colleague at a table by the water.

"Good to see you," Erik said, patting Thomas's shoulder. "It's been a while!"

Thomas sat down, noting that Erik's hair was as carefully styled as always. His Ray-Ban sunglasses looked new, and the well-fitting jacket and casual cotton shirt contributed to the image of a successful man.

Erik handed him the menu.

"Here you go. I've already decided on the scallops."

Thomas read aloud: "'The chef recommends grilled scallops on a bed of cauliflower puree with sautéed sage leaves.' Sounds good."

"I'm so pleased you were able to come," Erik said. "We don't meet up often enough."

"You know how things are."

It wasn't easy to keep in touch. During the week the job ate up most of Thomas's time, and on the weekends it was all about family. When they were going through their calendars on Sunday evenings, Pernilla sometimes joked that life had turned into a logistics operation, but there was an element of seriousness in her words.

"I'd like to show you something." Erik reached into his black leather briefcase and took out a folder. "This is our company brochure—it tells you who we are and what we do."

The brochure was printed on thick paper using bright, clear colors, with the Eagle Security logo on the front page. Below the company name was a picture of a smiling blonde in a crisp uniform standing in front of a reception desk. No doubt Pernilla would have found it overloaded but goal-oriented.

"Perhaps you're already aware that we operate in a dozen countries?" Erik continued, turning to a page showing a map of Europe with a number of countries highlighted in red.

Where was Erik going with this?

"Let me tell you something about Eagle Security. Our aim is to work in a wider context using, among other methods, a range of cutting-edge technological solutions. It's all about assessing risks, providing security solutions, and giving the client a sense of security in a world that's increasingly unsafe, unfortunately."

Erik paused briefly.

"We just want to help people. If they entrust us with their business, they'll be able to sleep soundly at night."

That's exactly what I do.

The thought came unbidden, accompanied by the inevitable weariness.

That's what I ought to be doing, Thomas corrected himself. *Instead I spend half my time filling out forms and writing reports.*

A harried waitress came over and took their orders. When she'd gone, Erik turned to another page and pushed the brochure across to Thomas.

"These are our core values, what we stand for: reliability, trust, and expertise."

This was beginning to sound a lot like a sales pitch.

"If you like the sound of it, you might be interested to hear that there's a vacancy for head of risk management in our Swedish division." Before Thomas had the chance to open his mouth, Erik added, "I know what you're capable of, Thomas, and you're perfect for this job. You'd be working with our major clients in the public sector; you'd be responsible for analyzing various scenarios, assessing threat levels, coming up with suggestions for solutions together with the team you'd be leading."

Thomas took a few sips of his drink as he tried to gather his thoughts. He gazed out across the water. It was a beautiful summer day, and the air was mild. Directly opposite the restaurant lay Djurgården, the small island right in the center of Stockholm that had once been the king's hunting ground.

After this week the city would empty as the majority of its residents headed off to their summer cottages or overseas. They wouldn't return until the middle of August.

What if Thomas came back to a completely different job? In a normal workplace with no violent crime, no human misery on a daily basis? A head office in the city, where everyone wore civilian clothes.

He picked up his sunglasses and put them on; somehow they gave him breathing space.

Erik didn't appear to have noticed that Thomas was at a loss for words.

"Isn't it time to cut loose? Ditch the bureaucracy and the in-fighting, the constant pressure from the media? Wouldn't you like to work in a place where people are at the heart of the operation?"

Erik clearly couldn't help reverting to clichés, Thomas thought. But the conviction of the newly redeemed was definitely shining in his eyes.

At that moment the waitress appeared with two plates of beautifully arranged scallops. Her attention was already on the next table, where a man was beckoning her over.

"Looks good," Erik said.

He kept talking about Eagle Security, sounding for all the world like a company boss on TV. His pitch was peppered with phrases from the brochure: holistic perspective, customer benefit, open dialogue. It was clear that he no longer identified with his former profession as a police officer.

Will I sound like him after a few years?

Thomas wasn't naïve. He knew perfectly well that Eagle Security was driven by profit targets and required returns, regardless of how many "core values" Erik came up with.

However, the police service was also subject to financial parameters. Nobody escaped budget targets and cuts.

I work for society.

He'd been a police officer all of his working life; could he really walk away? He cut another piece of scallop as he listened. This was definitely a business lunch.

"The terms are very good," Erik said, wiping his mouth. "Excellent salary, company car, of course. Six weeks' vacation. So what do you think? Are you interested?"

CHAPTER 13

They couldn't be far from Sandhamn now. The skipper had said it would take around half an hour, and twenty minutes had already passed.

Sarah was on Maria's lap, and Oliver was sitting beside her, playing with Celia's iPhone. Maria knew that Carsten didn't like it, but Celia would slip it to him quietly. His face looked hot beneath his little blue cap. It was a lovely day but warm inside the boat. She'd bought him a Coke, and he'd drunk it quickly.

She gazed in fascination at the boats they passed, their sails filled with the wind, the Swedish flag fluttering from the stern of every single one. Yachts, motorboats, smaller launches . . .

She loved the skerries and the low pine trees growing crooked because of the wind. Here and there, she glimpsed red-painted cottages, but mostly she saw nothing but forest and rocks. So different from the landscape of her native Småland.

A sound from behind made her glance in Carsten's direction; it was his iPad. He was sitting at the far end of the curved sofa with the tablet in his hand. He hadn't taken his eyes off it since they came aboard. He'd worked during the flight, too, and had hardly exchanged a word with Celia or anyone else.

Maria adjusted her position. Sarah had fallen asleep, thumb in her mouth. It was hardly surprising; they'd been up since six. Celia had curled up with her eyes closed, her forehead resting against the window. She seemed to be asleep, too, hands lying limply on top of her roomy snakeskin purse.

"Are we there yet?" Oliver asked.

"Nearly, sweetheart. Isn't it exciting? Soon you'll see your new house and your new room!"

"I need to pee-pee."

Needless to say, the Coke had worked its way through. Typical—she should have expected that from the start.

"Can't you hold on? We haven't got long to go."

Oliver shook his head.

"OK, let's go find the bathroom."

Maria looked around, unsure if there was one on board the taxi boat. She couldn't get up without disturbing Sarah and didn't really want to wake her unnecessarily. She was bound to start bawling.

"Ask Daddy to take you."

Oliver made a face but went over to Carsten. A sudden swell made the boat lurch; the little boy almost fell but managed to regain his balance.

"Daddy, I need to go pee-pee."

Carsten didn't seem to have heard him. He was still staring at the screen.

"Daddy." Oliver tried again, a little louder this time. He started moving his feet up and down; Maria could see it was urgent.

Carsten glanced up and frowned as Oliver tugged at his arm.

"What do you want?"

"Can you take me to the bathroom? I don't know where it is."

"You're a big boy now. Surely you can go on your own, just like you do in school?"

Carsten's phone rang, and he reached into his pocket.

Maria looked at Oliver's face; he was very pale. Was he feeling seasick? *Please don't let him start throwing up . . .*

"Maria!" Carsten shouted over the noise of the engine, waving his phone. "Can you help Oliver please? I'm busy."

Maria did her best to put Sarah down gently, hoping she'd stay asleep, but her eyes flew open, and she immediately burst into tears.

"Hush, sweetheart. We're almost there."

"Maria!" There was desperation in Oliver's voice. "I really need to pee right now!"

Maria picked up the sobbing Sarah and hurried over to Oliver.

"Try to hold on," she whispered as she took his hand and led him over to the toilet, which she'd just spotted tucked away between the cabin and the cockpit. The door was hard to open, and she had to let go of Oliver and tug at the handle. Sarah was still crying.

At last it opened, but when she turned around she saw that it was too late. A large wet patch was spreading from Oliver's crotch. His lower lip was trembling.

"In here, sweetheart." Maria bundled him into the cramped toilet. "Don't worry about it, these things happen."

As she closed the door, she glanced in Carsten's direction. He was sitting with his back to them, totally absorbed in the phone call. Celia was still asleep.

"It's fine," Maria reassured the little boy once more. "Sometimes you just don't make it in time."

"Please don't tell Daddy," Oliver whispered.

CHAPTER 14

The reflections of the sunlight dancing on the water hurt Celia's eyes as she stepped ashore from the taxi boat. She stood for a moment on the jetty. On the other side lay a large gray dinghy, plus a smaller boat with peeling paint on the engine hood.

She looked up and saw the enormous white house on the beach. Carsten had shown her photographs in London, but they hadn't conveyed the sheer scale of the place.

"Come on," he shouted over his shoulder. "Come and take a look. We'll bring the luggage in later."

Celia tottered along the wooden planks in her high heels.

"Don't rush me!" She sounded snappy and regretted the words as soon as they'd left her mouth.

Oliver suddenly let go of Maria's hand and ran after his father.

"Careful, Oliver! You're not wearing a lifejacket!" Celia called out. He couldn't really swim yet, and Carsten had already said that Sarah and Oliver would have to go to swimming classes on Sandhamn. They were scheduled to start on Monday.

Carsten waited for her at the end of the jetty and chivalrously held out his hand to help her onto the sand. Celia smiled at him, a spark of hope firing in her breast.

"Thank you, darling. It's stunning."

Her husband beamed. "It's beautiful, isn't it?" He picked up a pebble and sent it skimming across the surface of the water. It bounced several times, which pleased him even more.

"How about that?" He sounded so delighted that Celia stopped for a moment.

This is his dream. He's happy now.

Oliver came running. "Show me how to do that, Daddy! Show me!"

Carsten laughed and ruffled his son's hair.

"Find a flat stone and I'll show you—it's not difficult."

Celia's heart leaped when she saw how thrilled Oliver was because his father was paying him some attention. If only Carsten could always be like that with the children. If only *she* could be like that.

Oliver immediately started searching for a stone. His face was glowing; Celia had never seen him smile with such excitement. She would have liked to join in the game, too, but neither Carsten nor Oliver took any notice of her, so she set off toward the house. Maria followed with Sarah in her arms.

The black front door was already ajar, much to Celia's surprise. She stepped inside and stared at the vast open-plan living space. *It looks as if someone already lives here.* Carsten had said he'd take care of everything, but she hadn't realized he meant it so literally.

The room was fully furnished, with two gray sofas in an L-shape and a glass coffee table with a bowl of fruit on it. There were books on the shelves, both English and Swedish titles, and a large flat-screen TV on the wall. A music system had also been installed.

In the middle of the oval table stood a vase of fresh flowers.

A discreet cough made her turn around.

"Welcome to Sandhamn."

A tall woman was standing in the doorway. The light was behind her, partially concealing her face, but when she came closer Celia could see that she was in her forties with clearly defined features and several dark liver spots on one cheek. Her weather-beaten complexion suggested that she was a resident of the archipelago.

"Good afternoon. My name is Linda Öberg. I'll be working for you this summer."

Celia couldn't hide her surprise.

"I'm sorry?"

"I'm your housekeeper," the woman clarified. She sounded a little uncertain, as if she couldn't understand the confusion. She pulled off the rubber band securing her ponytail and redid it with a practiced hand.

Celia put down her purse while Maria gently laid a drowsy Sarah on the sofa. She sat beside her and stroked the child's hair. Celia forced herself to look away.

"I need to speak to my husband about this," she said, conscious that her English accent was more noticeable than usual. It always happened when she was upset. At that moment Carsten came in, with Oliver skipping along behind him.

"I've been skimming stones!" he shouted, eyes sparkling. "Daddy showed me how! One of mine bounced three times!"

"Hi, Linda." Carsten held out his hand. "Here we are at last."

He inspected the room with an air of satisfaction.

"You've done a fantastic job. Thank you so much."

He turned to Celia and registered her inquiring expression.

"Linda's the one who made sure everything was ready for our arrival," he explained. "All we have to do is move in." He pointed to the vase. "Look—beautiful flowers. You always like to have flowers in the house. There's everything we need for breakfast and fresh bread from the bakery."

He went over to the refrigerator and removed a bottle with a familiar yellow label.

"Champagne." He produced two elegant crystal glasses. "The Widow welcomes us to Sandhamn."

As he removed the cork, Celia draped her jacket over the back of a chair and sat down at the table. She realized that Carsten was expecting something, possibly enthusiasm, and took a deep breath. Didn't he understand that she would have liked to be involved in deciding the décor? It should have been a shared project; it might even have brought them closer together.

But now she had nothing to contribute; everything was already done. She was a part of the furniture, just like the new sofas.

He didn't need her. The children didn't need her. She felt the tears burning behind her eyelids.

Linda Öberg coughed discreetly.

"If there's nothing else, I'll be on my way. Leave you to settle in," she said, picking up a cloth bag from the floor.

"When will you be back?" Carsten asked.

"On Monday—twelve o'clock, if that's OK. We said five hours a day to begin with."

"Linda will be taking care of the laundry and generally helping out with the housework. That's what we agreed, wasn't it?"

Linda nodded. "Just tell me what you want me to do. I've left my cell phone number on a piece of paper on the kitchen counter; give me a call if you need me to come in over the weekend or if you'd like to change my hours."

She left via the patio doors, and Celia watched her walk down to the jetty and clamber into the smaller boat. The engine started right away, and she was gone.

"Let's look at the rest of the house," Carsten said, pouring two glasses of Champagne.

He wants us to celebrate.

"Your room's down there, Maria, in the other wing." Carsten pointed to a hallway to the right of the main door.

He handed Celia a glass, the tiny bubbles rising toward the surface.

Outside the window, someone started hammering.

"The guest accommodation isn't quite ready yet," Carsten said with a smile. "The builders are going to need a few more weeks to finish it off, but it'll be well worth waiting for. We can go and check it out when they're done for the day."

He raised his glass in a toast, but Celia put hers down without taking a sip. She knew she'd disappointed him, but she couldn't shake off the numbness that enveloped her like a thick blanket. Her lips felt stiff; her face was frozen in a grimace.

"I need to go and lie down for a while," she said, pretending to search for something in her purse in order to avoid looking at him. "I'm exhausted after the journey."

She reached for her jacket; she didn't need to glance up to know that Carsten's face had closed down.

"Don't you want to see the rest of the house?"

"Later."

CHAPTER 15

Monday, July 8

Nora was slightly out of breath when she pulled up on her bike by the flowerbed next to the pool. She climbed off and lifted Julia down from the child seat. They were late, and she'd cycled through the village as fast as she could.

"Come on, sweetheart," she said, undoing her daughter's pink helmet. "Time for your swimming lesson."

She took Julia's hand and went inside. A dozen or so parents had already gathered by the pool, while other four-year-olds were running around, screaming and shouting. The teacher, the daughter of a family who lived in Seglarstaden, was wearing a black wetsuit and checking off the participants on her list.

How many years had Nora come here with Adam and Simon? And now it was time to start all over again, with another little one learning to swim. The early-morning class was always for the beginners, starting at eight o'clock. Four might seem young, but the ability to swim was essential in the archipelago.

Nora said hello to people she recognized. They were all younger than her, but then she was an older mom. What would it be like when Julia was at school? She would probably feel ancient . . .

The teacher called the children over and handed out armbands and floats. Nora sat down on one of the sun loungers beside a serious-looking woman with dark wavy hair. Nora held out her hand. There was something familiar about her neighbor, but she couldn't quite figure out what.

"Hi, I'm Nora, Julia's mom."

She pointed to her daughter, who was busy trying to use the orange float. The cold didn't seem to bother her at all; she giggled at something and disappeared beneath the surface as the float tipped over.

"She's the one in the pink swimsuit," she added.

"I'm Celia," the woman said. Her English accent was unmistakable. "My daughter's Sarah—she's next to your little girl."

Nora searched her memory; had they met before?

"Are you new to the island?"

"Yes." Celia pushed back a strand of hair but didn't elaborate. A heavy gold charm bracelet glinted in the sunlight as she raised her arm. Nora couldn't help noticing the expensive twinset and high-heeled sandals.

"So whereabouts do you live?"

Celia fiddled with her bracelet.

"I'm not sure what direction it's in; we've only been here for a few days. My husband's picking us up after the lesson." She suddenly sounded embarrassed. "I need to find my way around. We're going to be here all summer."

"But you're from Sweden?"

Celia shook her head. "No. London. We flew to Stockholm on Friday."

The penny dropped; Celia and her husband must be the new owners of Fyrudden. That was why she'd seemed familiar; Celia was the
elegant woman by Carsten Jonsson's side at the movie premiere.

"Your Swedish is really good," Nora said after a little while. "Where
did you learn?"

Celia's face lit up at the compliment.

"Do you think so?" she said with real warmth in her voice. "Thank
you! My husband wanted me to learn. At first it seemed impossible, but
I'm actually doing OK now. We have a Swedish nanny—Maria—and
I try to practice with her."

She was beautiful when she smiled; the slight air of discontent
vanished.

She's probably just shy.

"Where did you say you lived?" she asked, just to check.

"On the other side of the island."

"The new house at Fyrudden?"

"That's right."

"Oh dear." The words just slipped out. Celia looked at her in surprise, and Nora felt her cheeks flush. She could hardly say anything
about the unpleasant gossip in the village. She tried to fix things. "It's
very different from other houses on the island. How do the neighbors
feel about it?"

She immediately wished she hadn't mentioned the neighbors; she'd
just made the conversation more awkward.

Celia adjusted her position on the lounger.

"It's my husband's project; I haven't had much to do with it. In fact
I'm sick of all the tradesmen who are still on site."

Nora was grateful for the change of subject. "Are you employing
locals?"

"No, our builders come from all over the place—Poland, Ukraine.
Carsten hired them."

Suddenly she stood up and waved to someone. She had obviously lost interest in Nora; she didn't move until a tall blond man came over, carrying several white paper bags. Nora recognized him from the picture she'd found.

"I've been to the bakery," Carsten said, holding up the bags. "Fresh buns and a spiced sailor's loaf."

When he noticed Nora, he immediately held out his hand. His handshake was firm, firmer than she was used to. Her little finger was crushed against his signet ring.

"Nora Linde."

"Is your child learning to swim, too?" Carsten asked, sounding anything but relaxed.

"Yes, my little girl, Julia."

Nora had hardly finished the sentence before Carsten was speaking again.

"How nice. Maybe our girls could get together for a playdate? It would be good for the children to make some friends on the island."

Celia fixed her gaze on the pool.

"Absolutely," Nora said.

Carsten gave his wife a little push.

"You can arrange that, can't you, darling? Take Nora's number before we leave."

He reached into one of the bags and took out a bun. It smelled of raisins and pearl sugar. He offered the bag to Nora. "Would you like one?"

"I'm fine, thanks. I just had breakfast."

Nora knew how old Carsten was, but he gave the impression of a younger man. All at once she felt guilty about snooping online. Surfing the net was one thing; meeting the person in real life was another matter altogether.

"By the way, we're thinking of having a housewarming party," Carsten said before taking a voracious bite of his bun. "On Saturday.

We'd be very pleased if you and your husband could come—around six? Bring the children if you'd like. Everyone's welcome."

He paused and his eyes flicked to Nora's left hand, checking if she was wearing a wedding ring. The action was so obvious that Nora felt compelled to clarify.

"My partner and I aren't married, but thanks for the invitation."

Suddenly Carsten reached up to one eye and blinked several times. He rubbed at the corner of the eye and blinked again. "My lens has slipped," he said, poking around.

"Are you OK? Let me see." Celia moved toward him to help, but Carsten turned away from his wife, leaving her hand in midair.

"You ought to wear glasses sometimes," she said. "Give your eyes a rest."

"I hate glasses, as you well know."

Carsten screwed up his eye, then a look of relief came over his face. "There you go. I'm fine now."

Julia came running over, and Nora wrapped her in a big green towel.

"I'm freezing, Mommy. The water was really cold."

"Come on, we'll go and warm up in the sauna."

Nora picked up her things and nodded to Carsten and Celia.

"I'm in the local telephone directory if you want to get ahold of me—Nora Linde."

"We hope to see you on Saturday," Carsten said.

CHAPTER 16

Celia held Sarah's hand as they walked toward the bicycle rack. Carsten followed them.

"It'll be lovely to have a big party in our new house," he said. "I met some business acquaintances at the bakery and invited them, too. I'm going to ask all the neighbors—after all, we want to build good relationships now that we're going to be living here."

Celia didn't say a word as she strapped Sarah into her bike seat.

"Let me do that." Carsten took over, adjusting the harness and tightening the last buckle. "Apparently the Divers Bar caters for parties. I thought I'd go over and have a word with them right away, while you take Sarah home."

Celia opened her purse, took out her lip gloss, and applied a fresh layer with the small brush, then carefully put it away.

"Isn't it a bit early for a housewarming?" she said. "We've only just got here. The guest lodge isn't even finished."

Carsten's face darkened, and she knew he was thinking it was typical of her to focus on the negatives. Why did she always have to raise objections instead of appreciating his efforts?

You could have asked me what I thought before you started inviting people.

"Nonsense. The sooner we get to know people, the better. The kids need friends."

He put the bags from the bakery into the basket on his bike. "Nora seemed nice."

Celia saw his smile and couldn't help reacting.

"She needs a haircut, and the nail polish on her toes was chipped."

Carsten sighed. "Do you have to be so critical?"

"Who goes out without makeup, for God's sake?" Celia went on. She didn't actually have anything against Nora, but she knew it would annoy Carsten. She was still struggling with the idea of a party. It was way too soon; she hadn't yet digested the fact that he'd decorated and furnished the whole place with no input from her.

"She wasn't even wearing mascara," she couldn't help adding.

Carsten ignored her. He unlocked his bike and slipped the key into his pocket.

"Are you sure those are the kinds of children you want Sarah and Oliver to be friends with?" she said, knowing she'd scored a direct hit this time.

Carsten was very particular about his children associating with the right playmates. He would check out the parents' social status and income whenever they got to know someone new; she'd seen him googling names on many occasions.

She kept going. "She's not even married. Have you any idea what circles she moves in? What does her partner do, for example?"

"You could have found that out—you were the one who was sitting there talking to her."

Carsten ran a hand through his hair, then produced that special smile, the one she used to love. The smile that said he'd made up his mind about something, and nothing was going to get in his way. He stroked the back of Sarah's neck; she was tired, and her head was drooping.

The look he then gave Celia had turned chilly to say the least.

"I think it will be a lovely evening. Especially if you're prepared to make an effort for once."

Celia bit her lip.

"Wear the red dress I bought you. It's perfect." He swung his leg over the bike. "Can you find your way home? Up the hill behind the Sailors Hotel, keep going until you reach the tennis courts, then you'll see the track through the forest." He rode off without a backward glance.

Celia stayed where she was, fighting back the tears. She knew what this party was about: Carsten's need to show off his new house to anyone and everyone. He wanted people to admire his amazing achievement.

There was no point in her making any suggestions; she'd learned that he wanted to do things his own way.

A single tear trickled down her cheek. She brushed it away, put on her sunglasses, and headed back to the house with Sarah.

CHAPTER 17

Sometimes Celia was absolutely impossible, Carsten thought as he stopped outside the Divers Bar. He propped his bicycle against the wall and gazed out across the harbor. The day's delivery of groceries was being unloaded on the steamboat jetty. He noticed how skillfully the forklift truck drivers maneuvered in the limited space without getting in one another's way.

Nothing was good enough for Celia when she was in that mood. Was it too much to ask for a little enthusiasm?

However, the sun was shining and the taste of the sweet bun lingered in his mouth. It was going to be a wonderful summer, he decided. And knowing that KiberPay would be floated on the stock market in the fall didn't hurt.

There had been no further proposals from the lawyer representing the anonymous buyers. He was supposed to have come back to them with a concrete offer by the day before yesterday at the latest, but Anatoly had heard nothing.

It was just as Carsten had suspected from the start: hot air. There had been some discussion, but as soon as he insisted that it was time to put the money on the table, as soon as Anatoly revealed the size of the price tag, the buyers had disappeared in a puff of smoke.

What had they expected? Did they think he was going to practically give away the shares so close to a flotation just because they asked? Very naïve.

Anatoly was of the same opinion. The whole thing had been a fishing expedition, a failed attempt to exploit a situation that didn't exist. There were so many people in Russia trying to make a fast buck at the moment—it was ridiculous but also sad that Russian society had reached this point.

He just had to keep a cool head, refuse to give in to any kind of pressure.

"We stick to the original plan," he'd told Anatoly on the phone.

A ferry sounded its horn three times and began to reverse away from the quayside. There was already a line of people at the fruit and vegetable stall outside the grocery store, attracted by boxes of tempting red strawberries.

Carsten started whistling and ran up the steps of the Divers Bar. This was going to be a fantastic party, regardless of Celia's views.

Nora stopped at the bakery on her way home. About a dozen people were waiting in line while the three girls behind the counter were working with impressive speed and efficiency.

The smell of fresh bread filled the air, and she could almost taste a spiced bun. It would go perfectly with a cup of coffee later.

The white wrought-iron chairs outside were filled with tourists enjoying the sunshine. Cups and thermoses of coffee were set out on a long table by the doorway.

Ahead of Nora in the line stood a woman with shoulder-length blond hair. She was talking loudly to a gray-haired man in his sixties; Nora recognized him from the Trouville Society. Suddenly the woman made such a forceful gesture that she almost knocked over one of the flasks. When she turned to save it, Nora realized who she was: Anna Agaton. She lived near Fyrudden with her husband, Per-Anders.

The Agaton family had been Sandhamn residents for many years. They owned some of the smaller islands farther out in the archipelago and were active members of the residents' association. Nora vaguely recalled that her maternal grandmother had been a close friend of Per-Anders's mother.

"It's appalling," Anna proclaimed, not caring who might be listening. "Those people ought to be ashamed of themselves, but I don't suppose they've got a decent bone in their bodies. It's obvious that part of the jetty's in our waters, and they haven't even bothered to introduce themselves, let alone ask our permission!"

"So what are you going to do?" the gray-haired man asked.

"We've reported them, of course. We can hardly bring in a crane and remove the jetty. That would make us guilty of criminal behavior, unauthorized removal of property."

"It's a tricky situation."

"We've written to the council as well, but we haven't had a reply yet."

Anna Agaton's phone rang. She took it out of her pocket and answered. The line moved forward; soon it would be Nora's turn. She sensed what the call had been about: the Jonsson family at Fyrudden.

CHAPTER 18

Celia cycled home as fast as she could. She needed to take a Sobril. Right now. Her heart was pounding, but she pedaled even faster. All the way through the forest, she'd been thinking in detail about what she should have said to Carsten when he told her about the party.

When she finally came to a stop behind the house, Maria was just heading off to the village with Oliver. He was already perched on his bike, and Maria was about to lock the door.

"Can you take care of Sarah? I'm going to lie down for a while."

Maria hesitated. She looked at Sarah, who was yawning.

"She's tired."

Why did Maria have to undermine her in front of the children? Why was everyone against her today?

"Please do as I ask." Celia parked the bike so that Maria could transfer Sarah. She rummaged in her purse and found a hundred-kronor note.

"Here. Take them to the kiosk and buy them an ice cream after Oliver's swimming lesson."

"Mommy!" Sarah shouted as Maria strapped her into the child seat on the other bike.

Celia hurried inside and closed the door so that she wouldn't have to listen to her daughter. She went into the kitchen and gripped the edge of the counter with both hands, tried to take a few deep breaths.

She watched Maria cycle away with Sarah behind her, Oliver following on his own little bike, his colorful bicycle helmet pulled down over his fair hair, his little legs pedaling fast.

She'd done it again, dumped everything on Maria instead of taking care of her own children, but the look Carsten had given her made it impossible to behave normally.

I can't cope.

After a while, she took out a glass and half filled it with water, then placed a Sobril tablet on her tongue. Her hand shook as she raised the glass to her lips.

A big housewarming party was a crazy idea; why didn't Carsten realize that? Celia had seen the way the other parents had given her the side-eye by the pool. She'd known there was something not right the second she introduced herself.

Nora Linde had also reacted when she figured out who Celia was. Talked about how the neighbors felt. The other day, Celia had overheard one of the English-speaking laborers say something similar; apparently the neighbors were angry about the new construction and the jetty in particular.

Celia went back to the window, but Maria and the children were out of sight.

The glass suddenly felt heavy. She put it down and headed for the bedroom to get changed. She was hot and sweaty from cycling through the forest with Sarah.

She opened the middle drawer to choose a clean T-shirt but stopped in midmovement.

Everything was arranged in neat piles, but surely the pink Michael Kors blouse had been on top? It was brand-new and she'd been very careful when she unpacked it. Now it lay beneath a navy-blue sweater instead of vice versa.

Celia ran her hand over the fabric and tried to remember. Was she mistaken? Or had Maria rearranged things? But why would she do that? She had no reason to go into their room, and Carsten wouldn't touch her clothes.

She caught a movement out of the corner of her eye and turned to look out the window.

The shore was deserted.

CHAPTER 19

Julia had fallen asleep on the sofa on the veranda after a long day in the sun. Her fair hair was plastered to her temples with sweat, and her thumb was firmly in her mouth. Nora gently kissed her forehead before calling Jonas. It was three o'clock, so he should be awake in spite of the six-hour time difference.

She listened as the signals rang out on the other side of the Atlantic. This was his last flight before the holiday; he was due to land in Stockholm via Copenhagen late tomorrow afternoon.

They would have four glorious weeks together in the archipelago; in two weeks Simon and Adam would be back from their vacation in Greece with Henrik.

The thought of her boys made her long to see them. She would never get used to sharing custody with their father.

Voice mail kicked in, and Jonas informed her that he couldn't take her call right now. As usual his cheerful tone made Nora smile.

Maybe he's still sleeping, she thought. She left a message and glanced out the window after ending the call. The bright sunlight showed how dirty the glass was, but the pink and red roses outside were glorious.

It was her former neighbor, Aunt Signe, who'd planted the beautiful rose bushes. She had left the Brand villa to Nora in her will some years earlier.

When Nora wandered around with Signe's old metal watering can, she could almost feel the old lady's presence, hear her whispering that this bush needed some extra water or more fertilizer.

Signe would have snorted at the couple she'd met by the pool today, called them nouveau riche, and insisted they didn't belong on Sandhamn.

Celia had seemed uncomfortable, and Carsten was strange—restless, almost manic. Nora had had the feeling they were trying to categorize her but hadn't succeeded, because she wasn't carrying the usual class markers—no jewelry or purse to indicate where she belonged.

There was a knock on the door, followed by a familiar voice.

"Hi—anyone home?"

"Come on in, Eva. Coffee? I picked up fresh pastries from the bakery."

Eva sat down in the kitchen and pushed up the sleeves of her loose-fitting top. She obviously couldn't wait to share her news.

"We've been invited to a party by Carsten Jonsson and his wife! You know, the people who've built the new house at Fyrudden. Filip met Carsten in the grocery store, and Carsten invited him on the spot."

"Are you going?"

"Are you kidding me? That place is the hot topic of the year. Of course we're going."

"We've been invited, too. I met them at the pool earlier today. Julia's in the same swimming class as their little girl." Nora put two cups of coffee on the table, then fetched milk and sugar. "But I'm kind of torn. I was standing behind Anna Agaton in the line at the bakery; she had nothing good to say about the Jonssons, and she didn't care who heard her."

Eva smiled.

"I can promise you the Agatons will be at the party. Filip heard that Carsten's asked the Divers Bar to take care of both the catering and the guest list. They've been instructed to ask every single person who means anything here on Sandhamn. I can't imagine the Agatons will stay away—they'll want to see the place just like the rest of us."

Nora thought back to her encounter with Celia. The whole time they'd been sitting by the pool, she'd never stopped fiddling with her wedding and engagement rings, twirling them around and around while the girls took their first tentative strokes in the water.

Joyless.

Did she realize how much people were gossiping about her family? Nora wished Celia had done a better job of keeping the mask in place.

"I don't understand them at all," Eva said, stirring her coffee with such vigor that a few drops splashed over onto the table. "Why come and live on an island like this if you're determined to step on your neighbors' toes? Sandhamn is too small; you have to take other people and their feelings into account. There are rules that can't just be ignored."

"I'm sure they'll settle down eventually. After five or six years, like every other newcomer." Nora winked at her friend. "Even if Carsten Jonsson doesn't seem like the kind of guy who caves because of someone else's opinion."

"He ought to learn a lesson from that family over in the west. They put up a fence and great big notices informing everyone that the beach was private, but the locals tore them down that very winter. In the end they had to give up."

Eva's expression suddenly grew serious.

"By the way, have you seen all that ugly rubble in the harbor, near the promenade? Apparently it's leftover rock from the Jonssons' jetty; the builders didn't bother taking it away, they just dumped it."

"Are you sure?"

"Well, I don't have any proof, but that's what everyone's saying in the village."

Eva put down her steaming cup of coffee and cupped both hands around it.

"You can't go against tradition on this island. If you do, you have to be prepared for the consequences."

CHAPTER 20

Wednesday, July 10

What was that? Celia opened her eyes and looked around in confusion.

It was already light outside, but she got the feeling it was still early. The thin beams of light finding their way in suggested that the sun had only just risen above the horizon. Her body felt heavy and anything but rested.

She groped for her cell phone to check the time. Five fifteen—she'd slept for only a few hours. She had gone to bed long before Carsten and pretended to be asleep when he came in. Then she lay awake for what seemed like an eternity, listening to him breathing.

She glanced over at him. He was lying on his back, mouth half-open, the sheets up to his chest. Totally at ease, as usual.

Celia longed for thick English curtains and darkness; these light Nordic nights made it impossible to sleep. No point in staying in bed. With a sigh she got up, went over to the window, and lifted a corner of the blind. A milky mist met her gaze; the sun was still trying to penetrate its veils.

Nothing outside to explain what had woken her. There wasn't a breath of wind, and the water was barely moving. She wrapped herself in her robe and opened the door as quietly as she could.

Carsten didn't move. Not a sound from the children's rooms either. She headed for the kitchen in her bare feet.

Outside the window stood ranks of bare tree trunks topped with sparse branches, and the odd green patch of low-growing blueberries here and there. If it had been anywhere else, in a place she'd chosen, it would have been beautiful.

She opened the refrigerator and took out a carton of milk. Filled a mug to the brim and put it in the microwave. Pressed "Stop" just before it pinged so that she wouldn't disturb the children.

The sun was winning its battle with the mist.

A noise from outside made her jump. It sounded like a branch breaking, the dry crack of old wood snapping. As if someone was stomping around in heavy boots.

The tiles were cold beneath her feet, and the chill spread upward through her body. Celia shuddered and felt the hairs stand up on her arms. In the distance, gulls began to scream; their shrill cries came without warning, as if they'd been startled into flight.

There's someone out there.

The thought filled her head. The main living area had no curtains to draw, no blinds to close. Nothing to stop anyone looking straight in.

That had been Carsten's choice; he wanted the house to be filled with light.

Her heart was pounding so hard it hurt, but she didn't dare turn around. She stayed where she was, frozen to the spot, head down, eyes squeezed tightly shut.

If I don't look, there's no one there.

The handle of the mug was digging into her palm, and she forced herself to loosen her grip. Her breathing grew shallower, more rapid.

Eventually she turned and stared at the huge window.

Nothing.

The wave of relief was so powerful that Celia sank to the floor with her back to the refrigerator. Her hand was shaking so much she spilled milk on the tiles.

The yard looked exactly the same as usual, except that the little vase of wildflowers that Sarah had picked was lying on its side. The water had run out onto the table, and there were petals on the ground.

It had all been a figment of her imagination.

She sipped the warm milk. It tasted just like when she was a little girl and couldn't sleep; her mom used to heat up some milk on the stove, then add honey and cinnamon.

I want to go home.

Celia drew her knees up to her chin and rested her forehead on them. Yesterday she'd sent some pictures of Fyrudden to her parents and told them everything was wonderful in Sweden, the kids loved the new house and the fantastic sandy beach.

She sat there until her legs started to feel numb. She forced herself to get up, and after one last glance outside, she went back to the bedroom.

Carsten hadn't stirred, hadn't noticed a thing.

Once upon a time she would have curled up beside him, woken him, and felt his arms around her. Back then, she couldn't stop touching him.

The bathroom door was ajar. Celia hesitated; she shouldn't really take a sleeping tablet at this hour. But she did it anyway.

As she was getting into bed she heard a scraping noise outside; it sounded as if it was somewhere near the door.

She held her breath.

Then she pulled the covers over her head and hoped the tablet would work fast.

CHAPTER 21

"Sarah, we have to go now, sweetheart."

Maria tried to hurry the little girl along without upsetting her. The swimming lesson was due to start in twenty minutes, but Sarah was sitting at the table with her head down, too tired to eat her cheese sandwich. Maria didn't want to go either; she'd slept badly and had weird dreams all night. At one point she'd woken up, convinced there was someone outside her window, but then she'd dozed off again.

Her head was beginning to throb; she could tell that a vicious headache was on its way.

"We mustn't be late—your teacher and your new friends will be waiting," she cajoled. "Maybe you can play with Julia today?"

Neither of the children liked getting up early; presumably Oliver was still asleep. Just like his mother. There had been no sign of Carsten either, but Maria knew he usually went out through the French doors in the bedroom to go for his run. Sometimes he stopped off at the bakery for a coffee.

She wiped Sarah's mouth and cleared away her plate and mug. She threw the sandwich in the trash even though it was only half eaten. If they didn't leave now, they wouldn't get there in time.

Maria slung the bag containing Sarah's towel and swimsuit over her shoulder.

"OK, let's go!"

Sarah didn't move. Maria had to bend down and pick her up. She pushed down the door handle with one hand, balancing the child on her hip. Sarah was in no mood to cooperate; she kicked out at the bag, which swung wide, then banged against Maria's back just as she was opening the door. She stumbled forward, stepped on something soft and slimy, and involuntarily kicked it.

The white—no, gray—thing landed on the next step down as the door flew open.

Blood, Maria thought.

The white feathers stuck up from the dead body, and the two wing tips were stuck together. Dead eyes stared up at her. The yellow beak was smeared with red.

She did her best to suppress the scream that was trying to force its way out.

"Close your eyes, Sarah!" she said sharply, pressing the girl's face into her shoulder as she backed into the house.

"Ow! Ow, you're hurting me!" Sarah's muffled voice protested. Maria knew she was holding her too tightly, but she couldn't let her see what was out there.

The bird's head had been twisted at an unnatural angle, because someone had carefully slit its throat. The gaping wound had shocked her; the blood had run down the steps, staining the pale wood dark red. A grubby note lay beside the body, with the words *GO AWAY* printed in capital letters.

"Put me down!" Sarah yelled, arms flailing. "Put me down! You're hurting me!" She started thumping Maria with clenched fists and almost punched her in the eye.

Maria blinked and nearly lost her balance again. Sarah twisted free and landed on her feet, while Maria fell backward onto the floor. Sarah was about to make a run for it, but Maria managed to grab her T-shirt and hold on tight.

Sarah screamed at the top of her voice. Maria struggled to stand up; through the open door she could see the mutilated body of the bird.

"Close your eyes, Sarah!" she shouted again. "Don't look!"

CHAPTER 22

Jonas gave Nora a gentle shake before switching off the old-fashioned metal alarm clock that had just gone off on the bedside table. It had belonged to Aunt Signe, and Nora couldn't bring herself to throw it away.

"Who's taking Julia to her swimming lesson?" he murmured in her ear.

If I close my eyes, maybe he'll think I'm still asleep, Nora thought. She didn't move a muscle, as if she hadn't heard the insistent ringing of the alarm.

"Are you awake?"

"Mmm."

"Do you want me to take Julia today?"

"Mmm."

Nora snuggled deeper into the pillow. She was lying on her stomach, with one arm and one leg drawn up. She knew perfectly well that she ought to be the one to get up, let Jonas sleep. This was the first day of his vacation; he'd arrived back from the US yesterday. She'd picked him up from Stavsnäs in the dinghy, because the Vaxholm ferry no longer ran in the evenings.

But she was so tired, and he was always so kind.

The alarm went off again, and Nora heard him reach out and press the button to stop the infernal racket.

Silence. Sleep.

Nora was still in bed when Jonas returned an hour and a half later, but at least she was awake.

"Thank you," she said with a yawn, feeling guilty. "I promise I'll take her for the rest of the week."

He stroked her cheek, and Nora curled up contentedly beneath the covers. Jonas opened the blinds, and the sunlight came pouring in. It was going to be another beautiful day.

"By the way, do you remember me telling you about that couple who've built a new house at Fyrudden? Carsten and Celia Jonsson. They've invited us to a party on Saturday. Eva and Filip will be there, too," Nora informed him.

Jonas went over to the closet and took out his sports bag. He rolled up a blue towel with the SAS logo and pushed it into the bag; he was off to play tennis with Filip.

"It's all kind of weird," Nora went on. "He's throwing this huge party, and yet at the same time he seems to be going out of his way to upset people."

"How do you mean?"

Nora clasped her hands behind her head. The sky was bright blue, but a jet must have just passed by, because she could see its long white vapor trail.

"Carsten's already fallen out with his closest neighbors, the Agatons, and a lot of people are annoyed about the construction traffic. The builders have been transporting all the materials through the forest on great big quad bikes and forklift trucks. Do you know it can take twenty years for heather to grow back again?"

"If there's a problem, maybe we'd better stay home."

Jonas could be so practical sometimes.

"I really want to see the house, though . . . ," Nora said, feeling slightly embarrassed by her curiosity.

"We'll do whatever you want," Jonas said with a smile.

Nora didn't really know what she wanted, but something told her the party wasn't going to go the way Carsten Jonsson had planned. If she'd been in his situation, it would never have occurred to her to throw a party.

CHAPTER 23

Carsten was sitting on the patio, staring out over the sea. It was a lovely day, but he didn't have time to admire the view. Again and again his eyes were drawn to the other headland, where the Agatons lived. He couldn't see the house, but he knew exactly where it was.

A half-full cup of black coffee stood on the table, with his cell phone beside it. The black crocodile case shimmered in the sunlight.

He turned his head when he heard Eklund's heavy footsteps approaching. He didn't bother taking off his sunglasses.

"Finished?"

"We've scrubbed down the steps and put everything in a garbage bag. We'll take it with us when we leave this afternoon, get rid of it."

Carsten nodded pensively. "Any idea where it came from? Or who wrote the note?"

"Not a clue." Mats Eklund followed Carsten's gaze to the Agaton property. "As I said before, there are a few locals who aren't too happy about this project," he added after a brief pause. "You never quite know out here in the archipelago. There's been the odd nasty comment when the boys have been eating lunch at the Sandhamn Inn, and people can do stupid things when they've had too much to drink."

It almost sounded as if Eklund thought Carsten had only himself to blame.

"I want motion-sensor lights all the way around the house as soon as possible. And I want two CCTV cameras, one above this door and one at the front."

"Don't you need permission for something like that?"

Carsten didn't even bother to reply.

The sound of an engine caught their attention, and Linda Öberg's little boat appeared. She slowed, gently reversing the engine near the jetty. As if she realized they were watching her, she raised her head and stared straight at Eklund. Carsten noticed that he avoided her gaze.

Linda moored the boat and climbed out, then she picked up her cloth bag and started walking toward them.

"Thank you for coming in early," Carsten said as soon as she was within earshot. "Can I have a quick word?"

"Of course."

"We've had a few problems this morning." He altered his position so that he could see her properly.

"Has something happened?" Linda frowned, a deep furrow appearing between her eyebrows.

"Maria was about to take Sarah to her swimming lesson when she found a dead bird on the steps."

"A dead bird?" Linda adjusted the elastic band securing her ponytail.

"Someone had cut the throat of a herring gull and left it outside our house with a message telling us to go away. Maria stepped on it when she opened the door. She and Sarah were shocked and scared, which I assume was the intention."

"Oh my goodness!" Linda's hand flew to her mouth. "How are they now?"

Carsten ignored the question. "We don't know who's behind it. None of us saw or heard anything."

"Do you suspect anyone in particular?"

Carsten shook his head. "Let's hope it was just a tasteless joke by a couple of kids who have nothing better to do."

"There are always idiots around," Eklund agreed.

The dead bird had been surprisingly slimy. Carsten was glad the Poles had been around to deal with it and scrub the steps. "Anyway, it's gone now," he said to Linda. "No need to worry about going into the house. The steps have been cleaned, and the bloodstains have more or less gone."

"What are you going to do?"

He shrugged. "There's not much I can do about such a stupid prank."

"You could report it to the police," Eklund suggested.

Carsten had to laugh at his naivety. "Why would I hand the press something like that on a plate? It would just backfire on me and my family." He took off his sunglasses. "This never happened, OK? Celia doesn't know anything about it; she was asleep when Maria found the bird, and she's still sleeping now."

"But Sarah was there?"

Linda was right, but Carsten had dealt with the matter.

"She's only little, she didn't understand what had happened. I've told her it's our secret, and Maria will be paid a bonus this month as a sweetener for keeping her mouth shut."

Linda switched her bag from one shoulder to the other.

"What would you like me to do?"

"I want you to have a word with Maria, make sure she understands she mustn't talk. I think it might be better coming from you—as a woman, I mean. I would have asked Celia, but as I said, she knows nothing about the incident."

Carsten jerked his head in the direction of the bedroom; the blinds were still closed. "Under no circumstances do I want Celia to find out about this." He knew she would go crazy. He lowered his voice. "Maria has had a terrible shock; she's resting at the moment. I'm sure she'll get over it; at her age it's easy to put something like this behind her."

"Daddy, can I play on your phone? Mummy's asleep," Oliver said from the doorway.

Not again, for fuck's sake.

"No. You know perfectly well you're not allowed to touch our cell phones."

Oliver's shoulders slumped, and he disappeared into the living room.

"This stays between us. I don't want people gossiping about it in the village. Is that clear?" Carsten said, looking from Linda to Eklund.

He had no intention of letting anything spoil the housewarming party. The invitations had gone out and preparations were well underway. He was determined to overcome the resistance on the island; he was more than capable of fighting, but sometimes a charm offensive was even more effective. He knew exactly how to change those sour expressions to admiration.

Everything must be perfect on Saturday.

CHAPTER 24

Maria was woken by a knock on the bedroom door. She felt dizzy and groggy, almost as if she'd been drugged. Her T-shirt clung damply to her skin.

Slowly the memory came back.

The dead bird on the steps, the words on that grubby piece of paper.

She couldn't help glancing out the window to make sure no one was peering in.

Carsten had come rushing and grabbed Sarah, then he'd given Maria a sleeping tablet and sent her off to bed before Celia or Oliver woke up. How long had she been asleep? The room was so warm—it must be late afternoon. She reached for her phone, but before she could pick it up, the door opened and Linda Öberg came in with a glass of orange juice. Maria felt horribly exposed; she didn't like lying there in front of Linda in nothing but her T-shirt and panties.

"So how are you feeling?" Linda asked, sitting down on the bed.

Maria groped for the sheet, which was in a tangled heap at her feet, and pulled it over her. Linda held out the juice, but when Maria didn't take it, she placed the glass on the bedside table.

"What time is it?" Maria mumbled. It was an effort to get the words out; her lips felt thick and unmanageable. *I'm never, ever going to take a sleeping tablet again.*

"Just after four. You've had a good, long sleep. That was exactly what you needed. You had a terrible shock this morning."

"It was horrible." The tears weren't far away as the image of the bird with its throat slit came back to her. The bloodstained mess she'd walked in. However, she didn't want to break down with Linda sitting there.

"Carsten asked me to have a word with you," Linda said after a moment.

"Why?"

Linda folded her arms. At such close quarters, Maria could see the acne scars scattered over her cheeks in an irregular pattern. She hadn't noticed them before.

"He doesn't want you to mention the bird to Celia."

"But Sarah was there, too—she's bound to tell her!"

"Sarah won't remember a thing. She's too little. By tomorrow she'll have forgotten all about it. Carsten's already spoken to her, said it's their secret."

"So I'm supposed to pretend nothing's happened?"

Linda nodded. "I've told Celia you're not feeling too good, that you've got a touch of sunstroke. It often happens in the archipelago when the sun is strong."

Maria curled up, the pillow against her back.

"It's best if you don't talk about this to anyone," Linda went on. "Carsten doesn't want any gossip in the village, he was very clear on that point. He's also asked the builders to keep it to themselves. He's keen to make sure Celia isn't worried or upset."

Celia must be protected. "But what about me," Maria wanted to shout. "Who's thinking about me? I was the one who found the gull!" She pictured it in her mind's eye yet again.

"So I just pretend nothing's happened?" she said, not caring that she was repeating herself.

"There'll be a bonus in your paycheck this month, as a kind of compensation."

"How much?" Maria was well aware that she sounded pathetic rather than angry. She was still so tired.

"Carsten didn't say, but I'm sure he'll be generous. He's prepared to pay well if you promise not to say anything to his wife." When Maria didn't speak, Linda added, "We want the family to be happy here, don't we?"

Maria could tell that Linda was expecting her to agree, but her head felt as if it were stuffed with cotton wool. All she could think of was sleep.

"I want to leave," she whispered as the tears began to flow. She couldn't stop them. Linda looked unsure of herself, as if she didn't know how to handle this development. She got up and went over to the window, threw it wide open so that the fresh air came pouring in.

"I don't think that's a good idea," she said without turning around. "Celia would ask why, and I can imagine how she'd react." She put the window on the latch. "I'm sure Carsten wouldn't agree either. What would the children say if you simply disappeared?"

Maria let out a sob.

"It'll be fine, Maria," Linda said in a gentler tone as she headed for the door. "Have a good rest, and I'll see you tomorrow. The party is on Saturday. You need to be back on your feet by then."

"Saturday?" Maria remembered Carsten talking about the house-warming party on Monday evening. Celia hadn't been keen on the idea at all, hadn't wanted to discuss food or drink or the guest list. Every time Carsten brought it up, Celia found something else to do.

Maria had also noticed the looks Celia had gotten from the other parents around the pool at Sarah's swimming lessons; she knew there was already plenty of gossip about the Jonsson family, and she could understand Celia's misgivings.

"Don't forget to drink your juice," Linda said as she left the room. "I'll help out with the children today, so you've nothing to worry about."

Maria curled up beneath the covers. It was kind of Linda to look after the children, but the way she'd said it made Maria feel guilty.

"I want to go home," she whispered into her pillow.

CHAPTER 25

Thursday, July 11

Morning briefing was over, and Thomas went back to his office with a cup of tea. The room felt stuffy; he opened the window, sat down at his computer to work through the emails that had piled up overnight.

During the meeting, they'd discussed, among other things, a series of car thefts in Saltsjöbaden, the wealthier part of their area. Only vehicles from the luxury end of the market had been targeted: Mercedes, BMW, Lexus. All missing from the driveway when the owners stepped out to go to work; the MO pointed to a professional gang from the Baltic states, which meant the cars had probably already been transported across the sea.

The computer hummed to life.

It wasn't as if the victims were exactly in the breadline, Thomas thought as he finished his tea. He'd left the tea bag in for too long, and the taste of tannin lingered on his tongue.

He was looking forward to his vacation. They'd decided on a two-week overlap for Elin's sake, and Pernilla was already on vacation. His four weeks were due to start on Saturday, and the plan had been to clear his desk of everything that had piled up during the spring before he took off.

It hadn't gone particularly well.

Every day he encouraged his team to achieve the closed-case quota, but to tell the truth, he didn't give a damn about the stolen cars or their owners.

The room was like a sauna; he felt restless, unable to concentrate. The paperwork in front of him held no appeal whatsoever. If only it had been Friday, then he could have headed out to Harö straight after work.

He propped open the door in an attempt to create a draft, then went across the hallway to Aram's office. Mercifully it was in the shade at this time of day, so it was considerably cooler.

"How are you doing with the owners of the stolen cars?" he asked his colleague. "I assume they're brightening your day."

Aram gave him a dirty look, then sat back and sighed. "Do you really want to know, or are you just razzing me?"

Thomas sat down and crossed his legs. He knew Aram would do his best, even though the chances of recovering the vehicles were small. It was going to cost the insurance companies a fortune.

Next to Aram's computer was a photograph of his wife, Sonja, and their two little girls. There was only a year between Elin and Aram's youngest daughter, Maryam, and they were playmates.

"Have you ever thought about changing direction, leaving the police?" Thomas couldn't help himself; the words came tumbling out. Aram looked at him in surprise.

"No—no, I haven't."

"Never?"

"No. I've wanted to be a cop for as long as I can remember. From the day we arrived in Sweden and I knew we could stay here."

Thomas remembered what Aram had told him about the family's flight from Iraq. They had endured horrific conditions until they finally reached Sweden; his younger sister had died en route. It had taken a long time before they were granted permanent residence.

His friendship with Aram had opened Thomas's eyes to the cold winds blowing through Swedish society these days, the growing racism and general antipathy toward foreigners. In the recent election, an openly nationalistic party had gained seats for the first time.

Aram gave Thomas a searching look. "Why do you ask?"

Should he mention his dissatisfaction, Erik's offer, the thoughts that came and went? He knew Aram would listen, but he hesitated. It was too soon.

"I was just wondering. Good luck with the car owners. Let me know when you're ready for lunch. I'll come with you."

CHAPTER 26

Celia had spent all afternoon lying on her bed with the blinds closed, crippled by a headache. She could still feel the tension in her temples in spite of the painkillers she'd taken. In the living room, she found Maria sitting on the sofa with Sarah and Oliver, watching a children's show on TV. Sarah was lying across Maria's lap, while Oliver's head was resting on her shoulder.

It was almost six thirty—didn't the girl realize the time?

"Maria, could you fix the children's dinner? I don't want them eating too late."

She waited, but nothing happened.

She raised her voice. "Maria!"

The girl leaped to her feet. "Sorry, I didn't hear you."

Celia massaged her throbbing forehead and tried to stay calm. Carsten had gone over to Stockholm for the day and would return by taxi boat at around nine. There had been a brief note on the chest of drawers when she woke up this morning.

"It's time for the children's dinner."

"What would you like me to give them?"

Celia opened the refrigerator so that Maria could see what was in there.

"Just make something they'll eat. You don't have to ask me every single day. Give them something, anything."

Celia forced a smile to compensate for the sharpness in her tone; it wasn't Maria's fault there were problems between her and Carsten. Fortunately she didn't seem to have taken offense and smiled back.

"Will you be eating with the children?" she asked, opening a packet of ready-made meatballs.

Meatballs with pasta—the Swedish staple, Celia thought. She shook her head.

"I'm not hungry right now. I'll wait for Carsten."

She'd bought seafood in the small deli and put a bottle of white wine in the refrigerator as she always did when he came home late. He was very fussy about his food; he hated heavy sauces and unnecessary calories. He was more particular about keeping his weight under control than she was.

When the children were asleep, she'd try to talk to him again. He'd seemed so distant over the past few days, so hard to reach.

"How many guests will there be on Saturday?" Maria wondered as she took out a large pan to cook the pasta.

Celia couldn't help checking out her hair in the shiny stainless-steel surface of the refrigerator door. The dampness from the sea made it frizzy instead of wavy. It was impossible to keep it looking nice for more than five minutes after she'd blow-dried it. Carsten liked heavy curls tumbling down over her shoulders. Then again, it was a long time since he'd stroked her hair or run his fingers through those curls.

She realized Maria had asked her a question.

"Sorry, what did you say?"

"How many guests will there be on Saturday?"

Celia didn't want to think about that, about all those people inspecting the place, eyeing her up and down as if she were a lump of meat in a butcher's store.

"Around a hundred and fifty, I think. At least that's the number Carsten gave the caterers." She tried to smooth down her hair. "What was the name again . . . ? Oh yes, the Divers Bar has promised to have everything laid out by five. The children need to be changed and ready by quarter to six at the latest so they can be with us to greet the guests as they arrive. Then you can take care of them, make sure they don't get in the way."

Maria nodded.

"By the way, I wanted to ask you something," Celia went on. "There are some dark patches on the outside steps. Any idea where they've come from?"

Maria turned the faucet on to fill up the pan; the water splashed over the top and a few drops landed on the floor. She immediately cleaned it up with a Handi Wipe.

"No," she said over her shoulder. "I haven't a clue."

"I saw them yesterday, but I forgot to mention it. It looks as if something dark has run down the steps—maybe from a torn garbage bag? You haven't noticed anything?"

Maria bent down to get a frying pan from the drawer next to the stove. "No," she mumbled again.

Celia sighed. It was probably Maria who'd put down a leaking bag and didn't want to admit it. No matter, she'd bring it up with Carsten later. Maybe one of the contractors could get rid of the stains—otherwise two of the steps would have to be replaced. She opened the refrigerator and took out the bottle of white wine, in spite of the fact that her head was still pounding. She unscrewed the cap and poured herself a glass.

"I'm going down to the jetty for a little while."

The children were still watching TV and didn't react as she walked past. Sarah was wearing her swimsuit, for some reason, and Oliver was clutching his teddy bear. Celia knew he took his chances when Carsten wasn't there; Daddy thought he was too old to be messing around with cuddly toys.

She paused; should she go and sit with them instead? At that moment, Sarah scrambled down and ran to Maria. She wrapped both arms around Maria's legs and held on tight. Maria removed the pan from the heat and picked up the little girl, smiling warmly.

"Would you like to help me cook dinner?" she said, kissing Sarah's forehead. "Come on, we'll do it together."

Celia walked out onto the terrace, glass in hand.

CHAPTER 27

Celia continued down to the paved area by the jetty, which was bathed in evening sunshine. There were several sets of outdoor furniture arranged in various places around the house and a table and chairs on the terrace. However, she preferred this spot, which was a little more isolated.

She put her glass on the low table and settled down on one of the Adirondack chairs. The sun was still warm even though it was almost seven o'clock; she wasn't cold even in shorts and a low-cut top.

Carsten had told her the evenings were often chilly in Sweden, but this week had been very pleasant. She hoped it would stay that way until Saturday; if it rained, everyone would end up indoors, and she didn't want that.

She realized the guests would want to see the house and that Carsten would have no objection. Quite the reverse; his childish delight had been clear from the moment they landed on Sandhamn. This desire to show off his new possession was beneath his dignity; it diminished him. It just simply wasn't done—at least not in England.

But he wasn't English, he was Swedish, she reminded herself. And there was no point in her continuing to brood about the party; it was going to happen, however she felt about it.

She reached for her wine. Sauvignon Blanc, Marlborough. It had the perfect aftertaste of green gooseberries that she loved. The label was Dog Point; that would have been a good name for this place rather than the picturesque Fyrudden.

A loud banging noise attracted her attention. She turned her head and saw one of the workmen a short distance away along the shore, just by a small copse of pine trees. He was busy erecting the new fence that would enclose the entire property all the way down to the water's edge. There had to be a gate in order to allow access, a nod to the traditions of the island, but Carsten had assured her that it would be kept locked at all times.

"We can't help it if we lose the key," he'd said with a wink.

It would be nice when the fence was up. Celia didn't like the openness, the fact that anyone could wander past the house.

The workman had noticed her watching him and raised a hand in greeting. It was the tall guy with fair hair, the one who seemed to work most closely with Mats Eklund. Celia waved back; she didn't want to seem rude, although she really didn't want any kind of closer contact. She was sick and tired of the builders being on site the whole time. However, it couldn't be helped; there were still things to finish.

She longed for the guest lodge to be ready so that she could invite friends over from England, maybe Sophie and her family. She needed something to look forward to.

And it would be so nice to get rid of all the workmen, stop feeling as if she was constantly being watched. They would turn up at the most inconvenient times, when she was least expecting them. Only the other day she'd been getting changed in the bedroom when she saw a figure outside the window—one of the carpenters had passed by only seconds after she'd been standing naked in front of the big mirror. She'd quickly closed the blinds but couldn't shake off the feeling that he'd been peeking.

On a positive note, Carsten had persuaded the builders to work both evenings and weekends in order to get the job done as quickly as possible, although on Saturday they would be off site a few hours before his party.

That was how she thought of it. Carsten's party.

The sound of voices brought her back to the present moment. She looked up and saw an elderly man next to the Polish carpenter. He seemed agitated; she could hear him speaking loudly in Swedish, but she couldn't understand what he was saying. The carpenter spread his hands wide.

Celia lay back and held her breath; she didn't want to get involved. Eventually the voices fell silent, and when she risked a glance toward the fence, she saw the stranger disappearing into the forest.

She gave a sigh of relief and took a big gulp of her wine. She closed her eyes, tried to relax her jangling nerves.

Suddenly she was in shadow. She gave a start and spilled wine on her thigh.

"Sorry, I didn't mean to startle you."

The words were spoken in Swedish but with a heavy accent. When Celia looked up, she was blinded; the man who had spoken to her had the sun behind him, and all she could see was his silhouette, making it impossible to distinguish his features.

She shaded her eyes; the man stepped to one side, and she realized he was the Polish carpenter. He was holding a sledgehammer with patches of dried paint on the handle.

"Sorry," he said again. "That was your neighbor, the guy who complains all the time. He doesn't like the new fence, but I told him to clear off."

Celia didn't really know what to say. "You need to talk to my husband." She hoped he would go away, but he didn't seem to get the message.

"Am I disturbing you, working on the fence? I can come back to it tomorrow if you prefer."

"It's fine. The sooner it's up, the better."

She began to wipe away the wine on her thigh but stopped when she saw him watching her movements. Suddenly her shorts felt much too short.

"The noise doesn't bother me at all," she added quickly in order to get rid of him. "It's fine, you carry on."

"Just say the word if you're bothered," he said, and turned away, swinging the hammer in time with his footsteps as he headed back to the fence.

Chapter 28

Friday, July 12

There was a thick morning mist lying over the sea when Carsten opened the door and stepped outside. The dampness hit him like a wall. Shapes were blurred and indistinct, and sounds were muffled. Not even the birdsong penetrated the dense, gray-white mass.

Far away in the distance, he could hear the foghorn.

The stains left by the bird were still visible, dark shadows on the top two or three steps, but anyone who didn't know the truth couldn't guess what had happened.

He started jogging southward, in the direction of Trouville. His cell phone was safely strapped to his arm, just in case Anatoly should ring. Carsten had sent him a text before he set off: Call me! Then he'd pulled on his running shoes, hoping to find an outlet for the restlessness in his body.

During the week, he'd emailed a number of questions to both Sergei and Roman, but the information that came back was both vague and unsatisfactory, nowhere near as precise as usual.

His anxiety was growing.

He didn't like the answers he was getting, and Anatoly hadn't contacted him, in spite of his leaving several messages. Thoughts of the Russian legal firm lingered in the back of his mind. Had there been substance behind Beketov's offer after all? Should he have been more cooperative? Then again, Anatoly had assured him that nothing had come of it, that he should forget the whole thing.

Carsten ran along the water's edge, his new Nike sneakers leaving broad impressions on the firm, damp sand. After a while he increased his pace, sprinted up a slope behind a summer cottage with closed curtains.

Why hadn't Anatoly been in touch?

He had reached Trouville; the mist was starting to lift, and it was possible to make out the contours of the islands opposite. He could just about see the spit of land that extended between the large and small beaches.

At that moment his phone began to vibrate. Carsten stopped dead. The call was from Russia. *About time.*

"Hello?"

"Carsten, how are you?"

Anatoly's familiar voice and nasal tone.

"Fine," Carsten said, in spite of his concerns. He went over to a pine tree and leaned against the trunk, automatically stretching his thigh muscles. He did his best not to sound out of breath. "How's it going?"

"I must apologize for not calling you sooner, but I've been stuck in one meeting after another over the past few days. I'm afraid I have some bad news."

Carsten stiffened. "What are you talking about?"

"The timing of the stock market flotation. It seems there are objections . . ." Anatoly broke off.

Carsten kept perfectly still, as if the slightest movement on his part could be key to a positive or negative outcome.

"I've been picking up ominous signals from GZ3," Anatoly continued. "It looks as if they want to postpone the flotation."

"For what reason?"

Carsten's own voice sounded strange to him, as if it were coming from someone else.

"They claim the time's not right."

Carsten gazed at the horizon. The foghorn could be heard more clearly here, even though the milky mist was dispersing fast.

"We've been working toward this for years," he said, stressing every single word. "Everything's going according to plan. We're almost there."

"I know."

They'd already invested millions in legal and financial advisers. Made vital contacts, because it was impossible to achieve a stock market flotation in Russia without knowing the right people higher up. The road to the New York stock exchange lay wide open; the goal was in sight.

"It's too late to change the date now."

The silence on the other end of the line didn't bode well.

"Anatoly, talk to me."

"They've persuaded Sergei that we ought to wait. He's with them."

"You're kidding me!"

Carsten realized how angry he sounded, even though he was trying to hold back. "I met him in May. He didn't say a word back then! On the contrary, he seemed more eager than ever to float the company. How can he possibly have changed his mind, just like that?"

Anatoly's deep sigh made Carsten long for a whisky. Or something even stronger.

"Well, he sounds as if he has a different opinion now," Anatoly said wearily. "We've met several times over the past few days, which is why I didn't call you. I've been trying to get a handle on what's going on, and I didn't want to worry you unnecessarily."

"But why? What's he saying?"

"He's highlighted a number of problems that need to be sorted out, impediments that weren't on the table before but have now begun to appear. The software is too unstable, it requires further development and testing in order to cope with the planned influx of new clients."

Carsten tried to force his brain to think logically.

"So what kind of time frame are we looking at?"

"Hard to say. Possibly spring 2014, but it could be later."

"2014," he repeated for no good reason. The loan was due for repayment in October 2013. He'd already spent millions on the house on Sandhamn.

"I'm flying to Moscow tonight." The decision was easy.

Anatoly cleared his throat, and Carsten knew he didn't think that was a good idea.

"Jumping on a plane won't improve the situation. Let me talk to Sergei again before you come over. There's a risk that he'll dig his heels in even more if you back him into a corner. I'm still trying to get him to stick to the original plan."

Carsten squeezed the phone so hard that it dug into his palm. Instinct told him he ought to go to Moscow right away, but the party was tomorrow. The party he'd insisted on, in spite of Celia's protests. One hundred and fifty people, people he wanted to build relationships with, get to know. Plus of course he wanted to show off his house.

"I promise I'll do my best," Anatoly said in his ear. "If I can get him on our side, then the bank will come on board, too."

And if it doesn't?

"Trust me, Carsten."

Celia crept into Oliver's room to say good night, but he'd already fallen asleep, just like Sarah. He was lying on his back; his forehead was slightly damp, so she turned down the covers. There was his teddy bear, carefully hidden from anyone who might happen to look in. Even in his sleep Oliver was clutching it tightly.

She perched on the edge of the bed and gently stroked his hair. The little night-light was shining; Oliver was afraid of the dark and couldn't get to sleep without it.

Yet another thing Carsten disapproved of.

Oliver was a sensitive soul; Carsten didn't understand, and Celia didn't know how to explain it without making him despise his son's "weakness" even more.

He looked like an angel lying there, his round cheeks dusted with a fresh crop of freckles. He'd really caught the sun this week. A wave of love overwhelmed her as she sat perfectly still, listening to his snuffles. She wanted to put her arms around him, hold him tight. Stop time, so that he would be her precious little boy forever.

Why couldn't she show the children how much she loved them? Why did she get so mad at them?

Celia felt the pressure in her chest.

When they were both clinging to her with sticky hands, it was as if her patience disappeared in a second, and she had to call Maria. Tonight she would have preferred to stay with Oliver, but dinner was ready and Carsten was waiting for her.

And tomorrow—the party. She was resigned to the idea now; she knew there was no getting out of it.

She patted Oliver's cheek and stood up, but lingered in the doorway. It was several minutes before she finally went to join Carsten.

CHAPTER 29

Saturday, July 13

Thomas lifted Elin down into the boat and placed her on the seat next to the wheel. The orange lifejacket was far too big for her, but she waited obediently while Thomas reached for the fishing rods and picnic basket from the jetty.

It was the first day of his vacation. He didn't really want to admit to himself how much he'd been looking forward to some time off. Yesterday he'd locked away the last files with a sigh of relief. Closed the door behind him and left Nacka with a strong sense of liberation.

"Have fun with Daddy," Pernilla said, waving from the jetty.

Elin raised her little hand and waved back. "Bye, Mommy!"

"Have you got everything?"

"We have. It'll be interesting to see what Elin thinks of the bait." Thomas nodded at the jar of maggots next to the rods. It was a beautiful day, sunny and with hardly a breath of wind; perfect for a fishing trip.

Pernilla had invited some of her girlfriends over, and Thomas had instantly offered to take Elin on a boat trip so they could have some time to themselves. He longed for those undemanding hours out at sea, just him and Elin and a fishing rod.

"You'll put them on the hook, won't you?" Pernilla couldn't help sounding slightly disgusted. "Elin's way too little to touch them. She'd just put them right into her mouth."

"Don't you worry about a thing," Thomas responded with a grin.

He cast off and started the Buster. He was planning on heading over to Alskär, maybe stop there for a swim, then find an inlet where they could try their luck at fishing.

The jetty disappeared behind them.

His phone rang just as he was passing through Käringpinan, the narrow sound between Harö and Lisslö. He glanced at the display: Erik. His former colleague got straight to the point.

"Hi. Have you given any more thought to my offer?"

Thomas had put the proposal aside for the past few days; he'd had only just enough energy to do what had to be done before he went on leave. Erik didn't seem to notice his hesitation.

"I think our company would be the perfect fit for you," he went on. "Just look how well I've done."

That could have been construed as boasting, but Thomas knew him well enough to realize it was nothing more than his usual self-confidence. He remembered other occasions when he'd envied his younger colleague, wished he had the same belief in his own abilities.

"To be honest, I've really sung your praises to my boss. You've got a lot of police work experience, and you've closed a number of high-profile cases. You're tailor-made for us."

A white Vaxholm ferry was coming toward them; Thomas moved over, leaving plenty of room.

Maybe this was what he'd been longing for, at least on some level? The chance for a fresh start.

"This has all come out of the blue," he heard himself say. "I've had so much to do this last week—you know what it's like before a vacation."

Excuses. What was wrong with him? Part of him wanted to hear more; he knew he was already dreading going back to work in four weeks. But the very thought of leaving made him feel disloyal.

Erik burst out laughing. "Oh, come on, Thomas! It's time for you to do something different now, after all these years."

A short distance away, the ferry docked at Harö jetty. The swell made the Buster bob up and down, and Thomas put his arm around Elin to make sure she didn't lose her balance. She seemed perfectly happy; she'd just spotted a shoal of fish close to the surface and was following the silvery movements in the water with unconcealed delight. Her little body was warm against his, and Thomas gave her an extra hug before he let go.

"I've just started my vacation," he said to Erik. "Let me think things over. I'll call you in a few days."

CHAPTER 30

Carsten caught himself whistling as he stood on the terrace, inspecting the shore in front of the house. The catering staff was busy laying everything out, the Swedish flag had been hoisted, and the sun was sparkling on the sea. The DJ was setting up over in the corner.

It was all perfect; not even the Russian situation could spoil his mood. Keeping a cool head, that was what it was all about. Not losing control at the first sign of a problem. No one ever said it would be easy to make a fortune.

Besides, Anatoly also had a lot to lose if the flotation was postponed. His commission would be delayed, and it involved big money—more than a year's income for most people. It was in his interest to stick to the original plan.

Everything will fall into place, Carsten repeated to himself.

If worst came to worst, he would fly to Moscow after the weekend, speak to both Sergei and the bank in person. He had never doubted his powers of persuasion, his ability to get his own way.

He walked across the terrace. The flower arrangements were perfect, capturing the Swedish summer with a touch of international finesse. Tasteful and opulent. He smiled with satisfaction.

There were long tables on the shore, and the delivery from the liquor store had already arrived, thanks to Eklund's quad bike. Box after box containing a wide variety of spirits, the finest wines, and Champagne, which was already on ice.

He hadn't cut corners on anything; he regarded this as an investment that would pay off. It was a cheap way of appeasing those who objected to the building project. Everyone who counted had been invited, and Carsten was sure they'd turn up.

"Give people plenty of booze," his father always used to say. "It's better to be drunk than miserable."

His father.

"You could never have imagined this," he murmured, glancing over at the window. In the bright sunlight he saw his father for a second before he realized it was his own reflection.

A long-buried memory surfaced, making him clench his jaw. How old had he been back then? Twelve?

He remembered sobbing as he stood in front of the bathroom mirror with a bloody, swollen nose. It had been hard to breathe with the blood bubbling in his nostrils, the mucus filling his throat. Every time he tried to inhale, he almost choked; he could taste the metallic bitterness on his tongue right now. He had panicked, thinking he was going to die right there in the bathroom. Could a person drown in their own blood? He was sure that was what was happening to him.

Suddenly the door flew open, and his father was standing there.

Fear made him swallow hard, but somehow the worst of the hysteria abated. His lungs began to work, and he found he could breathe again.

"You only have yourself to blame," his father had said with barely suppressed rage. "I hope you've learned your lesson."

Carsten still hadn't forgiven him for the coldness in his voice.

"Bastard," he said out loud, and realized he was talking to himself. His father had never understood.

"Excuse me, can I ask you a question?"

Someone was calling to him from the shore, and he turned around, grateful for the distraction. One of the waitresses was coming toward him. Her long hair was pinned up in a messy bun, and the silver hoops in her ears moved in time with her footsteps. Carsten blinked and tried to shake off the unpleasant thoughts.

"I was just wondering how you want us to arrange the buffet. Is it OK if we put the dishes on the table for everyone to serve themselves, or would you prefer something different?"

In a few hours the place would be filled with chatting, laughing Sandhamn residents who wanted to see his new house. He had to focus, not allow himself to be distracted by the past.

This party was going to be his triumph.

"We can serve the guests if you like—it's your decision."

It would be a lot more fancy that way, make a better impression, but it wasn't practical. He didn't want people getting stuck in a long line.

"Let them help themselves," he decided. "But I'd like you to serve the wine. And make sure you don't pour the Champagne in advance; otherwise the bubbles will disappear." He wanted those expensive bottles to be at their very best. "If there's anything else, just ask."

"Great, thanks."

Out of the corner of his eye, Carsten saw Eklund disappearing around the side of the house with one of the Poles, the tall guy who acted as foreman. The one Celia had seen talking to some old man the other day.

They were working hard, just as he'd demanded, but it was best if they stayed out of the way for the rest of the weekend. They were due to stop very soon; he didn't want any builders hanging around when his guests arrived.

There wasn't much more to do. Maybe Celia would be in a better mood once the project was finished. Last night she'd hardly said a word during dinner, she'd just poked at her food with a look on her face like a Catholic martyr. Then she'd gone straight to bed.

She was resting right now, saving her energy for the party.

He still had that metallic taste in his mouth.

He went and fetched a bottle of Champagne. He removed the foil and wire cage, and with a few expert twists, the cork shot out and landed in the water fifteen yards away.

Ignoring the catering staff, he lifted the bottle to his mouth and gulped down a third of the contents.

Nothing was going to ruin his party, especially not his father.

Celia was standing on the terrace with Carsten, ready to welcome their guests.

Everything was perfect, she had to admit. Colorful pennants fluttered on the flagpole, and a delicious aroma drifted over from the buffet table.

He smiled at her. "You look lovely. I like your dress."

"Thank you, darling." She didn't bother pointing out that he'd told her what to wear.

A red-faced, overweight man was approaching from the shore. He was wearing a dark-blue peacoat with shiny buttons. A woman who was presumably his wife was plodding along beside him; she had bleached blond hair and was clutching a potted plant.

"Per-Anders Agaton." He held out his hand to Celia; she noticed a small patch of shaving foam by one corner of his mouth. "My wife and I are your nearest neighbors."

She recognized him now; he was the guy who'd been having a less-than-civil conversation with the carpenter the other evening when she'd been trying to relax down by the jetty. She'd told Carsten about him, but Carsten had barely reacted; he'd just kept on talking about the party.

"This is my wife, Anna." Agaton stepped aside to let his wife come forward. She handed over the plant, and Celia was immediately struck by a wave of antipathy coming from their guest.

She doesn't like me.

She thanked Anna politely as she accepted the gift.

Agaton turned to Carsten. "We need to talk. Didn't you get my letters?"

There was something about his tone of voice that made Celia feel uneasy.

"Sorry?" she said. "What letters?"

Carsten, however, seemed unconcerned. He raised his glass in a toast to the new arrivals.

"This is our housewarming party. We can discuss all that later. There's no hurry."

Agaton's expression darkened.

"This is important. I'm not prepared to wait until it suits you!"

Celia glanced at his wife, but Anna didn't respond.

"Another time," Carsten insisted. "Now, if you'll excuse me . . ." He'd made eye contact with another couple who'd just arrived and went over to say hello.

Celia stood there, holding the plant. It was a prickly cactus, and she couldn't help wondering if it had been chosen deliberately.

"Tell your husband we need to talk!" Agaton snapped, then turned his back on her.

"Welcome," Celia murmured, wishing they'd both leave.

CHAPTER 31

Nora was cycling through the forest, ahead of Jonas. Even though she hadn't been at all sure about this party, she was excited. There was a kind of happy anticipation in the air. The back of the new house appeared among the trees, and she coasted down to the clearing, where several bicycles had already been left.

The lawn looked fresh and new, as if it had been rolled out in ready-made lengths of turf. An inviting hum of voices was coming from the front of the house. Nora knew there would be a lot of people here tonight; she'd seen plenty of dressed-up couples walking toward Fyrudden along the Trouville road.

She took her purse out of the basket along with the present she'd bought in the village gift store. It hadn't been easy to find something suitable for Carsten and Celia, with all their millions, but in the end she'd chosen a framed black-and-white photograph of the Almagrundet lighthouse taken by the store owner himself.

"OK, here we go," she said to Jonas, adjusting the turquoise dress that had seemed way too much when she tried it on in front of the mirror.

"You look fantastic," he whispered in her ear, taking her hand as they rounded the corner of the house.

"Wow!" Nora exclaimed as she took in the view that met them.

The warm evening glow illuminated the façade of the Jonssons' house, while the sun sparkled on the calm surface of the sea as if it had been specially arranged for the occasion. Tall pots were dotted here and there, filled with flowering plants in a riot of colors, dark-green ivy tumbling over the edges like a waterfall. Together with the round tables and freestanding heaters, the scene was more reminiscent of a villa in the south of France than a summer property in the Swedish archipelago.

"It's enormous," she said quietly. "How the hell did they get planning permission to build something this size? And so close to the water?"

She looked over and saw the long tables set out on the shore, laden with food. In the middle stood two huge zinc tubs containing countless bottles of white wine and Champagne in iced water; the red wine was on a table nearby.

"Is there anyone on the island he hasn't invited?" Jonas wondered, gazing at the crowded terrace.

Nora was looking for Carsten or Celia, but instead she spotted the nanny sitting in a corner with a tired and fractious Sarah. Maria was pale, definitely not in the party mood, just like the little girl on her lap.

"Hi, Maria. Any idea where Carsten or Celia might be? We've brought them a little present."

Maria shook her head. "They could be anywhere. There are so many people here." She waved a hand in the direction of the mingling guests; the terrace was so packed that many had made their way down onto the shore.

It was very noisy. Nora noticed a DJ in dark glasses sitting behind a huge sound system. It was hardly surprising that this was all too much for Sarah.

"Thanks anyway. We'll see if we can find them."

"You could give the present to Linda," Maria suggested, pointing to a skinny woman who had just emerged from the house, carrying a tray.

At that moment Nora caught sight of Celia. She was wearing a close-fitting strapless red dress. Nora was no fashion expert, but it had to be a designer label. Nora was nowhere near as elegant as her hostess, but she was pleased she'd chosen the turquoise dress rather than white jeans, like so many of the other guests.

She tried to catch Celia's attention and somehow managed it, against all odds. Celia glided over, and for a brief moment her face lit up. Nora held out the beautifully wrapped gift.

"A little something to welcome you to your new home. It's nothing special, but it does come from the island. This is my partner, Jonas Sköld—Julia's father."

"This is amazing," Jonas said, waving his hand in the general direction of the house and terrace.

Celia looked uncomfortable. "My husband's responsible for the whole thing. He's been heavily involved in the project right from the start."

Carsten joined them. He appeared to be in an excellent mood; his blond hair looked almost white in the sun, and he was wearing red pants. The sleeves of his pale-blue shirt were casually rolled up.

"Welcome," he said with a big smile. "So pleased you could come. What do you think of our little summer cottage?"

"It's wonderful," Nora said quickly. "Fantastic."

Carsten greeted Jonas with a hearty handshake. "I believe you play tennis?"

Jonas couldn't hide his surprise. "How do you know that?"

"I happened to see you on the court the other day. We could play a couple of sets one day if you fancy it?"

"Sure," Jonas said, still clearly taken aback.

"Make yourselves at home," their host continued. "The food's over there, and coffee and dessert will be served later. And Cognac, of course. How about a glass of Champagne to start with?"

He was speaking so quickly that it was hard to make out the words.

"Why not," Nora said, glancing at Jonas. He still looked as if he'd turned up in Disneyland.

Carsten disappeared but came right back with a glass of Champagne in each hand.

"Pol Roger," he said enthusiastically. "It's my favorite—it was Winston Churchill's, too. This is the Cuvée—not that easy to get ahold of in the archipelago."

His eyes had a slightly glassy look. Celia said something quietly in English. It sounded as if she was asking Carsten to stop boasting, but Nora couldn't make out the words; it was more of a feeling.

"Enjoy yourselves," Carsten said, ignoring his wife. "Feel free to go inside the house if you like, see what we've done."

Celia watched him as he headed for the shore.

She's unhappy, Nora thought. Then Celia raised her chin, and the cool, elegant hostess was back. *Maybe it was my imagination.*

"Excuse me. I just need to check on something in the kitchen." Celia disappeared into the crowd.

"Shall we get something to eat?" Jonas suggested. There was a vast array of food: dishes of peppery veal steaks, rosemary chicken, stuffed salmon parcels, and a wide range of salads, pickles, and chutneys. There was fresh sourdough bread with bowls of delicious dips, and goodness knows what else.

Jonas led the way, helping himself to just about everything.

"Are you eating for the next week?" Nora teased him when he'd covered every inch of his plate and balanced a slice of bread on top.

At that moment someone tapped a knife against a glass, calling for silence. The buzz of conversation died away, and everyone looked over toward the terrace. Carsten pulled out a chair and climbed onto it. He seemed to be enjoying the attention. Celia stood beside him, gazing up at her husband.

Nora glanced around, saw the curiosity on the faces of the guests. Was there any warmth behind it? Hard to say.

"Dear friends," Carsten began, "Celia and I are delighted that so many of you were able to come this evening. It feels like a good start to our new summer life in Sweden."

A faint smile from Celia.

"A good start would have been to respect the traditions of this island," someone muttered behind Nora. She turned her head a fraction and immediately recognized Per-Anders Agaton and his wife, Anna.

"It's a fucking liberty if you ask me, building a jetty in someone else's water," Per-Anders said, a little more loudly. Anna placed a hand on her husband's arm and pinched him.

"I told you we shouldn't come here!" she hissed so angrily that her earrings swung to and fro.

"We're looking forward to many wonderful summers on Sandhamn," Carsten proclaimed. "Celia and I and our two children, Sarah and Oliver." He raised his glass, ready for a toast. "And of course we're hoping to get to know you all as time goes by. It's so beautiful out here in the archipelago. As expat Swedes, it's a tremendous privilege to be able to spend the summers here with such friendly people. Isn't that right, darling?"

He broke off and stroked Celia's cheek before going on.

"*Skål*, everyone! I hope you have a great evening here at Fyrudden."

"You can take your fucking money and go to hell!" Per-Anders grunted, much too loudly. Fortunately his words were lost in the general clamor of voices responding to Carsten's little speech.

Nora felt embarrassed, although she wasn't quite sure on whose behalf. She looked over at Jonas, but he was a short distance away and didn't seem to have heard anything.

The DJ started playing a lively party track.

"Will you stop this!" Anna Agaton snapped. "There's no point in coming if you're just going to make trouble. Either you stop right now or I'm leaving!"

"It's not me you should be moaning at," Per-Anders responded. "It's him—he shouldn't trample all over other people's property!" He jabbed a thick index finger in Carsten's direction. Their host was still standing on the chair with an empty glass in his hand. He was beaming; he clearly hadn't heard what Per-Anders had said.

"At least if he knows what's good for him," his neighbor growled.

Chapter 32

Carsten was on the terrace in the middle of a group of people, telling a story. Celia could see from the way he was talking that he was drunk; he was almost babbling, and his gestures were exaggerated. *He started early,* she thought. She'd seen him through the bedroom window, guzzling a bottle of Champagne.

She'd had a bad feeling from then on. She hated it when he got drunk; she knew he was capable of saying anything. He became unpredictable; the slightest thing could trigger his temper. Half the time she didn't even know what was wrong. It had taken her years to learn the signs. Her body knew, too: the knot in her stomach that grew when he opened another bottle.

Celia leaned against the wall of the house, hoping that the gathering dusk would enable her to remain unnoticed.

There was a woman with long blond hair standing next to Carsten, a Swede in her early thirties from Trouville. She was laughing much too loudly at his jokes; it was clear that she wasn't entirely sober either. Carsten put his arm around her shoulders as if it were the most natural thing in the world.

Celia dug her nails into the palm of her hand and turned away.

The DJ had switched to easy-listening music. The food had been removed, and the staff was now serving various brands of whisky and Cognac. Dozens of red torches burned along the water's edge, and the eager chatter had been replaced by muted conversations. From time to time, there was a burst of laughter. Several couples were dancing on the shore.

Celia moved from group to group, trying to avoid eye contact so she wouldn't have to stay and chat. She was looking for Carsten.

The sun had gone down, and even if wasn't as dark as back home in England, it was still hard to see properly. She couldn't figure out who the silhouettes on the sofas on the terrace were. She felt a little dizzy; she shouldn't have drunk so much red wine, and she'd eaten nothing. She'd had no appetite, and it had been easier to grab another glass rather than attempt to fill a plate with food.

Besides, the wine helped her relax. It loosened her tense nerves and made the evening bearable. In spite of the fact that she knew it wasn't a good idea, she took another gulp of Bordeaux, holding the wine in her mouth for a moment before swallowing.

She hadn't taken a Sobril today; she tried not to when she knew she'd be drinking.

"What an amazing house you've built," someone said from one of the deep wicker armchairs. Celia smiled automatically, even though she had no idea who it was. How many times had she heard that same comment during the course of the evening? Ten? Twenty?

She gazed around in a last attempt to find Carsten.

The lantern at the far end of the jetty was casting a long shadow over Linda's little boat. She heard a woman giggling, saw a small group moving toward the guest lodge, Champagne glasses in their hands.

Even though she didn't recognize anyone around her, she didn't want them to know she was searching for her husband. She went down to the well-stocked bar on the shore and topped off her glass. A few drops splashed over the side, but she didn't take any notice.

It was a clear, starlit night, with a pale crescent moon just above the horizon. It reminded her of family vacations in Cornwall when she was a little girl.

Now she was among strangers in a country that wasn't hers.

She took a swig of her wine and decided she might as well help herself to another refill before she set off. Her heels sank into the sand. She stopped, put down her glass, and impatiently wrenched off her shoes.

Somehow she couldn't help looking back at the house. The brightly lit façade looked festive and appealing, but beyond the range of the spotlights it was darker, as if someone had cut the power there.

You can see straight in.

Every detail inside the house was crystal clear, every piece of furniture, every lamp, every vase. The television in one corner, the open fireplace in another, even an open book on the coffee table.

Celia picked up her glass and knocked back half the contents. She turned and gazed at the sea. Far away on the horizon, she could just make out the contours of a sail illuminated by a red navigation light. The vessel was heading east. Away from Sandhamn.

Slowly she scanned the shore, trying to sort out where Carsten could have gone. She'd looked everywhere. How could he simply disappear from his own party? He'd already left her to cope on her own for far too long, among all these people who spoke Swedish so quickly that she couldn't keep up.

In the dim light, she saw a dot of red a short distance away—a cigarette? Maybe it was Carsten, enjoying one of the cigarillos he was so fond of.

With a surge of relief, she made her way toward the faint glow, shoes dangling from her hand.

"Carsten? Is that you?"

Chapter 33

Sunday, July 14

Nora went upstairs and into the bedroom without switching on the light. Julia was spending the night with Granny and Granddad, so Nora and Jonas were home alone and could look forward to sleeping in.

She went over to the window. It was still so dark that the distant skerries merged into a single gray mass, but beyond Telegrafholmen there was just a hint of light, no more than a change of shading, but nevertheless a whisper of the sunrise.

Nora's ears were still ringing; she danced a couple of steps to the melody in her head. Her eyes began to get used to the gloom. She was able to make out the boats down by the jetties, lying completely motionless. The sea was smooth and glossy, like virgin olive oil.

She heard footsteps on the stairs.

"Oh, there you are," Jonas said.

"It's so peaceful at this time of night. Isn't it beautiful?"

Jonas wrapped his arms around her waist and interlocked his fingers over her belly. He'd already taken off his shirt, and she could feel the warmth of his upper body and the arms enfolding her.

"Did you have a good time?" he asked, nuzzling into her neck.

"Mmm."

The effects of the Champagne still lingered; she'd drunk far more than usual, but not enough to make her ill. It had been great fun, apart from Per-Anders Agaton's outburst. Carsten had been charming and Celia unexpectedly pleasant, even if there was an element of reserve there.

Jonas and Nora stood in silence for a few seconds. Nora could still hear the last song that had been playing as they left the party. They'd danced barefoot on the shore, holding each other close.

"I hope you're not too sleepy?"

Jonas's voice, teasing and hopeful. So loved, so irresistible.

He kissed the nape of her neck. His fingers found the zipper of her dress and pulled it down in a single movement. The dress fell to her feet, and Nora leaned against him once more.

Skin to skin.

He began to caress her shoulders, his hand following the curve of her back. He struggled a little with the clasp of her bra, but seconds later it joined the dress on the floor. His fingers traced a path over her stomach, around her navel, down and up again.

She could feel each warm fingertip on its voyage of discovery. She turned and kissed him, slowly at first, then with increasing passion.

"Let's go to bed," she murmured, taking his hand and leading him away from the window. Every fiber of her body was tingling, her muscles contracting as if they knew what was to come.

Nora lay down and watched Jonas through half-closed eyes. His hair was tousled and the skin on his nose was flaking a little. He was so beautiful, lying there on his side, his face close to hers. She reached out and stroked the taut muscles in his upper arm.

His stubble rasped against her skin as he pressed his mouth to hers.

A feather-light hand slid across her hipbone, finding its way over her belly and between her legs. A warm, throbbing sensation was gathering strength, as if every blood vessel was working together to pump the blood to one single spot. She could feel him hardening against her thigh.

His hand found her breast, and Nora arched her back to meet him. His breath was like a puff of steam against the thin skin over her collarbone. His tongue moved in slow circles, his lips brushed her stomach.

Nora fell back against the pillow.

"I love you," she whispered.

CHAPTER 34

The hour of the wolf.

Soon it would be time for the darkness to give way as the dawn came creeping over the horizon. On the other side of the island, the sun would rise through the morning mist beyond Korsö Tower.

But now it was still night.

The torches had burned out, and the catering staff had cleared everything away before they left Fyrudden. The lanterns were out, the heaters switched off.

The guests had gone home.

The yellow flame from the slender cigarette lighter showed clearly against the wall of the house. It was possible to see both the door and the steps. Brown pine needles lay scattered among the trampled-down heather.

The flame burned strongly.

Then it flickered; for a moment it seemed as if it might go out, in spite of the fact that there wasn't a breath of wind, but then it recovered, steadied.

The hand that brought the lighter to its target did not waver.

At first the wood resisted. The flame went out. It took three attempts to spark it to life.

This time the accelerant that had been used to drench the steps, the door, and the four corners of the building did its job.

There was a burst of flame, and the fire took hold.

"Fuck!"

The lighter fell to the ground, but that didn't matter; it had served its purpose.

The blaze grew with astonishing speed, spreading up the steps and across the façade. It ate its way through the door, into the hallway, racing toward the living room and the bedrooms.

On the other side of the house, new flames found more wood drenched in accelerant.

A pillar of black smoke rose into the sky, reeking of soot and sulfur. By this time the appearance of the fire had changed; the bright-yellow flames now contained shades of deep-orange, tipped with lilac. They advanced in all directions, like a hydra proliferating by the second as they found fresh fuel.

The steps were no more than a blackened skeleton glowing in the intense heat.

There was a loud crash; the first window had shattered. Several others immediately followed it.

Clouds of smoke and tongues of fire burst out through the broken windows, feeding on the surge of oxygen. Sparks rained down, landing on the ground with the fragments of glass. Soon the pine needles began to burn.

Someone coughed in one of the bedrooms.

Then the flames reached the roof.

CHAPTER 35

As soon as he moored the Buster at Fyrudden's jetty, Thomas was struck by the acrid stench of smoke. The call from the communications center had come through forty minutes earlier. As Thomas was on Harö, it hadn't taken him long to get dressed and head over to Sandhamn.

He stood in front of the charred ruin, processing his first impressions. The smoke brought tears to his eyes; he blinked over and over again, but it didn't help much.

The birds were chirruping happily, as if in some rural idyll. He realized he couldn't expect a respectful silence from the local wildlife. It was ten o'clock, and the bright sunshine exposed every detail of the devastation before him.

Smoke was still rising from the remains of the building, and the ground was burned and thick with soot in a wide circle all around the seat of the blaze. Here and there he could see charred beams, and a distorted tangle of metal in one corner suggested it might have been a bathroom. A collapsed chimneystack showed the location of an open fireplace.

Things could have gone very badly if the fire had spread to the property nearby or to the forest behind; the ground was tinder-dry at this time of year. Presumably the speedy intervention of Sandhamn's voluntary firefighters had averted this disaster. Thomas had already exchanged a few words with their chief, whose red jeep was parked a short distance away. A small group of islanders who'd helped out were standing next to the driver's door, talking quietly.

Staffan Nilsson, Nacka's most experienced CSI, came over to join Thomas. They knew each other well and had worked together for many years.

"Where's the family?" Thomas asked.

"Over there, in the main house."

Thomas glanced across and saw Adrian Karlsson approaching, wiping a smut of soot from his forehead. They, too, had worked together in the past.

"I just heard that your colleague is on the way," Adrian said. "The police launch picked him up in Stavsnäs, but you were quicker."

"Aram's coming from the mainland—Harö is closer, and I've got my own boat."

Staffan cleared his throat. "The body's on the far side, behind the collapsed wall. Do you want to take a look now?"

Thomas nodded.

"It's not a pretty sight," Staffan informed him, lifting up the blue-and-white police tape. Adrian seemed to be steeling himself; Thomas could see the tension in his face. Staffan led the way, then stepped aside.

A blackened body lay facedown, knees drawn up. It was impossible to distinguish any facial features, and the hands were no more than stumps. Nothing remained of the clothing, apart from odd scraps in a grotesque patchwork of red and black. It was as if muscles, fat, tissues had dissolved and melted into the bones. The head was tilted slightly to one side, with holes where the eyes had been. The corpse had stiffened in the fetal position.

The stench was unmistakable.

Thomas grimaced and couldn't help turning away for a second. He forced himself to focus on the details that would be vital to the investigation.

Which way was the body facing? Had the dead man or woman been trying to crawl away, but collapsed as a result of the heat, or smoke inhalation? Or had he or she been asleep and never even woken up?

It was impossible to answer any of his questions at this stage, but Thomas hoped that Staffan Nilsson would be able to come up with something today. It would be good if they didn't have to wait days for results from the lab.

There was one thing they had to know as soon as possible: Was this a homicide investigation, or were they dealing with an accidental death?

Staffan pointed to the corpse.

"I spoke to the chief of the local volunteer firefighters. He said all four walls were already ablaze by the time they got here."

The fire had been spotted by a dog owner who had been out unusually early, just before dawn. However, it had been impossible to save the house. Instead the firefighters had concentrated on protecting the surrounding area.

"There's no sign of the seat of the fire indoors," Staffan went on. Thomas knew what that meant; the place had been set alight from the outside. He trusted his colleague's judgment completely.

"You think it's deliberate?" he asked.

"I've taken samples, but I think we should bring in a dog. That will give us the answer right away; otherwise we'll have to wait weeks for the analysis results."

A specially trained dog would mark the presence of an accelerant. Their capabilities were impressive, sometimes bordering on the supernatural.

"We should be able to get one over here in an hour or two. I'll arrange it."

"Have you any idea if it's a man or a woman?" Adrian said from behind them. Thomas realized he was trying to avoid being downwind of the corpse.

"What do you think?" he said in turn, wishing they had something more to go on, such as shoes or clothing.

"Hard to say."

Thomas crouched down, getting as close as he could without jeopardizing the forensic investigation. It was almost unbearable; he had to cover his nose to stop himself from throwing up. He breathed through his mouth, concentrating on what was in front of him. He didn't want to think about the fact that this had been a living person just a few hours ago.

The right side of the head was pressed against the ground, and something glinted behind it. Thomas leaned forward.

A broken glass. A Champagne glass?

He stared at the body for a moment. *I think it's a man.* He felt quite certain, even though there were no facts to back up his instinctive reaction.

A man who was alive when the fire broke out.

Chapter 36

The maritime police boat moored at the far end of the jetty. Aram stepped ashore and waved to Thomas as the vessel backed away and sped off toward the mainland. There were very few vessels to cover a wide area.

Thomas went to meet Aram and greeted him with a handshake.

"Welcome. Good to see you, as always."

Aram raised an eyebrow. "I thought your vacation started this weekend?"

Thomas shrugged as he set off.

"What can you tell me?"

"Come and take a look for yourself."

It was best if Aram formed his own impressions. There was no need for Thomas to describe the unpleasant details; Aram would soon see them with his own eyes. He wondered if the image of the blackened corpse would haunt his colleague when he tried to get to sleep tonight.

"I've never liked fires," Aram said.

There was no wind, no fresh morning breeze to chase away the heavy smoke that had settled like a lid over the shore at Fyrudden.

"It stinks," Aram added, putting on his aviator shades. As usual he was wearing a white shirt under his V-necked sweater.

"You wait till we get closer," Thomas said helpfully.

"Thanks."

"Shall we talk to the family when you've taken a look around? I wanted to wait until you arrived."

Thomas led the way and pointed out the scene of the fire, even though it was completely unnecessary.

"Did you manage to find out anything about the owners?"

"I did the best I could on the way over," Aram replied. "The property belongs to a Carsten Jonsson. He's an expat Swede who's lived in London for many years. Not short of money, although you've probably already worked that out looking at this place."

Thomas contemplated the outdoor seating areas, the lavish pots of flowers everywhere.

"The wife's name is Celia Jonsson," Aram continued. "She's a British citizen. They have two children—Oliver's seven and Sarah's four. Both have dual nationality."

He made a sweeping gesture with his right hand.

"This is all new. They've only just moved in. This is their first summer on Sandhamn."

The shore was littered with cigarette butts, and an empty wine bottle bobbed at the water's edge. A short distance away, a couple of broken glasses lay half buried in the sand along with several beer cans.

"Party?"

Thomas nodded. "According to the fire chief, they had a housewarming party yesterday evening. Apparently it was a big event—dozens of people celebrating into the wee hours."

Aram rubbed his chin, where a patch of stubble gave away the fact that he'd had to rush when the call came through.

"Do you think things might have gotten out of hand?"

"Too soon to tell, but Staffan Nilsson thinks the fire was started deliberately."

CHAPTER 37

Thomas knocked on the black door. *At least the family still had the main house,* he thought. If the fire had spread, the situation could have been much worse, in terms of both human life and property. However, he realized that was probably little consolation right now. As if he'd read Thomas's mind, Aram said quietly, "There would have been one hell of a blaze if this place had gone up, too. You could fit four apartments like ours into this space."

The door opened to reveal a pale, slim woman with her hair tied back in a messy ponytail.

Thomas introduced himself and Aram.

"Celia Jonsson."

"Could we have a little chat?" Thomas asked.

"Of course. Come in."

In the living room, two children were curled up on the sofa with a young woman of about twenty. She was reading aloud from a story-book; it sounded like *Pippi in the South Seas.* The little girl looked about the same age as Elin. The twenty-year-old, dressed in a cotton top and a pair of sweatpants, was even paler than Celia.

"This is Maria, our nanny," Celia explained. "She's Swedish." Her eyes were darting all over the place, and Thomas sensed that she didn't want to talk about the fire in front of the children. However, the open-plan design made it difficult to find a spot for a private conversation.

"Maybe we should go and sit on the terrace?" he suggested. "We don't want to disturb story time."

Celia led the way through the glass doors. She chose the chair nearest the window so that she could keep an eye on her son and daughter.

"Is your husband around?" Thomas began. "We'll need to have a word with him as well."

"I don't know where he is." Celia spoke so quietly it was difficult to hear what she was saying.

Thomas leaned forward.

"He's not home," Celia went on, a fraction louder. "I haven't seen him today."

Red patches had appeared on her cheeks, spreading to her throat and chest.

Thomas had a sinking feeling in the pit of his stomach.

"When did you last see him?" Aram took out his black notebook and slipped off the rubber band securing the pages.

"Last night. We had a big party, a housewarming." The laugh that followed was unexpectedly bitter.

"Could you be a little more precise?" Thomas said gently.

Celia rubbed her forehead. "It was around eleven. I looked for him at midnight, but I couldn't find him. I thought he was down at the shore, but I was mistaken."

"What do you mean?" Aram's tone was as gentle as Thomas's.

"It wasn't my husband. Someone else was standing there, smoking. As I said, I was mistaken."

"So what did you do then?"

"Nothing." There was something else in her voice now—anger? What was the truth about the relationship between Celia and Carsten Jonsson? "I went to bed. I assumed he'd gone off with . . ."

She broke off.

"Gone where?"

"That doesn't matter."

"But you thought he was with someone else?"

There was a brief silence before Celia answered. "I don't know."

Thomas hoped she would provide some kind of further explanation, and eventually Aram asked, "Then what happened? After you'd gone to bed?"

"I woke up a few hours later because someone was banging on the door. A man said the guest lodge was on fire." Her hand flew to her throat. "My God, we could all have been killed. What if Sarah or Oliver had been hurt? I was terrified, I thought the fire was going to spread to the house."

"I understand," Thomas reassured her. "It must have been dreadful. Are you OK to carry on?"

Celia blinked several times.

"Maria had woken up, too, and together we managed to get the children out; we didn't dare stay indoors. We sat on the terrace so they wouldn't see what was going on." She pointed to a pile of blankets over in the corner and let out a sob. "I didn't want them to be even more frightened."

"I presume you've tried to call your husband?" Aram said.

"Of course, but there's no point. His cell phone's on the chest of drawers in our bedroom."

"Does he usually leave his phone behind?"

"It's charging."

That didn't necessarily mean anything, Thomas thought. It didn't prove that the dead man was Celia's husband. "Do you have a photograph of him?"

Celia wiped away a few tears, then got to her feet and went indoors. After a minute or so she came back with a phone and showed them a photo that must have been taken on the island quite recently. "There you go."

Carsten Jonsson was standing on the jetty with Oliver beside him. He was tan, smiling into the camera. His son was wearing a blue base-ball cap and a lifejacket.

Thomas knew he had to tell Celia about the body, even though they had no information about the identity of the deceased at this stage.

"Unfortunately I have some bad news. We found the remains of a person who died in connection with the fire."

"Is it Carsten?"

The color drained from Celia's face.

"We can't tell at this stage," Thomas told her, knowing that what he had to say next would only make things worse. "However, it could well be a man's body."

Celia made a whimpering sound.

"Unfortunately identification is impossible at this stage," Thomas added quickly. "However, we do need to ask whether Carsten had any distinguishing features that might help us to . . ."

"Oh God," Celia whispered, and collapsed.

CHAPTER 38

Aram glanced at his watch and realized that several hours had passed since he arrived at the scene. Celia had been in no state to continue, and they were now sitting with Maria, the nanny. She'd just told them someone banging on the door had waked her.

"Did you notice anything unusual yesterday evening?" Aram asked. "Any of the guests or catering staff who behaved oddly, any sign of trouble?"

"No. I was busy taking care of Sarah and Oliver, making sure they didn't disturb anyone."

"How were things between Celia and Carsten at the party?"

"OK."

Maria was constantly plucking at her top, and Aram had a strong feeling that there was something she wasn't telling them.

"Could you expand on that?"

"They've argued a lot about this house."

"Why?"

"Celia didn't want a house in Sweden, but Carsten decided they're going to spend the summers here."

"So he's the one who makes all the decisions?"

Maria nodded. "Well, most of the time. Celia never really stands up to him, at least not when I'm around, but then afterward she's pretty down, and there's a weird atmosphere. Then Carsten gets mad because she's miserable."

No point pussyfooting around, Aram thought.

"So what do you really think of Carsten?"

Maria continued to pluck at the fabric of her top.

"I won't say anything to him," Aram assured her. "You've got nothing to worry about."

"He seems very nice when you first meet him."

"But . . . ?"

"He's not always nice," she said after a long pause. "He can be horrible when he's stressed or when he's had a few drinks. He gives Celia a little push or a pinch, says stuff about her even when the kids are in the room. And he's always working—he's away a lot."

"Would you say he's been stressed recently?"

The girl nodded again. "Last Friday he was up half the night. I got up to fetch a glass of water around three, and he was sitting on the terrace, drinking. There was a half-empty bottle of whisky on the table beside him."

"Can you tell us a little more about the party?" Aram said. "Do you remember anything in particular about yesterday?"

"No. Once the children were asleep, I went to bed."

"Wasn't it hard to sleep with so much going on outside?"

"Yes, but I was so tired. I haven't been sleeping very well lately." She tugged at her sleeve.

"Why not?"

Maria glanced over at the window of Celia's bedroom.

"You can tell us anything." Aram made a huge effort to sound reassuring. "Whatever you say to the police is confidential. It's essential that we have as much information as possible so we can find out how the fire started."

"Something bad happened on Wednesday."

Maria pushed her hands under her thighs. Her shoulders went up, and she hunched her back.

"Go on."

Maria glanced at the bedroom again before answering.

"I was going to take Sarah to her swimming lesson on Wednesday morning, and when . . . when I opened the door, there was a dead bird on the steps."

"A dead bird?" Aram pictured a bullfinch that had flown into a pane of glass.

"A dead herring gull. Its throat had been cut."

Aram raised his eyebrows, but Maria didn't appear to notice. She kept her head down as she continued.

"There was blood everywhere—it was horrible. Carsten told me I wasn't to say a word to Celia about the bird or the note."

"The note?"

"There was a note next to the bird. It said *GO AWAY!*" Maria swallowed.

Well, that's pretty clear, Aram thought.

"Have I understood correctly?" he asked. "Celia knows nothing about this?"

"Linda insisted that was what Carsten wanted. I didn't dare ask any questions."

"Who's Linda?"

"She's the housekeeper—she does the cleaning, the laundry, and so on."

A housekeeper, too.

"What's her surname?"

"I don't remember. She lives on another island. She comes over in her boat every day."

"No problem, we can easily find out."

Aram looked at Thomas, who had remained silent throughout the interview. He'd barely reacted when she mentioned the bird; he seemed to be lost in his own thoughts. Aram turned back to Maria.

"Do the two of you get along well?"

The girl shuffled uncomfortably. "She's really old, like forty or something."

Aram couldn't help smiling. He made a note; they needed to speak to Linda right away. Celia was bound to know her surname.

Thomas's cell buzzed. He read the text message and held the phone out to Aram so that he could see the screen. It was from Staffan Nilsson.

Come and take a look at something when you're done.

"Does anyone else live here, apart from you and the family?"

Maria shrugged. "The Polish workers who've built the house stay in the guest lodge during the week."

"Were they here yesterday?"

"I think they went into town in the afternoon, because of the party. I heard Carsten telling the general contractor he didn't want them around."

"The bird," Thomas said unexpectedly. "What happened after you found it?"

"What do you mean?"

"Did anyone report the incident to the police?"

"I don't know." Maria seemed even more anxious now, as if it was her fault that she didn't know.

A dead bird on the steps, Aram thought. *Part of a serious threat, or just a grisly way of trying to drive the family away?* He would have liked to see the note.

Thomas drummed his fingers slowly on the arm of the chair, gazing in the direction of the ruined lodge.

"I can finish here if you like," Aram said.

Thomas stood up. "Maybe I can have a chat with you later." He handed Maria his card. "If you remember anything else, give me a call."

Maria stared at the card as if she had no idea what she was supposed to do with it. Out of the corner of his eye, Aram caught a glimpse of a shadow at the window of the bedroom opposite them. Was Celia watching them through the gap in the curtains?

CHAPTER 39

"How's it going?" Thomas asked Staffan Nilsson, who was on his knees, poking around in the ashes.

It was a relief to get away from the interview with the nanny. He'd found it hard to concentrate after they'd spoken to Celia. Aram had had to take over.

Thomas knew he should have been more engaged, but Celia's collapse was another reminder of how difficult it was to deal with the sorrow and confusion of the victims of a crime. They had so many questions, and he had no answers.

They were at the back of the lodge, a short distance away from the body that would soon be collected by the maritime police for transportation to the forensics lab in Solna. Åsa, Staffan's colleague, was busy documenting every inch of one of the fire-damaged walls with her camera.

Thomas hoped that Staffan's text message wasn't going to lead to any kind of close contact with the deceased. He had deliberately positioned himself with his back to the corpse; he didn't even want it in his field of vision. This wasn't the first time he'd encountered a charred body, but today he was finding it almost impossible to deal with.

Like everything else.

"So there's plenty to think about," Staffan began.

Thomas remembered that he'd written a number of articles about pyromania and arson; this was one of his specialist areas.

"Go on," he said. As far as he could see, Staffan was concentrating on a pile of gray ash, but no doubt he knew what he was talking about.

Staffan didn't answer immediately. He turned to a collection of samples ready to be taken back to Nacka, removed a clear plastic bag containing something black, and showed it to Thomas.

When Thomas took a closer look, he saw a flash of silver beneath the soot. Then he understood: it was the half-melted case of a cigarette lighter. *Interesting.* He found it easier to focus on inanimate objects.

"What do you think this might be?" Staffan said, holding out the bag so that Thomas could see more clearly.

It was a rhetorical question, but Thomas answered anyway. "Presumably a cigarette lighter."

"I agree. And wouldn't it be interesting to find out why it's ended up here? It was partly hidden under one of the bricks of the collapsed wall; otherwise it would probably have been completely destroyed."

"Someone could have dropped it on a separate occasion," Thomas suggested against his better judgment.

"Anything's possible," Staffan said as he replaced the bag. Suddenly they heard eager barking, which meant the police dog was doing its job. It was good that they'd managed to bring it in so quickly.

"The dog's detected accelerant in several places," Staffan went on. "I'll show you."

He set off toward what must have been the front door of the lodge and stopped by the remains of a burned-out flight of steps. The sea was behind them, the big house to their right, closer to the shore.

"These steps led up to the door. The dog clearly marked this spot, and as you can see, the wooden planks have been subjected to such intense heat that they've turned to charcoal. I'm assuming we'll find some kind of accelerant when the analysis is completed."

The remains of the walls and chimneystack were virtually the only elements remaining of the original building; everything else had been reduced to ashes.

"We can also see that it happened very fast; the flames spread with great speed, and coupled with the intensity of the blaze, it suggests a highly flammable accelerant distributed over a wide area."

Thomas knew where he was going with this.

"I'd bet a bottle of wine that this fire was started deliberately," Staffan said. "I think the perpetrator soaked the façade in several places to make sure the flames would catch."

"What kind of quantity are we looking at?"

"Hard to say at this stage. It depends on the depth of penetration, the viscosity of the liquid—a range of factors."

"Are we talking about one gallon or more?" Thomas persisted.

"I'd guess several gallons." Staffan pulled up one plastic glove that had slipped down his wrist. "Enough to make sure virtually nothing would be left."

Thomas studied the scene of the fire, trying to see it through his colleague's eyes. He thought he could smell the unmistakable stench of burned flesh, even though it must have been his brain playing tricks on him. "Gas?"

"Possibly, but it could also be the stuff you use to get the barbecue going. Gas is certainly the most common accelerant used in arson attacks. According to American statistics, it's almost five times more prevalent than other flammable materials in these circumstances." He bounced lightly on his heels, as if he were giving a lecture. "It's easy to get ahold of and extremely effective."

"Especially when there's a lighter around," Thomas couldn't help pointing out.

Staffan nodded in agreement. That was enough for Thomas; someone had deliberately set fire to the Jonssons' guest lodge.

"One more thing. What's your take on the dead body?"

"You mean the guy who burned to death inside?"

"You're sure it's a man? I couldn't decide."

"I'd expect forensics to confirm that the body is male," Staffan said. "Both the jaw and occipital bone gave me that impression. If nothing else, the pelvis will give us the answer; it's very different in men and women. Just as you thought, there was what appears to be a broken Champagne glass beside him. It seems likely that he was at the party."

Staffan Nilsson is good, Thomas thought once again. He relied on Staffan's instincts almost as much as his scientifically proven discoveries.

The sound of an engine made him look around. The maritime police boat had returned to transport the body to the mainland. He was very glad that wasn't his job.

"How did it go with the family?" Staffan asked. "Did they have any idea who the deceased might be?"

"The husband is missing; his wife hasn't seen him since yesterday evening, and he hasn't been in touch. He left his phone in the house."

"That doesn't sound good."

"No. She broke down a while ago, so she's resting now. I'll continue questioning her as soon as she's up to it."

"So you don't know why he decided to sleep in the lodge? Had they quarreled?"

"According to the nanny, they argued pretty frequently about the new house. Apparently the wife doesn't want to be here."

"Could she have set fire to the lodge to show him she's serious?"

The question took Thomas by surprise; the idea hadn't even occurred to him. Staffan reached for his camera, but Thomas stopped him.

"One more thing: Can you tell whether the deceased was alive or dead when the fire broke out?"

Staffan shook his head. "That's not my area, as you well know. You'll have to wait for the autopsy."

That was exactly the response Thomas had expected, but he'd still hoped for something else. However, he knew there was no point in pushing his colleague.

"One thing's for sure," Staffan added, almost in passing as he adjusted the camera lens. "Whoever did this was determined to cause a major blaze. It was a very thorough job; otherwise the fire wouldn't have caught and spread so fast."

Flakes of ash drifted through the air. The firefighters had left. The lush summer vegetation framed the blackened ruins of the lodge.

Is this over? Thomas wondered. *Or is it just the beginning?*

CHAPTER 40

He woke up with an aching head, as if someone had driven an iron spike through his skull. His whole brain seemed to be throbbing, and his tongue was rough and dry. He had a vile taste in his mouth; he'd smoked way too many cigarettes.

He propped himself up on one elbow in an attempt to orient himself. He was lying on the shore, actually on the ground, in the shade of a group of pine trees. A branch scraped his cheek when he moved.

He must have fallen asleep here last night.

How much had he had to drink yesterday? He didn't want to know, but it was definitely too much.

He flopped back on the damp sand, exhausted. His shirt felt cold and was sticking to his back. He'd have done anything for a bottle of Coke right now, but realized that raising it to his mouth would probably have been beyond him. He tried to lick his lips, but there was no saliva. Every mucus membrane was as dry as a fresh sheet of sandpaper.

A sudden wave of nausea overwhelmed him, and he only just managed to turn his head to the side before a cascade of sour vomit spurted out. His stomach heaved; he dragged himself to his knees, hoping that each burst would be the last. Eventually it was over and he collapsed. It was a long time before he managed to wipe his mouth with his shirtsleeve.

He ought to get up, go home, but all he could do was shuffle a few feet along the sand, away from the stinking pile.

Carsten Jonsson rolled over onto his back and stared up at the blue sky. The sun was shining, so it must be morning. But was it early, or closer to lunchtime?

Did he really want to know?

He'd lost control last night.

It was all because of that girl from Trouville, with her low-cut dress and her long blond hair. She'd made it very clear that she was interested. He'd held the Champagne bottle in his hand and invited her to sample the bubbles. She'd laughed and followed him without the slightest hesitation.

The music had been playing in the background as they wandered away. No one had noticed their departure; all cats are gray in the dark. They'd both been equally tipsy, and she hadn't objected when he stuck his hand down her dress and caressed her soft, full breasts. Before long he'd removed both the thin dress and her panties and unzipped his own pants.

Had it been good?

He had no idea; that was all he could remember. He didn't even recall her leaving. His brain was littered with tiny fragments, shards of what had happened yesterday evening.

The hum of conversation, guests coming and going in the summer night. The clinking of glasses, bottles being emptied. Warm bodies dancing on the shore.

However, he did remember that time had stopped occasionally, that he'd stared at all those people having fun and wondered what the hell they were doing there.

He'd done his best to numb the angst that came creeping up on him, opened another bottle of Champagne, poured another whisky. Thrown himself into the role of host with determination.

Something was cutting through the disgusting stench of vomit. Carsten tried to get his woolly brain to function, to understand where this new smell was coming from.

Smoke—it was definitely smoke, as if someone had lit a huge bonfire nearby.

CHAPTER 41

There was a knock on the bedroom door.

"Celia?" Maria said quietly. "The police would like to speak to you again. Are you up to it?"

"I'll be there in a minute," Celia replied in a faint voice.

She was lying on her side, staring at the white wall. Eventually she rolled over and forced herself to get to her feet.

She couldn't hide away in here forever.

How was she going to tell the children their father was dead? The detective had told her the body hadn't been identified, but she'd seen the truth in his eyes. He thought it was Carsten who'd died in the flames.

Who hates us that much? What have we done?

Her stomach contracted. *Please don't make me identify him. I can't do it.*

She heard Sarah calling to Maria and made herself take several deep breaths. She went over to the door, but when she reached out to open it, her hand was shaking so much that she could barely close her fingers around the handle. It took her more than one attempt to accomplish the simple task.

Sarah was laughing at something, and the innocent sound almost made Celia lose control. She pressed her clenched fist to her mouth to stop herself from sobbing out loud, then took one more deep breath and walked into the living room.

She glanced out the window and started to scream.

Just as Thomas rounded the corner of the house, he heard a scream from the living room, then Celia shot out through the door and raced toward a man on the shore. She threw her arms around his neck, sobbing helplessly.

Aram was still on the terrace with the nanny. They both stared at the scene playing out before them. Thomas went to join them.

"Is that Carsten?" he asked Maria.

"Yes."

If this was Carsten, then who the hell was the guy who'd died in the fire?

Thomas massaged one temple. The time was only one o'clock, but it already felt like a long day. He had to pull himself together, focus. They were going to be here for quite a while.

After a few seconds Carsten Jonsson freed himself from his wife's clutches and came toward the house. As he got closer, Thomas caught the unmistakable smell of vomit and stale booze. Jonsson's pants were creased, his shirt stained, his eyes no more than narrow slits. When he reached the terrace, with Celia right behind him, Thomas couldn't help taking a step back.

"He's not dead!" Celia said, staring accusingly at Thomas. Telling her about the body had been a mistake, but there was no point in having any regrets now. He'd acted with the best of intentions.

"My wife tells me you're from the police?" Carsten sounded as if he wanted to take control of the situation by adopting an authoritative tone in spite of his disheveled appearance.

"That's correct." Thomas introduced himself and Aram.

"What's happened?"

"I'm afraid your guest lodge has been destroyed by a fire. Someone died in the blaze, and we suspect an arson attack."

Something glinted in the man's eyes. Suspicion, or something else?

"We'd like to ask you a few questions as soon as possible," Thomas added.

"Do you mind if I shower first?"

Thomas got the feeling he was playing for time, but it would be unreasonable to refuse the request.

"We'll wait here, but I'd appreciate it if you don't take too long."

Carsten disappeared indoors, and Thomas sat down next to Aram.

"Maria, could you fix the children something to eat? It's getting late and they need their lunch."

Without waiting for a reply, Celia swept past and followed her husband.

"Sorry," Maria said. Was she speaking to Celia or the two police officers? Hard to say. She got up and went into the house.

Thomas realized he was thirsty. Maybe he could ask Maria for some water when they'd finished with the Jonssons.

"If Carsten's alive, who's the guy in the lodge?" he said without expecting an answer.

"There were almost a hundred and fifty guests at the party," Aram informed him, leafing through his notebook. "Maybe one of them stayed over?"

"According to Maria, the lodge was used by the construction workers during the week. Would there be room for guests as well?"

"The workers all left the island yesterday, before the party; they're not due back until tomorrow. We'll have to wait to speak to them until then."

"If we assume the deceased was a guest, has anyone been reported missing? We'll call Karin back at HQ as soon as we're done here, ask her to check," Thomas said.

Was it pure chance that the Jonssons' property had been targeted? It seemed unlikely. And then there was the dead bird. A stalker, or an angry neighbor? Or some other enemy of Carsten Jonsson that they didn't know about? Had there been other incidents?

"The question is whether the victim was killed deliberately," Aram said. "We can't be sure if the arsonist knew there was someone in the lodge in view of what Maria told us about the workers."

Good point. The death could have been purely accidental. Someone wanted to scare the family and had assumed the lodge was empty. There were a number of alternatives and scenarios to consider.

"We need to start by finding out if the family had been threatened," Thomas said, stretching out his legs. "Or maybe one member of the family in particular."

"It's going to be a hell of a job interviewing all the guests who were here yesterday. And the catering staff . . . ," Aram said with a sigh.

"Kalle's going to have to come back from his vacation," Thomas decided. "There's no other option."

It occurred to him that Nora could well have been at the party. He'd give her a call as soon as he had a few minutes to spare. He looked over at the shore and saw two maritime police officers with a body bag secured to a gurney. They were heading for the jetty, where the boat was waiting with its engines running.

"I guess the autopsy will take a while," Aram commented.

Under normal circumstances they would have the autopsy report within a few days, but at this time of year when so many people were on vacation, everything took longer. There was a risk that Carl-Henrik Sachsen, Thomas's preferred forensic pathologist, might be on leave.

"I'll ask Margit to hurry it along."

Aram ran a finger over the scar beneath his chin. It was something he did so often that he probably didn't even think about it anymore. As always it reminded Thomas of the mindless violence xenophobic fanatics had perpetrated against his colleague a few years earlier. Aram had spent a long time in the hospital, followed by six months' convalescence before he was fit to return to work.

Ironically, his main assailant had also been a foreigner, an American who was a member of a racist organization. He was locked away in Kumla prison, serving a life sentence for homicide and assault.

The sound of children's laughter drifted out onto the terrace. Through the glass wall, Thomas saw Sarah, the four-year-old, run over to the nanny. Maria was standing at the stove, making pancakes. Oliver was sitting on the floor, playing with one of his toy cars.

It wasn't difficult to follow their every movement from outside. He could see exactly what each of them was doing.

CHAPTER 42

When Carsten emerged onto the terrace, he'd shaved and changed his clothes. His blond hair was still wet, slightly dampening the collar of the neatly ironed white polo shirt he'd put on. Celia was right behind him.

He looked a lot better than he had twenty-five minutes ago. He was carrying a cup that smelled strongly of freshly brewed espresso.

No one had asked the police officers if they'd like a drink.

Carsten sat down opposite Thomas and Aram, and Celia joined him. In contrast to her husband, the strain was etched on her face; she looked ill beneath the suntan.

Thomas went through the preliminary conclusions from the morning's investigation; he explained that the fire was probably the result of an arson attack and informed them that the body had been taken to Stockholm for the autopsy. He ended with a direct question to Carsten. "Can you think of any reason why someone would deliberately want to burn down your guest lodge?"

Carsten took his time, sipped his espresso. "No."

"Nothing unusual has happened lately?" Aram asked. "You haven't noticed anything?"

"No."

"No threats, no protests about the construction project, for example?"

Carsten shrugged. "The neighbors have complained, but that's pretty common with a new building project. There's always someone with a negative attitude."

"I assume there's a certain amount of controversy involved when you decide to put up a house like this right along the shore," Thomas said.

There was no way the residents of Sandhamn would appreciate such a monstrosity. Thomas had heard Nora's views on summer visitors often enough to know what the locals thought of those who didn't respect the island's traditions.

No doubt the fence cutting across the shore had infuriated plenty of people.

"Maybe." Carsten put down his cup.

"Nothing unpleasant has happened recently?"

Another shrug. Celia stared at Thomas, then tucked her hand under her husband's arm. "Isn't the fire enough?" she offered.

Thomas considered how best to proceed. He would have preferred it if Carsten had brought up the discovery of the dead bird, not least because according to Maria, Celia didn't know about it. However, if Carsten was determined to keep quiet, he had only himself to blame.

"I know what you mean, but we have heard about another incident. Apparently someone left a dead bird on your steps, with a note that said GO AWAY! What was your reaction at the time?"

Celia looked confused and turned to her husband. "What's he talking about?"

"It was just a silly prank. Nothing for you to worry about."

"I believe its throat had been cut," Aram interjected. "Wasn't there quite a lot of blood on the steps?"

"How did you find out about this?" Carsten snapped. "Have you been interrogating our nanny?"

"Maria knew? And you didn't say a word to me?" Celia said.

"Calm down, let me deal with this." Carsten was clearly running out of patience.

Thomas avoided the question about the nanny; he'd made a promise to Maria.

"I don't think you understand the seriousness of the situation," he said instead. "Someone has deliberately set fire to your property, and a person has died in connection with that attack. This is not a game."

Celia stared at her husband, ignoring Thomas and Aram. "Have you signed anyone else up to your secret pact without telling me? Does Linda know about this, too? And the builders? Am I the only one who hasn't a clue what's been going on?"

No response.

"Carsten?" Celia clenched her fists tightly, her white knuckles forming a sharp contrast to her wedding and engagement rings.

Thomas tried to regain control of the conversation.

"We'd really appreciate it if you'd cooperate with us so that we can move forward with the investigation," he said to Carsten. "Right now we need to know whether there have been any specific threats against you or your family."

The air seemed to go out of Celia when she heard the word *threats*.

"What if anything happens to Oliver or Sarah?" she whispered.

"I'm afraid I can't help you," Carsten said, before turning to his wife. "I thought the bird was just a dumb prank by a couple of teenagers. I was trying to protect you, that's all."

"We're going to want to speak to everyone who works here," Aram said. "I need a list—first and last names, please."

"I want to go home," Celia said quietly. "To London."

"I'd prefer it if you didn't do that," Thomas said immediately. "In view of what's happened, I must ask you not to leave the country, at least for the next few days."

"You mean we have to stay here on Sandhamn? Carsten, please!"

"Stockholm's fine if you'd prefer that," Thomas assured her. "However, if you do decide to remain on the island, I suggest you book a suite at the Sailors Hotel."

"Until we can establish whether your family is at risk," Aram added.

"Absolutely not," Carsten said firmly.

Thomas wondered what the hell was wrong with the guy.

"We can't exclude the possibility that the fire was directed at your family, and therefore it would be better if you go somewhere else for the time being. For your own safety."

Carsten's eyes narrowed.

"I'm perfectly prepared to face anyone who thinks they can attack us in this way. Nobody is going to drive me out of my home."

"Carsten, please!" Celia said again.

He took no notice of his wife's pleading, but stared defiantly at the two police officers. Suddenly he slammed his clenched fist down on the table. Both Aram and Thomas jumped.

"Nobody is going to drive me out of my home—nobody!"

Thomas decided to drop the matter—for now. He changed the subject.

"We're going to need a complete list of everyone who came to the party last night."

Carsten's breathing was still rapid. "I don't want any publicity. Do you really have to bother my guests?"

"I'm sorry you feel that way," Aram said, "but I'm afraid it's not your call. This is a criminal investigation, as my colleague has already pointed out. We need to know who was here last night."

"It'll be all over the press and social media."

Thomas tried to smooth things over. "It's just routine. I hope you'll bear with us."

Aram leaned forward. "By the way, where were you last night? According to your wife, you disappeared around midnight."

Celia stared at her husband, who picked up his coffee cup and raised it to his lips even though it was empty. There was a brief silence.

"I must have fallen asleep on the shore."

"Sorry?"

"I fell asleep on the shore."

"Outside? In the open air?"

It was clear that Carsten nearly blurted something else out, but chose to bite his tongue.

"Yes."

Aram exchanged a glance with Thomas.

"In that case perhaps you could explain why you decided to sleep outdoors all night. Wouldn't it have been easier to come home and go to bed?"

"I don't really have an explanation. I'm afraid the truth is that I passed out on the shore; I'd had way too much to drink."

"Is this a common occurrence?"

"No."

"But last night, at your own party, you drank so much that you couldn't find your way home?"

Aram was deliberately provoking Carsten; Thomas had seen him do the same thing in similar situations, with useful results. Carsten was definitely hiding something.

"I don't understand where you're going with this," Carsten snapped, putting down the cup and glancing at his watch.

"Were you alone when you fell asleep on the shore? Or is there someone who can confirm that you were there?"

Celia stopped playing with her rings.

"Of course I was alone!"

The answer came far too quickly. Realizing his mistake, he added, "Why wouldn't I have been alone?"

"Don't lie!" Celia exclaimed. "You were with that blonde, weren't you?"

She leaped to her feet, knocking over the coffee cup. "I saw you talking to her on the terrace—the bitch with the big tits. The two of you disappeared at the same time. I looked everywhere for you."

"I was alone," Carsten insisted, even though his cheeks were flushed.

Celia's lips were unnaturally pale. "And I thought you were dead!" She rushed indoors and slammed the door behind her with such force that the glass shook. Carsten stared after her, then turned back to Thomas and Aram.

"How the hell can you ask a question like that in front of my wife? Are you out of your fucking minds?"

He may have muttered "incompetent idiots" under his breath.

Thomas refrained from pointing out that the problem had been caused by Carsten himself and no one else.

Aram wasn't giving up. "If there's anyone who can confirm that you spent the night on the shore, then it would be very helpful if you'd give us her name. The sooner we can eliminate you from our inquiries, the better."

Carsten got to his feet and leaned across the table, pushing his face close to Aram's.

"Are you insinuating that I'm a suspect? If you think I'd burn down my own house, you really are fucking crazy."

Oliver had his nose pressed against the window; he was staring at them, eyes wide.

"Sit down, please." Aram's tone was significantly more polite than Carsten's. "We're almost done."

Carsten hesitated, then perched on the edge of his seat.

Thomas took over. "We're not insinuating anything, but the fact is that you just withheld important information when I asked you if anything unpleasant had happened recently."

Carsten Jonsson wouldn't be the first person who'd burned down his own property, he thought. They needed to take a look at his finances, particularly his insurance coverage.

"I'm afraid I do have to push you," Aram said. "If you have an alibi for last night, then I suggest you tell us right now. For your own sake."

Chapter 43

Nora was lying stretched out on the sofa in front of the TV. She'd spent most of the day on the sun lounger on the jetty, not saying very much.

It had been a fantastic party, but now she was paying the price. She'd woken with a pounding headache and still felt tired.

I've gotten out of the habit of partying, she thought.

Since Julia was born, she'd cut down on the amount of wine she drank. She couldn't cope with work if she'd been up drinking red wine the night before. Jonas didn't drink much either, because he was almost always due to fly within the next twenty-four hours.

You could say they'd both become boring, but at the same time Nora wanted nothing else.

The news headlines came on just as Jonas wandered in with a cup of coffee. Nora envied his ability to drink coffee this late without it affecting his ability to sleep.

An image on the screen caught her attention: it was Sandhamn harbor, the classic view with the red façade of the Sailors Hotel and a forest of masts.

"Look!" she said, turning up the volume.

"There has been a serious fire in Stockholm's archipelago," a reporter with perfectly styled dark hair informed them. "A house burned to the ground last night on the island of Sandhamn, a magnet for sailors from all over the country. According to the police, one person died at the scene, but the deceased has not yet been identified."

The camera swept slowly across the harbor and lingered on the nearby pine forest.

"We believe the property involved was on the south side of the island. Unfortunately this made the firefighters' task more difficult."

The angle of the shot changed, and the woman turned her head a fraction before continuing her report for the camera.

"The house was built comparatively recently by a wealthy private individual. There have been a number of question marks throughout the project, and the local council has been criticized for granting planning permission."

"It must be Carsten's house," Nora said, her voice far from steady. "Oh my God—what if he or Celia died in the fire?"

Jonas reached out and placed his hand over hers.

"As long as it's not the children," she added.

The news bulletin had moved on to an item on water pollution. Nora sat up. "I must give them a call."

"Don't you think you should wait until we know more? It might not even be their house."

"Nobody else has built a place like that on Sandhamn. You heard what the reporter said."

Then again, maybe Jonas was right. She didn't want to intrude or come across as a nosey neighbor.

"I'll call Thomas. He'll know which house it is."

Before Jonas could object, she grabbed her phone and called Thomas. He sounded stressed.

"Andreasson."

"Hi, it's Nora. Are you busy?"

His voice softened. "Yes, but I'm glad you called. I was going to contact you."

She decided to risk it. "About Carsten Jonsson's house?"

"Exactly."

"How are they? Are Celia and Carsten OK? Have they got somewhere to stay?"

"They're all fine. It was the guest lodge that burned down; the main house is undamaged."

Nora's shoulders dropped and her breathing slowed.

"But I've just been watching the news. They said someone died in the fire."

"Yes, but it wasn't a member of the family."

Someone called out Thomas's name in the background. Nora waited.

"Listen, I can't say much right now, but I wanted to ask if you were at the party last night."

"We were." Nora glanced at Jonas, but his attention was focused on the TV. She sensed where Thomas was going. "You're wondering if I noticed anything while we were there?"

"Something like that. And I'd appreciate it if you could make a list of everyone you recognized—tonight, if possible. We need to find out as much as we can—anything that comes to mind."

Should she mention that Per-Anders Agaton had threatened Carsten during his welcome speech? She didn't like to gossip, nor did she want to get anyone into trouble for no reason, but she knew she couldn't keep quiet about what she'd heard.

"Just so you know, Nora, it's possible that the family is in danger. If you did notice anything, it's really important that you tell me."

"You ought to speak to Per-Anders Agaton. He's their closest neighbor. He lives just a few hundred yards from the Jonssons."

"Go on."

"I was standing next to him while Carsten was giving a little welcome speech, and Agaton made several dumb comments."

She gave Thomas a brief summary of what had been said. "He sounded incredibly bitter," she concluded. "There was something about the way he looked at Carsten that made me really uncomfortable. His wife wasn't happy with him. They quarreled afterward."

"Do you think he could have transferred his words into actions later that night?"

The direct question took Nora by surprise. She didn't want to accuse another Sandhamn resident without concrete proof, but Thomas deserved the truth.

"You mean could he have started the fire?" It was a silly question; she knew she was playing for time.

"Yes."

"I don't know."

CHAPTER 44

Carsten was slumped on one of the wicker chairs on the terrace, and the wine bottle on the table was almost empty. The sun had gone down behind the clouds, and the dark sky was somehow threatening. He hadn't bothered to switch on the lights.

Celia had taken a sleeping tablet and gone to lie down, wearing her eye mask and with the bedroom blinds drawn. The children were asleep, and he assumed Maria was in her room.

He took a slug of red wine without even tasting it. He'd been so dumb, making out with that blonde. But in his defense, he'd been too drunk to know what he was doing.

He was annoyed that he hadn't been able to remember her name when the police asked. They'd obviously enjoyed coming out with their offensive questions, rubbing salt into the wound after Celia's outburst.

He forced himself to breathe slowly; he mustn't allow himself to be provoked. In England the police had a much more civilized attitude toward those with a certain social status, while here in Sweden everybody was supposed to be equal. He'd been determined to stay calm, but Celia's lack of control had taken him by surprise. Her darling daddy should have seen her then. No sign of that famous British stiff upper lip.

Everything was supposed to be perfect yesterday, he thought. He filled his mouth with wine, savored the taste, and swallowed it slowly this time.

He had no intention of letting the police poke around in recent events—the broken window, the dead bird. He had no faith in their ability to handle the situation with any level of discretion. The fire was already all over the news, proving his point.

He'd also received several calls during the evening from an unknown number. The press, no doubt. Which suggested that the police had leaked his contact details. He'd rejected each call, but knew the blaze would be in every newspaper tomorrow morning. The speculation would already have begun.

He'd felt an instinctive antipathy as soon as he saw the two detectives on the terrace.

A ferry on its way to Estonia was passing by beyond the jetty, lights twinkling in the hundreds of small windows above deck. Even as a cash-strapped student, he'd never gone on one of the popular Baltic crossings; he'd always detested the idea of a cheap outing fueled by duty-free booze and some crap dance band, people crowding around the buffet to make sure they got value for their money.

He'd known it was an easy way to get drunk and get laid, but it wasn't his kind of thing.

His thoughts returned to the fire. Arson, according to the police. They'd asked him about the victim. They seemed inclined to believe it was one of the guests; they'd had so many questions about who'd been at the party and how well he knew them. Carsten had had the feeling they thought both victim and murderer were among the guests, but he'd never even seen half of them before. It was impossible for him to say who might have died or who'd started the fire.

He leaned back and gazed up at the sky. The stars were hidden by dense cloud cover.

Could it be one of Eklund's workmen? But no, they'd all left in the afternoon. He hadn't seen any of them before the party, and there was no reason for them to stay on the island.

It didn't make sense.

Thinking of Eklund reminded him of the trouble with the neighbors. A few days ago he'd convinced himself that the dead herring gull had been nothing more than a sick joke, but now he wasn't so sure.

He stared suspiciously at the deserted shore. Eklund had warned him that the locals were on the warpath, but there was a big difference between being annoyed about a building project and deliberately setting fire to the place. It was hard to believe that envy could drive a person to those lengths.

Or was he mistaken?

He took out his cell phone. He could hear the waves crashing in, the swell of the ferry reaching the shore.

Eklund and his men would be back tomorrow, and the police were planning to interview each of them.

He didn't want to wait until then. He called Eklund, who answered almost right away. Carsten could hear voices in the background—possibly the television.

"It's Carsten Jonsson. Have you heard what's happened?" He explained the situation, told Eklund about the fire and the charred body, the fact that the police had been asking questions about the guests.

"They're going to want to speak to you. I've given them your phone number and told them you'd be here first thing tomorrow."

"I'm so sorry about the fire. We'll be over on the early boat. Can the guest lodge be saved?"

"It was totally destroyed."

Carsten had gone to take a look when the police had finally left. Stared at the blackened foundations, the blue-and-white police tape fluttering in the breeze. Smelled the acrid stench that still lingered.

"The police wanted to know if there had been any threats against the family recently, any unusual events. It's probably best if our answers match."

"What did you tell them?"

"They already knew about the dead bird, but I didn't mention the broken window. They don't need to hear about that, and I don't want even more crap in the press."

"But surely they ought to know, if they're trying to solve a crime?"

"I don't believe there's any connection."

There was a big difference between a broken window and arson, and the window incident had happened over a month ago. Carsten couldn't see how the two could possibly be linked.

"Besides, Celia doesn't know about that," he went on. "She's already upset about the bird; I don't want to make her even more hysterical."

Eklund coughed—a deep, rasping cough.

"There might have been one more thing," he said slowly.

"What?"

"I'm not sure . . . Maybe I should have mentioned it before."

The unhappy tone gave him away; Eklund thought he'd made a mistake.

Carsten's jaw tightened. "What are you talking about?"

"It was back at the beginning of June. When me and a couple of the guys came out of the Sandhamn Inn after lunch, we found a flat tire on the quad bike. I thought it was just one of those things, but now I'm not so sure."

Sabotage, Carsten thought.

"I saw some of the guys talking to Per-Anders Agaton on the same day," Eklund went on. "But of course that doesn't prove he had anything to do with the tire."

Carsten gripped the arm of the chair in an attempt to remain calm. A picture was beginning to emerge.

"Do you trust your team?"

Eklund sounded surprised. "I told them all to go into town on Saturday, just as we'd agreed. And they wouldn't sabotage their own job. What the hell are you suggesting?"

"I'm just wondering if someone slipped them some cash to make life difficult for me and my family. Someone on the island who's angry, who isn't content with a dead bird . . . You built the lodge. Your team would know exactly where to set a fire so that it would catch in no time."

Carsten could hear heavy breathing on the other end of the line, but Eklund didn't speak.

"Would they refuse? Can you guarantee that?"

Last Thursday Celia had seen one of the carpenters talking to an older man. Carsten now realized it must have been Per-Anders Agaton. His name kept on coming up. Agaton had been on Carsten's property. According to the Pole, he'd come to complain about the fence, but maybe that wasn't the case at all, maybe he'd just said that to put Celia off the scent.

"One of your guys was seen with our neighbor on Thursday—the tall Pole with blond hair."

"That must have been Marek."

"I don't care what his name is. Celia caught them having a pretty intense conversation."

"Are you saying Marek started the fire? No way!"

Carsten didn't trust anyone, and that included Mats Eklund.

"I hope you're right. See you tomorrow."

He ended the call and slipped his phone into his pocket. He didn't feel any calmer. He knew wine and spirits had gone missing from the storeroom on several occasions. The builders stole from him, whatever Eklund might say. The Poles were there purely to earn money; there was no personal loyalty. Someone could easily have paid them to set fire to the lodge.

The dew had settled. The wineglass was beaded with moisture when he picked it up, and the red wine was too cold, but he knocked it back anyway.

The bottle was empty, but it wasn't enough. He reached into his back pocket for the little bag he kept hidden in the house, the one he always had around, just to be on the safe side. He'd promised himself that he'd never do another line, but right now he needed the focus it brought.

He weighed the bag in his hand. Another ship was passing by; he could see the lights of an American cruise ship leaving Stockholm far behind. All those passengers without a care in the world.

He took out a hundred-kronor note, shook out a line of white powder, and inhaled.

His eyes widened; the effect was instant.

His mind became crystal clear; it was a long time since he'd been able to see everything with such clarity.

Someone was out to get him and his family.

Could it have anything to do with the Russian deal?

No, that was ridiculous. Anatoly had already told him they wanted to postpone the flotation; there was no reason to try to scare him by starting a fire.

And yet the thought of KiberPay made his pulse spike.

Nothing was going his way right now. Was it too much to ask for a little bit of luck, for something to work out—just for once?

If this wasn't about KiberPay, then it had to be someone on the island.

He saw Agaton's red face, the pile of angry letters.

If Per-Anders Agaton was trying to fuck up his life, then he would have cause to regret it.

CHAPTER 45

Thomas yawned. The screen flickered before his eyes, and he was making more and more spelling mistakes. He'd come into HQ to write up the day's events before tomorrow's briefing. It was quarter past eleven now, and he'd gotten virtually nowhere. He couldn't concentrate; he was going around in circles.

Pernilla and Elin were still on Harö, and that was where he wanted to be.

He stood up and opened the window to clear his head. The cool night air swept in, carrying the scent of the weeping birch outside.

After spending the day at Fyrudden, it was a joy to fill his lungs with something that didn't smell of smoke. He rubbed his forehead. He'd been longing for this vacation, for the chance to get away from the job and think about something else. Gain a fresh perspective on his life. However, now he had no choice but to postpone his break under the circumstances. He could hardly expect his colleagues to stick around while he took off.

Pernilla hadn't complained when he left home this morning, but he knew she wasn't happy. The same thing had happened so many times in the past—plans that had to be scrapped, outings canceled. He was going to have to tell her that his vacation was on hold, but then again, she'd probably figured that out already.

She was a patient woman, but Thomas knew she worried about him. He couldn't hide the dark episodes from her, even though they were less frequent these days. Occasionally he sank down into a black hole when the images of his near-death experience on the ice came crowding in.

Six years had passed, but the memory still lay just beneath the surface. Involuntarily he tried to spread the toes on his left foot. The toes that were no longer there.

If he left the police, he wouldn't be in danger to the same extent. His physical safety wouldn't be at risk in the same way.

He left the window ajar and returned to his desk.

Pernilla would probably be delighted if he accepted Erik's offer. He was well aware that she couldn't help feeling anxious whenever he came home late from work, which was why he tried to call her several times a day. He wanted her to know he was fine, that nothing bad had happened to him.

He stared at the screen, the few sentences he'd managed to cobble together.

Erik had sounded so enthusiastic, so full of energy.

Thomas couldn't remember when he'd last felt that way as he headed off to work in the morning.

CHAPTER 46

Monday, July 15

Morning briefing was due to begin at seven thirty. When Thomas arrived, Margit was already at the table, together with Karin Ek. Both women looked fresh and well rested. Margit had acquired a deep tan, and her sinewy arms were almost chocolate brown.

"Did you get any sleep?" she asked.

"A few hours." Thomas felt as if he had grit in his eyes. He pushed aside his guilty conscience at not having achieved more the previous evening. It had been after midnight by the time he returned to the apartment in the Söder district, and by then he'd been too hyped up to go to bed. When he did manage to get to sleep, he was haunted by weird dreams.

Aram arrived with a striped paper cup from 7-Eleven. He was closely followed by Adrian Karlsson and three additional officers; Margit must have brought them in to help out.

When Thomas sat down, he discovered that Karin had already put up the pictures Staffan Nilsson had taken. They formed a checkerboard pattern, showing the remains of the guest lodge from various angles. On the right were photographs of the charred body, displaying the predations of the fire with horrible clarity. Some of the enlarged details were repulsive.

Thomas felt a wave of nausea, even though he'd seen everything in person.

"Kalle will be here in a few hours," Karin announced. "He was on the west coast when I managed to contact him, so he's flying up this morning. He wasn't very happy about having to postpone his vacation."

"It can't be helped," Margit said briskly. "He's in good company, if that's any consolation." She turned to Thomas. "I guess you were supposed to start your vacation today, as it's my first day back."

She'd already assumed that Thomas would be in, even though he hadn't managed to speak to her.

They knew each other well.

And there it was again, that same thought: if he accepted Erik's offer, his summer vacation next year would be guaranteed.

"Would you like to begin?" Margit went on.

Thomas pulled himself together and briefly summarized the situation, the previous day's interviews, and the information he'd received from Nora. He didn't bother highlighting the scope of the investigation; the fact that the fire had occurred shortly after the housewarming party meant that there were dozens of people who would have to be contacted and checked out before they could be eliminated from the inquiry. It would take weeks to go through the guest list Carsten Jonsson had eventually provided, and he also wanted to compare it with the list Nora had promised to send him later.

When Thomas had finished, Aram reported back on his conversation with Maria.

"This Carsten Jonsson sounds pretty difficult to handle," Margit said. "You two have met him. What do you think?"

"Well, he's cheated on his wife, he drinks too much, and he's extremely wealthy," Aram replied. "He's got everything, and he doesn't appreciate any of it."

Thomas glanced at his colleague. The comment was far from typical of Aram, but Jonsson's attitude had clearly gotten under his skin.

"He wasn't exactly cooperative," Thomas conceded.

"Could that be significant? Do you think he might be involved in some way?"

"His main concern seemed to be negative publicity," Aram said. "He didn't want anything about the fire or his family in the papers or on social media."

Karin smiled. "It's a bit too late for that. They're calling him the Venture Capitalist on the news, and the tabloid press have already posted a photograph of his house online."

"There goes his anonymity," Margit said dryly.

Thomas wasn't surprised. There had been too many scandals surrounding the involvement of venture capitalists in various companies; the newspapers were bound to go at Jonsson. Plus of course it was July, so news was thin on the ground.

"There's a lot of media speculation about both the identity of the victim and the cause of the fire," Adrian pointed out.

"Well, we know it was a man," Thomas said. "I had a call on the way in. The autopsy will be today or tomorrow, hopefully—Wednesday at the latest."

Karin frowned.

"There are a couple of missing-persons reports in the Stockholm area that could be a match for our victim."

"So does that make it more likely that it was one of the partygoers?" Margit wondered.

Aram leafed through his notebook.

"There were almost one hundred and fifty guests there; we'll have to go through the list and see if there's a match to either of the missing-persons reports. Even if there isn't, it could still be a guest whose absence hasn't been noticed or reported yet."

"It's only been about thirty hours since the body was discovered," Adrian added. The police wouldn't normally take action on a report until the individual had been missing for at least twenty-four hours.

Margit clasped her hands behind her head. "I don't like this at all. An arson attack in a little place like Sandhamn. Given their limited capability when it comes to fighting fires, I hope it's a one-off." She stood up, went over to the display board, and tapped the largest picture. "Do we have anything concrete to go on? Where do we start?" She turned to Staffan Nilsson. "You're the expert."

"Most arson attacks are carried out deliberately with the aim of achieving a specific goal," he replied. "Unless we're dealing with a pyromaniac, which is very unusual, we should regard the fire as a means to an end. The intention is to frighten or threaten or to destroy something precious."

Thomas thought that made sense. He remembered Celia's white face when she believed her husband had died in the fire. If someone had wanted to scare Carsten's wife, he or she had definitely succeeded.

"And which do you think we're looking at here?" he asked Staffan.

"I'm not convinced the perpetrator intended to kill."

Margit picked up on his reasoning.

"Because otherwise he would have set fire to the main house."

Staffan nodded. "Exactly. It would have been just as easy to target the house rather than the guest lodge, but he didn't do it."

"But someone died," Aram said. His Norrköping accent was unusually strong today. It hid the faint Assyrian accent that always became more noticeable when Aram had spent time with his relatives.

"We don't know if the perpetrator was aware that there was anyone in the guest lodge," Staffan countered. "The broken Champagne glass could well indicate that the victim was a guest who'd had a bit too much to drink and had the misfortune to stagger into the lodge and fall asleep."

Thomas tended to agree with him. The lodge wasn't finished, and as Maria had told them, it was supposed to be empty over the weekend.

"So was the fire some kind of threat or an expression of hatred?" he said. "A signal, maybe?"

It was certainly a powerful message. The incident of the dead gull with its throat cut couldn't be ignored, and the neighbor's comments overheard by Nora must be followed up on.

"The note that was left next to the dead bird makes it clear that someone wants the Jonssons off the island," Aram said. "Unfortunately Maria didn't know where it had gone."

According to Nora, there had been lots of gossip about the family. Thomas had seen the house for himself, and after interviewing Carsten, it wasn't hard to imagine that he would have made enemies along the way.

Where was the line between gossip and pure malice?

"I'm just wondering if there's anything else going on," he said.

"We can't answer that without talking to Carsten Jonsson again," Aram replied, tossing his empty coffee cup in the trashcan.

"He's not in any of our databases," Margit said. "He's clean."

Adrian spoke up again. "If the perpetrator was counting on the lodge being empty, that means he must have been familiar with the family's routines."

"Which suggests he's an islander or a summer resident, someone who lives there and could keep an eye on them," Margit agreed.

"We can hardly regard the entire population as suspects," Thomas objected. The expression on Margit's face told him she understood.

Once again he thought about what the neighbor had said, the vicious words he'd spat out at the party with Nora standing close by.

"Right now I'm most interested in Per-Anders Agaton. The fire wasn't necessarily planned. Sometimes stupid things happen in the spur of the moment, maybe because someone's had too much to drink."

It wouldn't be the first time booze and bitterness had made even the most reasonable person do something indefensible.

"I agree, the neighbor's our best lead right now," Margit said.

Thomas turned to Karin. "Can you see what you can find out about Agaton and his wife while Aram and I head back to Sandhamn to continue the interviews?"

"No problem. I'll call you."

Margit leafed through her notes. "We also need to start going through the guest list, run the names against our records, and see if anything comes up." She handed a copy of the list to Adrian. "If you make a start, Kalle can easily jump in when he gets here. A civilian analyst will be in at nine to help you." Then she turned her attention to Staffan Nilsson.

"One last question. Do you think there's a risk of more arson attacks?"

"It's impossible to say, Margit. You know that as well as I do."

Margit wasn't giving up. "But what's your best guess?"

"I don't deal in speculation."

"Come on, Staffan!"

"It depends entirely on the reason behind the original fire. *If* it was a message to Carsten Jonsson, and *if* that message has hit home, then there shouldn't be any further danger."

"And if not?"

"Then there's a significant risk of another fire."

CHAPTER 47

When Carsten got back from his morning jog, the red quad bike was already parked behind the house. Mats Eklund had arrived. *Good.*

Today he'd run much farther than usual, pushed himself until all he could hear was the pounding of his heart. Even the taste of blood in his mouth hadn't slowed him down. His head was thumping, and his eyelids felt heavy.

He'd had less than three hours of sleep during the night; he'd lain awake most of the time, his rage growing by the minute.

He couldn't allow it to take over, he had to stay in control.

He found Eklund by the tool shed, his cap pulled far down. In spite of the heat, he was wearing grubby denim dungarees and a long-sleeved T-shirt. Carsten nodded a greeting and wiped his face with a towel he'd grabbed on the way.

Eklund returned the nod. "I've seen the lodge. You were right, it's totally destroyed."

Carsten was still sweating; he wiped his forehead again.

"You'd better get started on clearing the site," he said. "I want the lodge rebuilt exactly as it was."

"You mean you'd like us to start today?"

"Of course."

Eklund frowned.

"Do you have a problem with that?"

"Well, it's still cordoned off. I don't think we're allowed to touch anything yet—not until we have permission from the police."

Carsten screwed up the towel in his fist. Why did he have to explain everything in detail to these idiots?

"The quicker the lodge is rebuilt, the better. I need to show everyone on this island that I'm not going anywhere. Whatever happens. Otherwise we'll never be accepted here."

Eklund pulled off his cap and scratched his head. A few flakes of dandruff drifted down and settled on his shoulders, creating white specks against the blue fabric.

"I think we should wait, speak to the police first. They can get pretty mad if you mess up a crime scene. I don't want any problems with work permits, that kind of thing. I had to bring in extra men to finish the job."

Carsten wanted to leave him to it, go shower away both the sweat and the rage.

"The police will be here soon—I'll talk to them. Nothing for you to worry about."

Eklund seemed relieved, but didn't move.

"Was there something else?" Carsten asked.

"I don't know if this is important, but one of the guys didn't turn up to catch the boat from Stavsnäs this morning."

"Oh?"

"It's Marek, my foreman."

Marek? Wasn't he the one Celia had seen talking to Agaton?

"So what's wrong with him?"

"I can't get ahold of him. I've tried his cell, but there's no answer."

Suddenly everything was perfectly clear. How could Eklund be so dumb?

"Do you remember what I asked you yesterday evening? I asked you if you trusted your team."

Carsten took a step forward, pushed his face close to Mats Eklund's.

"I do," Eklund stated firmly.

"Well, you shouldn't. It was obviously Marek who started the fire!"

"What are you talking about? Marek would never do something like that!"

"And yet he's clearly taken off!"

"It's impossible."

Eklund stepped back. The blotches on his face turned bright red. Carsten moved forward again and pushed the older man in the chest.

"Marek and Per-Anders Agaton were working together," he explained slowly. "Agaton's done all he could to sabotage this project from day one. You mentioned the flat tire on the quad bike. Who do you think was responsible for that and the broken window? Who left a dead bird on my steps?"

"Agaton?" Eklund mumbled. He didn't sound quite so sure of himself now.

"Celia saw Marek talking to him," Carsten went on. "Maybe they were chatting about the weather, but it seems unlikely." He kicked at a few pinecones on the ground; dry brown needles flew up in the air.

"Our fucking neighbor has written letter after letter, all about the same thing. He wants me to stop building my house and tear down the jetty. Don't you get it? He's determined to get me out, at any price." He pushed the damp hair back from his forehead and exhaled through his nose.

"Presumably he was too much of a coward to do the job himself, so he paid the Pole instead. Marek set fire to the guest lodge when my family had gone to bed and were totally vulnerable." He almost spat out the words. It all made sense now.

Eklund blinked rapidly several times, looking embarrassed.

"We were together on the steamboat jetty on Saturday," he said hesitantly. "I was waiting for the taxi boat to Stavsnäs. Marek was going to catch the direct service to Stockholm, but it leaves five minutes later, so I didn't actually see him go on board. I had no idea . . ."

The defeated tone of voice confirmed Carsten's suspicions. Agaton had bribed one of Carsten's own workmen, paying Marek to sabotage the project and destroy everything Carsten had achieved.

There was no doubt in his mind. All the pieces of the puzzle fit together.

"I presume Marek panicked when he found out one of the guests had died in the fire," Carsten said, forcing himself to stay calm. "Instead of criminal damage, he was looking at a homicide charge. A life sentence—Agaton hadn't paid him enough to compensate for that."

No further proof was needed. Per-Anders Fucking Agaton was behind the whole thing.

A red mist began to descend before his eyes.

"My guess is that Marek decided to disappear. He's probably on the ferry to Gdańsk by now, counting his money. He's fooled us all, including you."

Marek wouldn't go unpunished, nor would the man who'd paid him to burn down the lodge. Carsten clenched his fist in his pocket. His brain was already working overtime.

Without another word, he turned his back on Mats Eklund and walked away.

Chapter 48

Thomas didn't take the seat in the cockpit next to his sturdy colleague from the maritime police. Instead he sat down on the wooden bench and closed his eyes. Aram had decided to stay on deck in order to enjoy the view.

Thomas tried to find a more comfortable position on the hard surface. The lack of sleep was making itself felt, but he knew he was unlikely to doze off during the journey to Fyrudden.

The image of the charred body kept coming back to him: the thighbone drawn up to the stomach, the crouching position, shoulders pressed to the ground. He could almost smell the stench of burned flesh.

During the night he'd dreamed of flames licking at the walls of Elin's bedroom. The house on Harö was pretty isolated; it was a converted barn, which would no doubt catch fire in a second if someone put a match to it. A grove of trees screened their home from Thomas's parents' place.

Pernilla had called late in the evening to ask how he was feeling. She had an uncanny ability to sense his mood and always knew when he was on the way down.

This time, however, it was about something else: a vague, inexplicable shame. The police were supposed to prevent crimes like this. If they couldn't do that, then what was the point of all those long hours, the late nights when he stayed on at work instead of going home to his family?

Deep down he knew that thinking this way was a waste of time. As an individual, he couldn't possibly make much difference when it came to the evil in this world. And yet . . . there was that invisible weight of failure that had come over him as soon as he arrived at Fyrudden and saw the body.

The launch slowed to counter the swell from an oncoming Vaxholm ferry. The prow bobbed as the waves reached the hull, rolling back and forth several times before the boat was able to continue on its way to Sandhamn.

Thomas knew by exactly how much the speed needed to be reduced in order to meet the swell; he could almost feel the tiller in his hand. He had spent more than ten years traveling the archipelago with the maritime police and had always enjoyed the work, particularly the opportunity to spend so much time in the open air.

The only reason he'd moved across to Nacka HQ was Emily. Shortly before she was born, he'd asked to be reassigned; he didn't like the idea of being out at sea for days on end, leaving Pernilla alone with the baby.

Now he realized he missed that life. They'd been good years, very good.

Life as a maritime officer had been simpler in many ways. He'd dealt mainly with sailors drunk at the wheel or the recovery of boats that had run aground or capsized. Sometimes he'd been involved in other initiatives, particularly around Midsummer when drunken teenagers got into fights. He'd transport officers from the mainland, just as his colleague was doing today, or take care of injured revelers.

He stretched, hoping to give himself a fresh burst of energy. He was tired and cold in spite of the fine weather.

He should have been sitting on the jetty in the sunshine on Harö, maybe trying his luck with his fishing rod or building a sandcastle for his daughter. Instead he would be questioning people who might have had something to do with an arson attack. Talking to neighbors and construction workers, noting down the small details while staying alert to any hesitation or contradictions.

He already knew how suspicious they would all be; nobody was going to be pleased to see him.

The fact that Carsten seemed to have fallen out with half the population of Sandhamn didn't exactly help. And yet they'd all turned up to his party, including the neighbor who'd spoken out against him.

Nora had been there, too.

Apparently it was fine to gossip behind someone's back, but when you were invited to a party, you didn't refuse.

But who was he to judge?

Thomas opened his eyes and gazed out the oval window. They were just passing Getholmen Lighthouse, which meant they would reach Sandhamn in a few minutes. They overtook a lone windsurfer, the breeze filling the colorful sail.

Hopefully Carsten would be feeling more cooperative today; his challenging attitude and supercilious tone had made Thomas adopt a defensive position, which wasn't particularly professional.

Carsten Jonsson was the victim of a crime and must be treated accordingly. However, it was hard not to react when he was so condescending; he clearly regarded Thomas and Aram as bumbling idiots.

The boat juddered, and Thomas held on to the edge of the bench to steady himself.

He must maintain a professional approach, whether Carsten provoked him or not. There were plenty of his sort around these days, and there was no point in taking whatever he said personally.

Today he would do his job, and that was the end of it.

"Where do you want to go ashore?" his colleague called out over the noise of the engine.

"You can drop us off at Fyrudden. We'll start there."

Chapter 49

Carsten Jonsson was waiting for them when Thomas and Aram landed.

"I saw the police launch, so I knew you were on your way," he said, holding out a cold, damp hand. He almost stumbled over the words, and his eyes were red-rimmed. He'd shown no sign of shock yesterday, but Thomas knew the reaction could be delayed.

"Do you remember what I said about not wanting any publicity? Everything's already all over the papers; there are even pictures of our house online. And someone's leaked my phone number to the press. We've got journalists calling all the time."

"I'm sorry," Thomas said. "I hope that hasn't come from us. We're doing our best to handle this as discreetly as possible."

"You're doing your best . . ."

Carsten let out a bark of laughter, then turned and headed for the shore. He stopped at the end of the jetty.

"Have you found out any more about the person who died? Have you got a name?"

"We think it might be one of your guests," Aram said. "The identification process is underway, and we're working through the list you gave us."

"How long is that going to take?"

"I'm afraid I can't say." Aram was unfailingly polite. "We're working as fast as we can. The next step is to speak to your builders, if you don't mind?"

Carsten waved a hand in the direction of the forest, behind the dark-gray façade of the house. "They're over there, working on the fence."

As if on command, the sound of hammer blows filled the air. Carsten stared belligerently at the two detectives.

"Is that all you're going to do today? Speak to a few builders?"

Thomas decided to ignore the challenge. His intuition told him that Carsten was disturbed by the thought that one of his neighbors could be behind the fire. Besides, it was much too early to name anyone; he wanted to talk to Agaton himself first, form his own opinion.

"Is that all?" Carsten said again, positioning himself right in front of Aram. "Aren't you going to contact anyone else on the island?"

"We'll probably have a word with your neighbors."

"Why?"

Thomas sighed. They were going to have to come clean.

"We've heard there have been some disagreements lately. I believe one of your neighbors has expressed his objections to your building project in an aggressive manner. We need to follow up on that."

"How do you know about that?"

"We have witnesses who heard him."

"Are we talking about Per-Anders Agaton?"

"That's correct," Aram said before Thomas could stop him. "How do you know?"

Carsten simply shrugged and walked away. Thomas got the impression he was pleased. As if he'd expected them to be interested in Agaton.

CHAPTER 50

Celia examined her face in the bathroom mirror. Her eyes were puffy, and she could see the beginnings of a cold sore on her lower lip. The transparent blister was painful, yet she couldn't help touching it repeatedly with her tongue, even though she knew that made it worse.

Another pill had finally sent her to sleep, but she didn't feel rested. On the contrary, her body was slow and heavy, and she couldn't seem to wake up properly even though the sun was high in the sky.

The house was silent. Presumably Maria had taken the children to their swimming lessons.

Celia left the bathroom and opened the bedroom door. Was Carsten still in the house?

"Hello?" she called out. She wasn't sure whether the silence was a relief, or whether it was making her nervous. There was no simple answer, but she knew she couldn't hide away in the bedroom forever.

They needed to talk.

She headed for the kitchen area. There was a dirty espresso cup on the granite counter, so Carsten must have been around. Maria didn't drink espresso. She stared at the cup, fighting the urge to hurl it through the window, shattering the glass.

Everything that had happened over the past few days was Carsten's fault.

If he hadn't insisted on throwing a housewarming party, she and the children wouldn't have been exposed to danger; they would still feel safe.

Her legs were unsteady, and she realized she hadn't eaten for a long time. She opened the refrigerator, but the sight of cheese and salami disgusted her. She poured herself a glass of orange juice, drank half, and threw the rest away.

The sound of the door to the terrace made her turn, and she saw Carsten standing there, staring at her. He hadn't shaved; he was usually so particular about his grooming regime.

"Where have you been?" she said. Now that he was actually here, she wanted him to go away.

"I've been finding out who was responsible for the fire."

"What do you mean?" She put down her empty glass.

"It was Marek, the Pole you saw by the fence the other day. He was trying to sabotage the project." Carsten was swaying back and forth; he seemed unable to keep still.

"Why would he do that?"

"Money, of course. Our neighbor paid him to do it. Do you remember the fat guy and his wife who came to the party and gave us that ugly cactus? Anna and Per-Anders Agaton."

Celia nodded. She'd wondered why they'd bothered to come when they clearly had such a low opinion of both her and Carsten.

"Agaton objected to the planning application from the start. He's been trying to stop the build from the get-go."

"Are you sure about this?" Carsten's feverish intensity frightened her.

"I spoke to Eklund this morning. According to him, all the workers were supposed to travel over to Stavsnäs on Saturday, but presumably Marek stayed on the island. When the party was over and everyone had left or gone to bed, he set fire to the lodge."

Celia started to shake. Marek had been only a few feet away from her on Thursday. Did he know then that he was going to put their lives in danger? The fire could easily have spread to the main house while they were sleeping.

She and the children.

Marek had been nearby the whole time.

"I've also spoken to the police," Carsten continued. "They arrived a while ago and told me that Agaton made threatening remarks against us at the party. There are witnesses who heard him."

He slammed his hand against the doorframe. It must have hurt, but he didn't seem to notice. "It wasn't difficult to figure it out, especially in view of what Eklund said earlier." He folded his arms as if he was waiting for her reaction.

Celia swallowed. "Have you told the police it was Marek?"

"There's no point. They're not up to this." His cell phone buzzed; he took it out of his pocket and glanced at the display.

"I know exactly what's going to happen," he said, not looking at Celia. "They'll talk to Agaton, ask a few questions. He'll deny the whole thing, and of course the Pole's already disappeared. But don't worry, I've got the situation under control."

"Carsten, please, can't you just let the police handle this? We could go away—go back to London."

Carsten grabbed her arm.

"Nobody puts me and my family in danger! We're not going anywhere. I'll protect you if Agaton tries anything again."

Celia tried to free herself; Carsten didn't seem to realize that he was hurting her. At close quarters she could see how bloodshot his eyes were.

"Can't we just go back to London?" she said again.

"That bastard needs to be taught a lesson. I've got contacts of my own!"

His phone buzzed once more, and Celia could see that his attention was on the text message rather than on her.

"Who was the person who died in the fire?" she asked, trying to divert him.

"The police think it was one of the guests from the party, someone who'd had too much to drink and gone to sleep it off. They're busy going through the list."

Celia didn't want to ask the next question, but she had to do it.

"Did Marek know there was someone in the lodge when he set fire to it? Did he do it on purpose?"

"I've no idea," Carsten said impatiently. "What does it matter? He was just a means to an end; he was paid to do what he did."

"But do you think he knew?"

"Forget Marek. This is about Per-Anders Agaton."

CHAPTER 51

The hundred-year-old steamboat *Norrskär* had just passed the Brand villa packed with tourists. Nora was sitting in the garden; she folded up the newspaper and put it down on the table. Some journalist had tracked down the same photo of Carsten Jonsson that she'd found online: a man in an elegant dinner jacket, smiling broadly. Both the article and the picture made him seem kind of flashy, a playboy with no concept of how ordinary people lived their lives.

Of course it was easy to target Carsten and his ridiculous building project. The words "venture capitalist" had acquired entirely negative connotations in Sweden; there had been too many scandals involving nursing homes and senior housing for the elderly recently, situations where financial gain had taken priority over the well-being of the residents.

The pages fluttered in the breeze as Nora gazed down at the front page. The headline was bound to sell copies; she didn't usually buy the local tabloid, but today she'd been unable to resist.

She still felt torn over her decision to accept the invitation to the housewarming party; she didn't like the ostentatious house or the fence along the shore, but Carsten and Celia had seemed pleasant and polite—perfectly normal people.

Had it been hypocritical of her to attend?

She answered her own question: yes. But would it have made any difference if she'd refused on a point of principle?

Eva's voice interrupted her train of thought.

"All by yourself? Where's everyone else?"

Nora smiled and gestured toward a chair.

"Hi. Jonas and Julia have gone shopping. Have you seen the paper?"

Eva nodded. She was holding an apple, which she rubbed against her skirt.

"What a story! It's lucky no one in the family was hurt. Who do you think died?"

"I don't know any more than you."

Technically that was true. Thomas hadn't said much and had refused to go into detail. Nora was used to his reticence by now; she'd learned a great deal about police work by following her best friend's career. Plus she was part of the system herself now; she had a lot of contact with the police through her work in the Economic Crimes Authority, sometimes on a daily basis. She was well aware of the need for confidentiality during an investigation.

"You were at the party," she said to Eva. "Can I ask you something?"

They'd left at the same time, wobbling along Trouvillevägen on their bicycles behind Jonas and Filip, each clutching a flashlight.

"Did you hear anyone bad-mouthing Carsten or Celia on Saturday? Someone who might have been mad at them?"

"Are you thinking one of the guests might have started the fire?"

Nora hesitated. She hadn't mentioned Per-Anders Agaton's outburst. Eva was her best friend on the island, but she wasn't exactly famous for her discretion. On the other hand, there wasn't much Eva didn't know about on Sandhamn.

"Go on—you've started, so you might as well finish," Eva encouraged her.

"Remember early on, when Carsten was giving his welcome speech?" Nora explained what she'd heard Per-Anders say.

"He's crazy," Eva said when she was done.

"Why do you say that?"

"Because it's true. You know he's a lawyer, like you?"

No, Nora didn't know that, but then she'd never been quite as conscientious as Eva when it came to keeping tabs on those around her.

"But unlike you, he's obsessed with the law—the type who's always taking someone to court. He's a real pest. I know a lot of people who can't stand the guy."

"Do you think he objected to the Jonssons' planning application? I'm guessing he would have done, from what you just said."

"Normally I'd say yes, but he's been ill. I think he had a heart attack last year and went overseas to convalesce. They've got a place in Spain, on the Costa del Sol. So he had something else on his mind apart from the Jonssons' building project, or I'm sure they'd have had to wait a lot longer for the planning permission to come through. Agaton would have dragged them through every possible legal procedure and then some."

Eva really did know everything about everybody.

"I don't suppose he was too pleased when he arrived home and saw what had happened at Fyrudden while he'd been away," she added.

Nora considered whether to ask the next question.

"Does he have a reputation for being violent?" she said eventually.

"Agaton?" The sunlight sparkled on the water, just as it had done on the evening of the party. "No. You wouldn't want him as your neighbor, but not for that reason."

"What about his wife?"

"She's OK, I think. I haven't heard people complaining about her, but I can ask around if you like."

"Without causing more gossip?"

Eva leaned back on her chair. "You know me."

That's the problem.

"What else do you know about the Agaton family?"

"Let me see." Eva wiped some apple juice from her chin. "I think they bought the house sometime in the thirties. They've lived on the island for a long time, but always as summer visitors; they've never been permanent residents like your family and mine."

Nora moved her chair into the shade of the parasol; the sun was a little too hot for her.

"Where does Per-Anders work?"

"He has his own practice."

That explained why Nora had never heard of him in legal circles. If he had his own business, that was hardly surprising. It also explained why he had the time and resources to take the world to court on a whim.

His words still echoed in her mind.

"You do realize those two guys have something in common," Eva said. "Carsten Jonsson and Per-Anders Agaton."

"In what way?"

"They make enemies all the time. That's never going to end well."

CHAPTER 52

Thomas was trying to read Mats Eklund. They were sitting in the area of the terrace that couldn't be seen from the house, and Eklund had just stubbed out a cigarette.

"Any thoughts about the fire?" Thomas began. "Any idea who might have started it?"

"No."

"No suspicions?" Aram asked. "We're trying to find out if the family had been threatened, if anyone on the island wished them harm."

Eklund slipped his cigarette packet into his pocket. "The neighbors complained about a couple of things, but I don't know if they were involved." He jerked a thumb in the direction of the Agatons' house. "They're not too happy about the jetty or the fence."

"We'll be speaking to them later. Anyone else you think we should contact?"

Eklund shrugged.

"Are you aware that someone left a dead bird on the steps?"

"Yes. I was the one who had to clean up the mess."

"And the incident didn't make you wonder?"

Eklund shook his head. "I just removed it. None of my business."

"What about the note? Where did that go?"

"I think I threw it away."

"You really have no idea who could be behind all this?" Aram persisted.

Eklund shifted his position on the wicker sofa. He was wearing a tool belt around his substantial belly, including a knife in a black leather sheath.

"Like I said, none of my business. I'm just doing my job."

"So are we," Thomas countered, wondering why Eklund was being so unforthcoming. Was he afraid of Carsten Jonsson? Or was he worried about getting fired if he said too much?

"Do you think Carsten might have set fire to the house to get the insurance payout?"

The question had to be asked, even if it seemed farfetched under the circumstances.

"Why would he do that? He's rolling in money."

"Maybe he's made a few bad deals lately?"

"The insurance on the guest lodge wouldn't cover that much."

"This place must have cost a fortune to build," Aram said, waving a hand in the direction of the main house.

For the first time Eklund became animated.

"It sure did. There isn't a more expensive property in the archipelago. We worked around the clock to get everything ready for the summer."

From this angle Thomas could see the lights fixed beneath the eaves. The electricity bill for the exterior lighting alone probably corresponded to a year's consumption at his house on Harö.

"By the way, has Carsten said anything to you about clearing the site?" Eklund added.

Thomas frowned. "What do you mean?"

211

"He wants the lodge rebuilt right away. He told me to get started today."

"You'll have to wait until the forensic examination's finished," Aram informed him.

"That's what I told him, but he wouldn't listen. As usual."

At last, a comment that came from the heart. Thomas wanted to know more about Eklund's opinion of Carsten Jonsson.

"So is he difficult to work for?"

"He's paying the bills."

The shutters had come down again.

"Tell us about your association with Carsten," Aram said.

"We have a contract."

"What's he like as a person?"

"Haven't you spoken to him already?"

"We have, yes."

"There you go, then."

They waited, but Eklund was clearly disinclined to continue. Sometimes it was worth being patient, allowing the silence to hang in the air until the other person felt compelled to share some deep-seated confidence.

Not today.

"It can't have been easy having your employer in London when the work was being carried out in Sweden," Aram ventured in the hope of provoking a reaction.

Eklund shuffled again; the knife on his belt ended up pointing at Aram.

"It makes things a little more tricky."

"Did he fly over to Stockholm often?"

"We dealt with most things on the phone or by email."

"So you had a debrief maybe once a week?"

"More like every day."

"Sorry?"

"Carsten's perfectly capable of emailing ten times a day if he's in that kind of mood. No detail is too small for him to concern himself with."

"Sounds intense," Thomas said.

Eklund scratched an angry red mosquito bite on his chin.

"Or crazy," he said.

Anna and Per-Anders Agaton lived out of sight of the Jonsson property, even though their place was no more than five minutes' walk away.

After doing their best to get something out of Mats Eklund, Thomas and Aram had spoken to the Polish and Ukrainian tradesmen who'd sworn in broken Swedish that they hadn't been on the island over the weekend.

Thomas had the feeling that maybe all their papers weren't in order, but he didn't bother investigating that point. It was the tax office's problem, not his.

The Agatons' home was also substantial, but the style was completely different. It was a typical 1920s house with a pale-green metal roof and leaded windows. Several bicycles were propped up outside, along with an old-fashioned cart with the name "Agaton" on the side.

Thomas knocked on the white-painted door. There was no bell. A woman in a red sundress over a matching swimsuit appeared.

"Police," Aram said. "We'd like to ask you a few questions about the fire next door. I'm sure you've heard about it."

Anna Agaton frowned. "If you want to speak to my husband, I'm afraid he's not home right now. He went into town a couple of hours ago."

"When will he be back?"

"This afternoon, I think. I'm not sure which boat he was going to catch."

"Do you have a phone number for him?"

"Sure."

She read out a number and Aram jotted it down.

"He's not always easy to get ahold of," she added. "He usually switches off his cell when he's on vacation; otherwise his clients keep calling him. He's a lawyer."

"Perhaps we could have a word with you while we're here?" Aram said.

Anna glanced at her watch. "I'm afraid it's not convenient at the moment. I was just about to go into the village."

Thomas hesitated. It was after one, and they needed something to eat anyway.

"In that case we'll come back later—around three?"

CHAPTER 53

Thomas finished off his oven-baked cod and put down his knife and fork. They were sitting on the veranda at the Sailors Hotel bistro. Thomas was drinking low-alcohol beer, while Aram had settled for mineral water.

Thomas was thinking about the morning's interviews. What had they actually learned?

"Eklund didn't seem too keen on Jonsson," Aram said, as if he'd read Thomas's mind.

Just before he left, Eklund had muttered something about Jonsson's controlling behavior. Reading between the lines, it was clear that the collaboration hadn't been entirely painless, especially if some tiny detail deviated from the specifications.

"So far no one has had a good word to say about Jonsson," Aram added.

Thomas realized he was right. Even Celia had been furious with her husband the last time they'd seen her.

"No. And it doesn't make our job any easier."

"It certainly increases the number of people who might have wanted to frighten or harm him," Aram said, crumpling his paper napkin. "We need to get ahold of Per-Anders Agaton, see what he has to say for himself. If he bothers to turn up. We could end up stuck here all evening."

"Possibly, but the last boat doesn't leave until eight, so you don't have to worry about swimming home."

Aram ignored the comment. They were surrounded by casually dressed diners; Thomas noted that he and Aram were the only ones wearing long pants in the summer heat. "Would you like a coffee?"

He went over to the table at the far end of the bar in the old clubhouse, where cookies and flasks of coffee were laid out. The walls were adorned with black-and-white photographs of yacht races in the 1920s, and pennants bearing the emblems of various sailing societies were displayed on the archway.

Thomas filled two cups and returned to his colleague.

"This is beautiful," Aram said, waving a hand in the direction of the marina below the wide terrace. "It's easy to forget that."

Across the bay lay the Sandhamn Inn, and the promenade was busy with day-trippers and summer residents. The long, narrow jetties were packed with motorboats and sailboats, a forest of white masts high above the surface of the water.

"Yes," Thomas said, although he couldn't summon up the same pleasure in the idyllic scene before them. He would rather have been somewhere else—at home on Harö. He pictured the inlet, the little jetty, the seaweed at the water's edge where Elin loved to play.

"I guess I prefer the off-season," he went on. "There are too many people for my taste at this time of year."

"Doesn't it get pretty desolate in the winter, when everyone's gone?"

"It's certainly quiet, but there's a peace you don't find anywhere else." It was easier to breathe. "Harö is a lot less busy in the summer— fewer tourists, no marina, no shops and restaurants. The houses are scattered over the whole island."

Pernilla and Thomas had invited Aram and his family over, but they hadn't managed to arrange it yet.

"You must come and visit us this year."

Thomas's phone rang; it was Karin Ek. He switched to speaker-phone so that Aram could hear.

"Hi, Karin. Have you found anything on Per-Anders Agaton?"

"I certainly have. He reported Carsten Jonsson to the police in the late spring."

"Why?"

"It seems as if Jonsson has built his jetty partly in Agaton's waters. Not by much, but enough to make Agaton hit the roof. I've got his complaint in front of me; it's ten pages long."

Under normal circumstances, the issue could probably have been resolved with a couple of bottles of wine and a joint barbecue, but instead Agaton had written an essay and handed it over to the police. Which said a great deal about the relationship between the neighbors.

"Anything else?"

"I spoke to someone from the council. According to the planning department, there have been several complaints against Jonsson. One claims he's erected a building without permission, another accuses him of illegally felling trees around the periphery of his land."

"And these came from Agaton?"

"They were anonymous; it's not possible to see who submitted them. Apparently that's pretty common in these situations; not every-one is prepared to give their name if they're reporting a neighbor."

"And what is the council going to do about it?"

"Every complaint is dealt with in due course, but it doesn't sound as if they've gotten very far. It was kind of funny. I have a feeling they're not too keen on going after Jonsson. It sounds as if he's already given them a bloody nose more than once."

"Thanks, Karin. Well done."

"There you go," Aram said. "Building your jetty in someone else's waters is unlikely to make you very popular out here in the archipelago."

Thomas nodded. "You're not kidding. You never know what that kind of thing can lead to."

"Sounds like willful disregard to me."

It wasn't a major offense; the consequence was usually a fine or six months in jail.

Thomas could almost hear the prosecutor sighing over yet another feud between neighbors that was going to cost taxpayers' money. Agaton would have to contact the Swedish Enforcement Authority to request an order for the removal of the jetty.

Which of course Jonsson would ignore or oppose through every possible legal process. It would take years, and Thomas assumed Jonsson had known that right from the start.

Maybe Per-Anders Agaton had come to the same conclusion and decided to take matters into his own hands?

The clock struck two.

"Shall we go and find the housekeeper—Linda Öberg—before we go back to the Agatons? She should be at Fyrudden at this time of day."

"I wonder if she's as shaken as the nanny," Aram said pensively.

Poor Maria, Thomas thought. She seemed scared of her own shadow.

CHAPTER 54

Carsten emerged from the bathroom with wet hands and went over to the table to pick up his phone. He had to call Anatoly; his life depended on KiberPay. The chaos since the party was the last thing he needed right now.

He couldn't afford to let himself be distracted.

Agaton would have even more to answer for if Carsten didn't get the issue of the stock market flotation sorted.

He looked around the living room. He could have sworn he'd left his cell phone in the middle of the table when he went to the bathroom, but it wasn't there.

Maybe he was mistaken. Was it on the coffee table instead?

But there was no phone next to the vase of flowers or the books with their glossy covers.

He'd been gone for ten minutes at the most. Where the hell could it be?

He had to call Anatoly, get a grip on the situation. Several days had passed since he last spoke to the Russian; his anxiety increased as he thought of the time that had elapsed.

Where was his phone, for fuck's sake?

There was no sign of it. His mouth went dry.

"Celia!" he yelled in the direction of the bedroom. "Have you seen my iPhone?"

No response. She'd been in there all day; she was obviously avoiding him.

"Celia!" He dropped to his knees by the coffee table and rummaged among the magazines on the shelf below, scattering them across the rug. He hurled the sofa cushions onto the floor.

Nothing.

He got to his feet with a curse and managed to knock over the vase. The water went everywhere, but he ignored the puddle around his feet and kept searching.

His phone had to be here somewhere.

The sound of a child's laughter outside caught his attention. He opened the door and gazed out across the shore. Maria was playing with Sarah down by the water's edge. They were building a sandcastle. Sarah was filling her plastic bucket while Maria was busy digging a moat. Oliver was standing a short distance away, completely absorbed in something he was holding.

Carsten's jaw tightened. Had the little fucker taken his phone without asking for permission?

"Oliver!" he shouted as he set off across the terrace. "Is that my phone? Come here right now!"

The child didn't seem to hear; there was a faint breeze, and Carsten's words got lost on the way.

Don't let him press the wrong command, don't let him delete something important from the address book.

"This is the last thing I need," Carsten muttered as he increased his speed. "Oliver, come here!"

This time Oliver heard him. He looked up and saw his father, then stepped onto the jetty, one hand behind his back. He kept on moving backward even though he wasn't wearing a lifejacket.

"Do as I say, Oliver! Come here at once!"

Oliver didn't speak; he had almost reached the end of the jetty.

"Give me the phone, Oliver, before I get really mad."

Carsten strode along the jetty. He reached out and grabbed his son, but the boy crouched down and tried to escape. He wriggled and kicked out, and when Carsten tightened his grip, the phone slipped out of the child's hand. It fell to the ground, then got caught in a narrow gap in the wooden planks.

Carsten let go of Oliver and fell to his knees. He retrieved the phone, put it in his pocket, and stood up. He'd scratched his fingertips; they were bleeding slightly as he seized Oliver by the shoulders.

"Never, ever touch my phone again!" he shouted, shaking the boy so hard that his little head flew back and forth. "Touch anything that belongs to me, and you'll be sorry. Do you understand?"

All his contacts, the information he'd just acquired about Agaton's business affairs—it would all have been lost if he hadn't managed to get his phone back. He was fighting for the very existence of his family, and everybody was working against him.

"Mommy said I could borrow it," Oliver sobbed.

Celia, of course. Why must she always do the exact opposite of what he wanted? Why couldn't anyone simply obey him?

The sound was unexpectedly loud when the palm of his hand struck Oliver's face.

"My phone is nothing to do with your mother, and you can tell her that from me."

Oliver stared at him as an angry red patch appeared on the boy's cheek. Carsten dragged him off the jetty. Maria and Sarah were still sitting on the sand; Maria was staring at him with her mouth open.

"If you'd been doing your job, this wouldn't have happened," he snapped. "You're supposed to look after the kids, make sure they're behaving themselves. What the hell do you think I'm paying you for?"

He pushed Oliver toward the nanny.

"Keep him away from my stuff in the future."

CHAPTER 55

The heartrending sobs reached Aram and Thomas as they made their way toward the house along the forest path. Then Carsten Jonsson appeared, striding along with a cell phone in his hand. His expression was grim. He stopped dead when he saw the two officers.

"Back again? What do you want this time?"

"We need to speak to your housekeeper," Thomas informed him.

"She's not here."

"When is she due to arrive?" Aram asked.

"Shortly, I assume; I'm sure she said she'd be in later today."

Without another word, Carsten disappeared into the forest.

"That guy ought to talk to someone," Aram said. "Maybe we should give him the number for Victim Support."

They continued past the house and down to the shore, but there was no sign of Celia, Maria, or the children. No trace of whoever had been crying.

The doors leading onto the terrace were closed, but a skinny woman with a ponytail was tying up a small motorboat by the jetty.

"Excuse me," Thomas called out. "Are you Linda?"

The woman straightened up. "Who wants to know?"

"Police. We'd like a chat about the fire," Aram replied.

Linda secured the boat, then jumped ashore in one lithe movement and came to join them. "Linda Öberg," she said, holding out her hand to Thomas.

"Could we sit down for a few moments?" he said.

She led the way to the seating area where they'd interviewed Mats Eklund earlier. It was in the shade now, and it was good to get out of the sun for a while. Thomas was perspiring after the walk through the forest.

"How long have you worked for the Jonsson family?" Aram began when they were settled around the square wicker table.

"Only a few weeks. I started in May. I helped to get the house in order before they arrived on the island."

"What did you do?" Thomas asked.

"All kinds of things—took delivery of furniture and unpacked it, put the beds together, worked with the interior designer."

"The interior designer?"

Linda pushed back a few stray strands of hair.

"Carsten employed an interior design firm to style the house before the family arrived. All his wife and children had to do was walk in."

"What was the name of this firm?"

Linda frowned. Thomas wondered how old she was. It was hard to say—maybe forty, forty-five? She looked as if she'd had a hard life, or maybe her face was just weather-beaten. In which case she could well be younger.

"I'm sorry, I don't remember. You'd have to ask Carsten or Celia. The girl who was here was called Angelika, but I never knew her surname."

"And what are your duties now?"

"I do the laundry and the cleaning, make sure there are always fresh flowers around the house. The first thing I do when I arrive is to unload the dishwasher, then deal with the dishes from lunch."

"Do you do the shopping?"

"No, Maria does that—and I think Carsten likes to go to the deli."

"How did you get the job?" Thomas asked.

Linda seemed to consider each question before answering.

"I read an ad in the local paper. They wanted someone to work for them while they're on Sandhamn and keep an eye on the house when they're in England." She tugged at the sleeve of her blue top. "It's not always easy to make ends meet out here in the archipelago, so it sounded like a good deal. It's nice to know there's money coming in every month."

"What else do you do?" Aram asked.

"This and that. I work in assisted living sometimes; even those who live on the islands get old eventually. I do a few hours at the local nursery if they're short-staffed."

Thomas had noticed Linda's worn sneakers. "Is that enough?"

She shrugged. "I go fishing, and I pick berries and mushrooms. It's fine. I don't need much."

"Do you have a family? Children?" She wasn't wearing a wedding ring.

Linda looked away. "Unfortunately it never happened. We tried for a few years, but it didn't work out, and eventually we split up."

Thomas had the experience of trying to have a child without success and of the intrusive questions from other people. He decided to drop the subject.

"So where exactly do you live?"

"I rent a cottage on Runmarö, on the eastern side of the island. It only takes me twenty minutes to get here in my boat."

"What do you think of your employers?" Aram said, as if the question had only just occurred to him.

They'd asked Mats Eklund the same thing.

Linda's face closed down. Thomas guessed it wasn't a matter of loyalty, given the short time she'd been with the Jonssons. Presumably she was worried about her job, just like Eklund.

"They pay well," she said, confirming Thomas's suspicions.

"But what are they like as a family?" Aram persisted.

"Same as anyone else, I suppose."

As far as Thomas was concerned, that just didn't ring true. The money, the ostentation, the way they hired people—it all suggested a level of wealth that few could even dream of.

Before they'd ended their conversation yesterday, Nora had given him a quick summary of Carsten's career and what she'd found out about his parents. She had sounded a little embarrassed when she confessed to her online research.

"Doesn't it feel strange to be cleaning and doing the laundry for someone else?" Aram asked.

"No, why would it? What do you think an assisted living worker does?"

Thomas knew Aram well enough to understand what he was thinking. There was a significant difference between frail retirees and the Jonsson family.

"Do you get along well?" he asked.

"I guess so."

Maria hadn't seemed too keen on Linda, but Thomas had the impression she was a woman of great integrity.

"Has anything struck you since they moved in? Anything unusual, any strangers hanging around?"

"Not really."

"Can you think of any reason why someone would set fire to the guest lodge?"

"No. I don't understand any of it," she said with a deep sigh.

"You know about the dead bird on the steps?"

Linda seemed upset.

"I wasn't here at the time, but I'm sure it was horrible. I felt sorry for Maria—she was the one who found it, and she was terrified."

"Any information you can give us would be invaluable," Aram said. "Even if it's only a tiny detail."

"I don't know what to say. I haven't seen anything out of the ordinary. I really wish I could help you. The only . . ." She broke off.

"Go on," Thomas said encouragingly.

"It's nothing. Sorry, I don't want to badmouth foreigners." She glanced apologetically at Aram.

"It's fine," he said, holding up his hands. "I won't take offense. What did you want to say about foreigners?"

"It's those Poles."

"Yes?"

"One of them seems kind of . . . shifty. I don't trust him."

"Which one?"

"I don't know his name, but he's very tall—about the same height as Carsten. Eklund will be able to tell you who he is."

"And why don't you trust him?"

"Well . . . the other day I saw him talking to one of the neighbors. It seemed odd. I can't explain it any better than that."

At last, something concrete.

Thomas leaned forward. "When was this?"

"Last Thursday. It was late afternoon, and I was heading down to my boat to go home." She pointed. "They were over there, by the new fence."

"And something caught your attention?"

"Yes—the conversation seemed so . . . intense. They didn't even notice me, but I couldn't help wondering . . ."

"Could you describe the man who was talking to the Pole?"

"They were quite a distance away. I was on the jetty."

"Was he fat or thin, tall or short?" Thomas pushed her.

"I'd say he was well-built—fat, maybe."

"Any idea how old he was?"

Per-Anders Agaton came into his mind.

"Around sixty?"

"And have you seen him since? Would you recognize him?"

This time there was no hesitation.

"I saw him on Saturday night. He was at the party."

CHAPTER 56

Nora was heading for the gas station at the Royal Swedish Yacht Club marina. As usual there were plenty of boats all along the pontoon jetties; the station served both Sandhamn and the surrounding islands.

She'd just spoken to Simon, who didn't seem to be missing his mother in the slightest. She'd had to drag every word out of him during their short conversation. After only a couple of minutes he'd announced that he was going swimming, and that was the end of that. She'd try calling Adam later; maybe he might want to talk to his mom.

She needed a new bowline for the dinghy; she was hoping the gas-station store would have something suitable, because she'd forgotten to buy one in town. She crossed the narrow aluminum walkway and went inside. A motorboat owner was paying for his fuel: one hundred and thirty-two gallons of diesel. That wasn't going to be cheap.

Let's see, where are the ropes? Nora worked her way along the shelves: paperback books, candy, all kinds of chandlery. Fenders, shackles . . . ropes.

Over in the corner by the kerosene and lighter fluid, she noticed a man in shorts and a white polo shirt. She thought she recognized him, even though he had his back to her. The white-blond hair . . . It had to be Carsten. She hadn't seen him or Celia since the party, nor had she called them, in spite of the fact that she'd thought of doing so several times.

Now she felt guilty.

"Hi, Carsten."

He spun around. At first he didn't seem to know who she was, then he gave a brief nod.

"What do you want?"

Nora was completely taken aback.

"How are you?" she said. "I heard about the fire. Such a terrible thing after that lovely party."

"We're fine."

"Thank goodness no one in the family was hurt."

"Yes."

"If there's anything we can do, you only have to ask."

"We'd prefer to be left in peace."

"OK."

Nora didn't know what to say. She hadn't expected Carsten to be so brusque, but maybe that was his way of dealing with the shock. After all, the fire was very recent. At close quarters, she could see the dark shadows under his eyes, and the skin around his nostrils was red and flaking.

"How's Celia?" she asked, shifting her weight to the other foot. The silence was beginning to feel uncomfortable.

"Fine."

"And the children?"

"Fine."

"Things could have been much worse if the fire had spread," Nora plowed on. "We've thought about you so much over the past couple of days. Honestly, you only have to say if there's anything at all we can do."

"You can stop poking your nose in."

Nora felt her face turn bright red. Carsten glanced at his watch, a tiny muscle twitching at the corner of his mouth. Nora stared at the watch, not knowing what to say. *That must have cost a fortune,* she thought.

Behind them the motorboat owner had finished his transaction. The bell over the door pinged as he left the store, the assistant following him to fill up the tank.

Nora and Carsten were alone.

"I just came in to buy a new bowline," Nora said, wondering why the hell she felt obliged to explain herself. She focused on the shelf where a selection of ropes was laid out. This conversation was unbearable.

"Anyway, I hope things work out," she said. "Give Celia my best."

Almost before she'd finished speaking, Carsten had turned and walked out.

Nora stood there, staring after him.

CHAPTER 57

The front door of the Agatons' house lay in shade by the time Thomas and Aram returned.

"Back already?" Anna said, in spite of the fact that they'd agreed on the time. "I'm afraid my husband isn't here. He called and said he wouldn't be home until late this evening."

Thomas was more than a little annoyed. "Did you tell him we wanted to speak to him? It's urgent."

"I'm sorry, I didn't get around to it."

"May we come in?" Aram said politely. "As we said earlier, we have some questions for you as well."

Anna didn't seem too keen on the idea, but she stepped aside and held the door open.

"I really don't see how I can help you," she said, leading the way through the house and out onto a veranda facing the shore. "Take a seat."

The bright, airy space reminded Thomas of the Brand villa. Nora's house also had a glassed-in veranda overlooking the sea. He'd sat there countless times with a coffee or a beer, putting the world to rights.

But this was about Anna Agaton.

Aram was studying their hostess with those intense eyes. Thomas thought he knew what his colleague was pondering. Was it Anna's husband that Linda had seen with the Polish builder? According to Nora, the couple had quarreled openly at the party, but Thomas knew how difficult it could be for outsiders to understand what went on within a marriage.

Anna seemed younger than Per-Anders; they'd checked the records, and he was sixty-four. Thomas thought the age difference was probably around ten years. Anna was also much slimmer—almost petite, in fact.

She was drumming her fingers on the arm of her chair, making the skin on her forearms wobble with the movement. It was considerably looser than her face.

"Why did your husband report your new neighbor to the police?" Aram began in a tone as pleasant as if he'd offered Anna a cup of coffee.

"I'm sorry?"

"Is that how summer residents are usually welcomed to the island? Going to the police is pretty drastic—it's like something from a TV show."

"Building a jetty in someone else's waters is pretty drastic, too." Anna was clearly no stranger to the art of biting back.

"Couldn't you have come to some arrangement?"

"What do you mean?"

"Maybe you could have spoken to the Jonssons first, before contacting the police."

"I don't think you understand what kind of people we're dealing with here."

Anna didn't quite wrinkle her nose, but nearly.

"Perhaps you could tell us," Thomas said.

"Just because you've made a lot of money doesn't mean you can behave however you like when you move to a new place." Her nostrils flared in spite of her best efforts. "Here on Sandhamn there are certain rules that have to be respected, old customs and traditions. Anyone who isn't prepared to do so should consider buying elsewhere. There are twenty-four thousand other islands in the archipelago where you can do what you like."

She sounded like an echo of Nora. Thomas wondered if he had time to call in at the Brand villa. Maybe have a beer down by the jetty, clear his head for a while. It would be a perfect evening for sitting outside, and he would enjoy chatting with Nora and Jonas for a while.

"I realize that both you and your husband have been upset by your neighbors' behavior," Aram said, glancing at Thomas as if he knew that his colleague's thoughts were elsewhere. Thomas made an effort to pull himself together, concentrate.

"I've nothing against her—the wife," Anna said. "It's him I can't stand. He doesn't fit in here. He thinks money is the answer to everything."

"He sounds like a real cliché, but then that's sometimes the case." Aram's expression was sympathetic, suggesting that he knew exactly how difficult it could be to deal with new neighbors who hadn't a clue. His strategy seemed to work.

"I can guarantee that he comes from humbler beginnings," Anna said. "He wants revenge for something that happened when he was growing up. Believe me, I've seen this kind of thing before."

Her comment made Thomas think. She had a point; why had Carsten Jonsson chosen to build his house on Sandhamn rather than anywhere else? He must remember to follow up on that question.

"And yet you went to their party," Aram observed.

A faint flush appeared on Anna's cheeks, and she shifted uncomfortably.

"We didn't want to be standoffish."

"I'm sure they appreciated it," Thomas said, aware that his comment was on the verge of sarcasm. His job was to listen properly; she was keeping something back.

Get a grip.

He crossed his legs and gave Anna an encouraging smile. "How long did you stay at the party? What time did you leave?"

"Around eleven. We had a glass of wine and something to eat. The buffet was excellent, by the way. The Sailors Bar had done an excellent job. Then we had a coffee, said our good-byes, and left."

"What did you do when you got home?"

"Went to bed, of course. I made myself a cup of chamomile tea as I always do, and we turned off the light around midnight."

"I guess you sleep well out here?" Aram said with a nod toward the beautiful view. The surface of the water sparkled in the sunlight, and several swallows were swooping and darting around the house. A pleasant breeze drifted in through an open window. "The sound of the waves must be very soothing—very restful."

"Absolutely. And the air is good—clean and pure."

"And no traffic."

"No, it's lovely. There are no cars on Sandhamn, of course."

"Did your husband go to bed at the same time as you?" Aram asked, almost in passing.

"He was probably a little later. Per-Anders likes to stay up and read for a while. This is his favorite place; he enjoys looking out over the sea."

"So you don't actually know when he fell asleep."

Anna frowned. "If you've got something to say, then say it." She adjusted a cushion on the wicker sofa. The cushions were made of the same fabric as the seat pads—navy blue with diagonal pale-red stripes. The color was complemented by the flowering pelargoniums lined up along the windowsill.

"We're just trying to establish where you and your husband were during the evening and the night when the incident at the Jonssons' guest house took place." Aram stroked his chin with three fingers. "Arson is a serious matter."

"We were both at home," Anna insisted. "We had nothing to do with the fire." She raised her chin a fraction and stared at the two detectives. "I wouldn't be surprised if the Jonssons were trying to pin this on us; they wouldn't hesitate for a second. But they're wrong. We've done nothing."

"We have a witness who heard your husband threaten Carsten Jonsson on Saturday. I believe you were standing next to Per-Anders at the time."

"Nonsense." Anna shifted her position once more.

Thomas realized he'd hardly said a word for the last ten minutes. *Get a grip.*

"You think threatening someone in their own home is nonsense?"

"It wasn't a threat. You've been misinformed."

"So what was it? Please explain."

Anna swallowed so hard that the sinews in her neck stood out. The contrast between her smooth face and wrinkled neck made her look very odd.

"I think it's best you speak to my husband when he gets home," she said, straightening a cushion yet again.

"That's exactly what we're planning to do," Thomas said.

CHAPTER 58

Carsten was sitting at a table outside the Sandhamn Inn, in the far corner closest to the pilots' quay. He had chosen a slightly isolated spot with his back to the other customers; he didn't want to risk meeting anyone he knew. He'd had enough after bumping into Nosy Nora at the gas station. She'd looked like a frightened rabbit when he told her to get lost.

He'd tried to contact Anatoly several times during the course of the day, but his phone kept going straight to voice mail. He recognized the pattern, and it was far from reassuring. The last time they spoke, Anatoly had promised to get right back to him.

That was almost four days ago.

His phone rang, but it was only Celia. He rejected the call.

A waitress came over. "Can I get you another beer?"

Carsten looked at his glass. He must have emptied it without even noticing.

"Thanks. And bring me a whisky, too. Don't forget the ice."

She returned in a couple of minutes with his drinks and a bowl of nuts.

He shouldn't have hit Oliver; he'd never done anything like that before. It was as if someone else had raised his hand and delivered the blow. He took a swig of the cold beer. The boy had to learn not to touch other people's stuff. And it wasn't as if he'd hit him particularly hard.

He'd deal with it later.

The police had asked about Linda when he met them on the forest track. Maybe she'd seen Agaton hanging around, too. He called her.

"Hello?"

"It's Carsten Jonsson. Have you spoken to the police today?"

"I have," she replied, calm as ever.

"Did they mention Per-Anders Agaton?"

"In a way." There had been a slight hesitation before she spoke; was she trying to hide something from him, just like Eklund? He couldn't trust anyone anymore.

"What do you mean by that?" He took a slug of his whisky.

"We spoke briefly about your neighbor, because I happened to see him with one of the Poles the other day."

It was exactly as Carsten had thought. So far he'd been right on every single point.

"Tell me exactly what you said to the police."

Linda obliged. When the conversation was over, Carsten put down his phone and gazed out across the water. Linda had confirmed all his suspicions. She'd seen Agaton talking to Marek before the fire. Had Eklund known about the incident, too? Carsten wouldn't be surprised. He'd been so evasive. It had been like trying to get blood out of a stone.

All the pieces of the puzzle were falling into place. All he had to do now was decide on a course of action. He now knew significantly more about Per-Anders Agaton and how far he was prepared to go.

Not only had his neighbor reported him to the police back in the spring, he'd been responsible for a series of other complaints as well. The guy at the council had insisted that the complaints were made anonymously, but Carsten knew exactly who was behind them.

Make up your mind, he thought, sipping his whisky. The peaty flavor calmed him. It was exactly what he needed; he had way too much to take care of. His head was buzzing; every time he embarked on a thought, another came along and distracted him.

His phone rang: Celia again, for fuck's sake. He rejected the call. After a few seconds the display lit up again, but this time it was Anatoly's number, at long last. Carsten didn't bother with small talk.

"Why haven't you been in touch?"

"There was no point in calling until I had something to tell you."

"How did it go with the bank? Have they changed their minds?"

The reluctant pause told him the answer.

"I'm sorry. I did my best to persuade them to stick with the original plan, but to no avail. They refuse to budge. Everything's going to have to be postponed for at least six months, maybe more."

"What the hell does that mean?"

"There will be no stock market flotation for some considerable time. I'm afraid that's just the way it is."

"You're going to have to explain yourself better than that." Carsten knocked back the rest of the whisky.

"Believe me, I've spent days in meetings with the board, going over all the figures. Sergei's right, the concept still needs fine-tuning. There's no quick fix."

"This can't happen." Carsten made an angry gesture and knocked over the glass of beer. A waitress hurried over to clear up the mess, but he waved her away.

"I have no intention of accepting this! We go ahead with the flotation exactly as planned. It's too late to back out. I've seen the accounts, the customer base. I've gone over everything again and again. The company's ready."

"Carsten, we can't rush this. I really have tried, but there's something in what they're saying. The market's unstable, investors are wary. Everything has to be perfect before we press the button."

"No."

There was a humming noise in the background, but he could still hear Anatoly's deep sigh.

"You can't force the company onto the stock market on your own. You have to face facts, Carsten. Right now you're the only one who wants to go ahead."

Carsten tightened his grip on the phone. He was finding it difficult to breathe. He undid one button on his polo shirt, then another. He really wanted to swear at Anatoly, but knew he couldn't afford to lose control. He needed the Russian on his side. Sweat broke out on his forehead as he tried to analyze the situation.

"Hello? Carsten? Are you still there?"

"I'm thinking!"

"There is another possibility," Anatoly said hesitantly. "If you need money . . ."

He should never have mentioned the loan to Anatoly, never said a word about the burden of his debt.

"That legal practice has been in touch—Beketov & Partners. I don't know if this is the right moment to bring it up, but they wanted me to sound you out as soon as possible."

"Go on."

"Their client is still interested in taking over your share of KiberPay. Because of the delay, the bank will have no objections if you decide to sell."

"Why would I agree now when I refused before?" Carsten spat out the words in spite of his best efforts to sound cool and calm, not show any sign of weakness.

"They're prepared to pay the full amount in cash."

"How do you know?"

"That's the offer they've put forward to me. If you agree to a quick sale, they'll deposit the agreed sum in any bank of your choice outside Russia."

Carsten stared out over the harbor. He had to find enough money to repay the loan in October; otherwise he was fucked.

He could almost hear his father laughing. His father, who'd always thought he was good for nothing, always regarded him as a disappointment. He remembered the humiliation he'd felt, the determination to show them all one day.

No other options came to mind, however hard he tried to make his brain work.

"Think it over for a few days," Anatoly said. "The offer they've made is very generous, given how things have turned out."

"How generous?"

"They're willing to pay exactly the same amount as you put in, minus a premium of forty percent."

Forty percent.

The offer was nothing compared with the profit he stood to make when the company was floated. It didn't even cover his capital outlay, let alone the interest and fees on his loan.

He would have to sell the apartment in order to pay it off. He would lose Fyrudden. Above all, everything would come out. Celia's father would find out exactly what the situation was, together with the other investors.

He knew exactly how the UK Financial Conduct Authority regarded infringements of this kind.

There was a metallic taste in his mouth.

A Vaxholm ferry had just berthed at the steamboat jetty. The tourists who'd been waiting on the quayside poured over the gangplank like cattle rushing into a meadow full of clover on an early spring day. They had no idea that his world was about to collapse.

His polo shirt still felt tight around his neck. He ran a finger around inside the collar in an attempt to get some air.

He was being destroyed, but there was nothing he could do about it. Not from here, not even if he went to Moscow. It was too late.

"Of course you could always hold on to your investment," Anatoly said. "It's your decision. Just let me know what you want to do."

The Russian's voice brought Carsten back to the moment.

"I can sell the shares to someone else at a better price," he said, even though he knew it wasn't true.

A clause in the shareholders' contract meant that he needed permission from the other major investors once a certain date had passed. He hadn't taken much notice of that particular clause, because it had only applied to a brief period leading up to the flotation, after which he would be bound by stock market regulations anyway.

And now the trap had slammed shut. He was in the hands of the Russian bank.

He knew it, Anatoly knew it, and presumably the anonymous buyer knew it, too.

"It's your decision," Anatoly said again. "But if you can't afford to wait, then I'd advise you to take this chance before they change their minds."

"And if I don't?" He already knew the answer.

"Then you risk being stuck with the shares for some considerable time, maybe for the whole of next year or even longer. There are no guarantees."

With sudden clarity, Carsten realized who was his friend and who was his enemy.

"I'm prepared to sell, but on one condition. You bring all the necessary documentation over here right away."

CHAPTER 59

Thomas waved good-bye as Aram boarded the last ferry to Stavsnäs.

"See you tomorrow," he called out.

His plan was to drop by Nora's house and ask her to run him over to Harö so that he could spend a few hours with Pernilla and Elin. He would travel over to Stockholm on the first morning boat in time for the briefing at eight.

After that they would have to come back to Sandhamn. Per-Anders Agaton had neither showed up nor contacted them, in spite of the fact that Thomas had asked Anna to pass on the message. They had spent the past few hours interviewing some of the Jonssons' other neighbors, but were none the wiser.

Thomas passed the grocery store and turned off by the Sandhamn Inn. He continued past Barnberget, or the Children's Hill, where a four-year-old was sledding down the grass under the supervision of a woman who was presumably his grandmother. As he reached the old small-boat marina, he noticed that the land still continued to rise, recovering inch-meal from the crushing glaciers of the last ice age thousands of years ago; it was only just possible to moor at the inner jetties now.

The gate of the Brand villa was open. He knocked on the door several times, but there was no response.

"Hello? Anyone home?"

He went inside, through the hallway, and out onto the glassed-in veranda. Nora was down by the jetty with her back to him. He opened the door as quietly as he could and tiptoed up behind her.

"How loud do I have to shout for you to hear me?"

Nora shot to her feet.

"You scared me!"

She gave him a hug, then took a step back and gazed at him.

"You look tired. Is it the fire at the Jonssons' place?"

Thomas sank down on a chair.

"Maybe. It's all been a bit much. Pernilla and Elin are on Harö, and I wondered if you could take me over there. The last boat's already gone."

"No problem—as soon as Jonas gets back. He's out in the dinghy with Julia, laying nets. Would you like a drink while you're waiting?"

"A beer would be good—medium rather than strong, though."

Nora disappeared indoors and returned with a Carlsberg.

"There you go."

"So Jonas and Julia are out on their own?"

"Yes, he takes her out to sea whether she wants to go or not. He'd have been a fantastic dad to a little boy."

Was it Thomas's imagination, or could he hear a hint of wistfulness?

"Do you want more children?" he asked, knowing that he could easily put the same question to himself.

He was eternally grateful for Elin, but sometimes he couldn't help thinking of a son. A son who could play with the old toy cars that were still in a box in his parents' attic. Then again, maybe he should see if Elin would like to play with them.

"It's too late for that. At least as far as I'm concerned. Not for Jonas, of course."

Thomas knew that Nora sometimes worried about the age differ-ence, but if Jonas had been older than her, she wouldn't have given it a thought.

"I think Jonas is very happy to have you and Julia in his life."

Nora waved a hand dismissively.

"It's all good, I just get a little sentimental when I'm sitting here by myself. It's because I'm missing the boys so much. I just spoke to Adam, and they're having a great time in Greece with Henrik and his parents."

Nora couldn't help making a face; she didn't need to explain herself to Thomas. He'd met her ex-mother-in-law, Monica, often enough to understand.

"How's the investigation going?"

Thomas clasped his hands behind his head.

"He's quite a guy, Carsten Jonsson," he said.

"I bumped into him in the store at the gas station at about four o'clock. He wasn't in a very good mood—in fact he was very rude to me."

"What did he say?"

Nora shrugged. "It doesn't matter. They've had a rough few days, so I guess it's hardly surprising if he's not too cheerful."

"We spoke to their housekeeper today. Her name is Linda Öberg, and she lives on Runmarö. Do you know anything about her?"

"Öberg . . . That sounds like an old archipelago name, but it doesn't ring any bells."

"Early forties, tall and skinny, brown hair. Not exactly a bundle of laughs."

"Just like the nanny."

"Sorry?"

"Forget it. I shouldn't have said anything."

"So you've met Maria?"

"A few times. At the pool when I've taken Julia to her swimming lessons."

Thomas was still thinking about Anna Agaton and her opinion about Carsten: *He wants revenge for something that happened when he was growing up.* Revenge for what?

"Do you know if Carsten has any link to Sandhamn?" he asked, picking up a handful of gravel and letting it trickle through his fingers. "I'm trying to get a handle on the guy. Has he told you why he wanted to build his house here rather than anywhere else? It's not the cheapest place in the archipelago, after all."

"I guess that's exactly what he was looking for," Nora replied with an ironic smile. "A beautiful spot where he could build an even more beautiful house. That's why Sandhamn is so popular with those who have fat wallets."

Thomas knew that the transformation of the island worried Nora. The rising price of property meant that more and more houses were coming on the market, because siblings could no longer afford to buy one another out. But that was how things were these days. It was the same on the west coast and in southern Sweden. On Harö, too; there was nothing to be done about it. There were far too many picturesque communities that only came to life for a few weeks in the summer.

"If you could find out whether there is a link, I'd be very grateful. I can ask someone back at HQ to do it, but I'm sure you'll be much quicker."

Nora tilted her head to one side, and Thomas suddenly remembered fifteen-year-old Nora with long fair hair, sitting beside him in church before they went up to be confirmed.

"No problem. But as far as I'm aware, Carsten grew up north of Stockholm; he went to school in Vallentuna. I'll ask around, though. Eva might be able to help—she always knows what's going on."

She took out her phone and made a note.

"How's work?" Thomas asked.

Nora's face lit up. "It's great—in fact I've just been promoted to district prosecutor."

"Congratulations—well done!"

Thomas was impressed and genuinely pleased for his friend. However, he couldn't help feeling conflicted, as he had when Pernilla told him about her new job. Everyone seemed to be moving forward, while he was stuck.

"It's so exciting," Nora said. "I'm really happy with the Economic Crimes Authority. I can't believe it's been three years already."

Thomas recalled how upset Nora had been over the way she'd been treated by the bank. Personally he thought she should have reported her former boss for sexual harassment, but Nora had refused to go forward with any formal complaints. He ran a finger up and down the bottle of beer.

"Was it a big change, leaving banking?" he asked.

"You mean the transition from the private to the public sector?"

"Yes."

Nora leaned back and gazed up at the sky. A gull swooped down toward the water, grabbed a fish, and soared away.

"It was much easier than I'd expected," she said slowly. "And more difficult at the same time. But it was such a relief to get away from the bank by that stage that I didn't really think about it. Some things took a while to get used to—the principle of public access, for example, the fact that journalists can request emails and documents under certain circumstances, but I guess the same applies to most of those who work in the public domain."

She fiddled with a colorful bracelet made from beads; it looked like something Julia might have made at day care. Elin had presented Thomas with a similar one.

"I was thinking more about the sense of doing something useful," Thomas said.

The words came out of nowhere; he hadn't intended to ask the question or express himself that way. He continued anyway.

"Don't you ever feel that it doesn't matter what you do? That we can't change things, so it's pointless to try?"

Nora gave him a searching look. "Try . . . to do what?"

Thomas shrugged. "To do your best, make a difference."

Nora reached out and placed her hand on his. "Why don't you tell me what's actually on your mind instead of talking in riddles? Are you thinking about changing your job?"

Should he tell her about Erik's offer? He still hadn't mentioned it to Pernilla, hadn't wanted to burden her with his worries when she was so pleased about her new role. He would have to make a decision soon; he'd promised to get back to Erik later in the week. Time to bite the bullet.

However, just like the other day when Aram had asked him if there was anything on his mind, he couldn't get the words out.

"Thomas? I'm happy to listen if you want to talk."

No one knew him as well as Nora did; they'd been friends for more than half their lives. She'd always been there—when Emily died, when the divorce from Pernilla went through. She'd been so pleased when he and Pernilla got back together. He'd seen her tears when her marriage to Henrik collapsed and life was very dark.

An old gig puttered by; the two-stroke engine coughed, then recovered. Thomas's father had once had a boat just like that, but it was long gone, together with so many other things.

Everything changed, whether he wanted it to or not.

He was so close to confiding in Nora about his growing doubts, the thoughts Erik's offer had evoked. They were impossible to ignore.

But if he spoke to Nora, that would make it all real.

At that moment the dinghy rounded the jetty. Jonas waved when he saw Thomas and Nora.

"It's nothing," Thomas said, dismissing the matter. "It's been a long day, that's all. I'm looking forward to getting home."

CHAPTER 60

Carsten fiddled with his wallet, trying to extract a credit card. Several receipts fluttered to the floor, but he didn't bother picking them up.

"There you go," he said, handing the card to the waitress. It was a huge effort not to slur his words.

"Are you OK?" she said, glancing at the array of empty glasses on the table.

"I'm fine."

She took the card and inserted it into the machine. "Would you like me to enter the amount for you?"

The patronizing tone irritated Carsten, but he was too far gone to argue with her. When he stood up, he almost lost his balance and had to hold on to the edge of the table as he pushed his wallet into his pocket.

"Can you find your way home?" the girl asked behind his back.

He realized she was trying to provoke him and refrained from making a comment. He put on his sunglasses and left, keeping his head down and concentrating on not careening into any tourists as he made his way through the harbor area.

A red forklift came zooming along; the driver tooted angrily when Carsten didn't bother to step aside. Carsten gave him the finger.

When he reached the top of the steep hill behind the Sailors Hotel, the pressure on his chest was so intense that he had to stop. He bent forward, hands resting on his knees, struggling to catch his breath.

After a while he felt better. He wiped his forehead and set off again. By Dansberget he met a family heading down to the harbor; he staggered to the side and almost collided with the stroller.

"Watch out!" said the man, who was holding a little boy's hand. The child was about the same age as Oliver; he, too, was wearing a blue baseball cap. But he didn't look guilty the way Oliver had done out on the jetty, when he refused to give back Carsten's phone.

It was Celia's fault that he'd had to discipline the kid. She spoiled Oliver instead of teaching him the importance of obedience.

At the tennis courts he turned off onto the path through the forest. It was good to get away from the road, stop worrying about meeting anyone he knew.

But then he remembered Anatoly's call, and he suddenly couldn't take another step. He sank down on the ground with his back resting against a rough tree trunk. The sky above his head was clear blue, even though he was surrounded by darkness.

His phone rang; Celia again. The last thing he needed right now was her giving him a hard time.

He closed his eyes, and everything began to spin around. Once more he heard the echo of his father's voice.

He let out a sob and buried his face in his hands.

CHAPTER 61

An eerie silence fell when Carsten walked into the house, as if someone had unplugged a speaker.

The children were sitting on the sofa with Celia and Maria on either side of them. The aroma of hot chocolate rose from the mugs on the table.

"Hi, Oliver," Carsten said in an excessively loud voice, giving his son a big smile.

Oliver hid behind his mother and refused to meet his gaze.

"Come and give Daddy a hug."

His tongue felt thick and unmanageable in his mouth as he tried to form the words.

Oliver didn't move.

"Leave him alone." Celia put her arm around her son. Sarah looked at her parents in confusion. She was clutching her blond-haired doll. Celia stroked Oliver's cheek, then got to her feet. "Maria, could you please take the children outside for a while? I need to have a word with my husband."

Maria glanced in Carsten's direction, but didn't look him in the eye.

"It won't take long," Celia added. "Maybe you could build a sand-castle? I'll let you know when we're done."

"OK, let's go out and play," Maria said, taking Sarah and Oliver by the hand. They headed down toward the shore; Celia waited until they'd disappeared from view, then turned to Carsten.

"Maria told me you hit Oliver. Is that true?"

Carsten stared at his wife, trying not to sway. All he wanted was to lie down in his own bed, crash out.

"Where have you been all day?" Celia continued. "I've lost count of how many times I've called you. Why didn't you answer your phone?"

She'd gotten everything she wanted, he thought wearily. He knew there was no point in telling her what was really going on.

That everything was about to collapse.

A wife is meant to support her husband.

Celia came closer.

"Did you hit Oliver? Did you?"

"It's no big deal." Carsten had to lean on the dining table to stop himself from falling over.

"So you admit that you hit your own child. Are you out of your mind?"

"Oh come on, it was only a little slap. He took my cell phone."

Celia's voice went up to a falsetto. Her cheeks were bright red.

"Don't you ever touch him again, you hear me?"

"Just drop it," Carsten muttered, attempting to push past her. He had to get away from that shrill voice. Celia recoiled.

"You're drunk! What the hell is wrong with you?"

She grabbed him by the shoulder.

"Leave me alone!" He tried to shake her off. "Let go!"

Celia blocked his path.

I've had enough today.

"This can't go on, Carsten. Tomorrow I'm taking the children back to London."

You're not taking the children.

In a lightning movement, he gripped Celia's wrist so tightly that the skin whitened beneath his fingers.

"You're not going anywhere with Sarah and Oliver. You're all staying here until I say otherwise."

Celia's eyes widened.

"You're hurting me!"

She twisted and turned, but he refused to let go. Why couldn't she understand? He squeezed harder. "And don't ring your fucking father, whining and complaining. This stays within the family. Our family—is that clear?"

Celia whimpered.

One last squeeze, then he pushed her away. Maybe a little too hard. Celia fell, and the crack as the side of her head hit the wall echoed around the room. She landed with her cheek against the cold stone floor. It took a few seconds before she managed to drag herself to her knees.

"What have you done," she whispered, reaching up to touch her split eyebrow. Her fingertips came away red. Blood trickled down her cheek.

It was her own fault. She'd asked for it when she wouldn't stop nagging him.

Carsten turned away; he needed to lie down.

Just leave me in peace.

"You're sick in the head," Celia said.

Carsten stopped.

Turned back.

Raised his hand once more.

CHAPTER 62

Tuesday, July 16

Aram walked into the meeting room and nodded to Kalle, who'd already taken a seat.

"Welcome back from the west coast."

Kalle didn't respond to the comment about his interrupted vacation and merely grunted a greeting instead. Karin Ek arrived, together with Staffan Nilsson and Adrian Karlsson. Aram had heard a rumor that Adrian had applied for a transfer to the Investigations Unit, which seemed like a good idea. He was an extremely competent officer, and it was time for him to make a move, get out of uniform for a while.

Margit was over by the notice board studying photographs of Per-Anders Agaton and his wife. The couple certainly hadn't grown to look like each other during the course of their marriage.

"I've spoken to Thomas and told him not to bother coming over this morning, since we need to interview Agaton today anyway. There's no point in him traveling back and forth for a one-hour meeting. Aram, can you run us through what happened yesterday?"

Aram slipped the rubber band off his black notebook. It was an old habit, totally unnecessary, but for as long as he could remember, his father had carried an almost identical black notebook secured with a thick rubber band. He quickly summarized Monday's activities on Sandhamn.

"Mats Eklund confirmed that there's been a lot of trouble with the neighbors," he concluded.

Margit pointed to the photograph. "Per-Anders Agaton. Do you think he's deliberately trying to avoid you? He's a lawyer—he ought to know better."

"Even lawyers are human."

Aram checked the time. There was a boat to Sandhamn at nine forty-five; if the meeting was over within an hour, he should be able to make it.

He didn't like the fact that Agaton had stayed out of the way but didn't want to draw too many conclusions from that. They definitely needed to speak to Carsten Jonsson again; he seemed to have fallen out with half the island within a very short time. If that was his normal pattern of behavior, then there must be other enemies in his life. He also wanted to look into Carsten's connection with Sandhamn, try to understand more about his past. He'd expected Thomas to take on that aspect of the investigation, given his familiarity with the place, but Thomas hadn't mentioned it before they took their leave of each other last night. In fact his colleague had seemed pretty low recently, much less talkative than usual.

Sometimes Aram thought Thomas had a tendency to brood too much. There was no point in making life more complicated than necessary. *Chaton ela,* as his father used to say. Life was hard. It was just a matter of appreciating what you had and bearing difficulties with patience. Or at least enduring them.

The image of his little sister flashed through his mind. He would never forget the morning when she lay there dead in the Turkish container in which they'd hidden during their flight to Sweden.

He fingered the rubber band from his notebook.

Chaton ela.

"Any news on the autopsy?" he asked Margit, interrupting Kalle, who had just started talking about the guest list.

Margit checked her phone.

"Nothing yet. We might have to wait until tomorrow or even Thursday."

She turned to Kalle, who didn't appear to be in the least offended.

"OK, so where are we with the party?"

Kalle stood up and went over to the whiteboard. He picked up a pen and began to write.

"One hundred and forty-three people attended the party, most of them from the island. Twenty are permanent residents, the rest are summer visitors. Eighteen were staying at the Sailors Hotel, and four came from neighboring islands. Eight members of staff from the Divers Bar were also there, plus a DJ."

Kalle wrote the number twenty-five on the board and circled it.

"We're currently working on a plan to contact everyone, and we've identified twenty-five individuals that we'd like to start with."

"On what basis?" Karin asked, fiddling with the necklace she always wore. It was a gold chain with three initials, one for each of her sons.

"They all stand out in some way. For example, there are several who have a criminal record. We've also included those with a profession in which they come into contact with flammable materials—the chemical industry and so on."

Kalle put down the pen and returned to his seat. "Adrian's helping me, and we've asked for extra resources."

Margit nodded. "Karin, yesterday you said there were a couple of missing-persons reports that might fit the victim. Did you get any further with those?"

Karin leafed through her notes.

"I looked into two reports. One person's been found; he'd stayed over with his girlfriend without telling his parents. The other is still missing. His name is Svante Algren, but he's not on the guest list. We have no reason to believe he was on Sandhamn, so he's probably not our guy."

"So who's on the table at the forensics lab in Solna?" Kalle wondered.

"Good question," Margit said. "Aram, any ideas?"

Aram shook his head. Who was the man who'd been caught unawares by the fire? He could be a guest who hadn't yet been reported missing. Only three days had passed since the fire; people went away without letting anyone know, singletons lived their own lives without keeping in daily contact with relatives. It could be weeks before someone sounded the alarm. He focused on Fyrudden.

"The family and their staff are all accounted for. There's a team of builders, but we spoke to the project manager yesterday, and he didn't mention anyone being missing."

"If it was one of his guys, surely he'd have said something?" Kalle said.

The answer ought to be yes, and yet Aram wasn't sure. Mats Eklund had been less than forthcoming; Aram had gotten the impression that Eklund was worried about Jonsson's reaction if he said too much. He'd referred to his contract—was there a clause that was making him hold back? A nondisclosure agreement? Surely that wouldn't stop him in a situation like this?

Margit's phone rang.

"I have to take this," she said, getting to her feet. "Keep me informed."

Aram looked at his watch again; he had plenty of time to catch the boat. There were many reasons to return to Sandhamn.

CHAPTER 63

Carsten was lying on the bed with his iPad, reading through the email that had just come through from Anatoly. The Russian had forwarded the written offer from the legal practice and had also confirmed that he would be flying to Stockholm today. His flight left after lunch and was due to land at Arlanda at 4:25.

The documentation wasn't quite ready yet, but Anatoly would be bringing it with him. Soon Carsten would sign a bundle of papers that would destroy his life.

He put down the tablet and rested his head on the pillow. Stared at the ceiling, his eyes burning from a lack of sleep.

He'd lain awake all night. Every time he'd closed his eyes, Anatoly's words had come back to him.

Of course you could always hold on to your investment.

Anatoly knew perfectly well that Carsten had no choice. He had been openly sneering at him, just like Celia.

Carsten sat up and grabbed the iPad again. He looked at the email from Beketov & Partners, the offer with its derisory purchase price.

Then he googled the name of the company.

An elegant home page in blue and white appeared on the screen. He started randomly surfing the various pages in Cyrillic script, not understanding a single word until he realized there was an English version.

After a while he found the list of partners: names, photographs, academic qualifications, areas of expertise. He scrolled down the page, looking at the pictures of the men and women who worked for Beketov & Partners in Moscow.

Suddenly he stopped and stared at a beautiful dark-haired woman in a stylish jacket smiling into the camera. The same smile as earlier in the year.

And the final piece of the puzzle fell into place.

CHAPTER 64

The swimming lesson had already started when Nora arrived at the pool. She picked up Julia and hurried in through the gate.

"We're late, honey!"

"I want to go home!"

"No, you don't. You'll have fun."

Nora quickly put on Julia's armbands, and when the little girl saw the other children in the water, she happily jumped in, too.

Nora breathed a sigh of relief and looked around. Most of the parents were standing in a group over by the café, but the Jonssons' nanny was sitting in a corner by herself. There was something defeated about Maria's posture on the sun lounger. She was facing the sea and wearing sunglasses even though it was a cloudy day. Nora went to join her. She wanted to ask how Celia was; Carsten's behavior the previous day had made her reluctant to pick up the phone.

"Hi, how are you?"

Maria gave such a start that her sunglasses fell off and landed in her lap. It was obvious she'd been crying.

"Goodness, whatever's wrong?"

"I'm . . . I'm fine," Maria stammered. Then came the tears. Nora sat down beside her and put an arm around the girl's shoulders.

"It'll be all right," she murmured soothingly, as if she were consoling one of her own children. "Talk to me."

But Maria hid her face in her hands and kept on crying. Nora glanced in the direction of the pool, hoping the children wouldn't notice anything. Both Julia and Sarah were completely absorbed in learning how to dip their heads under the water.

"Tell me what's wrong," Nora said after a moment, when the sobs began to subside.

Maria shook her head. "Sorry," she mumbled.

Nora got up and fetched some paper napkins from the café. She handed them to Maria so that she could dry her eyes and blow her nose.

"Why are you so upset?" Nora said gently. "Has someone done something to you?"

Maria shook her head again. "No. Yes. I want to go home."

"Well, nobody's forcing you to stay, are they?"

"You don't understand," Maria whispered.

"I don't think you ought to cycle home in this state. Shall I call Celia, ask someone to come and pick you and Sarah up?"

"No, no!" The panic in Maria's eyes was unmistakable. Nora stroked her hair.

"Maria, can't you tell me what the problem is? I want to help you if I can. I'm happy to talk to Celia if you think that would do any good."

The swimming teacher clapped her hands; the lesson was over.

Nora made one last attempt. "Maria?"

"Sorry, I have to go." She stood up, wiped away the fresh tears, and put on her sunglasses. Then she stopped and turned to face Nora.

"Promise you won't mention this to Celia or Carsten. You mustn't tell them!"

CHAPTER 65

Celia pressed her knuckles against her eyes to stop the tears, but they just kept on flowing, exactly as they'd done all night.

What was she going to do? How was she going to get out of this mess?

She didn't even know how to leave the island; she had hardly any Swedish currency. Carsten had taken care of the passports when they landed at Arlanda.

Tentatively she touched the side of her head. She winced with pain; a scab had formed where she'd hit the wall, splitting the skin open. At least it had stopped bleeding, but the pillow was stained with dried blood, and the hip she'd landed on was still aching.

She'd never imagined that Carsten would hit her. She wasn't the kind of woman who let herself be abused. A wife who was afraid of her husband.

It was hard to admit that she was so scared now, but the fear when Carsten raised his hand had upended everything she'd believed up to that point.

Whenever she thought of him, her heart began to race. All those horrible names he'd called her last night. The tiles had been cold, but she'd lain on the floor for a long time after he'd slammed the bedroom door behind him. Eventually she'd managed to drag herself to the guest room and collapsed on the bed.

She'd spent the whole night listening for his footsteps, unable to sleep. Was he going to hurt her again? Was it her own fault? Maybe she shouldn't have provoked him like that, but when she found out he'd hit Oliver, she hadn't been able to stop herself.

Pain sliced through her hip, and she tried to shift her position. Her cheek was burning; it must be swollen. Her ear was throbbing, too, and there was a constant ringing noise filling her head. She buried her face in the pillow, wondering if she dared emerge from the bedroom.

Maria had had to take care of the children the previous day; Celia hadn't wanted them to see her, hadn't wanted to frighten them. When Maria had brought her a glass of water late in the evening, the expression on her face had told Celia how bad she must have looked.

The thought of the children brought on a fresh burst of sobbing. She had to be strong, for their sake. Nothing was more important than Oliver and Sarah. She was the only one who could protect them from Carsten.

She realized that now and wondered why she'd been blind for so long.

She would never let anyone else be responsible for her children again.

But Carsten wasn't going to let her go back to London with Oliver and Sarah.

Dad? He'd been against her marriage from the start, but he'd still put money into Carsten's business. For her sake. How could she tell her parents what had happened?

There was no one who could help her now.

Suddenly she heard something. It sounded like Carsten's cell phone. Fear sank its claws into her with renewed vigor.

Please don't let him be standing outside the door. Please don't let him come in. She could hardly breathe.

The phone rang again, and she realized it was coming from outside. Slowly she got out of bed and stumbled over to the window. The blind was closed, but she pulled it back a fraction with trembling fingers and peered out through the narrow gap.

Carsten was standing a few yards away with his back to her, talking on the phone and gesticulating with his free hand. She couldn't hear exactly what he was saying, but she thought he was speaking to Mats Eklund. Was he swearing? She made out the words "go away." She didn't dare open the window in case he saw her; he appeared to be even angrier than he'd been yesterday. His white polo shirt was crumpled; he hadn't changed his clothes, and he hadn't shaved.

The conversation ended, and he put the phone in his pocket. Celia quickly stepped back, but he didn't turn around. Instead he bent down and picked up something heavy. It was some kind of container—a gas can?

He walked away and disappeared from view.

CHAPTER 66

Thomas was waiting for Aram on the steamboat jetty when his phone buzzed: a text message from Erik.

Have you had time to think over my proposal?

Thomas ran a hand through his hair. That was the problem. He'd woken at five and been unable to get back to sleep. Everything was going around and around in his head. He had to make a decision.

There was no point in talking it over with Pernilla or Nora. He was the only one who could determine what he wanted to do in the future.

When Margit suggested he miss morning briefing, he'd raised no objections for once. Maybe she'd sensed that he was pretty low at the moment.

Or maybe she was just being practical.

Tärnan, the taxi boat from Stavsnäs, stopped a few yards along the jetty, and Aram appeared in the doorway. The sight of his colleague's familiar face made Thomas feel better.

A new day, a fresh start. He would approach the investigation with all his energy and concentration today. His private concerns would have to wait until this evening.

Aram leaped ashore.

"How did it go this morning?" Thomas asked. "Did I miss anything important?"

Aram shook his head.

"We kept it short. Margit says hi, by the way. Kalle and his team are working on the guest list, but it's going to take a while. Karin's checked the missing-persons reports, and none of them appear to match our victim."

They set off for Trouvillevägen, zigzagging between strollers and tourists. They were going to see Per-Anders Agaton first, then head over to Fyrudden. Two guys came toward them with plastic bags full of empty bottles, which they emptied into the recycling container. The sound of breaking glass as the bottles landed was deafening.

"How did it go with the neighbors?" Aram asked.

Thomas had spent the morning visiting the people who lived on the other side of the Jonsson property. In many ways the elderly couple was the polar opposite of the Agatons. And of Carsten Jonsson, to be fair. Bertil and Anna-Lena Lindberg enjoyed a beautiful sea view, but their house was much smaller—more like a little cabin than a fancy summer residence. The décor was tired, and the pine floors and ceilings had yellowed with age. The kitchen hadn't been updated in decades.

"They weren't at the party."

"Didn't they get an invite?"

"Yes, but they turned it down. He's eighty-one and she's seventy-nine. They're also quite frail. She uses a wheeled walker."

The faint smell often associated with the elderly had reached Thomas's nostrils when Bertil opened the door, the smell that seems to pervade the walls.

"What was your impression?" Aram took out a packet of gum and offered it to Thomas before taking a stick himself.

"That they're a sweet couple who don't get involved in other people's business. For example, they think it's a shame that Carsten wants to put up an ugly fence all around his land, but they said it's up to him. He's the owner."

"Not your typical arsonists, in other words."

They passed the back of the Sailors Hotel and continued up the steep hill toward Dansberget. There was a weary cyclist in front of them, pushing his bike instead of riding it.

"What did they say about Per-Anders?"

Agaton's failure to show up had annoyed Aram yesterday, but this morning he sounded more amenable.

"They try to avoid him whenever possible."

It had been difficult to get the Lindbergs to express an opinion, but it had gradually emerged that Agaton had challenged them on more than one occasion.

One incident had involved a shared water pipe, another a difference of opinion at a residents' association meeting.

"Carsten Jonsson and Per-Anders Agaton ought to get along," Thomas remarked. "They seem to be the same type."

"Yes, but you know how magnets work—negative poles repel each other!"

They reached the tennis courts, where a dozen or so children were being given a lesson by a fair-haired man in his midforties; Thomas had seen him around the village and thought Simon had had lessons with him for a while.

"By the way, I called on Nora yesterday. She promised to check out Carsten Jonsson on our behalf—see if she can find out why he chose to build his house here. We need to know if there's anything in his background that could be relevant for our investigation."

Aram gave him a quizzical look. "I wondered when you'd get around to that angle."

Was it so obvious that he was losing focus?

Thomas renewed his promise to himself; he wasn't going to let his mind wander today.

"I hope Agaton's home," Aram continued. "I've no desire to spend another day going back and forth between his place and Fyrudden."

Agaton had some explaining to do.

Linda Öberg had seen him arguing with the builders, Karin had found the complaints he'd made to the police. And the Lindbergs' experiences confirmed that he was the argumentative type.

He'd had both motive and opportunity. The question was whether he'd actually committed the crime.

CHAPTER 67

Nora couldn't stop thinking about Maria and how upset she'd been. What was going on in the house at Fyrudden? First Carsten's weird behavior in the store, and now the nanny.

If she hadn't promised Maria that she wouldn't say anything to Celia, she would have called her right away. After the swimming lesson, the girl had cycled off with Sarah in the child seat, leaving Nora standing there with a strong sense of inadequacy. If only she could help; but she didn't even know Maria's surname, let alone where her family lived.

She went upstairs to make the bed, only to discover that Jonas was fast asleep. He must have gone back to bed when he returned from his fishing trip. He'd set the alarm for six thirty so that he could head out and bring in the nets.

"Aren't you up yet?" she teased, tugging at the covers before sitting down beside him instead. "You're as bad as my boys," she said, stroking his hair.

"Why don't you join me?" Jonas reached out and drew her close. He yawned and settled down. "Perfect."

Nora rested her head on his warm, bare shoulder and sighed contentedly. Jonas smelled of morning—a mixture of sleepy warm body and clean sheets. With a hint of fish guts.

As so often before, there was a moment of surprise that they were so happy. When she was with Henrik, she'd often woken with the weight of the world on her shoulders; now she smiled every day.

"Any luck with the fish?" she asked after a while, running her index finger down his spine.

"Not bad—four perch and three whitefish, but I threw the smallest perch back."

"Fantastic. That's dinner taken care of for the next few days."

Nora turned and kissed his forehead. Julia was playing in the room next door, so there was no point in contemplating anything else.

"How was the swimming lesson?"

The anxiety came flooding back, and Nora sat up. "Good, but there's something odd about that family."

"What family?"

"The Jonssons. I met their nanny, and she was distraught. She was actually sitting by the pool, crying while the children were having their lesson."

"Maybe her boyfriend dumped her," Jonas said without opening his eyes.

"No, she was in a terrible state. This isn't about some boy. Plus she made me promise not to say anything to Celia or Carsten."

"So it's a personal matter."

"She seemed scared of her employer, and that's not right. I'm wondering whether I ought to mention it to Thomas."

Jonas stretched and looked at Nora. He yawned again.

"You're not responsible for the welfare of the Jonsson family, especially not their nanny."

"But she was so upset, poor kid. She can't be much older than Wilma. If I knew her mother's name, I'd call her."

"Doesn't she have a friend who can help?"

"Not that I'm aware of."

Just a minute—what did Thomas say about the housekeeper? Linda Öberg, that was her name. From Runmarö.

Nora stood up.

"Where are you going?" Jonas tried to grab hold of her, but Nora was having none of it.

"I just thought of something."

She'd promised Maria that she wouldn't contact Celia or Carsten, but nobody had told her she couldn't talk to the housekeeper. She was convinced this was something much more serious than a tiff with a boyfriend.

She went down to the kitchen, opened up her laptop, and clicked on her favorite search engine.

She found forty-eight Linda Öbergs, but only one was registered in the electoral district of Värmdö. No landline was listed, but there was a cell phone number.

Nora stared at the digits.

Would Linda think she was crazy if she called her up, asked how Maria was? Maybe, but she couldn't get the girl's red-rimmed eyes out of her mind.

She had no choice, even if Jonas thought she was interfering. She picked up her phone, keyed in the number, and waited. The call went straight to voice mail, and the automated voice didn't give the subscriber's name. Should she leave a message, or simply hang up?

"Hi, my name's Nora Linde," she said after a brief hesitation. "Could you please call me back? It's to do with the Jonsson family."

She left her number to be on the safe side, and ended the call. She immediately felt foolish, as if she'd poked her nose in for no reason.

I'll try one more time. Then I'll leave it. Jonas is probably right.

CHAPTER 68

This time Per-Anders Agaton opened the door to Thomas and Aram. It was almost eleven o'clock. He waved them in and led the way to the airy veranda. The wind was coming from the south, and the sea was choppy.

Thomas and Aram each took an armchair while Agaton sat down on the sofa opposite. He'd obviously decided to take the bull by the horns.

"My wife tells me you think I started the fire at the Jonssons' place. In which case I'd like to know what evidence you have."

Thomas ignored the supercilious tone. "We need to establish where you were at the time of the fire."

"I was here, of course. In my own house."

"But when we spoke to your wife, it became clear that there's no one who can confirm that," Aram said.

"You're mistaken. Anna definitely remembers that we both went to bed at the same time."

"That's not what she said yesterday."

Agaton shrugged. "You took her by surprise, she got confused. I'm sure it's not the first time that kind of thing has happened in an interview with the police."

Thomas could see Agaton in court. Polished, brimming with confidence, convinced of his ability to succeed through the words he used. He could also see why he wasn't popular with his neighbors.

"Joking aside," Agaton went on, "you can't seriously believe that I'd set fire to my neighbor's house like some kind of pyromaniac. Why would I do such a thing?"

"Because you were angry?"

"There are better ways of expressing my anger."

"Like what?"

"Legal procedures, for example."

"You mean you like to frighten people by suing them or threatening legal action?"

Thomas started to feel annoyed with himself. He'd allowed Agaton to provoke him and had bitten back immediately. That was no good.

"OK, let's calm down," Agaton said. "I'm no fan of unnecessary litigation, if that's what you're suggesting, but sometimes you have to draw a line when people do dumb things."

"We have witnesses who heard you threaten Carsten Jonsson," Aram informed him. "Could you clarify what that was about?"

"Who are your witnesses?"

The guy was a lawyer to his fingertips. Answer one question with another; go on the offensive if you find yourself in a tight spot. He was a living handbook on litigation. Thomas was finding it hard to listen to him; his concentration was slipping, in spite of his earlier resolve.

"That's irrelevant. The point is that other people took note of what you said and how you said it, which is why we're asking you to explain yourself." Aram paused and opened up his notebook. "Apparently you said that he could take his fucking money and go to hell and that he shouldn't trample all over other people's property—at least if he knew what was good for him."

Thomas forced himself to join in. "Those are harsh words."

"What did you mean by your final comment?" Aram asked. "If he knew what was good for him? That definitely sounds like a threat to me. Perhaps you'd like to explain what was going to happen if he didn't mend his ways?"

Agaton let out a snort of derision.

"I might have let my mouth run away with me, but I can't pretend that I haven't been infuriated by Jonsson's behavior. You don't build a jetty in someone else's waters."

"What was going to happen if he didn't mend his ways?" Aram repeated.

Agaton ignored the question and got to his feet. "Anyone thirsty?" Without waiting for a reply, he disappeared into the kitchen. A cupboard door opened, something clinked, then came the sound of running water.

Aram leaned forward and said quietly, "Do you think he's getting a little nervous? The Bar Association has rules about the kind of thing its lawyers are allowed to say."

Agaton returned carrying a tray with three glasses and a jug of water. He poured himself a glass.

"Please help yourselves."

"Thank you," Thomas said. "What was going to happen to Carsten Jonsson if he didn't mend his ways?"

"Nothing."

"So you didn't mean anything by what you said at the party?"

"It was foolish. I shouldn't have expressed myself in that way." Agaton spread his hands wide. Presumably he'd carefully considered his response while he was in the kitchen.

"So why did you?"

Agaton looked down at the floor. Maybe it was his professional instinct that made him keep quiet. If so, it must be taking its toll; he didn't seem like a man who went for self-censorship.

"Could you answer the question, please?"

"I'm afraid I don't remember."

Thomas suppressed a sigh. "It was only three days ago. You seem to have a very short memory."

"My apologies."

Down on the shore, a couple of tourists strolled by, carrying towels and a picnic basket. They stayed well away from the house; they were almost walking along the water's edge.

Agaton jerked his head in their direction.

"There's no need for fences on this island. Everyone who lives here knows that."

Aram leafed through his notebook, as if to make it clear that there were other witnesses.

"Tell me something else: Have you spoken to any of the Polish builders working for Jonsson?"

"Are you sure you won't have a glass of water?" Agaton said, as if he hadn't heard the question.

"I'm fine, thanks."

"We were wondering if you'd spoken to any of Jonsson's builders," Thomas said.

"Why?" Agaton refilled his own glass.

"We just need to know."

"I might have exchanged the odd word. Pleasantries in passing."

"Pleasantries in passing? Could you be a little more specific?"

"I don't really remember."

Aram was making copious notes. Thomas could see that Agaton was trying to read what he'd written; maybe he wasn't quite so self-assured as he'd first appeared.

"Let me put it this way," Aram said. "Have you attempted to persuade any of Jonsson's builders to do something that might cause trouble for the family or harm them in some way?"

"Absolutely not."

You're lying.

But Thomas knew there was no way of proving it. Not yet. Aram decided to change tactics.

"What would you like Carsten to do in order to improve relations between you?"

Agaton placed both hands on his thighs. His double chin wobbled as he leaned forward.

"I'd like him to leave. We don't want his sort on the island."

Chapter 69

Carsten had steered the rib north, toward the skerries around Björkösund. He would soon reach his goal, the little cabin on an islet.

It was exactly as he remembered it, even though it was such a long time since he'd been here. He knew the route well; he'd rowed here many times when he was a boy. That was how he'd found the cabin—by pure chance.

The islet was one of many that the military had used during the years when Sweden was preparing itself for an invasion from the east. The entire archipelago was crisscrossed with locations that had been requisitioned from the landowners. To begin with, they had all been equipped with military fortifications, barricades, and concrete jetties. Later, when the country began to scale down its defense operations, most of these fortifications had been destroyed, and the military had moved out.

But the jetties remained, as did the buildings they hadn't bothered to demolish. The gray cabin in front of him was one of these structures.

Carsten came up alongside the jetty and moored the rib. It must have been twenty years since he last stepped ashore here.

It was a tiny islet; it would take no more than twenty minutes to walk all the way around the perimeter. The odd pine tree had taken root and was clinging to the rock; otherwise there was nothing but juniper and heather, growing in the crevices. A thin layer of yellow lichen covered the surface of the inhospitable ground.

Carsten looked around, just to be on the safe side, but he was totally alone, with not even a yacht visible on the horizon.

The cabin door was secured with a rusty padlock. Someone else had clearly decided to make use of the place. He needed something to smash the padlock. He went down to the water's edge and picked up a heavy stone. In seconds the job was done. As he tossed the stone aside, he noticed that the knuckles on his right hand were still red and slightly swollen.

Celia.

She had only herself to blame. If she'd just stopped arguing with him, nothing would have happened. It wasn't his fault.

He opened the door and stepped inside.

A bunk bed, a table, two chairs. He'd often spent the night here as a teenager. There was a half-empty jar of coffee on the counter in the kitchen area, along with two tin mugs and a battered metal coffee pot. Presumably they belonged to whoever had fitted the padlock. Someone had hung thin curtains with a floral pattern; they were new.

He saw his face in the cracked mirror on the wall. He needed a shave, but his eyes were clearer than ever. His hair was standing on end because of the sea breeze.

Anatoly was due to land in Stockholm in a few hours; Carsten had arranged to pick him up in Stavsnäs at six thirty.

There was a lot to discuss, but out here they'd be able to talk without being disturbed.

Carsten touched the small plastic bag in his pocket. He still had some left. He blew on his right hand and nodded to his reflection.

Chapter 70

It was Maria who opened the door when Thomas and Aram arrived at the Jonssons'.

"What do you want?" she exclaimed.

She must have been crying; her face was puffy, her eyes red. She was clutching a scruffy rucksack.

"Are you OK?" Thomas asked.

"Things are a little difficult right now."

She dropped the rucksack on the floor and blinked several times. Aram gently placed a hand on her arm.

"Is there anything we can do to help?"

Maria glanced over her shoulder. "I don't think so."

"You can always call us if there's a problem," Aram said. "You do know that?"

They were interrupted by Sarah shouting from the living room.

"Maaariiiaaa!"

A hunted expression came over the girl's face. "Sorry, I have to go. I'm in the middle of making the children's lunch."

"We wanted a word with Carsten," Aram explained. "Is he home?"

"No."

"Any idea when he'll be back?"

"No, but you could try his cell phone."

Thomas had expected Carsten to be home at this time of day, even though they hadn't called to let him know they were coming.

"Is Celia here?"

"Yes, but she's resting." Maria's lower lip trembled. "She's not very well at the moment."

Thomas suspected that things weren't too good between the Jonssons after the revelation of Carsten's infidelity.

"I understand. When you see Carsten, tell him we were here and we'd like to speak to him."

Maria hesitated. "Celia's not very well at the moment," she repeated, her voice far from steady.

Thomas nodded. "I hope she soon feels better."

Maria chewed at her thumbnail, then said, "Thanks. Bye," and closed the door.

The forest was peaceful. It was hard to believe the busy harbor area was only twenty minutes' walk away.

"What now?" Aram said.

"Let's try to get ahold of Carsten."

Aram took out his phone and called Carsten's number. Straight to voice mail.

"No answer," Aram said unnecessarily.

A short distance away, the blue-and-white police tape fluttered around the blackened remains of the guest lodge. The faint smell of charred wood still lingered in the air.

"We're not going to get much further out here," Aram continued. "I'd rather spend time looking through the background material Margit's put together. Do some digging, see if we can find out more about any enemies Jonsson might have had."

"Back to Nacka, then."

Aram gazed around the site. "Where are all the builders?"

Good question, Thomas thought. The previous day they'd heard the sound of hammering, but now there was nothing. And the quad bike wasn't parked behind the house.

"Maybe we should speak to Eklund again before we leave," Aram suggested. "We can't be sure that the victim was one of the partygoers."

He took out his notebook and found Eklund's number. The general contractor answered right away; Thomas gathered that he was on the island but heading for the harbor, just as they were. Aram ended the call.

"He'll meet us by the tennis courts in ten minutes."

CHAPTER 71

When they emerged onto Trouvillevägen, Eklund was waiting about a hundred yards away. A cigarette dangled from the corner of his mouth, and there was a battered duffel bag at his feet.

"Finished for the day already?" Thomas asked.

"Finished for the summer. I'm going back to town with my boys."

Eklund took a final drag, then dropped the glowing stub. He ground it into the sand with his foot.

Aram couldn't hide his surprise. "But the week's hardly started."

"Carsten's orders. He changed his mind overnight. Yesterday he wanted us to start clearing the site after the fire; today he sent us home."

"When will you be back?"

"I haven't a clue."

Eklund sounded both surprised and angry, but made no further comment. Instead he changed the subject.

"Anything new on the fire, if I'm allowed to ask?"

"Of course you are, but it's too early to say."

Thomas was still puzzled. It was obvious that Eklund had expected to spend the whole week on the island as usual; what was going on?

Aram got down to business.

"I don't suppose any of your guys are missing?"

"Sorry?"

"I'm thinking about the person who died in the fire. You said none of your guys were missing, but I wondered if you might have changed your mind now that you've had time to think."

"But surely it was one of the guests from the party? That's what Carsten told me."

Why did he sound so shocked?

"The truth is, we don't know at this stage. We haven't yet established the victim's identity."

Eklund lit a fresh cigarette and took a long drag before picking up his duffel bag.

"I'm afraid I can't help you. I have to go; otherwise I'll miss the boat to Stavsnäs. The boys have already gone down to the harbor."

He turned away. Thomas was seized by an impulse to stop him, but at that moment his phone rang. It was Staffan Nilsson.

"I've got something interesting for you," he began as Eklund disappeared around the corner.

"Good."

"You remember that lighter I found at the crime scene?"

Thomas saw distorted metal in an evidence bag.

"Yes."

"I managed to lift a fingerprint. It was very faint, so I had to work on it, but eventually I had something that could be checked against our database."

"And?"

"The print belongs to a guy called Gustav Kronberg. He's from Stockholm, born in 1975."

"Does he have a criminal record?"

"Yes—a number of minor thefts to begin with, but then he upped his game and was convicted of robbing a post office in the midnineties."

Back when we still had post offices, Thomas thought.

"Has he continued to pursue a life of crime?"

"That's the problem. He's dead."

Thomas certainly hadn't been expecting that answer.

"He died in 2000," Nilsson continued. "A heroin overdose. He was an addict, in and out of treatment facilities for years. Same old story."

Thomas stepped aside to let two teenagers cycle past. "So how do we explain the lighter?"

"I've no idea."

"Could Kronberg have dropped it there a long time ago?" Even Thomas didn't believe what he was suggesting.

"I'd say that was highly unlikely," Staffan said. "That would mean it had been lying outdoors for thirteen years without the print being destroyed." He was beginning to sound a little stressed. "I have to go. I'm due in a meeting."

Thomas had one last question.

"Did you find anything else with a link to Kronberg at the scene?"

"No, that's up to you. I just wanted to let you know about the lighter; I've already done more than I really have time for."

"I appreciate it. But let me know if you come up with anything else."

Aram had heard most of the conversation, but Thomas quickly filled him in on the details.

"We need to look into Gustav Kronberg's background," he said. "At least it's a step forward."

Aram drew a line in the sand with his foot and stared at it, as if the answer might suddenly appear.

"I'd like to find out if there's a connection between Kronberg and Per-Anders Agaton," he said. "Dead men don't start fires."

CHAPTER 72

Holding Julia firmly by the hand, Nora opened the white garden gate and knocked on Olle Granlund's door. Uncle Olle was her oldest neighbor since Aunt Signe's death, and he knew most people on Sandhamn. He might have some information on Carsten Jonsson and his link to the island. She'd already spoken to Eva, but her friend had no idea why Carsten had chosen to build his house at Fyrudden.

Nora knocked again, but there was no response.

"I guess he's not home," she said to Julia.

Olle's black cat slid through the gate, lay down on his back, and started to roll around. Julia crouched down and stroked his soft tummy; he closed his eyes and began to purr.

It was one thirty and it was a lovely day; Olle was probably out in his boat. She'd just have to come back later. Nora allowed Julia to stroke the cat for a little longer before they returned to the Brand villa.

"Mommy, can I have a kitten? Please, Mommy, please please please!"

"We'll see, sweetheart."

Julia raced up to her room while Nora headed for the kitchen. She was getting nowhere. Linda Öberg hadn't called back, even though Nora had left another message.

Was there nothing else she could do to help Thomas? She had plenty of contacts in the banking world; maybe she could call Jonathan?

Jonathan Smythe was employed by the Financial Conduct Authority in the UK. They'd known each other for a long time and had worked together in the past when they were both in banking. Like Nora, Jonathan had moved over to the regulatory side, and as far as she knew, he was much happier in the public sector.

She picked up her phone and weighed it in her hand. She knew the British usually took their vacation later than the Swedes, so hopefully Jonathan would still be at work. She keyed in the international dialing code for the UK, followed by his number.

"Jonathan Smythe."

His accent always made her smile; it was an object lesson in Oxford English, even though he was anything but a stereotype with a rolled-up umbrella and a bowler hat. He was tall and slim and hated wearing a tie. More Bohemian than banker, in spite of the perfect enunciation.

"Hello, Jonathan. It's Nora, Nora Linde. How are you?"

After the usual small talk, she explained why she was calling and that it involved a police inquiry.

"I'm trying to gather information about a Swedish venture capitalist who's been operating in London for several years. His name is Carsten Jonsson. Have you heard of him?"

"Carsten Jonsson . . . Sounds familiar. Let me check."

Nora heard the sound of a computer keyboard, the click of the mouse. After a minute or so Jonathan came back to her.

"I've found him—I thought I recognized the name. He's the guy who was involved in the United Oil affair nine or ten years ago."

Nora had no idea what he was talking about, but then again she didn't follow the market in the UK. She sat down at the kitchen table and grabbed her notepad and pen.

"It was a huge scandal," Jonathan went on. "United Oil was prospecting for oil in the Sudan."

The Sudan. The name alone had such negative connotations; it made Nora think of warlords, violence, and human suffering. Needless to say, that didn't stop Western companies from moving in, including Swedish businesses.

Jonathan was reading from the screen, summarizing as he went along.

"Jonsson was engaged as a financial adviser when United Oil was floated on the stock market. Their work in the Sudan wasn't particularly successful nor politically correct. The local people were treated very badly; there was talk of bribery, all kinds of things. It was touted as a fantastic opportunity, but when it went down the tubes, which of course it did, a lot of small investors lost their money."

"That doesn't sound good."

"No. United Oil's attitude to its investors was brutal—ruthless, in fact. Both Jonsson and the broker he worked for were heavily criticized for their actions."

It all sounded very sordid. Dirty money.

Yesterday, before she bumped into Carsten at the gas station, Nora wouldn't have believed him to be capable of that kind of thing. Now she wasn't so sure. She couldn't forget the way he'd spoken to her. When he walked out of the door, she'd felt completely worthless.

"Was Carsten given any kind of official reprimand?"

"Let's have a look."

Nora waited, listening to the sound of the keyboard once more.

"No, not as far as I can see, but he left the brokerage firm shortly afterward. I wouldn't be surprised if they fired him, although that wouldn't have been the official line." Jonathan cleared his throat. "They don't like it when their employees get mixed up in a scandal—you know that as well as I do. But they wouldn't want to air their dirty laundry in public; they probably paid him off discreetly."

Nora trusted Jonathan's judgment; she knew he had no sympathy with the raw greed that sometimes pervaded London's financial circles.

"In other words, Carsten Jonsson isn't a name that inspires trust," she said.

"Definitely not."

"Do you know anything else about him? Everything's useful in this context."

Including gossip.

"In that case let's move from the facts to general rumors." Jonathan was always so correct, even now. "People say that Jonsson found his way back with the help of his father-in-law's money and contacts."

Nora wasn't surprised to learn that Celia came from a wealthy background, nor that Carsten had married into influence and connections.

"I think that's probably true," Jonathan continued. "There's no way he could have set up on his own after all the trouble surrounding United Oil."

"Do you know what kind of investments he's involved in nowadays?"

"He has interests in Russia."

"Russia?"

They say the burned child fears the fire—clearly not in Carsten's case.

"Well, at least that sounds better than the Sudan," Nora said.

"Not really. Doing business in Russia is complicated. Corruption is rife, and the bureaucracy is impenetrable. Any investment is undertaken at your own risk. Most of those who try to get rich quick come undone along the way."

Nora knew exactly where Russia stood on the international corruption index. Sudan was at the bottom of the 177 ranked countries, but Russia wasn't much better, in 127th place. Sweden was third on the list, which said a great deal about affairs on the other side of the Baltic.

"Why Russia?" Nora asked, even though she already knew the answer. The judicial system was rotten to the core, and the abuse of power was widespread; the little man didn't have very much say. However, the profits could be enormous if everything went well. Plenty of personal fortunes had been made in Russia over the past fifteen years.

How much had the development at Fyrudden cost?

"He lives dangerously," Jonathan commented. "And he's not afraid to take huge risks."

"Do you think he's made enemies?"

"A lot of people were ruined when United Oil collapsed."

"That was years ago."

"There are always those who have a long memory." There was an icy tone in Jonathan's voice. "One thing's for sure. If he behaves as ruthlessly in Russia as he did over at United Oil, then he ought to be looking over his shoulder. I find it hard to believe that his Russian associates would be as forgiving as his British investors."

CHAPTER 73

Thomas had just sat down at a window table in the stern of the Vaxholm ferry *Dalarö* when his phone rang. Aram had gone to fetch coffee.

"It's Nora. Am I disturbing you?"

"Not at all. I'm on the ferry."

"I've found out some information about Carsten Jonsson that might interest you."

Thomas leaned back and gazed out the window. They were just passing the island of Eknö. The population of Sandhamn had been brought over from here in the seventeenth century, when the king demanded that there should be pilots based on the unoccupied island of Swea Sandö.

"Go on."

"First of all, I forgot to tell you this yesterday. You know that Carsten's father worked as a sea captain before he joined the Customs Service? It occurred to me that the family might have lived on Sandhamn at some point. His father must have had a close relationship with the sea to take up that profession; maybe he applied to be posted to Sandhamn when he came ashore?"

"Wouldn't someone have recognized Carsten if that were the case?"

"Not necessarily. It's a long time ago, and Jonsson is one of the most common surnames in Sweden. And Carsten is his middle name—he's actually Lars Carsten. Maybe he decided he preferred it that way, once he was old enough to make up his own mind."

It was definitely worth checking out. Nora was very good at finding the small details; she had a real talent for it. She took a deep breath, and Thomas realized she'd saved the best till last.

"I had a very interesting conversation with Jonathan Smythe, an old friend of mine who now works for the Financial Conduct Authority in the UK. He told me about Carsten Jonsson's reputation over there."

Guaranteed to arouse Thomas's interest.

"And?"

"He was heavily involved in an oil company that went bust about ten years ago: United Oil."

Aram returned with the coffee. He put down a steaming paper cup in front of Thomas.

Nora passed on what Jonathan had told her about the dubious dealings in the Sudan.

"What happened with United Oil tells us a great deal about his business ethics," she said. "According to Jonathan, he was utterly ruthless. It's possible that someone from back then is still out for revenge."

Nora had done well; Thomas knew he probably wouldn't have been able to find out anywhere near as much as she had. He certainly wouldn't have known how to draw the right conclusions.

They were going to have to expand their assessment of the possible threat against Jonsson and his family.

Nora wasn't done yet.

"After United Oil collapsed, he lost his job and was out in the cold. He had to borrow money from Celia's father in order to set up on his own."

So he was dependent on his father-in-law's financial support. What effect would that have on the relationship between man and wife? *It was a lot worse than earning less than your partner,* Thomas thought. Suddenly the fact that Pernilla earned more than him didn't matter at all.

The ferry sounded its horn three times to let everyone know it was reversing away from Långvik on the north side of Runmarö. The captain swung her around and set his course for Styrsvik, the next port of call.

"Do you happen to know how he makes his money these days?" Thomas asked, taking a sip of his coffee.

"Apparently he's involved in some kind of deal in Russia."

"It seems to be very lucrative."

They both knew he was referring to the house at Fyrudden.

"But not without risk. Jonathan's going to keep digging; I gave him your number, in case he comes up with anything else."

Nora lowered her voice.

"I also made another call, to an old classmate of mine who now works for the Ministry for Foreign Affairs. She's had a lot to do with Russia, and she told me that there have been several incidents lately that have alarmed foreign investors. Domestic interests have tried to take over foreign-owned assets in a variety of ways—sometimes through subtle threats, sometimes by more violent methods."

She paused, as if she were trying to find the right words to summarize Carsten Jonsson's business affairs.

"He's swimming in murky waters," she said at last. "The fire might well have something to do with his Russian investments."

CHAPTER 74

Celia opened her eyes. She must have fallen asleep at some point, even though she'd been scared to drop her guard in case Carsten came in. The room had gotten way too warm in the afternoon sun, but Celia wished she could have gone on sleeping.

She didn't want to wake up and face reality.

She could hear the children laughing; that was probably what had disturbed her. Somehow she had to pull herself together, walk out of the bedroom, and pretend that life was just the same as always.

She just didn't know how.

Her head was throbbing, particularly at her temples and above her right eye. When she sat up she felt dizzy, but forced herself to her feet. She'd probably suffered a concussion.

Her robe was on the bed; she reached out a shaky hand and pulled it on.

She avoided looking at herself in the mirror, didn't want to see her puffy, tear-stained face. But she couldn't keep on hiding; she'd stayed away from the children for far too long, in far too many ways.

With a strange, numb feeling, she opened the door and went into the living room. Both Sarah and Oliver were on the floor, playing with the colorful bricks they loved so much. Maria was over by the refrigerator.

Sarah was the first to notice Celia.

"Mommy!" she shouted joyfully, and ran over to her mother. "Hi, Mommy!" She didn't react to Celia's appearance, but Oliver stared at her bruised, swollen face. When Celia held out her hand to him, he recoiled and refused to come to her.

That hurt, almost as much as when she'd found out that Carsten had hit him. She thought she could still see traces of the mark Carsten's hand had left on his cheek.

"We had spaghetti with ketchup for lunch today," Sarah said, chattering away happily. "Then we had ice cream for dessert. Chocolate ice cream."

Celia had already spotted a tiny fleck of dried ice cream at the corner of her mouth. She knelt down to hug her daughter, buried her face in the little girl's soft hair, and tried not to burst into tears. After a while she let her go. Maria was still standing by the refrigerator.

"Everything OK?" Celia said, forcing herself to smile and sound cheerful. But Maria wouldn't look at her. She kept her eyes fixed on a point on the wall and mumbled an inaudible response.

Something was wrong, Celia knew it. Then she saw the suitcase by the door and realized what was going on. Maria's rucksack was propped against the wall, with her jacket on top of it.

"I have to go home," Maria said in a flat voice.

"You can't!" Celia heard the shrillness in her tone.

Sarah looked scared and stuck her thumb in her mouth.

"Sorry, sweetheart, Mommy just overreacted a little. Everything's fine."

She stood up, using the table for support. Her legs were shaking, and she had to lean on the back of a chair to stop herself from falling over.

"I'm catching the four o'clock boat to Stavsnäs."

Oliver's little face crumpled; he ran to Maria and flung his arms around her legs.

"Are you going away?"

Maria patted his cheek.

"I'm afraid so, honey. I have to. Mommy will take care of you—it'll be fine."

"Please don't go!"

Celia took control. "Sarah, Oliver, go into the bedroom and wait for me. I'll be there in a couple of minutes."

Oliver didn't want to let go of Maria, but she prised his little hands away. A tear glinted in the corner of her eye before she lowered her head so that her hair covered her face. Eventually Oliver gave in and followed his sister into the bedroom.

"Please, Maria," Celia said quietly. "Stay for a little while—at least until the weekend? Surely a few days won't make much difference?"

When Maria didn't say anything, she went on: "Carsten and I are having a few problems at the moment."

Please don't leave me alone with him—that was what she really wanted to scream, but she couldn't bring herself to beg.

"I'll double your pay for this month if you stay."

"I don't want anything."

Maria still refused to meet her gaze.

"Just a day or two, please. Tell me what you want and I'll pay it. And I'll pay for your ticket home."

"I'm scared." Maria's voice was no more than a whisper. "Carsten warned me . . . He said I wasn't to tell anyone what happened yesterday . . ."

She didn't need to say any more; Celia understood.

"I'm sorry," Maria added.

The house was so silent.

There wasn't a sound from the bedroom; it was as if the children realized they mustn't make a noise. Only a few days ago, the terrace had been crowded with laughing, chatting guests. The music had played, and Carsten had stood on a chair, tan and smiling, welcoming everyone. She remembered how he had patted her on the cheek before raising his glass in a toast.

Maria walked to the door and put on her jacket. "I have to go; otherwise I'll miss the boat." She picked up her rucksack. She sounded almost embarrassed. "It's probably best if the children don't have to say good-bye. I don't want to upset them even more."

"I can't be on my own with them," Celia whispered, feeling more and more dizzy. "Please, Maria."

"You've still got Linda," Maria said, as if she were trying to convince herself. "She's just left, but she'll be back tomorrow."

Celia had forgotten all about Linda. She glanced out the window; Linda was heading down toward the water, her cloth bag over her shoulder as usual. However, just as she was about to step onto the jetty, she stopped and turned around. Her eyes met Celia's, then she flinched and her hand flew to her mouth. Celia crouched down, but knew it was too late; Linda had seen her battered face.

A wave of shame washed over her, and she couldn't suppress a sob.

Linda stood there for a moment as if she couldn't decide what to do, then she continued on her way and climbed into her boat.

Celia realized that the berth next to it was empty; the gray rib wasn't there.

"Has Carsten gone somewhere?" she said stupidly. "Where's he gone?"

"I don't know."

CHAPTER 75

Thomas got into the car and fastened his seat belt. Aram did the same in the passenger seat. The boat had arrived in Stavsnäs at three thirty, and it shouldn't take more than half an hour to get to the station at this time of day. There was no rush-hour traffic to speak of in July.

Thomas was eager to get away and quickly pulled out of the parking lot. Unfortunately he wound up right behind a bus that was in no hurry whatsoever.

His mind began to wander, creating fresh scenarios around Carsten Jonsson, the man who'd cheated small investors and was now doing business with the Russians.

There were many people who had good reason to hold a grudge against him, not just his irate neighbor on the island.

The difficulty lay in following up on the information Nora had given him. Moving forward without Jonsson's cooperation would be tricky. He still hadn't contacted them, even though many hours had passed since they'd tried to reach him. Maria had promised to pass on their message; surely he should have received it by now?

"Try Jonsson again," he said.

Aram took out his phone and keyed in the number, but when he started to speak, Thomas realized the call had gone to voice mail yet again.

Aram put the phone away. "So what do we do about Agaton? He definitely has a motive."

"We can't bring him in without evidence."

It was never easy to arrest a lawyer; in fact it rarely happened, possibly because the enterprise was usually doomed to failure. Margit wouldn't thank them if she had the president of the Bar Association giving her a hard time.

Aram rolled down the window for some fresh air, but let in a burst of diesel fumes from the bus in front of them instead.

"I can well imagine Agaton starting the fire to scare the Jonssons," he said. "You heard what he said. He wants them off the island, the sooner the better."

"But we still have no ID on the body."

Thomas knew he sounded irritable, but he was annoyed that they still didn't have the autopsy report. A lot of loose ends might be tied up once they had a name.

If Sachsen had been on duty, we wouldn't have had to wait so long, he thought, even though he knew that wasn't necessarily true. The lab in Solna dealt with suspicious deaths from many districts, not just Stockholm. They couldn't prioritize a case from Nacka just because Thomas was impatient.

"I'm becoming more and more convinced that it was an accident," Aram said. "Someone who'd gone into the lodge for a nap. Particularly if it turns out that Agaton is our man. I think he's capable of doing stupid things to get his point across, but I don't see him as a cold-blooded killer." He rubbed the bridge of his nose with his finger. "I wouldn't mind getting a search warrant to see what's in his shed or garage. Lighter fluid, maybe?"

"Everybody in the archipelago keeps a supply of that stuff," Thomas informed him. "And what *specific reason* would you give on the application for a warrant?"

They both knew the regulations when it came to searching the property of an individual who wasn't under "reasonable suspicion." They had nothing on Agaton that would fulfill those criteria.

"Let's hope Kalle and his team come up with something soon," Thomas went on. "We need a witness, somebody who's seen Agaton doing something more serious than bad-mouthing Jonsson. What he said at the party isn't enough."

His phone rang: Margit. He switched to speakerphone.

"Good news," she said immediately. "I've just received the autopsy report."

At last.

"What was the cause of death?"

"Smoke inhalation, but according to the pathologist, he was probably unconscious when the fire started. He had a very high blood-alcohol level."

"Have we identified him? Do we have a name?"

"No, but we do have an age. It looks as if he was between thirty-five and forty-five."

A drunken guest, in other words—exactly as they'd suspected from the start. Thomas began to make a mental to-do list.

"We still haven't found any missing-persons reports that match the victim," Margit continued, "but there is something else. He's probably not Swedish."

"How do they know?"

"His teeth. They're in a terrible state, and the pathologist is certain any work done hasn't been carried out by a Swedish dentist."

"Does she have any idea of his country of origin?" The bus had pulled up at a stop, and Thomas pushed on the gas to pass.

"Her guess would be eastern Europe."

Thomas breathed in sharply. This time he'd been too quick to jump to a conclusion.

"One of Eklund's builders," Aram said. "I'd put money on it."

Or someone of Russian origin with a completely different motive.

"We need to speak to Eklund as soon as possible," Thomas said. "We're on our way to Nacka now. We'll be there shortly. Can you try and get ahold of him?"

CHAPTER 76

Mats Eklund had arrived at the station at ten past five. When Thomas opened the door of the interview room, he saw that the general contractor was still wearing his work clothes: paint-stained dungarees.

A blood vessel had burst on one cheek.

"Thanks for coming in on such short notice," he said as he sat down. Aram joined him, switched on the tape recorder and gave the obligatory introduction.

"Why am I here?" Eklund demanded.

"We've had the results of the autopsy. We want to talk to you about the person who died in the fire," Aram said.

"I don't understand."

"It seems as if he came from eastern Europe," Thomas explained. "We believe he could be one of your builders."

"He was between thirty-five and forty-five years old and around six feet four inches tall," Aram added.

Eklund coughed, then ran his hand slowly over his thinning hair.

"Do you know who it is?"

"It could be Marek—Marek Kowalski. He's around that height. But Carsten said . . ."

He broke off.

"What did Carsten say?"

"He said it was one of the guests who'd died." Eklund's voice was subdued. He shook his head as if he didn't know what to believe. "Carsten accused Marek of having started the fire."

"Why would Marek do such a thing?"

"Carsten thought Agaton had paid him to burn down the lodge. He said Agaton was behind the other incidents, the broken window and the slashed tire. And the dead bird on the steps."

Of course Carsten hadn't mentioned anything about the window or the tire, Thomas thought.

Eklund blinked several times before continuing.

"When Carsten said that Marek must have gotten scared and taken off, I thought he was probably right. But if it was Marek who died in the fire . . ." His voice trailed away.

"The autopsy showed that the victim was very drunk," Aram explained. "Possibly on the verge of alcohol poisoning. If it's any consolation, he would hardly have noticed when the fire started. The cause of death was smoke inhalation, so it would have been pretty quick."

Eklund seemed grateful for the information.

"Would you like some water?" Eklund nodded, and Aram poured him a glass from the jug Karin had placed on the table.

"Could it have been an accident?" Eklund asked.

"No. The fire was started deliberately, from the outside. There were traces of an accelerant in several places," Thomas said.

"Is there any chance that Marek might have tried to take his own life?" Aram wondered. "Maybe he got drunk to help him pluck up the courage to do it?"

"I doubt it. He was over here to earn money so that his daughter could afford to finish college. Once he had enough he was planning to return to Poland; his family lives in Gdańsk." Eklund's shoulders slumped. "This doesn't make sense."

He was right, Thomas thought. It didn't make sense.

Someone else must have set fire to the lodge. Which meant they were back to square one, even though they now knew the identity of the victim. Once again he recalled what Nora had told him.

"What nationalities are your workers?" he asked.

Eklund looked confused, but answered the question anyway.

"Most of them are from Poland. A couple of the roofers are from Ukraine."

"Have you worked with them for long?"

"Yes, we've done plenty of jobs together. Marek takes care of the planning; he speaks both Polish and Russian."

"Russian?"

"Do you know anyone who speaks Ukrainian?" Eklund bared his teeth in something that might have been a smile. "They use Russian in the former Soviet states the way we use English. Everyone knows a little, enough to get by."

He took out his cigarettes. "Can I smoke in here?"

Thomas shook his head. "I'm afraid not."

Aram had opened his notebook and was checking his notes.

"You must have noticed yesterday that Marek was missing. Why didn't you say anything to us when we spoke to you?"

"I should have," Eklund admitted. "But Carsten was furious with me, and I didn't know what was best. He made it sound as if the whole thing was my fault—the fire, I mean, because one of my workers had started it."

He lowered his head. "I didn't want you to start poking around. It was stupid, I realize that now."

"When did you last see Marek?"

"Saturday."

"As we understand it, you stopped work in the afternoon," Thomas said. "Did you travel back to town together on the ferry?"

"No. I caught the taxi boat to Stavsnäs, and Marek was going to take the direct service to Stockholm. I was sure he'd boarded the boat that left five minutes after mine."

"I still don't get it," Aram persisted. "You must have noticed that he failed to show up yesterday?"

Eklund's regret was palpable.

"I mentioned it to Carsten, but he was so sure that Marek was responsible for the fire. He said his absence proved he'd done it, and I believed him. I know how it sounds now, but Carsten can be very convincing . . ."

"And do you yourself think Marek had something to do with the fire?" Aram asked, clasping his hands on the table.

"That doesn't fit with the Marek I knew."

"So what was he doing in the lodge? That's what I can't work out," Thomas said.

Eklund licked his dry lips.

"Marek had a drinking problem. I did wonder if he was stealing booze from Jonsson now and again."

"You mean he stayed because of the party? To help himself to everything that was being offered?"

Thomas could picture the scene. The Polish builder who wanted to taste the good life, who seized the opportunity when no one was looking. Maybe he'd picked up a couple of bottles and a Champagne glass, snuck off to the lodge. Fine wines he hadn't tried before. Champagne and whisky, expensive brands he would never have been able to afford. He knew the lodge was going to be empty, so there was no risk of being discovered. Presumably he'd gotten so drunk he'd fallen asleep.

With fatal consequences.

Aram interrupted Thomas's train of thought. "Can we go back to what you said about Carsten a moment ago? His accusations against Per-Anders Agaton?"

"Carsten's convinced that Agaton paid Marek to set fire to the lodge."

"Why would he do that?"

"To get the Jonssons off the island, of course—send them scuttling back to London."

"But if it was Marek who died in the fire, that can't be true."

Thomas had already drawn the same conclusion. Agaton could still be behind the arson attack, but the unfortunate Pole wasn't involved.

Eklund was starting to look stressed. He took a cigarette out of the packet, then put it back. A few flakes of tobacco landed on the table.

"You need to talk to Carsten. He was furious with Agaton the last time I spoke to him."

"And when was that?"

"Today, just before I saw you on Trouvillevägen. He made it sound as if Agaton was his worst enemy. And he'd called me late on Sunday evening about the same thing. The guy was bordering on crazy, if you ask me."

Thomas reacted to his choice of words; when they spoke to Eklund the previous day, he'd used the same term. Crazy.

Eklund chewed his lower lip. "I mean, Carsten can be difficult, but these last few days he's been worse than ever. It's as if he's stuck in a loop, he can't stop thinking about Agaton."

Thomas and Aram exchanged a glance.

"Sabotage, that's what he called it," Eklund added.

"Do you think he's capable of attacking Agaton—physically, I mean?" Thomas was hoping Eklund wouldn't clam up as he'd done previously when the questions about his employer became too intrusive.

"I couldn't say."

"Have you ever seen Carsten use violence?"

Eklund shook his head. "Not exactly."

"OK." Thomas sounded calmer than he felt. Was Jonsson refusing to cooperate with them because he'd decided to take matters into his own hands? Surely he couldn't be that dumb? Then again, it was almost six o'clock, and they hadn't heard from him all day, in spite of several messages asking him to contact the police.

"What do you mean by 'not exactly'?" Aram seemed determined to analyze every word the man said.

Eklund shifted uncomfortably on his chair. Why was he still so loyal to Jonsson, when it was obvious that he didn't even like him? Sometimes Thomas found the logic behind people's behavior difficult to understand, especially when they were being interviewed by the police.

Eventually Eklund decided to speak.

"Something unpleasant happened yesterday morning when Carsten found out that Marek had disappeared."

"Go on."

"He was furious. He pushed me in the chest, way too hard."

"You had a fight?"

"No, but I got the feeling he almost wanted me to come back at him. It was as if he needed an outlet for his anger."

Mats Eklund finally put his cards on the table.

"I've never seen him behave so aggressively. It was very unpleasant."

CHAPTER 77

As Carsten approached Stavsnäs, he saw that there were already several motorboats at the gas station where he'd intended to moor the rib, but then he spotted a space on the left side. He swung around so that he was coming from the right direction, and within a couple of minutes his boat was tied up at the rubber-covered pontoon.

He jumped ashore and gazed around the busy harbor, the hub for the Vaxholm ferries in the southern archipelago. There was a long line of people waiting at the fast-food kiosk, and every table outside the café was occupied. The parking lot was full.

No sign of Anatoly. He should be here by now; they'd arranged to meet at the gas station at six thirty. His flight had been due in at four thirty, and Anatoly hadn't let him know about any delay.

Then again, a few minutes didn't really matter. He had to fill up the tank; the afternoon's trip meant he was almost out of fuel. He'd traveled the last few hundred yards on fumes.

He had a can of gas on board, but he needed that for something else.

By this stage he felt perfectly calm, in spite of the fact that adrenaline was surging through his body and that he'd had no more than three hours' sleep in the last day or so. A line of coke had given him a fresh burst of energy. He knew exactly what he had to do.

Exactly how to put everything right.

He'd had plenty of time to think. Nothing could go wrong if he stuck to the plan.

One of the guys from the gas station, a teenager with a topknot, came over with a black fuel line in his hand. He nodded at Carsten and gestured toward the rib with his foot.

"Full tank?"

"Yes." Carsten kept searching for Anatoly in the crowd. There were so many tourists, so many families with strollers, all waiting for the next ferry to Sandhamn or one of the other islands. He noticed a mother holding a little girl by the hand; Carsten thought she looked like Sarah.

But she and Oliver were at Fyrudden, with Maria.

He'd had a chat with Maria that morning. He didn't want her gossiping about what had happened the previous evening. It had to stay within the family. She did understand that, didn't she?

Maria hadn't said a word. He'd hardly even needed to raise his voice. He felt secure in the knowledge that she'd take care of the children, keep her mouth shut.

Unlike his wife.

Last night Celia had openly challenged him. Threatened to leave with Oliver and Sarah. Did she really think he'd let her go?

The mere thought of it was enough to make him clench his fist in his pocket. He had to force himself to open his fingers, relax, take a couple of deep breaths. He couldn't afford to lose control.

Impatiently he glanced at his watch; where the hell was Anatoly?

A black cab drove up and stopped in the turning area a hundred yards away.

Anatoly got out. His dark-blue suit stood out among the casually dressed tourists on the quayside. His Church lace-up shoes were polished to perfection as usual, and the sun glinted from his expensive gold cuff links.

Carsten instantly felt calm. Anatoly was here.

Everything was going to be fine; he just had to deal with one thing at a time.

He took out his wallet and gave the teenager three five-hundred-kronor notes.

"Keep the change," he said as he set off to meet the Russian.

CHAPTER 78

Nora threw the last sheet over the line and secured it with three clothespins. It could stay out overnight. She loved the smell of laundry that had dried outdoors.

The evening was humid and oppressive; maybe there was a thunderstorm on the way. Hopefully not—that wouldn't do her wash any good.

They'd had dinner down by the jetty—oven-baked whitefish with new potatoes and horseradish sauce. Julia had been so proud of the fish she'd caught with her daddy, but even though Nora had enjoyed the food, she couldn't stop thinking about Maria. The nagging unease wouldn't go away. Linda Öberg hadn't called back, and there had been no answer when Nora tried again.

She knew she ought to let it go, but she was getting increasingly worried with every hour that passed. She couldn't wait until tomorrow's swimming lesson.

Jonas was reading by the jetty while Julia splashed around in a little blue wading pool. Nora gazed at the two of them. Would Jonas think she was interfering if she took a stroll over to Fyrudden? He hadn't wanted her to contact Celia and Carsten after the fire, nor had he been especially enthusiastic about attending a housewarming party given by people they hardly knew.

However, Nora felt a certain responsibility. It was hard to see a young girl in such a state; she didn't know how to dry Maria's tears. Sometimes logic and rational thought weren't enough. If it had been her own daughter, she would rather see a stranger get involved than no one at all.

She'd just drop by, make sure everything was OK. Have a word with Celia, see if they could arrange a play date for the girls.

Jonas . . . He would say she was overreacting. It was probably best if she didn't mention her plans. She picked up the empty laundry basket and went over to him.

"OK?" she said, stroking his brown hair. He put down his book, a thick biography of Steve Jobs, and reached for his beer.

"Come and sit down," he said, patting the chair beside him. "Take it easy. You seem to have been running around all day. I'll fetch you a glass of rosé."

"Actually, I feel like a walk," Nora said, as if the thought had just struck her.

"We could come with you. Julia's been in the water for long enough. It would be good to stretch our legs."

Sometimes Jonas was too nice.

"The thing is . . ." Nora hesitated. "I really wanted to do a proper power walk. We'd have to go much more slowly if Julia's with us. How about a glass of wine when I get back?"

It wasn't a lie, but she still felt guilty. He was so sweet, and she wasn't being entirely straight with him.

"No problem." Jonas picked up his book. "Enjoy your walk. See you soon."

Nora blew him a kiss.

"I won't be long."

CHAPTER 79

There weren't many boats around; the approaching cold front seemed to have scared most of them off. For the last twenty minutes they'd been more or less alone out in the bay. The white-tipped waves were choppy now; the water was lead-gray, and rain was threatening.

Carsten had deliberately kept his speed up so that the wind and the roar of the engine made it difficult to talk. A few times the swell had been against them; he'd slowed down, but not quite enough for the boat not to jolt and bounce.

Anatoly had clung on, trying to brace his body against each impact. It was obvious that he wasn't used to being at sea; his face had taken on a greenish tinge. From time to time he shifted his position, unable to hide his unease.

They were heading for a tiny islet with an old military jetty.

"Is this Sandhamn? The place I've heard so much about?" he shouted to Carsten. "I've been looking forward to seeing your new house and meeting your family again."

He had no idea that they were a long way from Sandhamn, northeast of Björkskär. They'd already been traveling for forty-five minutes.

Without answering Anatoly's question, Carsten reduced his speed as he assessed the distance from the shoreline. The wind was picking up, and he didn't want to crash into the jetty, which was disproportionately large in relation to the island.

"Can you jump ashore and catch the ropes?" he said to Anatoly, checking over the side to make sure there was nothing for the propeller to catch on. He didn't want to get stuck here overnight.

He swung around so that Anatoly could reach the jetty, and seconds later the ropes were secured to the black iron rings installed by the military all those years ago.

"We need to talk in peace and quiet, you and I," Carsten said, pointing to the cabin. "Come on."

Anatoly glanced at his expensive hand-stitched shoes, then at Carsten's deck shoes. He didn't have an overcoat, and Carsten could see he was shivering.

The temperature was dropping.

"You could have warned me that we were going right out into the archipelago," Anatoly said with a good-natured shrug as he reached into the boat for his briefcase. "I'm not dressed for this kind of outing."

Carsten forced the corners of his mouth up into something resembling a smile.

You could have warned me that you were planning on double-crossing me.

CHAPTER 80

The quickest route to Fyrudden was across Sandfälten and past the housing development on the hill above the harbor. Nora had supported the initiative to build rental property for those who wanted to live and work in the archipelago. If ordinary people couldn't afford to live on the island, Sandhamn wouldn't survive in the long term.

Today she walked quickly, head down, ignoring the new houses and neatly edged flowerbeds.

The thought of seeing Carsten was bothering her. With a bit of luck he wouldn't be there. After yesterday's uncomfortable encounter, she really didn't want to bump into him again. *It must have been the shock,* she said to herself, even though she didn't believe it.

Maybe it was Carsten who'd upset Maria so much? If he'd been as unpleasant to her as he had to Nora, it would explain a great deal.

The information she'd found out from Jonathan Smythe didn't make her feel any better. On the surface Carsten came across as a normal guy—maybe a little intense. Nora remembered the caring dad who'd sat with Sarah by the pool. He'd seemed so nice, almost boyish, dipping his hand into the bag of pastries from the bakery.

Now she knew he was partly responsible for thousands of small investors being conned out of their money; many had been ruined.

Carsten had put himself before others in every way, without showing a trace of empathy.

Did he ever think about those who'd lost everything?

Probably not; no doubt he felt they had only themselves to blame. There was always a way of rationalizing bad behavior.

The narrow lane wound its way past Seglarstaden, the area with its well-preserved houses from the 1930s where sailors had once stayed during regattas. Then she was in the pine forest, where buildings were few and far between.

Tomorrow she must speak to Olle Granlund; she'd stopped by before dinner, but he hadn't been home. She wanted to ask him about Carsten, see if he knew anything that could shed light on his behavior and why he'd been so determined to live on Sandhamn. The house at Fyrudden shouted out that he wanted to impress everyone around him. *Look at me, look at what I've achieved!*

Did he realize how much that revealed about his character?

No doubt all the disagreements with the neighbors came down to the same issue. Carsten couldn't help provoking others; he had to prove that he could do whatever he wanted, regardless of anyone else's opinion. It was a peculiar way to get attention, and his restless energy was wearing.

Nora wondered whether his smile during his welcome speech at the party had been genuine. Carsten Jonsson was a complex man, filled with the desire to possess. There must be something in his past that had created such a need to impress.

She wished they hadn't gone to the party; Jonas had been right all along.

She took the path leading to Fyrudden. She usually enjoyed spending time in the forest, but this evening it felt gloomy and desolate. There wasn't even a dog walker in sight, and the only sound was the roar of the sea on the other side of the island. A cold wind started to blow, and

Nora shivered. She should have brought a jacket; the temperature had dropped significantly.

The light had changed, too; big gray clouds hid the sun. Rain was on the way.

She increased her speed.

Should she have been honest with Jonas, told him where she was going instead of pretending she felt the need for a power walk? Then again, she only wanted to check that everything was OK at Fyrudden, have a quick word with Maria and Celia.

She'd soon be back home.

CHAPTER 81

Carsten pushed aside the pile of documents Anatoly had brought with him from Moscow.

The time had come.

He'd spent almost an hour reading through the densely written text, paragraph after paragraph detailing the transfer of ownership using a variety of legalistic terminology. Nothing was missing, everything was there, exactly as it should be.

Whenever Anatoly had tried to raise something, Carsten had held up his hand.

"Let me finish reading first."

It had grown darker, and the wind was howling around the little cabin.

Anatoly was standing with his back to Carsten, peering out the tiny window. His formal suit looked totally out of place in the sparsely furnished room. Every so often he checked his phone, but there was no service out here.

Carsten could sense his unease. Anatoly hadn't expected to travel so far into the archipelago, to a place where they were completely alone.

Carsten repeated the words silently to himself.

Completely alone.

We can reach an agreement here. No one can interrupt us, distract us, divert our attention.

The share transfer wasn't complicated, but Carsten had had to reread certain sections. Now and again his concentration wavered, the letters kind of jumped around in front of his eyes.

He couldn't allow himself to feel tired. He sat up a little straighter, pushed back his shoulders. He had to focus. He could sleep later, when everything had been put right.

He'd done one last line of coke a while ago. Just to be on the safe side. The document on the table would determine the rest of his life. It was essential to stay sharp. All that was needed to make the contract legally binding was his signature on the last page. The buyer had already signed.

According to the agreement, he was selling all of his personal shares in KiberPay to a company by the name of Pelagial Ltd, which was based in the tax haven of Guernsey, one of the British Channel Islands. As he'd expected, it was impossible to tell who was behind the company; "Pelagial" told him nothing.

Anatoly was still facing the window, where the paint had flaked off the wooden frame. Condensation had formed like a pale shadow on the glass, thanks to the kerosene lamp.

It's time, Carsten thought again. *Let's finish this.*

"Were you intending to double-cross me right from the start?" he said, taking care not to let his anger come through.

Anatoly spun around.

"What are you talking about?"

"When you offered me the additional block of shares—had you already decided to con me?"

Anatoly lifted his chin a fraction, then gave a nervous laugh.

"You're kidding, right?"

Carsten's face remained expressionless. "Answer me."

Anatoly spread his hands wide. "We've known each other . . . how long? It's almost fifteen years since we worked together in New York. You've met my family, I know your wife and children. We're old friends!"

"Answer the question."

Anatoly seemed to be searching for some hint of conciliation in those three short words. He gazed at Carsten for a long time.

"Why would I want to double-cross you?" he said eventually.

"I think you have plenty of good reasons. Sixty million dollars, for example."

"Sorry?"

"Sixty million dollars—the amount I could have gotten for my shares in KiberPay if we'd gone through with the stock market flotation in September. The value will probably double in two to three years."

Carsten pointed to the document.

"This offer doesn't even cover my original investment, never mind the interest on the loan that's due for repayment very soon. As you well know."

"Whether or not you sell is entirely your decision. Yours and yours alone. I told you that on the phone."

Carsten was unimpressed by Anatoly's attempt to sound pleasant and friendly. He knew that the Russian was thinking feverishly behind that calm façade.

But Carsten had already worked out exactly what had happened.

Anatoly must have persuaded Sergei to provide dubious figures for the Russian bank, which led them to postpone the flotation. Maybe Anatoly had promised Sergei a piece of the pie? Or convinced him that they needed to get rid of the Swede, keep the profits in Russia.

Carsten recalled Sergei's lack of enthusiasm when they'd discussed expanding the number of owners. At the time there had been no other option; in order to expand, they had to make a new issue of shares available, bring in more capital from overseas owners.

Now Sergei had seized the opportunity to change all that.

"You didn't think I could find out anything about the so-called client that Betekov & Partners were supposed to be representing," Carsten said.

Anatoly's face gave nothing away.

"In fact I do have my own sources," Carsten continued. "For example, how come your wife works for Betekov & Partners?"

He slammed his fist down on the table.

"How come? Explain that, if you can!"

As soon as he'd seen Irina Goldfarb's photograph on the legal firm's home page, any lingering doubts had disappeared. He didn't wait for an answer.

"You didn't think I'd bother to do my own research, did you? You thought I'd be so panic-stricken that I'd be prepared to sell at any price."

"You've misunderstood, Carsten," Anatoly ventured. "You've got it all wrong."

He sounded as if he were talking to a child.

"When did you decide to collude with Sergei? You knew I'd taken out a huge loan to buy the shares. You knew I was in deep shit." Carsten let out a bark of laughter. "I know exactly what's going on. My biggest mistake was trusting you. My so-called old friend."

"Carsten, stop. That just isn't true. Irina has nothing to do with any of this; there are over a hundred lawyers working for Betekov."

Carsten wasn't interested. "OK, so this is what we're going to do. You're going to amend the contract, correct the amount. When that's done, we can leave the island, and you and I will never have to see each other again."

"What do you mean?" Anatoly took a couple of steps toward Carsten.

"The contract is very well written," Carsten continued blithely. "Extremely professional, everything exactly as it should be. But it contains one major error. The sum of money is too low. Much too low."

He took out his pen and placed it on the document.

"There you go. All you have to do is change the amount. I want sixty million for my shares. Change the figure and add your initials to confirm the new agreement."

Beads of sweat had broken out on Anatoly's brow. He took a deep breath and looked Carsten in the eye.

"I can't do that, as you well know. The buyer has already signed. I can't alter it now."

Carsten picked up the pen and held it up in front of Anatoly's nose.

"Take it."

"What the hell is wrong with you? It's not possible to alter a signed contract. I can't take that back to Moscow!"

"Take the fucking pen!" Carsten said with such force that a globule of saliva landed on the other man's cheek.

Anatoly took the pen and put it down on the table.

"Listen to me, Carsten. I understand how disappointed you are over what's happened with KiberPay. So am I. I was convinced that everything would work out exactly as we'd planned. I've done all I could to get a better price for you, I swear on my life."

He pulled a handkerchief from his pocket and wiped his bushy eyebrows.

Carsten couldn't suppress a scornful grin, even though he'd been determined to maintain an ice-cool demeanor. How naïve did Anatoly think he was? He must have taken Carsten for a complete idiot. He pointed to the page where the purchase price was given in both figures and words.

"Change it to sixty million, then we can both get away before the storm comes. We can't stay here all night."

As if on demand, a broken branch crashed into the window. The wind howled all around the cabin; Anatoly didn't move until the eerie sound had died away. His pupils had contracted to tiny black dots.

"This is a waste of time, my friend."

"Change it to sixty million and I'll sign right away."

Anatoly's expression was sorrowful. "You're asking the impossible."

That look was more than Carsten could bear. He grabbed the pen and wrote in the new sum himself.

"There. All you have to do is endorse it with your initials. Go on."

"No, Carsten. I can't do that."

"Yes, you fucking can!"

Carsten's hand shot out, knocking the document to the floor. Papers flew in all directions. Anatoly got down on the uneven wooden floor and started scrabbling around, gathering them up with his slender fingers.

"We're leaving. This is pointless," he said over his shoulder.

Carsten was breathing heavily. A buzzing noise filled his ears, and a thick red mist descended before his eyes.

Don't tell me what to do.

"Can't we just sort this out like grown men?" Anatoly pleaded, still on his knees.

Carsten aimed a hard kick at his bowed head. It struck Anatoly's ear, and he crashed onto his side.

"I have no intention of allowing myself to be duped by you and your fucking friends!" Carsten said, kicking him again as hard as he could. This time the skin split, spattering blood all over the papers. Carsten couldn't stop; he kicked him over and over again, in the stomach, the shoulders, the back of the neck, the head. He kept on kicking him until he ran out of energy.

Anatoly was no longer moving.

He was lying facedown with the bloodstained papers fanned out around his head, a thin trickle of blood running from his ear.

"It's your own fucking fault," Carsten muttered breathlessly. He aimed one last kick at Anatoly's spine, then grabbed his jacket, blew out the kerosene lamp, and headed for the door.

Chapter 82

When Nora emerged from the forest, she saw that the house was in darkness. It looked as if no one was home. The sky had turned an ominous dark gray.

Please don't let it start raining before I get home.

Rapid changes in the weather weren't uncommon in the archipelago, but this had taken her by surprise.

She went up to the door. What would she say if Carsten opened it? She knocked and waited, but no one came. She decided to try around the side, see if she could make out any activity through the huge picture windows. It was significantly colder here; the wind was gusting, and the water was the color of lead.

Suddenly she saw a movement, and there was Sarah staring out at her.

"Hi there!" Nora waved, raising her voice above the sound of the wind. "Do you remember me? I'm Julia's mom. Is Maria home—or your mommy?"

Sarah's eyes were wide and serious.

"Can I come in, honey?"

There must be an adult in there with Sarah. Nora hoped it wasn't Carsten.

Sarah picked up a doll from the floor and disappeared. Nora tried the door leading to the terrace; it wasn't locked. Against her better instincts, she pushed it open and called out: "Hello? Anyone home?"

Silence. There were no lights on in the living room, but surely Sarah couldn't be in the house on her own?

"Hello? Celia, are you there? Maria?"

Should she go inside?

The wind seized the door and made the decision for her. Nora stepped in and closed it behind her.

"Is it OK if I come in?" She was uncomfortably aware that no one had invited her in.

Was that the sound of a door opening at the far end of the hallway? Nora was feeling more and more ill at ease, expecting Carsten to appear at any second. If he'd been unpleasant to her yesterday, he was unlikely to greet her warmly when he found her in his house.

She heard a faint voice.

"Who is it?"

"It's only me—Nora Linde, Julia's mom."

After a brief pause, Celia appeared in the living room. She was wearing enormous sunglasses, which seemed a little odd.

"Sorry to just come marching in," Nora said, wondering how to explain why she was there. *I found your nanny sobbing by the pool. Is everything OK?*

Celia was partly turned away, so Nora could only see her in profile. Her hair was lank, hanging over her face and the collar of her robe. Had she already gone to bed? It was only eight thirty.

Suddenly Sarah came running in behind her mother. Celia tried to stop her, but the little girl made straight for Nora.

"I'm hungry," she announced. "Can you make us something to eat? Mommy's not feeling very good."

Nora got a sinking feeling in her stomach. She crossed the living room.

"What's wrong?"

As she got closer to Celia, she almost gasped. The beautiful woman in the red dress who'd welcomed everyone to her party was a wreck. One side of her face was swollen and covered in a huge bruise. The sunglasses couldn't conceal the bandage over one eyebrow, and her lower lip was split.

"Jesus, what's happened?"

Celia swayed alarmingly.

Nora quickly tucked a hand under her elbow. "Come on, let's sit down and have a chat."

Celia didn't protest; she simply allowed herself to be steered over to the sofa, where she sank down. Silent tears began to flow.

"Where's Carsten?" Nora hardly dared ask the question; she felt slightly sick when she uttered his name.

"I don't know. He's taken the boat. I haven't seen him today."

"Where's Maria? Couldn't she help you?"

"She's left us."

Had Maria left Celia in this state? Now Nora understood why the girl had broken down by the pool, but walking away from Celia and the children at a time like this wasn't the right thing to do.

Celia was slurring her words, and she was still swaying.

Please don't faint.

"Have you eaten anything today?"

"No. I can't."

"Wait there. I'll get you a glass of water." Nora wondered why people always offered water in a difficult situation. As if that was going to fix things. She hurried over to the kitchen area, found a glass, and filled it with cold water. Her hands were shaking.

What a bastard.

She went back and held the glass to Celia's lips.

"Have a drink. It'll make you feel better."

When Celia reached for the glass, Nora saw the bruising on her wrist—livid marks left by four fingers and a thumb on the thin skin. She tried to think rationally, even though her heart was pounding.

She'd seen Sarah, but not the little boy.

"Where's Oliver?"

Celia tilted her head in the direction of a bedroom.

"In there."

"Have the children had anything to eat?"

"Some candy. I felt so bad, I just couldn't face cooking."

"Won't you take off your sunglasses so I can see how it looks?" Nora said gently. "And we need some light. Is that OK?"

Celia hesitated, then removed her glasses as Nora switched on the two lamps on either side of the coffee table.

The full horror was revealed.

The right side of Celia's face was black, blue, and yellow, and her swollen cheek gave her a clown-like appearance. She still had dried blood by her hairline and down toward her ear; strands of hair were stuck together with blood and plastered to her skin. Nora was aware of the slightly sweet smell of blood mingled with the smell of stale sweat. However, it was the fact that Celia was so groggy that worried her the most.

"You need to see a doctor."

"No. No doctor."

Celia had turned even paler, making the bruises still more grotesque. Nora gently stroked her hair, avoiding the injured side.

"Someone ought to take a look at you."

Celia blinked away her tears and clasped her hands tightly on her lap.

"Carsten will be angry . . ."

"You have to see a doctor. I think your eyebrow might need stitches, too, or you could be left with an ugly scar."

"You can't tell anyone about this." Celia grabbed Nora's arm, but her grip was as weak as a child's. "I'll be fine. I'll be better tomorrow."

Nora tried to think clearly. She wanted to call the emergency number right now, request the air ambulance, but could she do that against Celia's will?

"Promise you won't say a word to anybody!" Celia was on the brink of hysteria.

Nora made up her mind. No matter what Celia said, she was going to speak to Thomas and tell him what Carsten had done to his wife. But first she had to take care of Celia and make sure the children had something to eat. And she had to let Jonas know she'd be staying at Fyrudden.

Why hadn't she told him what she was planning to do?

One thing at a time, she said to herself, although it didn't help much.

"OK, I'm going to stay here and fix some dinner for the kids. But you have to see a doctor. That's nonnegotiable. There's a doctor I know here on the island—Andreas Brenner. He might be able to come over this evening."

Before Celia could protest, she added quickly: "Doctors are bound by a duty of confidentiality, so you don't have to worry about Andreas."

Celia was beginning to find it difficult to take anything in.

"I'm so tired," she murmured.

Nora didn't want to push her, in spite of her concerns.

"OK, why don't you go and lie down for a while? I'll see to Sarah and Oliver, and we can have a chat about the doctor later."

Celia didn't answer, but allowed Nora to help her to her feet and into the bedroom, where Oliver was curled up on the bed in front of the TV. His teddy bear was tucked under his arm, and he was sucking his thumb.

"Hi, Oliver," Nora said cheerfully. "Mommy needs a little rest. Why don't you come into the kitchen, help me make dinner for you and your sister?"

He didn't say a word, he just stared at Nora as she maneuvered Celia into bed. His silence and his frightened eyes made Nora want to weep. She tucked Celia in and stroked her damp forehead, which felt hot against her palm. Did Celia have a temperature?

She had to see a doctor, despite her objections.

"Everything will be OK," Nora said, doing her best to sound reassuring.

She lifted Oliver off the bed. He made no attempt to resist; he simply clung even more tightly to his teddy bear.

"Let's see what we can find for dinner!" Nora's smile wasn't returned. She was about to close the bedroom door when she heard Celia's voice.

"Nora?"

Nora went back to the bed. "What is it?"

"I saw Carsten earlier." Celia's words were almost inaudible. Nora crouched down and leaned forward in an attempt to hear better.

"This morning. With a gas can in his hand."

A tear formed on Celia's eyelashes, then slowly trickled down her swollen cheek.

"What are you talking about?" Was Celia becoming delirious?

"Carsten."

"What about him?"

"The fire, it was Agaton."

Nora inhaled sharply. "You mean Agaton started the fire?"

"That's what Carsten thinks."

"Then presumably he's spoken to the police."

Celia closed her eyes.

"Celia." Nora squeezed her shoulder gently. "What's Carsten planning to do?"

But Celia had already fallen asleep.

CHAPTER 83

Thomas was unlocking the door of the apartment on Östgötagatan. It was twenty to nine, and he'd spent the last hour wandering the streets and thinking.

Trying to make a decision.

What did he want to do with his life? Stay in the police service or move forward with something else? Keep trudging along the same familiar path or switch to a different track? It was time to make up his mind, but his evening walk hadn't provided any answers. There were just as many question marks as before.

Pernilla had called while he was crossing the square known as Medborgarplatsen. As soon as he answered, she'd handed the phone to Elin, but not even his daughter's cheerful voice could improve his mood.

He still hadn't mentioned Erik's proposal to Pernilla. If he told her, said it out loud, he would probably realize that it was too good to turn down.

His phone rang again: Aram.

"I've found some very interesting information on Gustav Kronberg. You ought to take a look at it."

His colleague sounded as eager as a terrier. Thomas wished he could summon up the same level of enthusiasm.

"Are you still at work?"

"Yes."

Thomas felt a sudden pang of guilt. He took his keys out of the door and set off down the stone steps. The car was parked on the corner, less than a hundred yards away.

"If you can wait fifteen minutes, I'll be there."

Aram appeared as soon as Thomas walked in.

"Thanks for coming."

Thomas followed Aram to his office and sat down in the visitor's chair. The glint in Aram's eyes revealed how pleased he was with the results of his research.

"OK, tell me what you've found."

Aram turned the computer screen around so that Thomas could see.

"Gustav Kronberg came from the archipelago. He grew up out there and lived on Sandhamn with his parents and sister until he was thirteen."

Thomas silently thanked Staffan Nilsson. The fingerprint on the lighter had led them in the right direction.

"He went to school on the island, but from the age of thirteen, children had to transfer to the mainland to continue their education. Gustav's parents decided to relocate. Their daughter was already boarding at the school, so the move meant she could become a day student."

Aram was a rock; he was carrying this investigation.

"Go on."

"Gustav started a program based around business studies, but dropped out after a couple of years. You know the rest. He got into drugs, went down for the post office robbery, died of a heroin overdose."

Aram leaned back, waiting for the obvious question. Thomas didn't disappoint him.

"So did you find a link between Gustav Kronberg and Per-Anders Agaton?"

"No, but I did find a completely different link. You said Nora mentioned that Carsten's father might have been posted to Sandhamn when he worked for the Customs Service; I decided to check it out."

Thomas should have done that himself, but he'd completely forgotten about it. As the glow of the desk lamp caught Aram's glasses, Thomas felt even guiltier. His colleague usually wore contact lenses, but this evening his eyes were bloodshot from a lack of sleep, so he'd had to resort to his glasses instead. While Thomas brooded over his own issues, Aram had discovered a key piece of the puzzle.

The hair shirt tightened around his shoulders.

"Do you realize that Carsten is exactly the same age as Gustav?" Aram said, dangling the bait in front of Thomas. "They were both born in 1975."

No, Thomas hadn't realized, but Aram's tone told him this was significant.

"In the mideighties, Carsten's father worked for the coast guard—that was before he started with the Customs Service. From 1986 to 1988 he was stationed on Sandhamn."

Very little happened by coincidence.

Thomas's phone rang; it was Nora. He rejected the call and switched the phone to silent. He would speak to her later.

"Carsten was eleven when they moved to the archipelago," Aram continued.

In other words, Carsten had lived on Sandhamn when he was a child. Nora hadn't known that, but she'd set them on the right track.

"So Carsten grew up on the island."

"No. They settled on one of the neighboring islands, Hagede."

Hagede, opposite Harö. Thomas could see it across the inlet, which meant the Jonsson family had been living right under his nose. Aram had certainly done his homework—and he wasn't finished yet.

"Carsten went to school on Sandhamn for two years, just like Gustav Kronberg. They were in the same class."

There was always a connection. Always. It was just a matter of finding it.

Thomas thought about snowflakes drifting down from the sky one by one until they formed a pattern. Tiny flakes that together became something else, something bigger.

"Do the Kronbergs still live in Stockholm?"

"No. The parents divorced after only a few years. The father moved to Norrland; he's on the electoral register in Haparanda. The mother still lives south of Huddinge."

We need to talk to her, Thomas thought. *Find out all we can about her son. There has to be an explanation for the fact that his lighter was found at Fyrudden.*

He instinctively felt that something was beginning to crystallize.

"You mentioned an older sister. Where's she now?"

Aram's gaze became even more intense.

"You've already met her: Linda Öberg."

CHAPTER 84

"Why don't you pick up?"

This was the third time Nora had tried to get ahold of Thomas. The first time the number had been engaged, then it went straight to voice mail. What the hell was he doing?

She put down the phone and turned her attention back to the frying pan. She'd found bacon and eggs in the refrigerator; they were sizzling away, but the familiar sound didn't make the situation any more normal.

The knot in her stomach was growing.

She hadn't been able to contact Andreas Brenner either, and she was seriously worried about Celia. If she didn't manage to speak to Thomas soon, she would have to call the emergency number, regardless of her promise to Celia.

Oliver was perched on a stool, following Nora's movements and still clutching his teddy bear. Nora chatted away, trying to distract him, but she could hear the strain in her voice.

"I bet you're as hungry as a wolf by now!" she said, reaching out to pat him on the cheek. Oliver recoiled so fast that her hand touched nothing but thin air. Nora focused on the pan, and a tear dropped onto one of the eggs.

The boy's silence was unnatural, and those big eyes never left her for a second. He was too little to have to experience all this.

Carsten had a lot to answer for.

Nora hoped the children hadn't been around when he beat up Celia, but she didn't dare ask them. Maybe Oliver had seen the whole thing; no seven-year-old should look or behave the way he did right now.

Carsten was tall, at least eight or nine inches taller than Celia, and a lot heavier. She wouldn't have stood a chance.

That swollen, discolored face . . .

Nora thought of Henrik and the terrible quarrel they'd had on the jetty some years ago. He'd struck her across the face, and she remembered her deep shock as she wiped the blood from her lower lip. That was the beginning of the end of their marriage, although Henrik had never done anything like that again and had apologized over and over.

Nora couldn't see how Carsten could ask Celia's forgiveness for what he'd done, nor how Celia would ever be able to feel safe with him in the future.

The recollection of how she'd been impressed by his extravagance just a few days ago made her despise herself.

The food was ready. She served it up on two plates, added some ketchup, and plastered on a smile.

Breathe, she thought, turning to Oliver.

"Can you fetch Sarah, sweetheart?"

She put the plates on the table and poured two glasses of milk. She felt like a robot. Then she picked up her phone again; she had to contact Thomas. And Jonas—darling Jonas, who would never even think of raising his hand to her.

Oliver sat down at the table, and Sarah clambered up onto her chair. She ignored the cutlery and began to eat with her fingers.

"Can you two sit here nicely while I make a phone call? Oliver, be a good boy and help Sarah if she needs a hand."

Nora went over to the door. If she spoke to Jonas, she'd have to explain the situation, and she just didn't have the time. Instead she sent a quick text:

Am at Fyrudden. Celia hurt. Will ring as soon as I can. Love N xx

Then she tried Thomas again.

Please, please pick up.

CHAPTER 85

Thomas's mouth went dry.

"Is Linda Öberg involved in all this?" he said, wondering why it hadn't occurred to him before.

"It looks that way."

Aram pushed a sheet of paper across the desk. Nora called again, but Thomas ignored her and stared at the document.

It was an extract from the electoral register. Date of birth and marital status for Linda Öberg. The years in which she'd married and divorced. The names of her parents and sibling. An entire life summarized in just a few lines.

"Her married name is Öberg, but her birth name is Kronberg. She's Gustav's older sister."

There are no coincidences.

"We'll bring her in tomorrow," Thomas decided. It was too late to contact her tonight; they didn't even know exactly where she lived. The address was only a box number; as on Sandhamn, there were no street names on the island of Runmarö.

"If she grew up on Sandhamn, she ought to know Per-Anders Agaton," Aram said.

Linda Öberg and Per-Anders Agaton. An unlikely duo.

The discovery of an old lighter wouldn't convince the prosecutor to charge either Linda or Per-Anders.

"What if she started the fire?" Thomas said slowly. "Why would she do that?"

"Either it was her own idea or someone else persuaded or forced her to do it."

Thomas found it easier to regard Per-Anders as the brains behind it all. He'd gotten the impression that Linda was pretty reserved, a woman who kept herself to herself.

Aram took off his rimless glasses, breathed on the lenses, then polished them with a gray cloth.

"You've been out there a lot more than I have. How far would they be prepared to go to get rid of an outsider?"

At least Agaton hadn't hidden his feelings toward Carsten Jonsson. Linda had been much less forthcoming; shouldn't her antipathy have been evident if she was prepared to commit arson?

Not if she was a skillful liar.

"Maybe Agaton has some kind of hold over Linda?" Thomas speculated. "Perhaps he was the one who made her apply for the job as housekeeper?"

"Did you manage to speak to Carsten, by the way?"

"Not yet."

After the interview with Mats Eklund, Thomas had tried to reach Carsten several times, but without success. He'd left a series of messages, but Carsten hadn't called back.

"No luck with the nanny," Aram said. "Her phone's switched off. I couldn't even leave a voice mail."

He got up and stood with his back to the open window. The sky was overcast, and it was beginning to grow dark, as if it were already fall rather than mid-July.

"Carsten Jonsson is deliberately staying out of the way," he went on. "I don't like it, especially in view of what Eklund told us."

Eklund had described his employer as crazy. The word had lodged in Thomas's brain, but he hadn't done anything about it.

"I'm wondering if Carsten is planning on doing something stupid." Aram turned and closed the window with unnecessary force.

They'd focused on the threat against Carsten—not the possibility that he might constitute a danger to someone else. Thomas glanced at his watch: after nine. There were no boats to Sandhamn at this hour.

"There's not much we can do until tomorrow."

Aram wasn't happy with that. "Maybe we ought to contact Agaton? Just to be on the safe side?"

Thomas's phone rang again. Withheld number. Could it be Carsten at last?

"Thomas Andreasson."

"Is that Nora Linde's friend Thomas?" a polite voice enquired in English.

"Yes . . . yes it is."

"Splendid. My name is Jonathan Smythe. Nora gave me your number and asked me to call you if I found out any more about Carsten Jonsson."

"And you have?"

"You could say that. I don't know how much Nora told you about the United Oil affair, but the small investors fared very badly in the aftermath. I discovered that one of them who lost a great deal actually went to see Jonsson."

"What happened?"

"When Jonsson was confronted with what he'd done, he lost his temper completely. Apparently he went crazy—we're talking about a serious assault. If others hadn't intervened, he'd have been in real trouble."

"Was he charged?"

"The police weren't involved. It was settled privately. I think he had to pay a lot of money to sweep it under the carpet."

The line crackled.

"Hello? Are you still there?" Thomas pressed the phone closer to his ear.

"Rumor has it that Jonsson had a drug problem back then," Jonathan Smythe continued.

Then the connection broke.

CHAPTER 86

The wind was strong now. Visibility had deteriorated, but Carsten knew exactly how to find his way back to Sandhamn even if the light went. The sky was thick with dark clouds, but it hadn't started raining yet. Perhaps the storm would pass.

That would suit him better.

The wind had changed direction, and the sea was against him, which meant that he had to reduce his speed. The crossing had taken longer than usual, but he would be there soon. Then he would take care of the final details. Deal with those who wanted to harm him.

He saw Agaton in his mind's eye. And Celia.

A huge wave came surging toward him; he cut the gas to counter the swell, but it still poured in over the prow and soaked his feet.

Maybe the salt water would wash away the bloodstains on his shoes.

The house at Fyrudden had been a mistake, he could see that now. He should never have returned to Sandhamn, but he was still proud of what he'd achieved. No one who saw that house could doubt his success.

With a practiced hand he steered through Korsö Sound and east of the island; that was the quickest way to the jetty. A light appeared, and he realized that the Svängen lighthouse was giving him a sign. The brief flashes were a secret signal, telling him he'd done the right thing in refusing to let himself be manipulated by Anatoly.

It had taken him some time to work out how everything hung together, but now he was in no doubt that it had all started much earlier than he'd suspected.

The "accident" in the parking lot.

Anatoly had already been trying to get to him back then. He'd somehow managed to persuade the insurance company to blame the explosion on a technical fault, but Carsten knew better. Anatoly had paid someone to sabotage the car. He'd been against Carsten right from the start.

And now Anatoly had gotten exactly what he deserved.

Carsten had nothing to reproach himself for.

The lighthouse flashed, and Carsten responded to its signal with a wave. He turned to check that the gas can was where it should be in the stern.

The outline of Sandhamn came into view, and he tightened his grip on the wheel.

The lights of the Sailors Hotel were unnaturally bright in the gathering darkness. The pine forest was nothing more than a shapeless mass, a black backdrop to the hotel's illuminated façade, but the little turret at the top glowed encouragingly at him.

It was almost nine thirty, although the dark sky made it seem much later. It didn't matter. The sooner night came, the better.

Carsten looked over his shoulder again. The can was definitely there, but he decided to swing by the gas station, pick up some more gas.

He had no intention of letting someone else take over the house at Fyrudden; it would be better to destroy it.

He had no intention of letting the children go either.

Chapter 87

When Thomas finally answered his phone, Nora almost wept with relief.

"It's me," she said, stumbling over her words. "I'm at the Jonsson house. Celia's been beaten up—she's in a bad way."

Everything came out in a slurred mess, but she couldn't help it.

"Nora, calm down. I can't understand what you're saying."

Nora took a deep breath. At that moment she wished she hadn't decided to come over to Fyrudden, then she wouldn't have had to see Celia's swollen face and Oliver's iron grip on his teddy bear.

She shouldn't think like that, but what she saw in this house was unbearable. She rested her head on the cold doorframe and tried to pull herself together.

"Did you say Celia's been beaten up? Do you know who did it?"

The sound of Thomas's voice made everything seem better, like cool water soothing a dry throat.

"It was Carsten. As I said, she's in a bad way. She needs help."

"Where's Carsten now?"

"I don't know, but his boat is gone."

"How are the children?"

The children.

Oliver was at the table, staring at his plate. He hadn't touched the food, presumably because he wasn't prepared to let go of his teddy in order to pick up his fork. At least Sarah was eating; she had ketchup all around her mouth.

"Not great. Sarah's OK, but Oliver's in shock. I don't think Carsten's done anything to them, but Oliver might have seen him attack Celia." She swallowed hard, took a deep breath, and continued.

"There's something else—something much worse."

"What do you mean?"

Thomas's brief questions calmed her. The police officer had taken over; he knew how to handle the situation. The words Celia had whispered came back to Nora.

"Before she fell asleep, Celia told me that Carsten blames Per-Anders Agaton for the fire." She couldn't remember exactly what Celia had said, but she knew Celia had been terrified; otherwise she wouldn't have made such an effort to warn Nora.

"It sounded as if he was intending to take his revenge," Nora said quietly, so that the children wouldn't hear.

"In what way?"

"She saw him with a gas can in his hand, and now he's disappeared."

Nora paused and took another deep breath. "After what he did to Celia, I think he's capable of anything. If you were here, you'd understand."

She could almost hear Thomas thinking feverishly.

"But you don't know where he is now?"

"No."

On the other end of the line, Nora heard a door opening, footsteps on the stairs, a voice in the background.

"Can you take Celia and the children to your place until we can get over to Sandhamn? So you're not there if Carsten comes back?"

"I can't move Celia. I've tried to get ahold of a doctor who lives here, but he's not answering. You need to send the air ambulance."

Her stomach muscles contracted as the impact of what Thomas had said hit home. Carsten could be a danger to everyone at Fyrudden. Including her. She had seen what he could do, the violence reflected in Celia's bruised and battered face.

"I'll try and contact the helicopter right away," Thomas said. "In the meantime, you need to make sure he can't get in."

"Do you really think he's planning on burning down Agaton's house?"

"I don't think anything. Lock all the doors and windows and take care of the children. I'll be there as soon as I can."

"OK."

"Call me immediately if he turns up—promise."

Chapter 88

Thomas was speeding up the highway with Aram beside him. The conversation with Nora had been like a bucket of ice-cold water poured over his head. A wake-up call.

The car tires squealed as he rounded the bend, but he didn't take his foot off the gas.

The police helicopter was picking them up from the helipad below Slussen, and the air ambulance was on its way to Sandhamn. It was going to be a rough journey; it was almost too windy to fly, but traveling by sea wasn't an option. It would take hours to get there that way.

A police launch had been called, but it was in Vaxholm.

"Per-Anders Agaton isn't answering," Aram said, putting down his phone.

"His wife said he rarely has his cell switched on, but surely they must have a landline?"

"I've already checked. Private number."

"Call Karin. There must be someone on duty at Telia who can override that."

Thomas stopped at a red light. They were almost there, but every minute was torture. It had taken forever to secure the helicopter, and they had to reach Sandhamn as soon as possible.

He hadn't heard from Nora and hoped that was a good sign.

Aram sent a text message to Karin.

"Try Agaton one more time," Thomas said as the lights changed.

Aram pressed "Redial," and against all expectation an authoritative voice responded.

"Per-Anders Agaton."

"This is Aram Gorgis from Nacka police. We spoke yesterday."

Aram explained the situation as concisely as possible.

"We have reason to believe that both you and your wife need to be extra vigilant over the next twenty-four hours."

We suspect that your neighbor is intending to burn down your house to get his revenge, Thomas added silently.

If they were wrong, then Carsten was being unfairly accused, but Thomas thought that what Nora had told him about Celia was sufficient cause for concern. Carsten was violent as well as ruthless. Thomas hadn't forgotten the enumeration of his activities in the UK.

It was as if he'd been swallowed up by the ground, but he must have gone off somewhere in the rib that had been moored by the jetty. It was both fast and expensive; Thomas was familiar with the model and knew its capacity. Carsten Jonsson could easily avoid being apprehended.

"It would be best if you spent the night elsewhere," Aram ventured. He was making a real effort, but Thomas could tell that Per-Anders wasn't prepared to listen.

"We're in the process of trying to locate Carsten Jonsson, but until we do, there's a risk that you and your wife could be in danger if you remain at home."

Per-Anders didn't seem to be taking the matter seriously at all. This was the third time Aram had tried to get his message across.

Do you think we're calling you for fun?

Thomas was driving way too fast, given that there was other traffic on the road.

"He's welcome to try," Per-Anders snapped so loudly that Thomas heard. "I have no intention of being hounded out of my house by that fucking waste of space!"

Aram held the phone away from his ear.

"It's Jonsson who doesn't belong in the archipelago. My family and I have lived here for years!" Per-Anders yelled. "He needs to keep away from us!"

Aram ended the call with a sigh.

Thomas understood the passionate attachment to the archipelago that lay behind the lawyer's rudeness. Unlike Carsten, he wasn't driven by a desperate need for affirmation. However, his reaction reminded Thomas of Carsten's on the day after the fire, when Thomas suggested that he and the family might like to check into the Sailors Hotel. His response had been just as blunt as his neighbor's: a flat refusal to leave his home.

Neither man was prepared to accept advice from the police.

"There's not much more we can do," Aram said. "At least he's been warned. We need to get there as fast as possible."

The clock on the dashboard clicked to 10:13 as Thomas turned off for the helipad, where the helicopter was waiting, its rotors already in motion. The pilot saw them and waved.

A black insect, about to take off.

"If only we knew where he's gone," Aram said. He didn't need to clarify who he was talking about.

"If he's out there in the rib, it'll be hard to find him."

"Not if he uses his cell phone."

"That won't help much."

Tracking the phone using the signals from transmission towers took time. It was relatively easy to map a person's movements using triangulation after the event, but difficult to establish his or her location at a specific moment. If the phone was switched off, it was impossible. Aram was grasping at straws, but Thomas couldn't blame him.

Forty minutes had elapsed since Nora's call. It would take at least another twenty to get there, however skillfully the pilot negotiated the strong winds. Which gave Carsten free rein for an hour, while Celia's condition deteriorated.

He should have read the signs, realized that Carsten would accuse his neighbor of having started the fire.

"He's dangerous," Thomas heard himself say and knew beyond all doubt that it was true.

"Shall we put out a call for him?" Aram asked, unfastening his seat belt even though Thomas hadn't yet parked the Volvo.

Nora's account meant that Carsten was already guilty of a serious crime. Arson would only make things worse, but that didn't matter to a man who'd already crossed the line.

"Do you think that'll help at this stage?" Thomas wondered if he was admitting his own sense of impotence. If he'd spent more time focusing on the investigation instead of his personal problems, they might have found the connection earlier.

The tension in Aram's jawline gave him the answer.

"Do we have any choice?" he shouted as he opened the door. "It seems as if Carsten Jonsson is capable of just about anything."

Thomas locked the car, and they both ran to the helicopter.

CHAPTER 89

Nora was checking on Celia more and more often. Her breathing was rapid and shallow; Nora couldn't tell whether she was asleep or had slipped into unconsciousness. One corner of her mouth was drooping slightly.

Nora tried to remember what she'd read about concussions. Didn't a hard blow to the head mean there was a risk of a brain hemorrhage? Was that why Celia had seemed so confused?

Her face was almost as white as the pillowcase, but the bruise seemed to be spreading. Or was it just Nora's anxiety that made it look worse?

Where was the helicopter?

The minutes crawled by. Nora did her best to occupy Sarah and Oliver; she read them a fairy tale, then put on a Disney movie she'd found on the shelf. Sarah was getting sleepy. Nora tucked her in at one end of the sofa with a pillow and a blanket. She didn't dare let the children out of her sight.

Immediately after her conversation with Thomas, she'd gone around the house locking the doors and checking that the windows were firmly closed. Then she'd switched on every light she could find. It was better than the long shadows in the corners, but on the other hand it meant that anyone could see in. She felt like a fish in an aquarium. If only there were curtains to draw, but there was nothing, not even blinds as in the bedrooms. The awnings outside provided protection from the sun, not privacy.

Suddenly Nora's phone began to buzz, and she gave a start. Oliver's eyes widened with fear, and she quickly reassured him.

"Everything's fine, sweetheart." She wished her nerves weren't quite so close to the surface. The slightest sound made her jump.

It was Jonas. Just the sight of his name on the display reminded her that there was a normal world where she actually belonged. She had a man who loved her, who would never think of hitting her.

"Hello?"

"Darling, is everything OK? You've been gone for hours."

His voice almost made her surrender to the tears burning behind her eyelids.

"Just a minute."

Nora got up from the sofa. She didn't want to frighten Oliver even more, but she had to explain the situation to Jonas.

"I won't be long, sweetheart," she whispered to the little boy. "You stay here. I'm just going to take this phone call. I'll be back very, very soon."

Oliver reached out and grabbed her sweater. Nora patted him on the cheek, and this time he didn't flinch.

"There's nothing to worry about, honey, I promise."

She went over to the front door so that Oliver could still see her, but turned her back and spoke quietly so that he wouldn't hear.

The strain was too much.

"Oh God, Jonas," she half sobbed.

"Nora, what the hell is going on?"

Where to start?

"It's Carsten. He's beaten Celia black and blue—she's in a terrible state. I'm waiting for the air ambulance to come and pick her up. That's why I haven't called."

Jonas inhaled sharply. "Are you OK?"

"Yes, but I'm worried that Celia might have a concussion or something. The kids are here with me, but it seems like ages since Thomas said the helicopter was on its way."

A sob fought its way through. Nora swallowed hard; she couldn't afford to lose it now. "I'm so sorry I didn't tell you I was coming here—that was so stupid of me."

"Doesn't matter. The main thing is that you're all right."

"I really am worried about Celia; I can't wake her, and the children are so scared."

"Do you want me to come over? I can be there in fifteen minutes on my bike."

Yes please, she wanted to say. *Please come!*

But Thomas had assured her that the helicopter was on its way, and someone had to take care of Julia.

"I'll be fine," she said shakily. "You stay there with Julia, and I'll be home as soon as the helicopter gets here. It shouldn't be long now."

"Are you absolutely certain?"

Nora caught sight of her hunched figure in the mirror, her terrified eyes.

"Yes." She straightened up. "Don't worry. I'll give Thomas another call."

"Look after yourself."

"I promise," she said, making a huge effort to sound positive rather than exhausted and afraid. She slipped the phone in her pocket and went to fetch a paper towel to blow her nose.

As she turned she happened to look out through the glass doors.

She almost stopped breathing.

The gray rib was moored by the jetty.

CHAPTER 90

There were several lights showing on the ground floor of Per-Anders Agaton's house, but the yard lay in darkness. The only sounds were the howling wind and the crashing waves.

It was even darker now; it was hard to make out Agaton's jetty.

Carsten was standing behind the thick trunk of a pine tree on the edge of the forest, with the gas can at his feet. He wondered if the Agatons were home.

Hopefully not; he didn't want anyone sounding the alarm and attempting to put out the fire before it had caught properly.

Stick to the plan, whispered a voice in his head.

His intention was to pour gas on the wooden wall of the veranda, the one facing the water. The wind was blowing in the right direction, so the flames should spread quickly. He would use the rest of the gas on the corners of the house. If he started a blaze in at least four places, there was no chance that the building could be saved in time.

A shiver of satisfaction ran down his spine. There was nothing wrong with his ability to analyze a situation. He was still capable of thinking clearly, even though he'd had only a few hours' sleep over the past four days.

They didn't appear to be home; he hadn't seen anyone while he'd been standing there. No one could stop him.

Carsten slid down into a sitting position with his back resting against a tree. After a minute or two he took out the hip flask from his inside pocket and took a few generous swigs. In seconds the warmth radiated throughout his body. It was his favorite brand, the one he always bought in London. Citrus and sherry notes lingered on his tongue, and for a moment he was sitting in his English library. He could smell his favorite leather armchair.

Nothing is more important than loyalty, he thought.

Celia didn't understand that. She wanted to take Oliver and Sarah away from him; she was poisoning his relationship with his children.

Nothing must come between him and those children.

He stretched out his legs, noticing a couple of brown stains on his right shoe. His pants were also spattered with blood.

If anyone found Anatoly, they would understand; the clause in the contract spoke for itself. His betrayal was right there in black and white.

Carsten rested his eyes without closing them. His body felt at ease, weightless; he couldn't even remember the sensation of being weary, exhausted. He'd wasted so many hours of his life sleeping. Why had he done that, when he was fine without it?

"So you dared to set foot on my property after all, you fucking asshole!" a voice bellowed behind him.

When Carsten twisted around, a powerful beam of light was shining straight in his eyes. At first he couldn't make out anything beyond the light, then it was lowered a fraction, and he saw Per-Anders Agaton with a large flashlight in one hand.

And an old axe in the other.

"Don't move," Per-Anders said, waving the axe around. "I found out what kind of man you really are."

Carsten got to his feet, as tense as a cat ready to pounce.

"Stand still! You come here with all your fucking money, and you think you can do whatever you like. Enough is enough—we don't want your sort on this island. Take your family and get out of here!"

The beam of the flashlight fell on the red gas can at Carsten's feet. The other man's eyes widened.

"Those cops were right—you've come here to burn down my house! Have you completely lost your mind?"

Clumsily he pushed the flashlight into his pocket and took out his cell phone.

"I'm calling the police. They can deal with you!"

He began to key in the number, keeping one eye on Carsten. When the hand holding the axe dropped a little, Carsten took his chance.

He threw himself sideways and grabbed the can. With a single sweeping movement he brought it up, striking Per-Anders with such force that he dropped both the axe and his phone.

"What the hell are you doing?" Per-Anders roared as Carsten swung the can again, this time making contact with his hip. The older man lost his balance; he dropped to his knees, and Carsten launched a fresh attack. With no hesitation, he raised the can high in the air and brought it down on Per-Anders's unprotected head as hard as he could.

There was a crunching sound as metal met flesh and bone, and Per-Anders collapsed. He made a gurgling noise and landed facedown. His fingers scrabbled among the pine needles for a few seconds, then . . . nothing.

Carsten dropped the can and bent over, hands resting on his thighs as he tried to catch his breath.

The bastard had been after him all along, just as he'd suspected. He felt a sharp pain in his abdomen; maybe he'd cracked a rib at some point. It hurt every time he took a breath.

He'd allowed himself to be taken by surprise. It was never going to happen again.

The night air was cold; he took shallow breaths to minimize the pain, and it was several minutes before he managed to straighten up and look around.

He could hardly see a thing; he used his cigarette lighter to provide a small amount of illumination. His hip flask glinted a short distance away, where he'd dropped it during the fight. Thank God it wasn't broken. He took several deep swigs and waited for the pounding of his heart to slow down.

Better now.

With a groan of relief, he sank to the ground and closed his eyes for a little while. His pulse rate was still too rapid, but the combination of alcohol and adrenaline eased the pain.

Rest for a while.

When he stumbled to his feet, Per-Anders Agaton was still lying facedown among the pine needles. Carsten nudged him with one foot, but there was no reaction. He kicked him several times; the body felt like a sack of cement.

The gas can was badly dented, but fortunately it hadn't sprung a leak. Carsten gave it a shake just to check, and it seemed fine.

There was more in the boat in any case.

The flashlight had fallen out of Per-Anders's pocket; it was still working, and when Carsten shone the beam around, he discovered the axe the old fool had been waving around. He picked it up; the blade was pitted with rust. He tested the weight and raised it above his head, preparing to face invisible enemies.

Everyone was against him. He had to defend himself.

When he turned around, the same lights were showing on the ground floor of the house.

Nothing's changed, the shadows whispered.

Carsten smiled and tightened his grip on the axe.

Then he set off toward the house with the gas can in one hand and the axe in the other.

CHAPTER 91

The noise inside the helicopter was deafening. Thomas was at the front next to the pilot, with Aram behind him.

"You need to land on the south shore," Thomas told the pilot over the radio. "We're heading for the new house at Fyrudden—you'll see the jetty."

The pilot gave him the thumbs-up. The lights of Sandhamn became visible; they would be there in minutes.

A strong gust of wind made the helicopter tilt slightly, and Thomas automatically tensed his stomach muscles.

His cell phone buzzed—a brief message from Nora. He saw that he had several missed calls, also from Nora. With a deep sense of unease, he read the few short words.

Think Carsten's here, his boat is back. Where are you?

He turned to Aram and showed him the text.

"So he's back on the island," Aram said via his own headset. "Have you heard anything from the police launch?"

"No, but there's no chance they'll get there before us."

Thomas sent a quick message to Nora even though the coverage wasn't great.

Almost there, you should be able to hear the helicopter soon.
Stay safe!

They had turned now and were flying toward Sandhamn's western
headland. Not far now. Thomas could already see the beam of the lighthouse on Skötkobben.

The helicopter shook and listed in the strong wind. Thomas rarely
felt seasick, but right now his stomach was beginning to protest. The
white-capped waves surged down below, and the curved windshield
seemed to offer inadequate protection from the worsening weather. An
unexpected bout of turbulence didn't help matters. He did his best to
keep his eyes fixed on the horizon straight ahead.

"Is that the house you mean?" the pilot asked, pointing to a rooftop
beyond the trees.

"That's the one."

Thomas could make out the jetties; the helicopter had lowered
its altitude now. Something reddish-orange beneath them caught his
attention.

"Hang on a minute."

He craned his neck to get a better view. Among the black shadows
on the ground, he caught a glimpse of a strange glow.

Another fire?

"What's that?" he said, pointing. Aram turned his head. "Over
there on the left, just before Jonsson's house," Thomas added.

Aram's sharp intake of breath confirmed Thomas's own fears.

"Can you go around so I can take another look?" he asked the pilot.
She, too, had seen the glow by this stage.

She moved in closer. "Do you think it's a fire?"

They could see the house now, and Thomas realized it was Per-
Anders Agaton's place.

Shit.

It looked different from the air, but there was no doubt in his mind.

The pilot had flown in a wide arc, and they were now approaching the front of the property from the other side.

The flames were clearly visible, shooting out from the veranda and climbing up the façade, licking the windows and changing the color of the white frames.

"Jesus!" Aram shouted.

Thomas was staring so hard that his eyes ached. It had to be Jonsson. Who else could it be?

Judging by the size of the flames, the fire hadn't yet caught hold. Which meant it had been set very recently. Was Jonsson still there? They had to land on the shore. Right now.

"Take her down," he said to the pilot.

"What? Here?"

"Wherever you like. Just take her down now."

Aram echoed Thomas's thought. "Do you think Carsten's still there?"

Thomas was calling the fire service.

"Contact the police launch, check where they are," he said to his colleague. "Tell them it's urgent; they have to get here as fast as they can, whatever it takes."

The helicopter swept over the house as the pilot searched for a place to land. From this angle the strip of shore seemed much too narrow to allow them to come down safely.

I hope she knows what she's doing.

The flames were taking hold now. They'd already reached the top of the ground floor windows and were spreading to the upper story with alarming speed.

The shower of sparks glowed brightly against the night sky.

If only they'd arrived half an hour earlier.

CHAPTER 92

Nora went around turning off the lights; she didn't dare have them on if Carsten was creeping around in the shadows outside. It was better to wait in the darkness, however frightening that might be.

At last she heard the sound of the approaching helicopter.

Thank God—she couldn't hold out much longer.

The throb of the engine grew louder, then fainter. Nora crept over to the window and peered out. She could see flashing lights, a silhouette above the treetops—but surely it was heading in the wrong direction?

No, no! It was coming down over by the Agatons' house.

She wanted to shout at the top of her voice: *Wait! That's the wrong house! We're here, this is where you're meant to be!* But she knew it was pointless; no one would hear her. What now? Her shirt was sticking to her skin, she could feel the tension in her jaw.

Oliver had fallen asleep beside his sister on the sofa. Celia was still in bed, her breathing rapid and shallow.

The lights of the helicopter disappeared behind the tall pine trees, and Nora realized it had landed on the other side of the headland. The pilot must have somehow misunderstood.

Nora felt like crying. She had to get some help for Celia. There was no point in calling Thomas; she'd tried several times, but he hadn't picked up. The thought that the helicopter might take off again at any minute was unbearable.

The children were fast asleep. They wouldn't notice if she ran over to the Agatons' place, it wouldn't take long.

She tried not to think about the fact that Carsten might be out there.

It's not me he's angry with.

With one last glance at Oliver and Sarah, she set off.

Thomas opened the door of the helicopter and ran as fast as he could, with Aram right behind him.

A dull explosion made him jump. The glass had begun to shatter, and the flames were now shooting out through every window on the ground floor as the fire grew stronger with each second.

The heat was intense. Was anyone still inside? There was nothing they could do until the fire service arrived. The front door was burning, and the veranda where they'd sat the previous day was filled with smoke.

Thomas looked around but couldn't see anyone moving outdoors, no broad-shouldered figure lurking in the darkness. His eyes watered as he tried to spot Carsten behind the billowing clouds of smoke.

"He has to be here somewhere," Aram said.

The burning wood crackled. Thomas felt his heart race. "Where the hell has he gone?"

CHAPTER 93

The wind struck Nora full in the face as soon as she stepped outside. A cold, damp wind that tore at her clothes. She glanced at the jetty, hoping the rib wouldn't be there. She didn't want to see it tugging at the mooring lines, shouting out that Carsten was back on the island.

But there it was, its dark gray rubber hull bobbing up and down.

The metal lines on the flagpoles clanged in the wind. The shore was deserted, but a tarpaulin covering the woodpile had come loose, and was flapping wildly.

Nora tried to shake off her fear of crossing Carsten's path. She peered into the darkness, trying to find the track that led to the Agatons' place. She used the light on her phone to help, then set off to the west, moving as fast as she could.

After a hundred yards or so she saw the glow up ahead. As she got closer she could see the orange flames reaching into the sky, and the acrid smell of smoke filled the air.

It was like a punch in the stomach. Another fire. The Agatons' house was on fire.

This was exactly what Celia had tried to tell her. Carsten had taken matters into his own hands, and no one had managed to stop him.

A wave of nausea came over Nora; she bent over and threw up. With her hands clutching her belly, she rocked back and forth. She retched again but nothing came up.

The smell brought her back to reality. The fire was getting stronger, and smoke was beginning to drift through the forest.

She had to get help before the blaze spread.

Olle Granlund was one of Sandhamn's voluntary firefighters. She searched the contacts list on her phone for his number, but she couldn't see properly because of the tears in her eyes. She knew his name was there, why couldn't she find it? She started to scroll up and down, almost hysterical by now.

At last—there it was!

Please answer. Someone has to answer my call this evening. Please, Olle.

"Hello?"

"There's a fire," Nora gasped. "The Agatons' house on the south shore is on fire. You have to come."

"We've already been called out—we're on our way. Speak to you later, Nora."

The strength drained from Nora's body, and she had to lean on a tree to stop her legs from giving way.

The smoke was thicker now; she could feel it entering her lungs, and the taste of ash was in her mouth.

She knew she had to keep going, get to the helicopter, find someone to take care of Celia.

But the fire brought old memories flooding back.

Nora had once been locked inside Grönskär Lighthouse and had almost died. She'd started a fire in the lantern room in order to attract attention, but she'd been convinced her life was going to end there. The same fear pulsated through her body now with such force that she could hear it throbbing in her ears.

She wiped her cheek and realized she was crying.

Sorry, Celia, she thought, squeezing her eyes tight shut. *I can't do it, I can't go and get help for you.*

The sound of a twig snapping underfoot made her open her eyes. She was no longer alone in the forest.

Someone else was moving through the trees, striding away from the Agatons' property and heading straight for Nora. She peered into the gloom and saw a man coming toward her. He was walking fast and purposefully, swinging something in one hand.

She knew immediately that it was Carsten; there was no mistaking his white-blond hair. In a few seconds she would be face-to-face with him.

In spite of the fact that she felt like throwing up again, she crouched down behind a broad tree trunk and tried to make herself as small and invisible as possible, arms wrapped around her body.

She just prayed that he hadn't seen her. She sat perfectly still, fear clawing at her throat.

Her lips began to move of their own volition.

Angels bless and angels keep,
Angels guard me . . .

Carsten was only yards away from her on the narrow track. He seemed to be holding some kind of metal object; it glinted as he passed her hiding place. Was it an axe?

Then he was gone.

In spite of the fact that Nora's panic-stricken breathing should have been audible for miles, he hadn't spotted her.

Carsten was heading home.

Celia and the children were alone in the house.

Nora gripped her phone so tightly that her fingers hurt. She had to call Thomas.

CHAPTER 94

"Thomas," Nora breathed into her phone. "He's here. Carsten's here."

Thomas was on the side of the Agatons' property that faced the sea, searching the woodshed by the jetty with his gun in his hand. It was dark and hard to see properly; it seemed unlikely that Carsten would have hidden in there, but he had to check.

"Where are you?"

"In the forest, a few hundred yards from Carsten's house. I'm hiding, but Celia and the children are still in there."

Thomas had already put away his gun and started to run. He beckoned for Aram to follow him and shouted over the roar of the fire: "He's on his way home! Let's go!"

They ran as fast as they could. Thomas stumbled over tree roots more than once, and a branch scratched his face before he could duck.

The dark bulk of the house rose up before them; the only light was a faint glow from the living room. Thomas stopped at the edge of the forest and held up his hand. Aram joined him, gasping for breath.

"So where is he?"

"Nora said he was heading this way. She saw him a few minutes ago."

"Thomas," Nora said quietly from behind him.

"Do you know if he's gone indoors?"

Nora shook her head. "I've no idea where he is."

"Is the front door locked?"

"No. I could lock it from the inside, but I don't have a key to lock it from the outside."

Thomas placed a reassuring hand on her shoulder.

"I want you to stay here. We need to go into the house, but you can't come with us. OK?"

Nora nodded.

"Good. Stay here until I call you."

Thomas drew his gun once more and turned to Aram, who was also armed.

"We can't wait for backup if Celia and the children are in there," Thomas said, as much to himself as to Aram.

A sudden gust of wind parted the clouds, and a thin moonbeam shimmered on the surface of the sea. The glow from the fire lit up the sky to the west.

Thomas moved silently toward the front door.

"On three," he mouthed. He counted one, two, three, then yanked the door open.

The hallway was empty. They continued into the house, trying to ascertain the layout. The children were tucked up on the sofa at the far end of the huge living room. The only light came from a lamp on the table nearest the little girl.

They were sleeping, which had to be a good sign.

"Do you think he's here?" Aram whispered.

Thomas listened intently. He could hear the faint hum of the refrigerator, but nothing else. In the half-light contours dissolved, furniture and ornaments became vague shadows, perspective was distorted.

"I don't know."

They couldn't tell whether Carsten had come inside or not. This was a big house, and they'd spent very little time here. Thomas was having difficulty orienting himself.

There was a fine sheen of perspiration on Aram's brow, and Thomas knew he was sweating, too.

A faint smell of gas drifted by. Thomas's stomach contracted.

"He must be here," Aram said quietly.

Thomas took a step toward the nearest door.

"I'll take this hallway, you go that way."

CHAPTER 95

Aram crept past the sofa as quietly as he could. The small lamp enabled him to see where he was going, but when he reached the hallway, the gray stone floor swallowed what little light there was.

The smell of gas grew stronger.

Silently he approached the first door and opened it quickly, ready to find himself face-to-face with Carsten Jonsson. Instead he saw a bedroom with blue curtains. A few toy cars were scattered across the floor, along with a fire engine.

Aram moved on.

His palms were sweating now; he tightened his grip on his gun.

The sand on the soles of his shoes was crunching much too loudly.

Next door.

He placed his left hand on the handle, took a deep breath, and flung it open with enough force to take anyone lurking inside by surprise.

This time the curtains were pink.

Only one door remained, at the far end of the hallway. That must be the parents' room, where Celia was.

Something had dripped on the floor outside. Aram felt a surge of adrenaline as he tried to think clearly.

Had Carsten gone looking for his wife? Was he waiting in the bedroom, ready to start a fire?

Aram stopped and listened, but couldn't hear anything. Thomas was still searching the other hallway, but he would have called out if he'd found Carsten.

So Carsten had to be behind this door if he was still in the house.

His heart pounding, Aram raised his gun and positioned himself to the side of the doorframe. He could hardly see; it was as if the tension was clouding his vision.

Silently he counted to three, kicked open the door, and looked straight into Carsten's staring eyes.

He was standing on the far side of the bed with a heavy axe in his hand. As soon as he saw Aram, he raised it above his head.

Between them lay Celia, eyes closed, her face as white as a corpse.

The stench of gas was overwhelming.

"Drop it or I'll fire!" Aram yelled, pointing his gun at Carsten's chest.

No reaction. Carsten's eyes were bloodshot, the pupils dilated. There was blood on his white polo shirt and his pale-blue jeans.

He's killed Per-Anders Agaton, Aram realized in a fraction of a second. He heard Thomas come rushing in behind him.

"Final warning!" Aram bellowed.

Then everything happened at lightning speed.

Carsten took a step forward and swung the axe.

"Drop it!" Aram shouted again, firing his service weapon at the same time. He lowered the barrel at the last second. The sound of the shot echoed around the room. Carsten's body jerked as the bullet hit his thigh, and the axe fell from his grasp.

Blood was pumping from the wound. The noise had woken the children, who started crying in the living room.

Only Celia hadn't moved, in spite of the deafening report and the blood spattering the bedclothes.

Carsten stared down at his leg, then slid soundlessly onto the floor with his back to the wall.

Blood continued to bubble through his jeans, spreading across the pale carpet like a red river. Aram stared at the gun in his hand.

Thomas was the first to react.

He moved the axe out of Carsten's reach, then grabbed a pillow and pressed it against the wound. Carsten was still staring at the blood; his breathing was shallow, his face almost as ashen as Celia's.

The children were screaming hysterically in the background.

"Aram, help me before he bleeds out! We need some kind of tourniquet."

There was a strange ringing noise in Aram's ears. He couldn't take his eyes off the gun in his hand—was the barrel still smoking?

"Aram! Find me something to wrap around his leg—now!"

Thomas was pushing the pillow down as hard as he could, using his own body weight, but the pressure from the femoral artery was too great.

"I can't stop the bleeding," he panted.

Aram looked around blankly, then he spotted a robe at the foot of the bed.

The belt.

He tore it free, and together he and Thomas wound it around the pillow and Carsten's thigh. Thomas pulled as hard as he could, and they raised the leg.

At last the blood stopped pumping. The flood became a trickle that slowly died away. The white belt was stained red, but it had served its purpose.

Carsten's eyes closed, and his head fell sideways as he went into shock.

Suddenly the room was bathed in a harsh white light.

The police launch had arrived at the jetty.

Chapter 96

Karin stuck her head around the doorway of Thomas's office.

"She's in room one."

"Thanks."

Thomas finished his coffee. His body was aching with weariness, but he couldn't put off the interview with Linda Öberg.

He hadn't left Sandhamn until two o'clock in the morning. The crime scene had been a constant procession of paramedics coming and going. The air ambulance had landed, and backup had arrived with the police launch.

Carsten and Celia had been transported to the hospital, while Nora had taken the children home with her.

Poor kids, Thomas thought, running a hand through his tousled hair. Their father would be in jail for a long time, and their mother's condition was still giving cause for concern.

He stood up with a sigh and put on his jacket. Margit was waiting in the hallway. Aram was already being questioned by Internal Affairs.

Linda was slumped on the chair when they entered the room. Her face was literally gray, reminding Thomas of the color of ash after the previous night's fire.

Per-Anders Agaton's house had burned to the ground. Fortunately his wife hadn't been home, but Per-Anders's body had been discovered not far away.

"Do you understand why you're here?" Margit began.

Thomas recognized the tactic and knew it expressed a silent hope on Margit's part that Linda would give them sufficient information to enable them to move on—an opening, because they didn't yet know how everything hung together. His ears were buzzing, and he was very glad that Margit had taken the lead.

"How's Celia?" Linda asked quietly.

"She's in the hospital. She suffered a subdural bleed when Carsten beat her up."

"Is she going to die?"

"No, but it's going to take her a long time to recover."

"Carsten's a pig." Linda lowered her head. "I never meant for Celia to get hurt."

Linda's words could only be interpreted as some kind of confession—but exactly what had she just confessed to?

Margit nodded sympathetically. "I can understand that. Why don't you tell us what happened?"

Linda looked as if she was on the verge of tears. She pressed her hands to her mouth for a moment, then she began to explain.

It had all started with the ad Carsten placed in the local newspaper. The opportunity sounded promising, and Linda and Carsten had met on Sandhamn when he came over to inspect the building project. She'd been delighted to get the job.

"I didn't recognize him at first—I mean, it was such a long time ago. He's much slimmer now, and he doesn't wear glasses anymore. Plus he's changed his name."

"Sorry?" Thomas said.

"He used to be called Lars—Lasse."

It was exactly as Nora had suspected. Maybe Jonsson had started using his middle name in order to stand out from the crowd. Lasse Jonsson was pretty ordinary. Carsten Jonsson, however—that was a name to remember.

"Then I realized who he was," Linda continued. "It took a while, but eventually I knew he was the same Lasse who'd been my brother's classmate."

"Were you at the school on Sandhamn with the two of them?" Margit asked.

"No. By the time Lasse—or Carsten—started, I'd already moved to boarding school."

Linda suddenly lifted her chin.

"That man destroyed my brother's life."

"What makes you say that?"

Thomas gazed at Linda as he tried to work out how everything hung together. The arson attacks, an abused wife, a neighbor who'd been beaten to death. Was Linda the catalyst for all of it?

"Carsten was a bully," Linda said. "He made Gustav's life a misery, took away every last scrap of self-esteem. Gustav never got over it."

Children could be horrible to one another.

"Why didn't the teacher step in?" Margit said.

Linda shrugged.

"You tell me. Maybe he didn't see what was going on, or maybe he just decided that boys will be boys, and it was only 'a game.'" She drew quotation marks in the air with her fingers. "It was a game that resulted in split lips, bruises, having his face pushed into snow that a dog had peed on, and having dog shit stuffed in his schoolbag."

Linda was talking to herself as much as to the two detectives. It sounded like a recital she had voiced many times in her head. The words carried her own sense of guilt, painful memories that had kept her awake during countless long nights.

"The physical bullying wasn't the worst of it," she added. Her tone of voice made Thomas think of a sleepwalker for some reason. "It was the relentless psychological campaign of terror that went much deeper. Gustav never felt safe; he could be attacked at any moment. Sandhamn is a small island; there was nowhere to hide."

It was as if a switch was flicked off inside Linda.

"I wasn't there to protect him. I was on the mainland."

"But then your family moved from Sandhamn," Thomas prompted her.

"And things went downhill fast. Gustav started dabbling with drugs in high school. Mom thought everything would be OK when we left the archipelago, but it was too late. She blamed my dad, said we'd stayed too long. He was the one who didn't want to go; he loved the archipelago, even though it was Mom who came from the island."

Thomas remembered that the parents had divorced only a few years later.

"I don't understand," Margit said. "Why didn't your parents take the matter up with the school if things were so bad?"

Thomas knew her well enough to pick up on her unease.

"I think Mom tried. She definitely spoke to Carsten's parents, and Carsten took a real beating from his father. He was a violent man. You can guess who suffered next day in school. There was no improvement."

"So you decided to avenge your brother?" Thomas said.

He could see the deep lines etched by grief on Linda's face. He'd thought her skin was weather-beaten, but now he realized that wasn't the case at all. It was all about the brother she'd tragically lost.

"It wasn't about revenge."

"So what was it about?"

"Justice."

Linda rubbed her forehead as if she wasn't sure how to explain.

"It wasn't fair," she said after a while. "Gustav was dead, and there was Carsten, moving into his fine house with his family. Everything was top quality. Celia had such lovely things, such beautiful jewelry; the closets were full of designer clothes. It made me sick to think that Carsten could come back that way. He didn't even seem to feel guilty about what he'd done; it was as if he didn't care at all."

"Maybe he didn't know?" Margit ventured.

Linda gave a contemptuous snort. "Does that make it any better?"

No.

"So when did you decide to take . . . action?" Thomas asked. He'd intended to say "take your revenge," but changed his mind at the last second.

Linda wrapped her arms around her body.

"I was on Sandhamn one evening in June. It was a weekend, so none of the builders were on site. I had to deliver something to Fyrudden, and it was so beautiful."

Her eyes shone with unshed tears.

"It was pretty late and still chilly, as it can be in June. But the sky was perfectly clear, and just . . . endless; it was twilight, everything was pale blue. The air was filled with the scent of lilac."

She ran a finger under her eyes.

"It was so unfair. The house was almost finished, and I could see how fantastic it was going to be. I hated the fact that Carsten would soon be moving in with his family, while my brother was . . ."

Margit pushed a box of tissues across the table.

"So I picked up a big stone and threw it at their bedroom window. I don't know why; it felt right. I wanted him to disappear, leave the island, and never come back. I had to do something."

Linda took one of the tissues and blew her nose.

"Was it you who left the dead bird on the steps?" Thomas asked.

Linda looked down at her hands; the cuticles were dry and cracked.

"It had gotten caught in my fishing net. When I lifted the net, it was almost dead, and one wing was broken. The idea just came to me. I had to put it out of its misery anyway, so I took it to Fyrudden."

"To frighten the family?"

"They didn't belong on Sandhamn. I wanted Carsten gone . . ."

The lines of sorrow around her mouth deepened.

"He had no right to come back. Not after what he'd done to Gustav."

"Was that why you decided to set fire to the guest lodge?" Margit was taking a chance, but Linda nodded.

"In the end, I couldn't sleep at night. I lay there, thinking about Gustav, hour after hour. The state he'd been in over the last few years, so gaunt and kind of . . . eaten away. Do you know what a heroin addict looks like toward the end?"

Linda reached for another tissue and blew her nose again.

"You've seen how Carsten treated Celia. A leopard never changes its spots. Why should he always get what he wanted?"

The bitterness in her voice revealed the sense of impotence she'd carried for so long. Both Celia and Linda's brother had found themselves in Carsten's shadow, and both had fared very badly.

It wasn't fair, but that didn't mean it was OK for Linda to take the matter into her own hands.

"Tell us more about the fire," Thomas prompted her. "We found your brother's cigarette lighter at the scene—with his fingerprints on it. Did you use it?"

Linda sighed.

"I just wanted to make them go away. Scare them so they didn't feel they could stay at Fyrudden. Using Gustav's lighter felt like the right thing to do."

She gripped Margit's arm.

"I had no idea there was anyone inside the lodge. You have to believe me. I'm no murderer."

Thomas knew instinctively that she was telling the truth, but it didn't help. A man had lost his life because of Linda Öberg, not to mention all the subsequent developments.

"So you set fire to the guest lodge to frighten them, make them leave the island," he summarized.

"Yes, but it was never my intention to kill anyone, I swear it. All the builders were meant to go home for the weekend. They weren't supposed to be around."

Linda slumped in her seat.

"He shouldn't have been there," she whispered.

Margit poured a glass of water and passed it to Linda. She waited until Linda had taken a few sips, then asked, "Why did you choose that particular evening?"

Linda's face was gray, her lips thin and bloodless. Thomas hoped she wasn't going to collapse before they were done.

"I stayed late because I'd been helping out with the party. The family had gone to bed. The party had been so extravagant; somehow that made everything worse."

"Had you planned it in advance?"

"No. I don't know where the idea came from; it just popped into my head when I was about to get in my boat and go home. There was lots of lighter fluid left over from the barbecues the caterers had used at the party. I always carried Gustav's lighter with me in its own little leather case. I'd kept it all those years; it was almost all I had left of him."

A random twist of fate, Thomas thought. As so often happened. No meticulously worked out plans, no evil intent. Just pain and grief and hatred that had festered for years.

And an opportunity that unexpectedly presented itself.

"What did you do afterward?" Margit asked.

"I went home. It didn't feel real, somehow. I almost believed I'd imagined the whole thing—at least until I came back the next day and saw the charred ruins, the smoke still rising into the air. That was when I found out someone had died."

Linda swallowed hard.

"I've felt so bad since then. It never occurred to me that Carsten would blame Per-Anders for starting the fire."

"How do you know he did?"

"I heard him talking to Mats Eklund the day before yesterday. Carsten was furious. I was terrified, but there was nothing I could do without revealing the truth."

Linda hid her face in her hands.

"I couldn't tell Carsten I was responsible for the fire."

She began to weep.

"I know the Agatons' house burned down last night. I know Per-Anders is dead. It's my fault, it's all my fault."

Chapter 97

It was two o'clock in the afternoon, and the team had gathered in the meeting room. Thomas and Margit had summarized the interview with Linda Öberg, telling their colleagues how Gustav had been bullied and about Carsten and his violent father. A vicious circle that had begun in a small school on Sandhamn.

"Linda is devastated," Margit said. "She swears she had no idea there was anyone inside the guest lodge."

"Will she be charged with arson?" Karin asked.

"I assume so."

Margit put down her pen and rotated her neck and shoulders.

"She started a fire that endangered both life and property, plus of course it could have spread. The question is whether the prosecutor decides to charge her with manslaughter, in which case she'll be in jail for a long time."

The sentence could be eighteen years, or even life. The minimum was six years.

Linda had been allocated a public defender who would no doubt argue strongly for the lesser offense.

Margit held up a sheet of paper.

"There's something else. The maritime police received a call about a badly beaten man in a cabin on an islet near Björkskär, which isn't far from Sandhamn. He appears to have been lying there since yesterday, and he's in a very serious condition. His name is Anatoly Goldfarb, and he's a Russian citizen."

Thomas looked up. Nora had mentioned Carsten's Russian business affairs.

"There was a pile of bloodstained documents beside him," Margit continued. "Carsten Jonsson's name was on several of these documents, and a pen was found with his name engraved on it." She paused briefly. "That means we're opening a new case of attempted homicide."

Someone else will have to take that on, Thomas thought. He needed to go home and sleep. His arm felt so heavy he could barely lift his coffee cup.

"We'll need to interview Carsten as soon as he's sufficiently recovered," Margit said. "CSI is examining the scene right now."

"Any news from the hospital on Carsten?" Kalle asked.

Margit frowned.

"I've spoken to both the emergency psych team and intensive care several times. The suggestion is that he may have suffered a psychotic episode, which can be triggered by extreme stress, an acute lack of sleep, and a combination of drugs and alcohol."

"That's some cocktail!" Karin exclaimed.

Thomas could actually see a new thought occur to Margit.

"If he had some kind of showdown with Anatoly Goldfarb, that could explain it," she said, making a note. "I'll pass the information on to the hospital."

She gave Thomas and Aram a grateful look. "The question is how things would have ended if you hadn't managed to stop him."

Thomas remembered Carsten's eyes as he stood over Celia, clutching the axe. That was a man who'd lost his grip on reality, but they would never know whether he'd really intended to attack Celia and burn down the house or whether he just felt the need to defend himself against the police. Somehow Thomas hoped it was the latter, for Celia's sake.

"What did Internal Affairs have to say, Aram?" Margit asked.

Aram was also pale with exhaustion, and he was wearing his glasses again.

"They want to talk to me again tomorrow."

Margit gave him an encouraging smile. "I can't see there being any problem, but you know how these things work."

She turned to Thomas. "Your statement confirms Aram's account."

Thomas had already completed his report.

"Sounds like self-defense to me," Margit concluded.

Thomas's phone vibrated in his pocket. He glanced at the display: Erik again. He rejected the call, but promised himself that he'd get back to Erik later that afternoon.

It was time to give him an answer.

Chapter 98

Nora was curled up on the sofa on the glassed-in veranda with a fleecy blanket over her legs. It was five o'clock in the afternoon. A light drizzle had been falling for the past few hours, but she didn't mind; it was nice to be cozy indoors.

She was still exhausted after the events of the previous night; she didn't have the energy to play with Julia or read a book. She couldn't sleep; every time she closed her eyes, she was back in the forest, with Carsten striding toward her, carrying an axe.

It was better to sit here and gaze out across the water, watching the boats pass by.

Oliver and Sarah's maternal grandparents had picked them up a while ago. They had been deeply shocked. Celia's mother had started crying as soon as she saw her grandchildren. Her father had been more composed, but was trembling with suppressed rage.

Nora hoped that Celia wouldn't wake up until her parents arrived at the hospital. She wanted her to be surrounded by people who loved her when she opened her eyes. She needed her mom and dad and her children right now.

Footsteps approached, and Jonas appeared with a cup of tea.

"Hi," he said. "How are you doing?"

"Not so bad." The question brought tears to her eyes. "A little fragile maybe."

Jonas came and sat down beside her. She leaned against his shoulder and relaxed, still ashamed of the fact that she hadn't been honest with him yesterday evening.

"I was so worried about you." His voice was rough with emotion, and Nora felt even more guilty. She took his hand and stroked it, brought it to her cheek, and held it there.

"I don't know what I was thinking, but I should have told you I was going to Fyrudden."

"It's just as well you did go there, for Celia's sake. Thank God everything worked out in the end."

A shadow passed over his face, and Nora realized he was feeling guilty, too.

"I wish I'd gone along with you, then you wouldn't have been alone with that madman."

He put his arm around Nora and drew her close. She could hear the calm, steady beating of his heart.

You're safe now, it assured her.

"Poor Celia," she whispered.

"Yes. And those poor kids."

Jonas passed her the cup of tea. Nora took a sip and tasted honey. He'd put too much in, but it didn't matter.

"I don't think you know how much I love you," he said, with a sharpness in his voice that took her by surprise. "Not really, you've no idea how scared I was when I called you and you told me what was going on. If anything had happened to you . . ."

Nora kissed his cheek. "I do know."

He was looking at her with a strange expression. She felt a fluttering sensation in her stomach.

"I want to ask you something," he said slowly, as if he were trying to make a decision.

"Go ahead."

She answered way too fast, but his sudden seriousness was making her uneasy.

"Can you close your eyes, please?"

"Why?"

"You don't always have to know *why*."

Nora closed her eyes.

Jonas took her hand and opened it gently. Then he placed something small on her palm. It felt cool against her skin.

"I was going to do this completely differently," he said quietly. "But after yesterday . . ."

Nora opened her eyes and looked at the ring, the sparkling diamond.

"Nora, will you marry me?"

Acknowledgments

In the Shadow of Power was the book that didn't want to be written. It was stubborn and reluctant and fought me almost nonstop. It took me a long time to realize that this might have been because the writing process coincided with a close relative's serious illness.

But now it's done, and I'm so glad I didn't give up. More than ever, I owe a huge thank you to those who helped me.

Karin Linge Nordh, my impressive publisher, thank you for being there with praise and encouragement when I needed it most. I don't think you have any idea how much it meant to me.

John Häggblom, no one could be a better editor than you! This time you carried me all the way on your (very broad) shoulders. Without you, this book would never have been finished, believe me.

Warm thanks to Alexander Izosimov, who helped me to understand how business is conducted in Moscow and patiently went through every detail of Carsten Jonsson's fictional business affairs.

As always, Detective Inspector Rolf Hansson has been a great help with various aspects of police work. Thank you, Rolf. You're an absolute rock!

An enormous thank you to Anna Remse, deputy chief prosecutor with the Economic Crimes Authority, who meticulously described the work of the Authority; to Dr. Petra Råsten Almqvist, an expert in forensic medicine, who clarified aspects of injuries sustained in a fire and of the autopsy process; and to Fredrik Ekman, who supplied background information on business in Russia.

Thanks also to family and friends who read and commented on the manuscript along the way: Lisbeth Bergstedt, Anette Brifalk, Helen Duphorn, and of course my darling daughter, Camilla Sten. My Sandhamn friend Gunilla Pettersson went through the entire text with her eagle eye for detail. The fact that you all give up your time to help means so much to me.

Sara Lindegren and everyone else at Forum who works on my books, you're fantastic, and it's a true pleasure to work with you. Lili and Rebecca at Assefa Communications, thank you for all the effort you put into the launch and promotion.

The team at Nordin Agency, including Anna Frankl and Joakim Hansson, who promote my books all over the world, your commitment is amazing, and you achieve miracles on a regular basis!

As a writer I have taken certain liberties. There is no headland on Sandhamn called Fyrudden, and no one has built a great big white luxury home on the southern shore. The old military cabin on the skerry is invented, as are all the characters in the book. Any resemblance to persons living or dead is entirely coincidental, and I take full responsibility for any possible errors.

Finally, darling Lennart, Camilla, Alexander, and Leo: you are everything to me. Thank you for your patience yet again.

Sandhamn, April 14, 2014
Viveca Sten

ABOUT THE AUTHOR

Photo © 2016

Since 2008, Swedish writer Viveca Sten has sold more than 4.5 million copies of her Sandhamn Murders series, which includes *Still Waters, Closed Circles, Guiltless, Tonight You're Dead, In the Heat of the Moment, In Harm's Way,* and *In the Shadow of Power.* They have cemented her place as one of the country's most popular authors, whose crime novels continue to top bestseller charts. Set on the tiny Swedish island of Sandhamn, the series has also been made into a Swedish-language TV miniseries seen by seventy million viewers around the world. Sten lives in Stockholm with her husband and three children, yet she prefers spending her time on Sandhamn Island, where she writes and vacations with her family. Follow her at www.vivecasten.com.

ABOUT THE TRANSLATOR

Marlaine Delargy lives in Shropshire in the United Kingdom. She studied Swedish and German at the University of Wales, Aberystwyth, and taught German for almost twenty years. She has translated novels by many authors, including Åsa Larsson, Kristina Ohlsson, Helene Tursten, John Ajvide Lindqvist, Therese Bohman, Ninni Holmqvist, and Johan Theorin, with whom she won the Crime Writers' Association International Dagger for *The Darkest Room* in 2010. Ms. Delargy also translated *Guiltless, Tonight You're Dead, In the Heat of the Moment, In Harm's Way,* and *In the Shadow of Power* in Viveca Sten's Sandhamn Murders series.

Made in the USA
Monee, IL
29 April 2024

57567266R00236